They Came at Night

Westley Smith

WATERTOWER HILL
PUBLISHING

WESTLEY SMITH

author of *In the Pale Light*

THEY CAME AT NIGHT

A novel

Published by Watertower Hill Publishing
Joshua Daughrity - Publisher
www.watertowerhill.com

Library of Congress Control Number: 2025950366

Hardback ISBN: 978-1-965546-16-1
Paperback ISBN: 978-1-965546-17-8
eBook ASIN: B0F9B1HNTG

Printed in the United States of America
10 9 8 7 6 5 4 3 2 1

For Sonnie, and every aunt who goes above and beyond.

Praise for *In the Pale Light*

"In The Pale Light is fast-paced and full of twists and surprises. The tension builds to a crescendo that had me reading well past my bedtime."

Goodreads User Avonna

"In The Pale Light's creative plot is razor-sharp! It aims to dazzle the reader by providing a sense of urgency, intensity, and vigor."

Goodreads Reviewer BookWormBecky

"The writing is super engaging… I was unable to put this book down… The characters are relatable, especially Terry -he is just so human, with problems like everyone else…the ending is explosive! Highly recommend this one to mystery and thriller fans!"

Goodreads Reviewer Country Mama

"If you like a tale that has a hidden meaning to its title, some good ol' fist fights that make you feel like you're in the fight, some shoot 'em up scenes … give this one a read; I'm sure you won't be disappointed. I thought I had this one figured out, but no. I didn't."

Goodreads Reviewer Melissa Ammons

"The writing was taut with increasing intensity. The characters were compelling, not only Terry and the detectives, but minor characters too. The villains here were twisted and as the novel progressed almost everyone was tainted by the cruelty of both fate and humankind. IN THE PALE LIGHT is a visceral novel of vengeance and the search for truth."

Goodreads Reviewer Katreader

"In the Pale Light serves up justice as a side dish almost a decade in the making."

Amy for Novels Alive

"A page turning mystery with heart stopping moments."
Goodreads Reviewer Leanne

In The Pale Light by Westley Smith is an intriguing and ingenious new crime thriller that hooked me from the very opening. With its complex, morally gray, but sympathetic characters and many twists and turns, this book is one of my favorites of the year
Karen Siddall

"This novel is a masterclass in suspense, rich with the same intricate storytelling and deep character exploration that makes Smith's work so unforgettable. The only "flaw" I can mention is that the intensity of the book left me emotionally drained—but in the best possible way."

Elicia's Book Haven

Praise for *They Came at Night*

"A gripping, action-packed psychological thriller about a troubled woman whose quiet family reunion in a strange small town suddenly turns into a deadly nightmare. You'll be cheering on every page as Sandra Leigh goes from being a victim to a heroic killing machine who will do whatever it takes to protect the ones she loves. Author Westley Smith really turns up the tension and the twists and the thrills in this fast-paced read all the way to the shocking ending."
R.G. Belsky, author of the Clare Carlson mystery series

"*They Came At Night* raises a harrowing question: what happens when the only things worse than the demons inside you are the demons outside you? This is a thriller that lives up to the name: a tale that grips you and pulls you relentlessly from one page to the next as you race toward its nerve-shattering climax."

Charles Philipp Martin, author of the Inspector Lok novels Rented Grave *and* Neon Panic

"Tense and violent, Smith shows us how far a woman will go to protect her own." "Action-packed but filled with heart." "Sandra Leigh is the best kind of kick-ass female lead. Smart, fearless, and not afraid to get dirty to protect those she loves."

Elena Taylor, award-winning, bestselling author

"Taut. Intriguing. Scary as hell… so be careful who you terrorize. Retribution is brutal."

Tj O'Connor, award-winning author of The Whisper Legacy

CHAPTER ONE

Sandra Leigh hadn't felt the phantom pain for several years—the perception of discomfort in a limb that was no longer there. But after receiving a phone call from her sister two weeks ago, the ghostly ache of her severed left ring finger had returned.

Hey, Sissy. William and I are renting a house with Emalyn for the weekend. We'd love for you to join us, Carrie had said in her normal chipper tone.

Was the pain telling her something? Perhaps a warning that she wasn't ready for a weekend excursion with her family just yet. Should she have declined the invitation and stayed hidden in the mountains of West Virginia, at the Compound, where she was safe from... well, everything since the attack?

Now, sitting in the rear seat of her brother-in-law's Toyota Sequoia, heading to the rental home Carrie had booked for their weekend gathering, these questions floated through her mind as she tried soothing the tingling sensation away from what remained of her finger.

Her brother-in-law, William, was driving, and Carrie, her elder sister of ten years, sat in the passenger seat. Beside Sandra, her fifteen-year-old niece, Emalyn, scrolled through her phone.

What were you thinking, Sandra? You're not ready for this.

The suture scar across the tip of her nub wiggled like a worm on a hook as if confirming her thoughts.

"I'm so glad you decided to come, Sissy," Carrie said, turning in the passenger seat, her Carolina-blue eyes twinkling with excitement, looking forward to their weekend.

This was the first time they had done anything together as a family since *he* attacked her while on the way to Carrie's house.

West Chester University, where she was studying music education, focusing on piano, had ordered all students and staff to return home in March 2020, fearing the threat of spreading COVID-19.

Nearly an hour into her two-hour drive, the driver's-side rear tire of her Toyota Corolla blew, leaving Sandra stranded in the middle of nowhere. Not knowing how to change a tire, she contacted AAA on her cell phone, feeling lucky to have gotten a signal at least. The operator told her they were sending someone out to make the repairs.

Five minutes later, the swirling yellow lights of an approaching tow truck cut the night. Relieved, knowing the tire would be fixed and she'd soon be on her way, Sandra had gotten out to greet the repairman.

2

But when the tow truck door opened with a rusty reeeek, and his snake-skin boots hit the frozen ground, Sandra felt a shift in the air that raised the gooseflesh from her toes to her scalp and caused a fear-hardening of her nipples.

Something wasn't right.

"You the one who called about the flat tire?"

"Me too," Sandra replied unenthusiastically, trying to suppress the horrible memory of that night unfolding in her mind.

Carrie smiled reassuringly as if she understood Sandra's hesitation to participate in the family trip.

You don't.

The sunlight breaking through the dense forest canopy caught Carrie's gold wedding band and cast a circulating light that made Sandra squint. The tingling sensation intensified as if a thousand tiny needles were simultaneously jabbing the tip of a finger that was no longer there—a memento of *their* night together.

Mixed feelings of irritation, envy, and sadness tightened her chest. She'd never be able to wear a wedding ring—not like an ordinary wife with all ten fingers, not like Carrie could.

Averting her gaze to the Mudmaster GG1000-1A5 watch strapped to her left wrist, Sandra saw it was almost noon. They had been in the car for about two hours. The watch's compass told her they were heading northwest to Little Hope, Pennsylvania.

The ride had been uneventful and quiet, which Sandra was thankful for. She didn't want to discuss what had happened, and she especially didn't want to discuss her life over the last five years living and working at the Compound.

But you're going to have to. You know that.

She did. The subject would come up this weekend. How could it not? It was the elephant in the room.

"Mom." Emalyn spoke for the first time in over an hour. Sitting forward, she pushed her round glasses up the bridge of her nose and fidgeted in her seat. "How much longer until we get there?"

"Five more minutes, hon," Carrie replied in a teasing, breathy mom tone.

She winked at Sandra playfully.

Emalyn rolled her dark eyes and sat back in the seat with a sigh, blowing a tuft of her curly brown hair out of her face. She scrolled through her phone several times before tiring of whatever had held her undivided attention for most of the ride and shifting her bored gaze to the passing forest.

Emalyn appeared very attached to her phone. Sandra wondered why Carrie, an elementary school teacher wasn't putting a stop it. She had to know phone addiction was a real thing. Sandra had learned from experience once she gave up using one herself.

In Sandra's five-year absence, Emalyn had turned from a chubby-cheek ten-year-old child who loved drawing and coloring, chicken nuggets with ketchup, and *Percy Jackson* into a budding young woman she didn't recognize and no longer knew.

Her niece had spoken little during the drive, and the space between them had filled with an uncomfortable heaviness, like sitting next to a stranger on a tour bus.

Hell, you are practically strangers at this point.

This bothered Sandra. She had been close with her niece, nearly inseparable, before leaving everything—family, friends, school, her life, what was left post-attack—behind to join the Compound.

According to Carrie, Emalyn's recollection of the loving, caring, always-there Aunt Sonnie—a nickname given to her when Emalyn was learning to say Aunt Sandy—was vague. To expect Emalyn to welcome Sandra back into her life as if nothing had changed between them was unrealistic.

4

And everything had changed. Sandra knew that happy, fun-loving, liberal college girl who was so optimistic about her future, looking forward to maybe playing piano for a symphony (if she was lucky) or teaching in a classroom like Carrie (if she wasn't), had died that cold March night along the side of the road.

Can't play or teach piano with only nine fingers.

She took a deep breath that rattled in her throat and looked out the window, hoping to quell the thoughts from her mind along with the irritating phantom pains. A metal For Sale sign at the mouth of a stone driveway caught her attention. A magnetic SOLD! was stuck across the front.

The colonial house sat partially hidden in dense woods about fifty feet from the main highway. The home wasn't quite dilapidated, but it needed serious rehab. She wondered how much the buyer had paid for it, knowing the work needed to make it livable.

Twenty-five yards further up the road, she saw another For Sale sign with another magnetic SOLD! across the front. This home was a double-wide trailer about to fold in on itself. Then, across the road, she saw yet another For Sale sign by a dirt driveway. This property was also marked SOLD!, though the house, a rancher, appeared in better shape than the previous two.

Why were so many properties sold on this stretch of the highway? Had the pandemic hit the area hard? It was possible. Many people had lost their homes while the world was shut down.

"You said this place was outside of a town called Little Hope, but you never said how you found it," Sandra said, looking away from the rancher as they passed.

"Online," Carrie replied, sweeping a long strand of auburn hair behind her ear. "A website called R&R."

"R&R?"

"Rest and Relax," Carrie said. "It's like Airbnb, but the site focuses on families looking for houses big enough to vacation together."

Hearing that Carrie had used a website to rent the house gave Sandra the heebie-jeebies. Corporations couldn't be trusted to keep personal information from falling into the wrong hands.

"William chose the house. I can't wait for you to see it, Sissy."

Carrie's blue eyes flicked to her husband with tender admiration. Even after fifteen years of marriage, her sister still swooned over William. Carrie's wedding ring caught the sunlight again, pulling Sandra's eyes back to it. The tip of her ghost finger twitched. She rubbed the nub, reminding her of its absence... of everything *he* had taken from her.

"I thought if there were any chance of getting you to come along this weekend, it would have to be somewhere remote, private," William said, shifting his dark brown eyes onto Sandra in the rearview mirror. At forty-seven, he was strikingly handsome, with short gray hair and a stubble of matching beard growth that she wasn't used to seeing him with.

"We'll be alone up there, surrounded by woods with hiking trails." He glanced at her in the mirror again and smiled.

Was he looking for her approval? A pat on the back for thinking of her and her growing distrust of civilization since the attack? Not knowing how to respond, Sandra just nodded.

A *ding* on William's cell phone caused him to shift his gaze to the center console, where his mobile rested in the cup holder. The GPS map was open on the screen, leading the way to their rental home.

"Can you check that?" William asked.

"I *am* happy you decided to join us, Sissy," Carrie said again, picking William's phone up.

How Carrie kept saying *Sissy* rubbed Sandra the wrong way. There wasn't necessarily a fakeness in her cadence—it was what Carrie had always called her, but now it felt forced, like her sister was tiptoeing around something.

Is she wondering if I'm... mentally stable?

By the fall of 2020, while the rest of the world was worrying if they were next on the virus's hitlist, Sandra had grown increasingly paranoid, convinced *he* was coming for her.

He was still out there, free to roam the desolate highways looking for other stranded females. *His* essence had invaded her like a malignant organism—a constant presence in her mind, leaving her to wonder why she'd been chosen to be *his* victim as if she were picked from some fucked-up lottery drawn by the devil.

She had quit college in the spring and had gone completely dark by that summer, deleting her social media accounts, closing her emails, and dropping her phone carrier so *he* couldn't track her down using the phone's GPS.

She didn't know if *he* had the skills to hack into her digital life, but she couldn't take that chance, and she didn't trust Facebook, Google, or Verizon to keep her personal information safe from a savvy and determined psychopath looking to hunt her down. She even considered changing her name for an extra measure of protection.

This consuming obsession, which had caused her to lock herself away in the guest room of her sister's house with the shades drawn, had finally led Sandra to seek professional help to deal with the emotional fallout of the attack. She couldn't deal with the mental torment and the fear of *him* for the rest of her life.

Using Carrie's laptop (so she didn't leave a digital footprint of her own), she started an online search for therapy centers. That's when Sandra had stumbled across what she knew immediately was her salvation.

The Compound—an unconventional rehabilitation center in the hills of West Virginia operated by ex-Navy SEAL Joel Conrad.

When she told her family of her plans to join the Compound, they objected to what they considered her rash decision. Janis, her mother, was certain the Compound was some militia group looking to overthrow the government to keep then-President Trump in power, which Sandra found asinine but something her faux-liberal-minded, CNN-watching mother would say and believe.

Carrie and William begged her not to leave, offering to let her live with them and pay for therapy for as long as needed. But she couldn't stay. If she did, she risked herself, and more importantly, her family's lives, positive that when *he* found her, *he'd* kill all of them.

Carrie dropped the phone into the cup holder, snapping Sandra back to reality. She shifted in her seat uncomfortably and felt the Smith &Wesson Model 442 revolver tucked into the rear of her pants press against her spine.

She'd never be helpless to defend herself again.

"Everything okay?" William asked with a concerned glance.

"It was Devin." Carrie shook her head, frustrated. "He said they got hung up but are on their way."

William had a twenty-three-year-old son from a previous marriage. From her chat with Carrie about the trip, Sandra knew that Devin and his girlfriend were also joining them for the weekend.

She didn't know the girlfriend's name and didn't care enough to ask. She wasn't planning on spending time with them anyway. She had other priorities this weekend, like rekindling her relationship with her sister. And especially with Emalyn.

It was why Sandra had decided to come along, despite her fears, the anxiety running the gamut, and the persistent phantom pains.

The attack hadn't just affected *her* life but the lives of those around her, too.

Well, except for maybe her mother, who didn't seem too bothered by the whole ordeal. Then again, she never made that much of a fuss over anything that happened in her second daughter's life, including when it was almost taken.

"It's already noon. That means they won't get here until..." Carrie trailed off.

William shook his head but didn't say anything—the silence of a disappointed father. Carrie took his hand and squeezed it reassuringly.

Sandra looked out the window and saw another SOLD property, though there was no house in sight, and again found it weird that so much land had been sold off.

"Mom, I have to pee."

"Five more—"

"Mom, I really have to go," Emalyn whined.

"Well, you're in luck, kiddo," William said. "We just arrived in Little Hope."

A one-way stone bridge was quickly approaching. Beyond it, Sandra saw a town tucked into the forest hills. A small sign on the bridge's right side read:

WELCOME TO LITTLE HOPE.

As they crossed the bridge, Sandra glanced into the creek gully. Four scruffy-looking boys stood on the bank, watching the Sequoia enter the town with stares so unwelcoming that her nub began to thump as if it were a warning.

CHAPTER TWO

Pappy's Gas & Garage was a small service station just past the stone bridge leading into Little Hope. According to the sign, it offered gas, oil changes, PA inspections, tires, and repairs.

William pulled off the main road and slowly brought the Sequoia beside the single pump. Sandra heard the *ding ding* of a bell go off inside the garage, alerting the attendant that customers were there.

Looking past Emalyn, Sandra saw a brick building with a small office and a single-bay garage. It looked to have been built in the 1950s.

The lack of upkeep concerned her; the building needed significant repainting, the gutters rehung, and the yellowed glass of the office window and door—from the sun and years of cigarette smoke—replaced. She wasn't sure this was the best place for Emalyn to use the restroom.

In the garage bay, a mechanic in blue overalls was bent over an engine, pulling on a ratchet. Righting himself with a groan, he looked in their direction, squinting against the sun. He was older than she would have expected; his face was a roadmap of wrinkles and smudged with grease.

"Be right wit ya," he shouted.

William waved that he understood.

"Mom, I need to pee," Emalyn moaned, squirming in her seat like a fussy toddler.

Carrie's eyes flicked back to the gas station, worry dancing through them.

"You think this place has a clean bathroom?"

Carrie's tone suggested that she hoped Emalyn could hold it until they got to the rental house. Both Sandra and Carrie had refused to use public bathrooms on multiple occasions over the years because of how filthy some were. There wasn't a chance in hell that Carrie wanted her daughter to use the one in this rundown gas station.

"Mom!"

"Could it be any worse than some of the others we've stopped at?" William asked.

"Yes, William, it can," Carrie shot back.

He was a man, so William didn't understand what it was like for females to use a public restroom.

If this old guy was the only person working here, how sanitary could the restroom be? Was the toilet covered with grease smudges, smelling of old man piss, and strewn with porn mags lying about to look at while he sat on the throne fantasizing about women that would never allow his dirty hands anywhere near them? It was possible in a place like this.

The mechanic approached the SUV, wiping his hands on a red rag stained with grease and oil. William lowered the window as the old man neared. He hooked his dirty hands over the side of the door and leaned down—the built-up black grit caked under his fingernails was so thick it looked like it would need to be surgically removed.

"What can I do fer ya?" he asked with a rubbery smile that allowed Sandra to see he was missing his two front teeth.

"Can you top it off?" William asked.

"Mom," Emalyn pleaded, wiggling in her seat.

"Sure. What me to check the earl, too?" the mechanic asked.

"Mom!"

"No. I think we're good," William replied.

"William," Carrie said hesitantly, touching his shoulder. She couldn't avoid Emalyn's pleas to use the restroom, and the way she squirmed around made Sandra believe it was an emergency.

"Do you have a restroom my daughter could use?" William asked.

The mechanic's eyes flipped to Emalyn, sitting behind William. He looked her up and down, slowly taking her in. An icky feeling slinked over Sandra, and a twist of white-hot pain shot from the tip of the nub into her wrist—it was similar to the gaze *he* had given Sandra when he first laid his fishy eyes on her that night.

"Round back," the mechanic said, looking at William while hitching a dirty thumb over his left shoulder.

"I can take her," Sandra offered, knowing Emalyn shouldn't go to the bathroom alone, without an adult there to keep an eye on her.

"No," Emalyn quickly said, glancing at her mother.

Sandra felt a pang of hurt. *We used to be so inseparable.* There was a time when Emalyn would have let—no, begged—for Aunt Sonnie walk her to the bathroom. Not anymore.

What do you expect? You up and left her—everyone—five years ago.

"I'll take her," Carrie said, opening the door and stepping out.

13

William's phone *pinged* again with an incoming text message, and he quickly snatched it from the cup holder.

Emalyn popped her door and slid out of the seat, slamming it behind her so hard the giant Sequoia shook to its treads. She met Carrie at the front of the SUV, and the two of them headed for the restroom in the rear of the shop.

The old mechanic watched them walk across the parking lot too closely for Sandra's comfort. The thought of popping his perverted eyes out of their sockets with her thumbs crossed her mind. Finally, he turned back to William, who hadn't noticed his leering since he was preoccupied with his phone.

"Where ya all headed?" the mechanic asked.

"We rented a place near here for the weekend," William said, closing the phone and looking at the mechanic.

"The Bemyer place?"

"I guess."

The mechanic's face tightened as if something had disturbed him.

What's that look about? A sharp phantom pain, like someone was cutting her open with a razor blade, sliced across the tip of Sandra's nub. She rubbed it, trying to soothe the stinging. What Sandra hated most about the renewed phantom pain was its persistence.

"You said to top her off?" the old man asked.

"If you don't mind."

He tapped the door with his greasy hand, leaving an oily palm print on the interior, and then headed to the pump.

The Sequoia was quickly warming without the air conditioning running, and the air inside had already grown stuffy and stale. Aching from the ride and needing fresh air, Sandra opened the door.

"Think I'll get out and stretch my legs, too."

"Not a bad idea," William agreed. His cell phone *pinged* once more.

The day was hot and humid, and Sandra felt beads of sweat break out across her body almost instantly. A slight breeze brought with it the tangy smell of blacktop baking in the August sun, and it did little to make the heat bearable.

Stretching her arms over her head, her red-and-gray western shirt rode up in the back, exposing the Smith & Wesson's handle. She quickly tugged the shirt back over the gun.

A laugh drew her attention across the street. The four scruffy-looking teenage boys she'd seen by the creek were walking up the sun-bleached sidewalk. All four were dressed in cutoff jeans, raggy t-shirts, and sneakers that looked like they had seen the inside of that creek more than a few times.

They were chatting until the dark-haired boy on the right spotted Sandra. He tapped his freckled, red-headed buddy to the left of him on the arm and whispered something before pointing at her.

The redhead locked eyes with Sandra, and a cold chill crept up her spine, setting off her internal warning system.

Something was threatening about that look. The kind of look one gets when they aren't particularly welcome.

She turned away from them, not wanting to ruffle their young feathers and cause a scene. Walking around the front of the SUV, she saw the town of Little Hope stretched out before her.

Sneeze and one would be through it. To her left was the Little Hope Grocery Store. The Main Street Diner was directly beside it, offering *Old Fashioned Milk Shakes* and burgers for $19.99. *That's a deal, said no one ever.*

On the right was the municipality building. Two satellite dishes were mounted to the roof with **MAX SATLINK** boldly written in blue and white lettering across the front. Mom-and-pop shops were peppered between residential homes, offering everything from shoe cobbling to sewing to electronic repairs.

There was also a record store, VIN'S RECORDS. This surprised Sandra. She hadn't seen a record store in years. Then again, Little Hope was so far off the beaten path that broadband probably hadn't reached this far into the hills, and physical records might be the only way for outside entertainment. It would explain why Max SatLink dishes were on the roof of the municipality building.

Max SatLink, Sandra knew, was a satellite internet provider focused on bringing the internet to rural areas. *Maximum connection anywhere, with minimum price* -was the companies slogan. At the far end of town, just before the road curved up into the hills, sat a large white church.

It looked like a typical northern Pennsylvania mountain town.

Except the place was a ghost town.

Other than the four punks across the street—who had now wandered past and were working toward the other end of town, there wasn't a soul in sight. Sandra wondered if the heat was keeping everyone inside.

Possible. It's hot as the pits of Hades out here.

William grumbled. Turning, Sandra saw him looking at his phone, annoyed by whatever had come through, rubbing his hand vigorously through the whiskers on his chin.

Lean from years of running and weight training, he claimed his fitness routine kept the stress of his job—selling insurance—from putting him into an early grave. Sandra knew nothing about the insurance business or the stressors that came with it, so she took William's word for it.

"Everything okay?" she asked.

"Just my son." William slipped his phone into his pocket and looked at her, jaw tight, lips pursed in annoyance. "He's so unreliable."

Sandra didn't respond. If he were looking for sympathy, he'd come to the wrong person for it. *That's what your wife's for.*

"Sure you don't want me to check the earl?" the mechanic asked, leaning against the side of the Sequoia while the pump shot gas into the tank.

"No, I think it's okay," William replied.

The old mechanic nodded but looked disappointed, probably because he couldn't milk extra cash from William for checking the *earl.*

Carrie and Emalyn came around from the back of the gas station. The relieved look on her sister's face told Sandra that the bathroom must have been at least tolerable. That was a good sign, considering the rest of the building.

Had she misread the mechanic's gaze earlier? Was he an upstanding man who was trying to be helpful and friendly to his customers? Joel , her mentor at the Compound, insisted she work on her judgment of character before jumping to conclusions about strangers. Trust had been a hard thing for Sandra to come by since the attack.

As they neared, Emalyn's cowboy boots clicked off the hot macadam and drew the mechanic's attention to her. A gust of hot summer air blew her orange dress against her young, flowering body. Sandra watched the mechanic's old eyes drift down to her niece's chest, where they lingered. But when his eyes drifted further down, her nub began to burn like someone was holding it to a flame.

Trust really is a hard thing to come by.

"How much do I owe you?" William asked, turning to the mechanic while reaching into his hip pocket for his wallet. He had not seen the old man eyeing his fourteen-year-old daughter.

"Fifty-nine-fifty-nine," the old man said.

"Here's sixty-five. Keep the change."

"Thank ya, kind sir. If you need anything while yer in town, just ask for Pappy. Okay?"

"Will do." William looked at his girls. "Ready to go?"

"Yeah!" Emalyn said, clearly excited now that her bladder was empty and she could think straight.

She walked past Sandra to hop back into the SUV, but Sandra grabbed her by the sleeve of her orange dress.

"Why don't we switch sides for the remainder of the ride."

Emalyn's eyes flipped to Carrie and then back to Sandra with a look of confusion. She didn't understand the need to switch, especially now that they were close to their destination.

When she saw that she wouldn't get an answer from her mother or aunt, she shrugged and started around the rear of the SUV to the other side.

"Anyone else need to use the restroom before we go?" William asked, glancing at Sandra.

She shook her head, not taking her eyes from Pappy, like a lioness watching its prey.

"Well, back into the truck then."

As the Campbells climbed into the SUV, Sandra meandered to the rear door, her eyes still on Pappy. Her nub no longer burned; it pulsated with fury. Her internal monster had risen from its slumber, and it was pissed.

"Get a good look, Pappy?" Sandra asked.

"Excuse me?" he said, playing dumb. But from the reddening of his cheeks and the impish smirk, he knew precisely what Sandra was talking about.

"I catch you ogling my niece again, and I'll rip your eyes out and feed them to you, understand?"

Pappy swallowed, his throat making a strange *clicking* sound. He took a step back, as if afraid Sandra might make good on her promise and open his skull, exposing his depraved thoughts for the entire town to see.

She knew how to remove a person's eyes with her bare hands. It was part of the Rapid Assault Tactics (R.A.T.) training Joel taught them at the Compound—fast disengagement and termination of engagement. In layman's terms: dirty fighting that inflicted the most damage or death to an aggressor.

Finally, Pappy turned on his heels and scurried back to the garage.

Sandra climbed into the SUV. The air conditioning had already cooled the cab, and it felt refreshing on her sweaty skin.

"Everything okay?" Carrie asked, her eyes boring into Sandra's with concern.

"Yeah. I was thanking Pappy for his hospitality."

From Carrie's skeptical look, Sandra knew her sister didn't buy the lie. Though they were ten years apart and looked nothing alike, they had always had a knack for reading each other well—the bond of sisterhood, Sandra supposed.

William took a left onto the road.

As Sandra settled in for the remainder of the ride, she watched the deserted town pass. It soon dawned on her that all the businesses, including the grocery store and the diner, had CLOSED signs on their doors or windows. *Odd.*

It was Friday afternoon, a prime business day. She supposed it could be because the town's population was small, and keeping the stores open all day was unnecessary. *But even on a Friday?*

She also saw SOLD signs on most of the residential homes, just like the houses on the outskirts of town. The homes were old and looked like they had been vacant for some time. Was this why the

19

stores weren't open and she didn't see anyone? Was it because there was hardly anyone living in Little Hope?

Coming to the bend where the white church sat on the corner, Sandra spotted the four boys from the creek. They had found a good spot in the shade of a maple tree beside the church to squat. *What the hell were they up to?*

They watched the SUV approach with a maniacal examination that unnerved Sandra, reminding her of how *he* ingested her with those beady little fisheyes of his. The redheaded boy with freckles then spit a large, green loogie as the SUV passed. The boys all laughed.

"You okay... Sandra?"

She looked back at Emalyn, who was watching her curiously. It was the first time her niece had spoken to her, other than looking up from her phone long enough to say *hey* when Sandra climbed into the SUV that morning. *She used to call you Aunt Sonnie. Now just Sandra.*

"I'm fine," Sandra replied.

"You don't look fine. You look... troubled."

She was. A disconcerting feeling was taking hold, causing the phantom pain to twist around her wrist like squid tentacles and tighten.

There *was* something strange, something off about Little Hope, and it wasn't just because of its lack of people, the shitheads by the church, or the perverted old mechanic. Though she supposed this was enough to raise alarm bells, it wasn't solely the root of the uncomfortable feeling causing her internal monster to stir.

Then what is?

She wished she knew.

You're just being paranoid again. Knock it off.

"What did you really say to that old dude back there before you got in?" Emalyn asked.

"What makes you think I said something different than what I told your mom?"

"His face. He got as red as an apple." She smiled, her big brown eyes brightening.

Expose the light to the darkness, and the darkness recedes.

Emalyn shifted uneasily in her seat, and the feeling that more questions were coming her way tightened Sandra's neck muscles—questions she wasn't ready to field. From the cold shoulder she'd gotten all morning, she'd thought Emalyn wouldn't say much to her this weekend.

"What's life like at a survivalist commune?"

"Emalyn—" Carrie's voice held a warning tone meant to tell her daughter not to broach the subject of the Compound.

"It's not a survivalist commune," Sandra replied, annoyed. She knew Emalyn's perception of her life at the Compound was coming from her grandmother, and it pissed her off. Leave it to her mother to pit Emalyn against her.

"But Grandma says—"

"Well, Grandma's a conniving *bitch* who will say anything to get you on her side."

"Jesus, Sandra!" Carrie said, shocked.

The words had exploded from Sandra's mouth before she could stop them, and she instantly regretted her actions—her monster was speaking for her, taking control.

Emalyn looked as stunned as the old man at the gas station had when Sandra confronted him. Her innocent eyes grew hurt and drifted down to Sandra's left hand, lingering on her missing finger as if understanding that its absence was the reason she was no longer her Aunt Sonnie but the hardened person she had become. Self-consciously, Sandra pulled her hand out of sight.

"Look, Emalyn, I'm sorry for snapping—"

21

"It's fine," she replied, with a tremor in her voice. She sat back in her seat, crossed her arms, and turned her gaze back to the window.

Sandra wanted to apologize again but she caught Carrie staring at her with a look reminiscent of how her mother had always glared at her—disappointment, resentment, a stain on her life that she couldn't wash off.

Unable to take Carrie's contemptuous sneer—a sneer she rightly deserved—Sandra averted her gaze to the passing forest, desperately wanting to be anywhere but where she was right now.

CHAPTER THREE

The rest of the ride to the rental property was tense and quiet. It was Sandra's fault, of course, for snapping at Emalyn. Her lifelong contention with her mother had unknowingly bled onto her niece for asking a simple question.

She suspected this was her mother's plan: to pollute Emalyn's mind with untruths about Sandra's life at the Compound. *What other lies had she told about me?*

Still, she wished to take her harsh words back. But, like the attack, it was in the past, and there was nothing she could do to change the outcome now.

You must move forward. One step at a time. One breath at a time. One day at a time, Joel preached.

Easier said than done.

Sandra knew if she wanted to fix her relationship with her family, she would have to face the moment. She couldn't do that by losing her temper or letting her monster show itself. What happened to her wasn't her family's fault. *It was his*. Allowing her irritation—at her mother—and her fear and anger—at *him*—to control her emotions wasn't fair to any of them, especially Emalyn.

Don't be a victim.

What she wouldn't stand for was her mother filling Emalyn's head with bullshit lies. The Compound wasn't some whacko commune full of doomsday preppers and right-wingers planning how to survive the collapse of the world or overthrow the government. It was a rehabilitation center for combat veterans and victims of assaults like Sandra.

At the Compound, they learned survival skills—bushcraft, hand-to-hand fighting, firearms, and melee weapons training, all so they could physically defend themselves if an altercation happened again and survive off the land if needed.

Everyone was assigned daily chores at the Compound. Joel often told them that a busy mind and a tired body don't have time to focus on the past. He was right, Sandra had quickly learned. She was too tired from training or working on the various camp chores like chopping and stacking wood or fetching water from the stream, to focus on *him*...

However, they didn't just train their bodies; they also trained their minds on how to deal with the aftermath of their ordeals with rigorous therapy sessions led by Joel and his team of licensed therapists.

Three times a week, Sandra sat down with Joel in a one-on-one session and spoke about her fears that *he* might find her, the concerns she had about dealing with a family who no longer understood or knew the person she'd become, and the anger that fed her monster from the life *he* stole from her.

Joel had a mantra that he ground into her head session after session, year after year, something she repeated often, but not nearly enough when she felt her anxiety taking hold and her monster itching for release.

Don't be a victim.

Sandra had no doubt it was her mother's lack of understanding, and more so her lack of compassion—for her daughter or any of the people at the Compound—that made her tell Emalyn it was a survivalist commune. It was Janis's way to turn that screw deeper and to convince Emalyn Sandra had gone off the deep end.

It wasn't going to work. Sandra wasn't going to let her mother corrupt her niece's impressionable mind, warping her views to fit Janis's hateful ideals. Though she felt she shouldn't have to explain herself—she was an adult and could make her own choices—she would if it meant dispelling mistruths her mother took pleasure in spreading.

"Here we are," William said, turning the SUV onto a gravel driveway shrouded in thick tree cover, blotting the sunlight.

Approaching the house, Sandra saw snippets of its structure come into view through the thicket of trees. Though she should have been excited, the sharp prickling of her missing finger ruined the moment. Again, she rubbed the nub, hoping to soothe the nervousness away.

You shouldn't have come.

"Look at this place," William said, bringing the SUV to a stop so they all could take in its beauty. "The pictures online don't do it justice." The excitement in his voice shone, and he squeezed Carrie's hand, her ring disappearing in his palm.

The house was a two-story log cabin made from spruce with a cross-gabled roof. It sat on nearly an acre of trimmed green grass surrounded by woods. A small work shed sat at the far end of the property.

"It's gorgeous," Carrie crooned.

25

Sandra agreed. The anxiety gripping her eased its hold, if only slightly. The house was big enough for all of them, with plenty of space to stretch out—or, in Sandra's case, step away if she had to.

As much as she wanted to rekindle old relationships, she needed time to get to know her family again. Not an easy feat for someone accustomed to living on the fringe of civilization, alone for the most part, with only other troubled individuals to commiserate with.

Still, the phantom pain persisted, though it had returned to its normal tingling.

"Look at that firepit," William said, pointing to a massive circular flagstone enclosure with a square pit in the middle, stacked with wood, ready to be lit. A stone path led back to a screened-in porch with an outdoor dining table under cabana lights and a ceiling fan. Above the porch, a deck ran the width of the west side of the house.

"This is so awesome," Emalyn said.

Sandra felt the excitement coming off her niece in pulsating waves, replacing the hurtful sadness that had filled the space between them. Sandra wondered if they could start anew now that they were here and put what happened behind them. She would like to show her niece that *Aunt Sonnie* was still in her, still alive; she just needed some gentle prodding from her long slumber.

"Can we have S'mores?" Emalyn asked. Her love of S'mores went back to when she was little. She and Sandra used to make them in the microwave on movie nights when Sandra was home from college and spent the weekend at her sister's house.

"Some more of what?" William glanced back at Emalyn, confused.

Emalyn rolled her eyes.

"Some more of what? We haven't cooked anything yet, so how can we have some more of something we didn't even cook?"

"Lame," Emalyn said.

William smiled, pleased with his dad joke. Carrie did, too. He stepped on the gas, bringing the SUV closer to the house, and parked it next to the front porch.

Getting out of the truck, the heat and humidity fell over Sandra like a moist wool blanket, causing her skin to feel tacky and itchy. Surprisingly, the woods surrounding the property were still, and she didn't hear a single bug, forest critter, or bird chirping.

Strange.

William got out and stretched his back, gazing at the house's grandeur.

"So, what do you think?" he asked Sandra.

"It's nice."

He glanced back at her, one eyebrow raised.

"Okay. Better than nice," Sandra admitted.

"Why don't you girls go inside and look around? I'll grab the bags and coolers and bring them in."

"I can help," Sandra said.

She didn't come along for William to cater to her needs like a wounded puppy. She'd carry her own bag. Besides, she had packed her rucksack with only —essentials—two sets of clothes, a toothbrush, deodorant, tampons and pads (just in case), and, of course, an all-purpose tool, matches, a lighter, rigger's tape, a few glow sticks, and a first aid kit, to be safe. What more did she need?

"Nonsense," William replied, waving her off as he went to the rear of the SUV and popped the rear hatch.

Turning away, she caught Emalyn hurrying toward the house, her cowboy boots swooshing through the grass. Her eyes were drawn back to the covered porch.

She saw a human silhouette move.

Could it be the owner of the immaculate rental property? Had they come to welcome them for the weekend? Then she remembered Carrie mentioning renting the home from Rest and Relax. *It's like Airbnb, but the site focuses on families looking for houses big enough to vacation together.*

If the house was owned by a corporation and not privately, then who had she seen slinking around under the porch?

Before Sandra could reposition herself to get a better look at the form she believed she saw lingering on the covered porch, Carrie slinked up beside her, smiling like the cat that had just caught the canary.

"Not too shabby, huh, Sissy?"

"Not at all." Her eyes flicked past Carrie to the porch. No one was there. *Odd. I could have sworn...*

"As soon as we saw it, we knew it was perfect for all of us," Carrie continued.

Sandra nodded. That awful feeling of snapping at Emalyn earlier nipped the back of her neck like a mosquito bite. She deserved Carrie's scorned look. Emalyn's quiet sulking.

They had gone out of their way to rent this place and to invite her on this trip, all so they could get to know one another again, to be a family again—that's what this weekend was about.

She should have handled the situation better. But her mother filling Emalyn's head with lies about her, about the Compound, was too much for her monster—which was already riled up because of Pappy's wondering eyes—to bear.

"Look, I need to apologize for earlier. For snapping at Emalyn. That was wrong." The words were bitter on her tongue, like sour candy, but she needed to say them.

"It's not me you should apologize to." Carrie shifted her gaze to Emalyn, now by the front porch steps, waiting for them, eager to get inside to look around. "It's that little girl who needs to hear it."

Sandra swallowed. Her throat was dry and rough like tree bark, and she felt as embarrassed as she had when her mother poked fun at her for missing a note while practicing piano. *A cat walking across those keys could make better music than you.* However, Carrie was right. She needed to talk with Emalyn and try to make things right between them.

"But not just about what happened earlier," Carrie said. "About everything. Emalyn was distraught after you left, Sandra. She couldn't understand why Aunt Sonnie abandoned her."

"I didn't abandon her."

Carrie leveled her blue eyes on her, tightening her lips into a thin white line.

Sandra lowered her eyes, shame falling on her like a powerful wave driving her into the silt. She *had* abandoned Emalyn. She *had* abandoned all of them to join the Compound.

"All you had to do was talk with Emalyn. Explain why you were leaving and that it had nothing to do with her."

"It was hard for me to articulate everything I felt back then. It's still hard."

"I know." Carrie's voice softened with sympathy. "But you have a chance this weekend to correct some of those rash decisions you made after the attack."

Sandra didn't think any of her decisions were rash. They had been months in the making as the fallout of her attack began to fester in her brain and take hold, as her fear and paranoia rose to a fever pitch that *he* was going to find her and finish what he had started, that she would be helpless to do anything about it again.

Don't be a victim.

"That little girl looks up to you, Sandra. And she still worships the ground you walk on, even if she's not showing it right now. Trust me."

A warm breeze blew, and with it came a muddy smell that Sandra instantly recognized. Carrie's face wrinkled at the scent.

"You smell that?" Carrie said, covering her nose.

"It's lime."

They used lime at the Compound to keep the latrines' smell down during summer. There was no indoor plumbing at the Compound, so water for drinking, bathing, and cleaning had to be fetched from the stream at the bottom of the hill—one of the many chores assigned to someone daily.

"There must be a lime quarry nearby. The air picks up the dusty powder from the rocks and spreads in the breeze."

"Ugh. I hope we don't have to smell it all weekend."

"Once the winds change, you won't even know it's there. Or you'll become nose blind to it by the time we leave."

Carrie's face twisted in thought.

"I hope this doesn't affect—" A sneeze drew her attention to the house, and her shoulders slumped. "Emalyn's allergies. I didn't bring any Benadryl. Shit. Maybe we can get some back in town."

Sandra looked around the property's perimeter and spotted some wild peppermint growing in a sunny spot. She picked a palm full and returned to Carrie, passing the leaves to her.

"These are peppermint leaves. Steep them in boiling water for about five minutes to create tea. It will help flush out Emalyn's sinuses."

Carrie looked at the leaves like they were a handful of gold. When her eyes met Sandra's, they shone with gratitude and admiration.

"Who are you?"

Sandra smiled. One of the Compound's mandatory rehabilitation treatments was for the patients to reconnect with nature. Joel believed, and Sandra now did too, that nature could heal the mind with its peaceful tranquility. It freed the mind of noise and allowed it to process the trauma so the healing could begin.

Could it erase what happened totally? Of course not. But it could make dealing with it bearable. Joel led the entire group on hiking trips deep into the woods twice a month, where they learned survival skills like fishing, trapping, and herbology. *The earth provides everything you need to survive,* Joel had said. *You just have to know how to find it.*

"Grandma!" Emalyn shouted.

Sandra's eyes shot to the house, and she found her mother coming out from the covered porch, her arms spread wide to embrace Emalyn as she rushed to greet her. Any enthusiasm she had accumulated about the weekend drained out of her as fast as money from a gambler's bank account.

It was her mother she'd seen on the porch.

What the hell is she doing here?

"How's my baby girl?" Janis said, rocking Emalyn back and forth. "I missed you so much."

A sharp pang of jealousy gripped Sandra's throat. Her mother had never hugged her like that. Never once had Janis told her she *missed her.* While Sandra was in the hospital, recovering, her mother had only visited once, complained about the food in the cafeteria, and never asked how she was feeling. The bitch even dared to suggest that Sandra brought the attack on herself.

"What is *she* doing here, Carrie?" Sandra barked.

"I-I," Carrie stammered, flabbergasted.

"What?"

"I didn't know she was coming. She said she had other plans this weekend."

"You invited her?" Sandra said through gritted teeth. Had she known her mother would be there, let alone invited, she would never have agreed to come along. Never.

"Yes. But…" Carrie trailed off, her eyes darting back and forth, trying to figure out their mother's angle.

"So, you *did* invite her? Was that before or after you invited me?"

31

"I—we, William and I—invited both of you. Mom responded first and said she couldn't make it. I was going to tell you when I called if Mom said she was coming, but since she said that she wasn't, I didn't see the need to bring it up. Sandra, I would never put—"

Carrie reached out to touch her arm, but Sandra stepped back. Betrayal tightened her chest and caused the phantom pain to shoot up her arm like she'd touched a live wire.

"How could you do this to me?"

"Sissy, I didn't know." Her eyes pleaded for Sandra to understand that she had no part in their mother being there. Was this what Carrie had been tiptoeing around? That their mother might show up as a surprise guest?

Manipulative bitch!

"Sandra, I had nothing to do with this. Honestly."

Carrie's words were worth squat. Whether she knew their mother was coming or not was beside the point. Carrie should have, at the least, suspected their mother capable of doing something like this when she invited her—when she invited them both to spend the weekend under the same roof, something they hadn't done since before Sandra left for college in 2018.

Carrie knew, just as Sandra knew, how cunningly manipulative their mother was. She thrived on her schemes, especially toward Sandra, whom she went out of her way to funnel her viciousness toward.

"I didn't know you were coming, Grandma," Emalyn said.

"Well, I wasn't going to. But I couldn't pass up a weekend with my favorite granddaughter."

They started across the lawn. Emalyn ran ahead of her grandmother and dashed up to Sandra and Carrie, happy as a clam in water.

"Did you know Grandma was coming? Was this a surprise?" Her face beamed with joy.

"I'm as surprised as you, sweetheart," Carrie said, her blue eyes narrowing on her mother.

As Janis strolled through the grass, Sandra was reminded how beautiful her sixty-seven-year-old mother truly was. With a thin, demure frame, shoulder-length silver hair, and only the slightest of wrinkles around her mouth and eyes, she beamed a classy, lady-like elegance.

Her 14K rose-gold wedding ring gleamed in the afternoon sun, a sign of her devoted love for Sandra's father, George, who passed away when Sandrea was sixteen. But the jewelry and beauty were a facade. Below the elegant veneer was a woman filled with spiteful hate.

"Mom," Carrie said, her voice rising as if she were excited to see her there. "Where's your car? How did you get here?"

"I used Uber."

That isn't an accident. You didn't want anyone to know you were here. What are you up to?

"I thought you couldn't make it?" Carrie said. "You told me you had other plans."

"Plans change, dear. And besides, how could I pass up spending the weekend with you girls?" Janis's eyes flipped to Sandra, and they quickly sized her up.

She noted her mother's disapproval of her outfit choice—camouflage pants, hiking boots, and an open western shirt with a tight black tank top underneath that fit her toned, muscular physique. But what cut her mother to the bone, Sandra knew, was her lack of makeup and the way her long strawberry-blonde hair was pulled into a tight ponytail.

33

You're a disappointment, her mother's voice echoed in her mind. She'd heard it enough growing up. *Ladies are never supposed to go out without their faces on and their hair done.*

"Isn't it great?" Emalyn said. "We're going to have the best weekend ever." She sneezed again and rubbed the back of her arm across her itchy nose.

"Oh, Emalyn. You need your allergy medication."

"I'll be fine, Grandma."

"Nonsense." Janis shifted her gaze to the green leaves cupped in Carrie's palm. "What do you have there?"

"Peppermint. Sandra said to steep these into tea. They'll help Emalyn's allergies."

"Really?" Emalyn looked at Sandra, astonished. "Is that true?"

"Oh, fiddlesticks. You're not feeding my grandchild wildflowers." Janis's eyes shot to Sandra with that familiar derisive gaze she'd grown up knowing, making her feel like she was ten all over again.

"It's a natural decongestant," Sandra said.

"So *you* say. But how do the rest of us know?"

Sandra was about to object, saying that she did indeed know what she was talking about, but Janis looked away—no, dismissed her—and returned her gaze to Carrie.

"It's good that one of us thought of bringing some allergy medicine." Janis looked at Emalyn, her face softening—the mask of the loving grandmother back in place. "Let's get you some."

With that said, Janis ushered Emalyn away, heading toward the house.

Sandra turned to her sister with a hard stare that could have bored a hole through Carrie's skull.

"I know, Sandra. I know."

"Do you?"

"What do you want me to do?" Carrie asked, turning to her. "You know how Mom is."

"Stand up to her."

"Oh." Carrie's eyes grew wide. "Like you do."

Sandra said nothing. She had never stood up to her mother in her twenty-seven years. Not. One. Single. Time. Even her monster was quiet—too scared to face the formidable Janis Leigh.

"Look, let's try to make the best of this weekend. What else can we do?"

Sandra could think of a few things. There was, after all, a lime quarry nearby.

"I thought your mother couldn't come?" William said from behind, several bags laced over his shoulders and a cooler full of food and drinks in each hand. He looked past them.

"Mom decided to come after all. Isn't that nice?"

"Oh." His face dropped, horrified at the prospect of spending the weekend with Janis. He knew his mother-in-law well enough to know there had to be an ulterior motive for why she had changed her mind and decided to come.

"Give me some of those. I don't need you throwing your back out." Carrie took two bags and one of the coolers from him and headed for the house.

Sandra didn't move a muscle. The house that had appeared so beautiful only moments ago now looked like a giant mausoleum meant to entomb her with her mother. The urge to leave was as strong as her need to escape *him* that night.

But she was too far from home to do anything about it now.

CHAPTER FOUR

As soon as Sandra stepped into the foyer, claustrophobia squeezed her so tightly that her bones ached. Although the house appeared large on the outside, inside, it felt small and cramped.

The chatter of voices and laughter brought her attention to the end of the narrow hallway where her family had gathered in the kitchen. The sound was unfamiliar to her ears, like eavesdropping on a foreign conversation and trying to understand what was being said.

It had been so long since she shared time with anyone outside the small group living at the Compound, where oftentimes it was a hotbed of sadness. It wasn't always the easiest place to live, to try and heal, since everyone there was dealing with their own fucked-up lives. But it had been what Sandra needed to overcome *him*.

And obviously you still do.

Maybe that was why she was getting the claustrophobic feeling. To try and fit in. To be normal? Happy? She had difficulty remembering what normal was and what true happiness felt like. She wasn't used to being with people who weren't walking that traumatic tightrope, fighting not to fall into the abyss. To be around souls who hadn't looked the devil in the eyes and lived to tell the tale was a way of life she no longer understood.

Janis stood at the island pouring tea from the cooler into four red plastic cups Carrie had packed with the drinks. Now that Sandra had a moment to study her mother, she appeared thinner than the last time she'd seen her. *How long ago was it?* Sandra couldn't remember.

Thinking of Janis brought up those old phantoms of her childhood that she didn't want to deal with, especially now that she had all-new ones to conquer.

William and Carrie stood opposite Janis. Emalyn was fidgeting on one of the barstools by the island, eagerly awaiting her glass to be filled with overly sweet tea so she could swallow the pink Benadryl pill she held. Sandra noticed there wasn't a red cup for her.

She wasn't surprised—another little dig.

William and Carrie had dumped the bags by the front door, next to a stand in the tight foyer. In the center of the stand was a black greeting card with WELCOME written in large silver letters across the front. A clear glass vase sat on the right, filled with freshly cut summer wildflowers that perfumed the air. To the left was an open guestbook.

Sandra found her rucksack amongst the piles of luggage William insisted on carrying in. She picked it up and hooked it over her shoulder. Glancing at the guestbook as she stood, she saw it was opened to the first page, with her mother's scrawling signature at the top, like some famous movie starlet. Next was Emalyn's.

Followed by Carrie and William's. It must have been a brand-new book since no other signatures were on the first page.

Are we the first people to stay here?

She looked back at the door, thinking about leaving again, and saw the electronic keypad beside it. She assumed one number locked the door and another armed and disarmed the alarm. She reminded herself to get those numbers from Carrie, just in case.

Can never be too cautious.

Starting down the hallway—*God, it's narrow*—Sandra passed an open stairwell on the right that led up to the loft suspended above the living room. She figured the three doors on the second floor led to two bedrooms separated by an adjoining bathroom.

In the living room, two sofas in an L shape were placed in front of a flat-screen TV mounted above a stone fireplace. A coffee table was in the center with a remote to the TV on top and more freshly cut wildflowers in a vase. There was a large bookshelf filled with hardbacks from various authors and genres and a copious amount of DVDs. A wall of windows with door access to the deck allowed an unobstructed view of the backyard, firepit, and woods.

"Would you like some tea?" Carrie asked, pulling Sandra's attention back to the kitchen.

"Oh, heavens," Janis said as if she had forgotten. "Where's my mind? I didn't grab a fifth glass for Sandra. I'm so used to it being just the four of us."

Dig that knife deeper, Mother. You haven't scraped my soul yet.

Sandra passed a door on her left that she presumed led to the basement and the covered porch below the deck. Following the door to the basement was another short, narrow hallway, just in front of the kitchen. Two more bedrooms were directly across from each other, and a bathroom was at the end of the hallway with the door open.

"It's fine. Where's my room? I want to get settled in," Sandra said, looking back to the others.

"William and I are taking the room on the right, just down the hallway there," Carrie said, pointing. "You and Emalyn can have the room directly across from ours."

The tingling of her missing finger turned to a hammering that matched her heartbeat. She had not planned to bunk with Emalyn. She knew her face must have shown the unease she felt at the idea by what Carrie said next.

"It's the only room with two single beds." Carrie's gaze shifted to Janis. "And since Mom decided to join us, we thought it best for her to have her own room."

Sandra's body tensed like a rattlesnake about to strike. *You ruin everything,* she wanted to scream at her mother.

"You don't mind, do you, sweetheart?" Janis asked Emalyn, running her hand through her granddaughter's thick, curly brown hair.

"No." Emalyn looked at Sandra, trepidation dancing the muscles around her eyes.

Sandra could tell she wasn't thrilled about sharing a room with a crazy aunt.

"I'm just happy that Grandma is here," she said, trying to hide her discomfort.

"Aww. And I'm happy to be here, too," Janis replied.

Just what are you doing here? Janis didn't do anything by accident. Her mother was meticulous about her schedule, writing down her daily activities on her Calendar of Power—the Cop for short, Sandra called it—because it seemed to be the law by which Janis lived and must never be broken.

She knew her mother wouldn't change her weekend plans at a whim to join them. There had to be some other reason why she was there.

40

But what?

"If you'd rather have the room to yourself, Emalyn can sleep on the sofa," William said. "It's really—"

"It's fine," Sandra said. "I don't mind, as long as Emalyn is okay with it."

"Of course she is," Janis said.

"Then let her say it," Sandra shot back, her eyes flicking from her mother to Emalyn, who quickly looked at the floor, admonishing her aunt's gaze.

"Are you okay bunking with me for the weekend?"

"I guess." She didn't sound convinced by the idea.

After the way she'd gone all Travis Bickel on her earlier, Sandra couldn't blame the kid for not wanting to sleep in the same room.

"If it's a problem, Sandra, I really don't mind sharing a room with Emalyn," Janis said.

"I'm good with it if she is," Sandra said. *Besides, I don't want you getting your talons in her further than they already are.* If she allowed Janis to continue beating that wedge between her and Emalyn, it would hinder her reconnecting with her niece.

"I just know how you like your privacy. I mean, you left us all to go live at that… commune."

"I said it's fine," Sandra said, ignoring her mother's snide remark.

There's not a well too deep that she won't go to hurt me.

Janis clapped her hands together. "William, would you be a dear and get the grill started? I bought salmon for dinner tonight and fresh vegetables at a nice produce stand."

"Mom… that's very kind of you," Carrie said hesitantly, "but we're just going to grill up some hotdogs and burgers we brought along."

41

"Honey," William said, thinking with his stomach like men often do. "We can grill those burgers and hotdogs tomorrow."

Carrie nodded apprehensively, deepening the lines around her eyes and mouth, making her look like a younger version of Janis. Sandra could tell Carrie was also questioning what game their mother was playing with the sudden change in plans and bringing food to share with the family—something Janis never did.

Something *was* up.

"Then it's settled." Janis had spoken, so should it be done. "William, get the grill going. Carrie and I will start getting things ready and bring it out to you."

"We should get settled in first," Carrie said. "We have a mound of bags in the foyer to take to our rooms."

"Oh, where are my manners? Of course."

Sandra headed to her room.

"Do you want a glass of tea before you go?" Janis asked.

"I'm fine," Sandra called over her shoulder. She stopped and turned back. "What are the numbers for the house lock and the alarm? Just in case I need them."

"House lock is 43115. The alarm is 83115," Carrie told her.

"Thanks."

Sandra headed down the hallway.

In the bedroom, she shut the door behind her.

Then she realized something.

It was pitch black in the room.

Finding the light switch, she flipped it up.

An overhead light blinked on, revealing a small, sky-blue room with two single beds separated by a wooden four-legged nightstand with a lamp. Nature paintings of birds, fields, and flowers hung on the walls. A bookshelf was next to the closet, filled with games for guests to play while visiting.

The room's motif was supposed to be serene and comforting. Sandra didn't get that feeling. The air in there was charged with an electric current like she'd felt in the computer labs in college. And there was something else that troubled her.

There were no windows.

Who builds a house without windows in the bedrooms?

Trying not to overthink the house's design oddities, Sandra slung her bag onto the bed and plopped down. The springs squeaked, and the bed bounced her up and down like she was on a trampoline.

The silence and solitude of the room fell upon her like a comfortable oversized sweater she could disappear in.

Exhaustion gripped her, and the sudden need to sleep overcame her with such force she had to lay back on the bed or fear passing out and falling face-first onto the floor. Her head had no sooner hit the pillow than she was out.

CHAPTER FIVE

"You the one who called about the flat tire?" His voice was muffled as if he were speaking through something pressed to his lips.

"Y-yes," Sandra called back, catching the hitch in her voice.

"Ah, shucks," he replied in a good-natured tone. "That's a bummer. And on a cold night like tonight."

He closed the tow truck's door; it *rrreeked*, followed by a *bang* that echoed through the chilly air and the open fields surrounding them like a gunshot. Stepping in front of the powerful headlights, Sandra couldn't see anything but his hulking silhouette.

"You have a spare in that shoebox of a trunk?"

Did she have a spare?

"Um? I think so." She hated relying on this stranger to help her with her predicament. "But I don't know how to remove the old one and put it on."

"Don't worry, little lady. That's why I'm here. We'll get you fixed up in no time at all."

He trudged toward her with a gait that was a mix of a waddle and limp. As he drew closer, and the shadows fell off him like a black sludge, Sandra saw he was a large, oddly shaped man. His torso was blubbery, supported by short, toothpick legs.

She wondered how his small ankles sustained such a bulky frame. The icy wind blew, and she smelled the metallic scent of grease and cigarette smoke coming off him.

He wore a KN95 mask. It explained his muffled voice. A Carhart jacket was zipped to the middle of his barrel chest, revealing a flannel shirt underneath. His blue jeans were held around his bulging gut by a black belt with the silver buckle of a nude –woman—the kind Sandra remembered seeing on eighteen-wheeler mudflaps when she was a kid.

A trucker's cap with a bulldog on the front and the word MACK underneath covered greasy, dark hair that nearly touched his shoulders. Behind a pair of bottle-thick glasses, his beady fisheyes watched her with a weird fascination, absorbing her in a way that was…

Unnerving.

"Let's see what we're dealing with," he said, turning his leer to the car. His knees cracked like dried branches when he squatted beside the rear tire.

The sound sent a deep shiver through Sandra's body. His mere presence gave her eerie vibes. She remembered how the air had grown colder when he first arrived, causing the gooseflesh to rise across her skin and her nipples to harden until they hurt.

Were these feelings misguided? Did they have nothing to do with him and everything to do with how helpless and afraid—yes, afraid—she felt being stranded out there in the middle of nowhere, dependent on someone—a stranger in a mask, no less—to get her out of the bind she found herself in?

Or was it something else?

He reached into the darkness of the wheel well and ran his thick, bloated hand over the tire's tread like he was petting it.

"Ah!"

"What?"

"Think I found your problem."

Sandra leaned closer, trying to see past his mass into the dark of the wheel well, where he dug at something in the tire's tread. When she'd left campus that morning, she hadn't seen anything wrong with the tire. Then again, she wouldn't know what to look for even if she had checked it before driving off.

He picked something out of the tread with a chewed-down, tobacco-stained nail. Turning in his squat to her, he raised his hand into the tow truck's lights. A roofing nail was pinched between his fingers.

"How did it get in there?" Sandra asked.

"Probably picked it up somewhere along the way," he replied, looking at it. "I'd say it's been in your tire for a while. The nail head kept the air in, but the driving probably caused the hole to open enough to create a slow leak."

"Great."

"Where you comin' from?"

"West Chester."

"College girl, eh?"

Sandra shivered and took a step back. How did he know she was in college? *A lucky guess?* She looked twenty-one, and it was common knowledge that West Chester had a university. *Power of deduction?*

"No biggie. You said you have a spare?" he asked.

"I guess it's in the trunk."

47

"Jack, too? And a tire iron to get the lug nuts off? If not, I got both in the truck."

Sandra shrugged. She didn't know what was in the trunk. Now that she was stuck on the side of the road with a flat, she wondered if laws should require a driver to know how to change a flat tire before issuing a driver's license. She'd support that bill if Congress stopped fighting and started working for the American people like they were supposed to.

"No worries." He stood, joints popping as he rose. He studied her again with a watery, gleeful glint that made Sandra wonder if he was undressing her with his eyes. "I'm happy to help."

She wrapped her arms around herself, hiding her body from him. Though she couldn't see beyond the mask covering his mouth and nose, Sandra knew by the lines around his eyes that he was smiling. An awful taste rose in the back of her throat, burning. There *was* something odd about this guy.

"You need a key to pop the trunk?"

"Huh?"

"Key." He turned his hand like he was starting an ignition. "Does the trunk need a key?"

"No. There's a lever on the floor."

"Open 'er up. I'll get everything out, change the tire, and you'll be on your way."

Sandra nodded and was about to turn but thought better of it. She didn't want her back to him. Backpedaling to the driver's side door while keeping her eyes on him, she pulled the trunk release lever on the floor. The lid unlocked with a *click* and popped open.

"There we go," he said, moving through the dead grass toward the trunk. His snakeskin cowboy boots fell heavy on the frozen ground with each step, like he was a giant stomping across some scary fairy tale world Sandra suddenly found herself in.

She tightened her arms across her chest to keep the shivers from reaching her bones. The air was crisp, with the slightest hint of snow sweetening the breeze.

"You're lucky you reached someone," he said from behind the open trunk lid.

Sandra couldn't see him, but she heard him moving her luggage around to get what he needed in the bottom of the trunk.

"Why's that?"

He peered around the trunk and studied her closely, his beady eyes slowly roaming over her body again. She swore she could hear him lick his lips like a ravenous dog.

"A crazy person could've come along and tried to take advantage of your situation."

Sandra's throat tightened. He ducked out of her sight, returning to what he was doing. She shuffled forward, arms still crossed over her chest, to see past the lid. But as she grew closer, he moved further away, as if he didn't want her to see him rooting through her belongings.

"Yeah, a pretty little thing like you. It wouldn't be hard for someone to snatch you up and take you with them." He chuckled in that good-natured way as if the idea of her kidnapping was amusing.

It wasn't.

Her teeth began to chatter.

"You sure you have a spare?"

"W-what?"

He looked around the open trunk lid at her again.

"A spare? Are you sure you have one?"

"It-it should b-be in t-there."

He bent back into the trunk. She saw the car dip as he leaned on the rear, the springs objecting to his weight, and heard her bags being shifted once more.

"I don't... No... I..."

49

Shit! Do I not have a spare fucking tire?

"Maybe I'm missing it," he said. "Would you mind coming around and showing me where it is?"

Sandra's breath caught in her throat, and her muscles instantly cramped, pinning her where she stood.

The car must have a spare. It must.

"Yeah, I'm not seeing… Nope." He looked at her quizzically. "It wouldn't be under the car, would it?"

Under the car?

"Sometimes the manufacturers put the spares under the car," he said as if reading her thoughts.

"Maybe. I-I don't know." She was as dumb as a sack of potatoes regarding automotive stuff.

"Well." He looked back into the trunk. "It's not in here. So, it must be under the car—if you *have* a spare."

"Okay."

He started to get into a squat, and Sandra heard one of his knees *pop*—a dagger to her ears.

"Ouch!" He shot back up.

"Are you okay?" Sandra asked, though she didn't hear any concern in her voice, only dread.

"Yeah." He rubbed his right knee. "I've got bad knees. You probably heard them crack when I bent down to look at your tire. Doing this work for too long. Takes its toll on the body."

Or it's your weight, Sandra thought, but she wouldn't dare fat shame anyone.

"If you wouldn't mind taking a peek under the car for me, that would be helpful."

The worry on her face must have shown. He picked up on it almost instantly.

"Look, I can tell you're concerned. Us being on this isolated road together. Me behind this mask—which I'd like to take off, but

I have asthma and don't need to catch the 'Rona. But I promise you, I'm only here to help."

She suddenly felt awful. He was risking his life to help her while a virus ravaged the earth that could kill him—an *essential worker*, the news had called them. *And you dare to judge him?*

"I didn't..." she trailed off, looking at her feet, not knowing what to say for herself. Shame sank through her chest into her belly like a lead weight.

"It's no big deal. I understand. Been doing this for twenty-five years. I've met countless women in your exact position. They're all the same."

"I'm sorry. Really."

"No need to apologize. You're just taking precautions, and that's smart."

At least he understood.

"What do you need me to do?"

She stepped beside the car but kept herself out of his reach. He might not be the weirdo she'd first thought, but she didn't want to be within his grasp, just in case.

"If you'd bend down and look under the trunk here." He jabbed a fat finger into the darkness directly under the license plate. "That's where the tire should be."

Sandra placed her left hand on the lip of the open trunk, hooking her pinky and ring finger inside as she bent down to look under the car.

That's when she saw him grip the trunk's lid and bring it down.

She tried to pull her hand away before the lid closed on her fingers, trapping her. She almost succeeded.

Almost.

The trunk lid slammed closed, catching the third finger of her left hand. She felt it snap backward at the second joint, the bone breaking through the skin.

51

Blinding pain shot through her like a lightning strike, and her scream fanned out into the desolate darkness, where it died unheard. She frantically tried to pull free but tripped in her panic, in her pain-fogged mind, over her own feet and fell to the cold, hard ground.

Her shoulder wrenched backward, over her head, and was nearly pulled from the socket. With her left ring finger still caught in the closed trunk overhead, blood started to run down her hand and soak into the cuff of her jacket.

"Ouch. That must've hurt," he said.

Tears of terror and pain filled her eyes. He had used her own emotions against her. To make her feel bad about his situation so he could draw her closer and lead her into *his* trap. *What was he going to do?*

"You women are all the same," he said. "That's what I've learned over the years."

Sandra understood what he was talking about, even as the insurmountable pain writhing through her made her feel lightheaded and sick to her stomach. There were other women—stranded travelers—he'd done this to.

Don't pass out. Don't pass—

He turned away and waddled back to the tow truck, leaving Sandra dangling like a rabbit caught in a snare.

Rrreeek! The tow truck's door opened. He rooted around inside the cab for something. Sandra tried to wiggle free from the trunk's grasp, but every little movement sent searing, intolerable tendrils of pain cascading down her arm into her shoulder and neck.

She broke out in a flop sweat that quickly cooled in the frigid night air and crystallized on her skin.

A moment later, he came back around the door, leaving it open this time. Sandra understood why—it gave him easier access to load her inside the cab. A fear blossomed across her body, unlike anything she had felt before.

She screamed.

There was no one to hear.

And no one would come.

When he returned, he was wheezing heavily through the mask. In his right hand, he held black plastic zip ties. But it was what was in his right hand that made Sandra lose control of her bladder.

A buck knife.

He reached down to grab her free hand, but Sandra snatched it from his bloated fingers and tried to wiggle under the car. He sighed like her fighting wasn't his idea of a good time. On the contrary, she knew he was enjoying himself. Her struggle, fright, and agony—it all charged him—turned him on.

"It will be easier for you if you don't resist," he said.

For a moment, Sandra considered his proposal. He could take the anguish away if she did listen and obey his commands. But she was also aware that the intense pain was clouding her rational thoughts. What kind of suffering would come later for the immediate gratification of relief? What were his plans for her after she was freed from the trunk, zip-tied, and in his tow truck? Torture? Rape?

Or something far, far worse?

She saw herself dead in her mind—nude bloody, and battered—in a shallow ditch somewhere deep in the woods, a place where her body would never be found.

Her thoughts shifted to Emalyn, her innocence stolen by Aunt Sonnie's disappearance and murder.

You can't allow him to take that too.

He reached again for her free hand. Sandra slapped him away. Huffing, he righted himself, his beady fisheyes ablaze with anticipation, the thrill of the struggle.

Sandra screamed again, praying her shrill cries would reach ears that could bring help.

He then arched his back and screamed into the night, mocking her.

"You can scream all you want. There's no one out there to hear you."

He reached out and grabbed her left wrist. His touch sent a chilling pain down her arm that hit her heart like an ice dagger.

"I hoped we could do this the easy way. But that's another thing I've learned about women over the years. You never make anything easy for us men."

He placed the buck knife on her third finger. Sandra's vision blurred from the tears, and she suddenly wanted to beg him to stop—*please please don't take my finger I need it to play piano*—but the words were trapped behind her swollen tongue.

"This night belongs to us," he said and began to cut.

Sandra jolted awake from the nightmare, grabbing at her missing finger, the phantom pains slicing through her hand like the knife's blade had so long ago.

"You okay?"

The voice drew her attention to Emalyn sitting on the opposite bed, pulling clothes from her suitcase and stacking them carefully beside it.

She must follow in her mother's footsteps. Carrie was always the neat freak of the two of them, a trait passed onto her from Janis, who couldn't have a dress out of color-coded order in her closet.

"Were you having a bad dream?" Emalyn asked.

Something like that. The sweat dampening her hairline and back reminded Sandra it was more than a bad dream. She swung her feet off the bed, continuing to rub the disquiet of her missing finger. *Settle now. It's over—just a bad dream—a nightmare.*

She hadn't had a nightmare about the attack in months, and it made her wonder if the stress of the day had kicked it loose from her subconscious.

"It must've been really bad because you thrashed around a lot."

Sandra had no idea that she *thrashed around* in her sleep. There was no one beside her at night to tell her. It had been years since she had shared a bed, let alone a room, with anyone.

At the Compound, guests had their own twelve-by-twelve-foot cabin with just enough room for a single bed, a small eating/working area, and a wood stove for warmth in the winter. There was no power in the cabin for lights or electronics.

The muscles in her lower back were stiff from the strange bed, and her mind felt wavy, as if she'd eaten a hallucinogenic mushroom—something she had done once when she was still new at the Compound and learning herbology. Her trip had taken her deep into her mind, where she was forced to relive the attack over and over and over and over—a mistake she never made again.

"What time is it?" Sandra asked.

"After three."

"After…" She looked at her watch, confirming the time. "Sorry. I didn't mean to sleep so long."

"Why?" Emalyn seemed stupefied. "You're on vacation. You're allowed to take a nap."

Sandra didn't respond. She couldn't remember the last time she had napped in the middle of the day. Her days were full of combat training, therapy sessions, or taking care of camp chores, which didn't leave time for much else.

"I should go help with food prep," Sandra said.

"Well… there's a bit of a hang-up with that," Emalyn said, pulling more clothes from her suitcase and laying them on the bed next to the others.

"A hang-up?"

"There aren't any utensils in the house."

"No... utensils?"

"Not a single one. No knives, forks, or spoons. Not even a spatula to flip eggs."

"What kind of house doesn't have utensils?"

"A really shitty one."

Sandra studied her.

"Where'd you learn adult words?"

"I'm fourteen," Emalyn said, as if the question was absurd. "You think I don't know cuss words?"

"I guess I still see you as that little girl I knew."

"Well, I'm not," Emalyn snapped. She looked back at her clothes and rearranged them on the bed as if they were out of order. "You'd know that if you'd been around the last five years."

Sandra heard the disappointment in her voice. She said nothing. What could she say? The kid was right.

Letting the subject go for now, she stood and arched her back, twisting both ways to loosen the tight muscles. Her western shirt flew out like a cape, revealing the pistol's handle at the small of her back.

"Is that a... gun?" Emalyn asked, eyes widening.

Sandra quickly tugged her shirt back over the weapon.

"Yes." There was no sense lying about it.

"Man, Mom's going to shit a brick if she knows you have a gun."

"Are you going to tell your mom?"

Emalyn considered the question for a moment.

"No," she decided, with a shake of her head.

"Good. Because I don't need her flipping out on me."

"None of us need that, trust me. She's already about to lose it because Grandma's here."

Sandra had forgotten about her mother's sudden –appearance— the wonders of a nap. Her shoulders sagged, and irritation warmed her, knowing they'd have to spend the entire weekend together. *Oh, piss.*

"You and Grandma don't get along, do you?" Emalyn asked, studying her.

"What makes you say that?"

She shrugged, looked back at the suitcase, and pulled the zipper, avoiding eye contact. "How you interact, like two cats in heat fighting over a Tom."

Emalyn was observant for fourteen; Sandra had to give her that.

"It's a long story."

"Is it because of what happened to you?" Emalyn persisted, her eyes shifting to Sandra's missing finger.

"Some of it," Sandra replied, slipping her left hand into her pocket.

"You mean there's something else?" Emalyn sat straighter. Her intrigue was piqued.

Sandra didn't take the bait. She wouldn't elaborate further on the rift between herself and Janis. Hell, she didn't even know why they had a rift. It had always been there as far back as she could remember.

Nevertheless, the fewer details Sandra elaborated on about Janis's nastiness, the better off she'd be down the road with Emalyn. If she badmouthed Janis in front of Emalyn, it would make her look like an asshole and would inevitably make Emalyn resent her more.

But if she gave Janis enough rope, she'd eventually hang herself. It was just a matter of time before Emalyn saw her grandmother for who she truly was.

"Let's go see what's going on," Sandra said.

Stepping into the hall, Sandra saw the door to William and Carrie's room hung open; their open suitcases were on the bed. Like her and Emalyn's bedroom, their room had no windows.

Strange.

"Hey, you two," Carrie said as Sandra and Emalyn entered the kitchen. "You want some chips?"

She grabbed an open bag of Doritos on the counter and shook it. Emalyn took a handful. Carrie offered some to Sandra, but she declined. She had hated Doritos her entire life—Carrie must not have remembered.

"It looks like we're in a bit of a pickle," Carrie said, dropping the bag onto the counter. "Can you believe this place doesn't have silverware?"

"It doesn't have *anything*," Janis added, opening a few cupboard doors to empty shelves. Sandra got a whiff of pine—the shelves must've been new, recently installed—that caused her to long for the refuge of the Compound and the forest hills of West Virginia, where the Table Mountain pine grew so thick the scent made the air sugary.

"That's odd, right?" Carrie asked.

"Very," Sandra replied. Yet having no silverware or pots and pans to cook with wasn't what was starting to perturb her in the kitchen, it was the lack of an exit. There wasn't a rear door or a window in the kitchen—just like in the bedroom.

Her nub tingled. She tried to quell it with a light massage. "What are you going to do?"

"I guess we'll have to go back into town and see if we can pick some up. What else can we do?"

"Everything was closed," Sandra said.

"Maybe it will be open by now?"

Carrie had a point. It was, after all, Friday afternoon. Someone around these parts would need supplies and have to go to town to get them.

The front door opened, and William started down the hall and entered the kitchen. The humidity had dampened his blue t-shirt around the collar and under the arms; sweat dotted his brow, which he dabbed with the back of his hand.

"There isn't anything in the shed behind the house—no mower, hedge trimmer, or even a shovel. Is that strange?" William asked.

"Maybe they have someone take care of the lawn," Janis said, leaning against the counter. "Don't need the lawn equipment if someone is doing the work for you."

"Okay. That's fair." William thought for a moment. "But why isn't there any silverware? Plates? Or pots and pans?" He opened a drawer and looked in like some had magically appeared since he last checked. "I don't get it."

Sandra remembered the guestbook lying on the small table in the foyer.

"The guestbook looks new. Maybe we're the first group to rent this place. The owners might not have gotten a chance to stock it fully. Did it say on the website to bring cookware or anything like that?"

"Not that I recall," Carrie said, shaking her head.

"Check," Sandra said.

"I tried. There isn't any cell service out here."

"And no Wi-Fi," Emalyn said, sulking. "How could you book us a place without Wi-Fi, Mom?"

"Hey." William's voice cut sharply at his daughter, followed by a warning look.

"It was an oversight on both of us in our excitement to book this place. I'm sure it said that there was no Wi-Fi. Still, you'd think they'd have SatLink way out here. That's what the municipal building was using back in town."

He was right. The house should've had such amenities if it wanted to attract visitors—it was a requirement nowadays when people couldn't be away from their phones, social media, email, or even Netflix while on vacation. Then again, some people went on vacation to disconnect from technology.

"Is there a landline, at least?" Sandra asked.

"Yes," Carrie pointed to the far wall of the kitchen, where a phone was mounted.

At least they could call for help in an emergency.

"I can run back into town and—"

"Dad?" a male voice called, interrupting William.

"Hey! Devin. Lacy." William's voice rose excitedly, and his face brightened at the realization that his son had finally arrived.

"We're in the kitchen."

Sandra turned just as Devin Campbell and his very attractive blonde girlfriend, Lacy, entered the kitchen, setting their luggage down. Devin was tall and lean like his father. His dark hair was styled in a side-swept fringe. He wore a white linen button-down shirt with the sleeves rolled to the elbows and brown linen pants. An expensive-looking watch sparkled on his wrist, and a pair of Oakley sunglasses hid his eyes.

"By God, you made it!"

William wrapped his son in a bear hug. Devin was anything but thrilled by the look on his face. It appeared he wished he was anywhere else right now, Sandra felt.

She had only met Devin a handful of times in the seventeen years Carrie and William had been together. He was five years younger than her and had lived with his mother, Carmilla, for most of his adolescence. According to Carrie, he rarely visited his father.

There was friction in their relationship that went back years, but Sandra had no idea what caused it.

It wasn't her business.

The pretty blonde girl introduced herself to William as Lacy Talbert before turning to the others in the room with a million-dollar smile and teeth so perfect Sandra wondered if they were real or if Lacy had some work done. She wore a blue sundress and stylish brown sandals that showed off her pedicured pink toenails. A purse hung from her wrist with Gucci embossed across the front.

To Sandra, the pair looked like they had just come from some trendy beach club on the coast of Florida.

"Did you guys have any trouble finding the place?" William asked.

"A little. The damn GPS led us the wrong way. We had to turn around. That's why we're late," Devin said. He pulled off his shades, revealing his sharply slanted dark eyes.

Mean eyes, Sandra thought.

"How was the ride up?" William asked.

"Beautiful," Lacy said. "I got some amazing shots for our Instas."

"That's good to hear," William replied, though he seemed anything but amazed.

"Look, I was just about to run back into town to get a few things. Do you want to come with me?"

Devin sniffed and rubbed his nose. Sandra wondered if he was allergic to the lime in the air like his half-sister.

"Well, Lacy and I just got here, so we wanted to get our stuff to our rooms first." He turned and looked at their luggage in the hall, which included two gray suitcases, three bright pink ones, and two backpacks.

How long were they planning on staying? A month?

61

Pack light. Always be ready to bug out. Joel's words of wisdom, which Sandra lived by.

"Oh. Well, we can talk when I get back," William said. He glanced at Carrie, disappointment showing in his eyes.

"Why don't I go to town and pick up what we need? That'll give you time to chat with Devin and Lacy," Sandra offered. The house was filling up too fast for her liking. She needed to distance herself from it all for a while—room to breathe and think.

"You don't mind?" William asked.

Sandra shook her head and caught Devin stuffing his hands in his pockets. His shoulders slumped with disappointment. He looked uninterested in catching up with his old man.

"Can I go?" Emalyn asked.

That stunned Sandra. She hadn't expected…

"I don't think—"

"No. It's fine," Sandra said, touching Carrie on the arm.

"Are you… sure Sandra can handle Emalyn on her own?" Janis asked in a tone meant to elicit concern from the others. "I mean, with all Sandra's… problems."

"Trust me, Emalyn's safe with me," Sandra said, glaring at her mother.

"Can I, Mom? Can I go?" Emalyn begged.

"I'm okay with it if your father is." Carrie looked at William.

"Yeah." He reached into his pocket, pulled out the SUV's keys, and tossed them to Sandra. "Have fun, you two."

CHAPTER SIX

Emalyn quietly thumbed through her phone on their drive back to Little Hope. After their conversation earlier in the bedroom, Sandra thought they would chat on the ride—that this was why Emalyn wanted to go back into town with her. That wasn't the case.

Give it time. Emalyn would talk when she was ready. There was no need to force a conversation.

As she drove silently, the nightmare swam in her mind like a shark circling bloody chum. The reoccurring dream came less frequently than it used to, which she was thankful for, but she knew no matter how much she willed her mind to let go of the past, *he* would always be with her, living in her subconscious rent-free.

This night belongs to us.

But it wasn't just *that* night that belonged to *them*. In a way, Sandra had unwillingly committed a lifetime to *their* special night together.

He had made sure of that.

Though there were snippets of the attack that she had blocked in her mind, the recurring dream accurately represented what she did recall about that night's hellish events.

Not the pain, though. You remember every second of that.

After severing her finger, *he* had grabbed her by the hair and dragged her across the hard, lumpy ground toward the open, waiting cab of his tow truck, kicking, squirming, and screaming until her throat was raw. No one came.

She was bleeding profusely, cradling her hand to her chest, the warm blood soaking through her jacket, her shirt, her bra, and onto her cold skin. She remembered him hoisting her up next to the truck, a great wheeze seeping through the mask from his efforts as he did.

She smacked his hands and clawed at his face, hoping to break his hold on her. But he resisted her weak strikes and was surprisingly strong for an out-of-shape man with a breathing problem.

Had it not been for the circling yellow lights of the real tow truck cresting the hill, bathing the dead grass and woods surrounding them a piss color, he would have gotten her in *his cage* and driven off, keeping her for himself, doing God-only-knew what with her.

Knowing *he* didn't have time to get her inside before unwanted attention arrived and spoiled his plan and his fun, he tossed her to the ground, jumped into his tow truck, and sped off into the night.

Never to be seen again.

A few days later, at the hospital, with her left hand wrapped in enough bandages that it looked like she wore a white boxing glove and on enough painkillers to put down a buffalo, a pair of detectives questioned her.

She told them what had transpired, surprising herself with her detailed recall in her doped-up state. She described what *he* looked like and wore—the snakeskin boots, glasses, the MACK trucker's cap, and the KN95 mask. She told them *he* claimed to be asthmatic, and she believed it true because of his wheezing.

The detectives were particularly interested in the tow truck— make, model, year, color, style. However, she couldn't give any details on it. They were disappointed. Looking back, she supposed it was one of those lost snippets of that night locked away somewhere in her mind.

Before the detectives left, she asked why they were so interested in the tow truck. What they told her chilled her to the core, and it was the first time she remembered feeling the phantom pain.

They suspected *he* was listening to tow truck drivers' conversations with their dispatchers via CB radio. By doing this, he found the location of the breakdown and who was involved—a man, a woman, or a family. He only targeted single female drivers and would rush to the scene before the real tow truck driver arrived, kidnap his victim, and disappear.

As far as they could tell, *he* had been using this tactic for years, and they were able to link him to nearly a dozen kidnappings of young women.

A faded sign sticking out of the brush came into view: SEWYER Co. QUARRY, snapping Sandra from her thoughts. Just beyond the sign, a large metal gate blocked a heavily overgrown access road leading to the quarry. A No Trespassing sign was attached to it. Sandra hadn't seen the quarry on their way to the house, and she wondered if this was where the smell of the lime emanated from.

"Creepy," Emalyn said as they passed.

Sandra agreed with a nod.

A moment later, the white church appeared before the road curved into Little Hope. As Sandra steered the SUV around the bend and came parallel to the church, she noticed a man standing by the front doors as if asking for permission to enter.

He was tall and well-built, with a thick brown beard. A tight black t-shirt exposed his muscled physique and was tucked into tan cargo pants. Just from his appearance, Sandra knew that he was in the military. He had that always on-guard look about him and the thousand-yard stare of a man who had been knee-deep in some serious shit. A look she saw in her own eyes in the mirror every morning. In his hand, he held a stack of white papers.

She wondered if he was a local but let that thought slip away as they started through the center of town. Besides the man at the church, the town was deserted, and most stores still had CLOSED signs in their windows. All residential homes that didn't have For Sale signs had their shades drawn, giving Sandra abandonment vibes. If there was life in this town, it hid itself well.

While parking the SUV in front of the Little Hope Grocery Store, Sandra saw that it and the diner were now open.

That's a plus.

Getting out, Sandra checked her six. No one was on the streets except the bearded man, who had made his way from the church's stoop and into town. The blast of an air gun from Pappy's Service Station broke the quiet summer afternoon. Other than that, Little Hope was still as deserted as Death Valley.

Weird.

Entering the grocery store, Sandra was hit with air so cold she thought she'd somehow crossed into the Arctic. The woman working the register was in her late forties and running a file across her nails. She wore horned-rimmed glasses, and her hair was styled in a 1950s beehive that made her look older than she was. A baby blue dress with red flowers connected by thorny, green vines covered her soft flesh. A name tag above her ample left bosom read PEGGY.

Peggy looked up from her filing and over her glasses, resting low on her nose, and said, "Welcome to Little Hope Grocery. Can I help yous?"

Emalyn had gotten distracted by the candy rack. Sandra ushered her away to the register.

"Hi. We're looking for cookware. Would you happen to have any?"

"Aisle Six, hon. At the far end of the store."

Peggy pointed behind her as if Sandra couldn't figure out where Aisle 6 was from the numbers hanging above each aisle.

"Thanks."

Leading them through the store, Sandra saw it was old and dingy, with yellow floor tile and lime-green walls reminiscent of those found in 1950s hospitals. The overhead lights did little to brighten it up, and the unmistakable tang of freshly butchered meat lingered in the air.

"Do you smell that?" Emalyn asked, pinching her nose shut.

"Yes."

"What is it?" she asked in a nasal voice.

"Meat."

"Really?"

"Yes."

"*Yarg!* How gross."

"You've never been in a butcher's shop before?" Sandra asked.

"Why would I go into a butcher's shop? Mom gets all our meats at the grocery store."

Of course she does.

"Fresher to buy meat from the butcher. Higher quality without all the additives."

"Additives?"

They rounded the corner into Aisle 6. Carrie had given Sandra a list before they left, and she found everything they needed: plastic plates, tin foil, disposable pans, cooking spray, olive oil, paper hot cups for morning coffee, and a box of a hundred plastic spoons, forks, and knives. No real utensils or plates were available for purchase, so plastic was the only option.

Why didn't the rental home have any of these everyday items? Was it an oversight in the rush to rent the property out? Or had Carrie missed the tidbit on R&R's website telling her they needed to bring culinary supplies? Regardless, it was as strange as the lack of bedroom windows and no rear exit from the house.

"Factory-owned farms shoot their animals full of steroids and antibiotics."

"Why?"

"To make them grow bigger so they can feed more people and make more profit."

Sandra had read *Meat Market: The Secret Takeover of America's Food Business* and was appalled by how soulless corporations like Tyson Foods destroyed people, small rural farms, and, most importantly, by the mistreatment of hundreds of thousands of animals they slaughtered every year to continue to feed an already overweight, out of shape, not to mention increasingly sickly population. To think of even supporting such a system made her irate.

"Oh. So you go to the *butcher* instead?"

"Sometimes. Or we hunt."

"Hunt? Like you kill deer?"

Sandra gathered what they needed and turned to Emalyn, not answering her question. "Do you need anything?"

"No," she said, her finger and thumb still pinching her nose shut.

Sandra yanked her hand away.

"Knock it off. Don't be disrespectful."

She walked past her toward the register. Emalyn followed.

"Find what you needed?" Peggy asked, filing her nails again. Sandra wondered if it was a health code violation. Not that it mattered in a deadbeat town like Little Hope; she doubted anyone from the Health Inspector's Office even bothered to visit this store regularly.

"Yes." Sandra laid the stuff on the counter.

"You new in town or just visiting?" Peggy asked.

"Just visiting." Sandra reached into her pocket for cash.

"You the folks renting the Bemyer place?"

Sandra knew it was a bad idea to divulge where they were staying. Though she wasn't particularly worried about Peggy visiting them, she obviously had the gift for gab, and if she told someone, someone with ulterior motives, it could bring trouble their way.

The four boys crossed her mind with their menacing gazes, the redhead spitting that nasty green loogie at them as they passed.

Peggy continued as if she already knew the answer to her question.

"That's a nice, new place up there."

"This is a beautiful little town," Sandra said, shifting the conversation away from where they were staying—if it was, in fact, the Bemyer place.

"Well, thank you. Little Hope isn't much. But it's home."

"Pretty quiet in town today, huh?" Sandra shifted her gaze to the barren street.

"Like that every day," Peggy said sadly. "Since the quarry closed."

"What do you mean?"

"The Sewyer Company employed most folks around these parts. But when the company decided to close after the ground was depleted, a lot of folks left."

Sandra got the picture. It reminded her of a book she'd read about California ghost towns in the wake of the 1848 Gold Rush once the mines dried up. Little Hope was no different; the economy thrived while the quarry was in operation and was wrecked with its closure. It explained all the vacant houses and businesses.

But not the sold signs?

"About how many people still live in Little Hope?" Sandra asked.

"Maybe fifty. A few still live in town, but most are on the outskirts, in the surrounding hills."

Sandra wondered how Little Hope would survive the coming years with the economy and inflation. *How had it survived this long?*

Peggy nodded as if reading Sandra's thoughts and said, "We're lucky, though."

"Oh? How's that?"

"That R&R came in when they did."

"R&R? As in Rest and Relax?"

"Yeah."

"The rental company?"

"The same. About two years ago, they bought up a bunch of places the banks had foreclosed on."

"Like the Bemyer place?" Sandra asked.

"Exactly. They bulldozed the old house and built that new fancy one you're staying in." Peggy sighed. "From what I hear through the grapevine, R&R is buying all the vacant properties in and around town."

That explains all the SOLD signs.

"How does that make you feel?"

70

Peggy sighed again. "On one hand, it is sad seeing the old homes vanish. But it's been a tough couple of years for this town and those of us who have remained. If what R&R is doing helps attract people back to Little Hope, it will take a lot of stress off us business owners."

Turning Little Hope from a mining town into a tourist town.

"Well, I hope it works out," Emalyn said. "I think this town is super neat, and I'd hate to see it disappear. It's... Americana."

"Aren't you just as cute as a button? I tell you what. I saw the way yous were lookin' at the candy. Why don't yous pick something yous like? On the house, of course." Peggy winked at Sandra.

"No. That's okay," Sandra replied. "Her mother wouldn't want her to spoil her dinner."

"Oh, you're not her momma?"

"My niece."

"But you two look so much alike."

She and Emalyn looked nothing alike. Peggy was just being polite.

Emalyn had Carrie's olive skin and auburn hair. Her dark brown eyes came from her father. Sandra was fair-skinned, with strawberry-blonde hair and vibrant green eyes. She always thought she looked of Irish descent, not English/French like everyone else in her family, leading her to wonder sometimes if she was adopted. Maybe that was why her mother showed such disdain for her.

"Can I have something? Please?" Emalyn begged.

"Go ahead." Sandra relented, not wanting to insult Peggy's kindness again. "Thank you for your hospitality."

Peggy waved the gesture off as if it were no big deal. All part of the small-town charm, Sandra guessed. Still, she wondered how Little Hope Grocery stayed in business. There weren't enough people in town or the surrounding area to keep it afloat, and it couldn't rely on tourists alone for income. Not yet, at least.

She thought it better not to overthink it and turned to Emalyn, looking over the candy.

"Find anything worth ruining your teeth?"

"Yes!" She grabbed a packet of Pop Rocks. "I love these things."

"Great." Sandra turned to Peggy. How much do I owe you?"

"Fifty-seven dollars."

Well, now she knew how they stayed in business. Overpriced goods. They were the only store nearby for miles, and people would pay for the convenience. *Smart.* She counted out the money from the wad of bills and passed it to Peggy. They said goodbye and headed out.

Starting back to the SUV, Emalyn stopped as if something of vast importance had caught her attention up the street.

"What?" Sandra asked, following her gaze.

"Can we get a milkshake before heading back to the house?"

Sandra was confused. Emalyn picked up on it right away. "It says in the diner window that they offer old-fashioned milkshakes. I never had one of those."

"It's just ice cream and milk," Sandra replied, remembering seeing the advertisement in the window earlier. "Nothing special."

"But maybe they do something different with *their* milkshakes."

"They don't."

"Oh, c'mon. It'll be fun. Just the two of us."

How could she say no to that? She wanted to spend time with Emalyn this weekend, and at least for the moment, it appeared her niece wanted the same.

"Fine."

They started up the sidewalk toward the diner. The bearded man Sandra had seen earlier was nowhere around. She wondered what had happened to him. Was he a store owner, a local, or, like them, a tourist checking out the town, staying at one of the other rental properties owned by R&R?

A bell *dinged* as they entered the diner. Inside, the place was right out of the 1950s, complete with a jukebox in the back Art Deco . It smelled of old fried grease and meat and the sour smell of dairy. A dark-haired man sat along the back wall, eating a sandwich. The waitress behind the counter picked up two menus and started to them.

"Just the two of ya?" the waitress asked. She was somewhere in her early twenties, with curly blonde hair, an unnaturally thin body with pale skin, and a gaunt face with deep purple bags under her eyes. She looked haggard and rundown, and Sandra couldn't help but wonder what cruel twist of fate had led her to this moment in her life.

"We came for your old-fashioned milkshakes," Sandra said.

"You can have a seat at the counter. I'll grab the dessert menus."

They took seats on hard, round stools attached to the floor. Emalyn spun around, taking in the place as she did, her eyes large ovals of fascination.

"This is so effing neat."

"Hey, watch the swears."

"I didn't swear. I said effing. Effing isn't a swear word."

"It's implied."

Emalyn smiled. She knew what she was doing—testing her boundaries with Sandra.

The waitress returned with the dessert menus.

"Do you have Wi-Fi?" Emalyn asked.

Sandra stopped herself from rolling her eyes.

"Sorry. No."

"Oh," Emalyn said, disappointed.

"I'll come back when you decide." The waitress strolled over to the man eating his sandwich along the back wall to check on him. "Is there anything else I can get you, Cleve?" Sandra heard her ask.

"How about we split a shake," Sandra said. "That way, neither of us ruin our dinner."

"Okay. What flavor do you like?"

"As hot as it is, I'll drink anything. You pick."

Emalyn ran her finger down the list of milkshake flavors and tapped one at the bottom.

"Ah, butter pecan?"

"A butter pecan milkshake?" Sandra asked, raising an eyebrow. "That's the flavor you want?"

"No. But it's the most disgusting ice cream ever, and you did say you'd drink anything."

"Okay. You got me. Pick something else."

She giggled and looked at the menu again. Her laugh was music to Sandra's ears and brought back memories of when they used to roll around on the floor in Carrie's living room, playing foolish kid games, laughing until their faces hurt. She missed those carefree times.

He took time from you, too.

"How about cookies and cream?"

"I can get behind that."

The waitress returned, pulling a pad from the apron around her waist.

"All ready?"

"Yeah. We'll have the Cookies and Cream milkshake."

"With malt?"

"Yes!"

"What's malt?" Emalyn asked, glancing at Sandra.

"It's a powder made of barley, wheat flour, and evaporated whole milk powder that gives milkshakes an extra nutty, milky flavor."

Emalyn's face scrunched like she smelled a foul odor.

"Don't knock it until you try it. And besides, you said you wanted to try an old-fashioned milkshake. Here's your opportunity."

This seemed to settle the debate.

"Whipped cream and cherry on top?"

"Duh," Emalyn said in a lighthearted tone meant to be funny.

The waitress glanced at Emalyn, but she didn't crack a smile. A haunting air hung around her, like she'd seen more than she should have for her age—a quality Sandra saw in herself and others at the Compound.

"Be right back." The waitress turned on her heels and entered the kitchen.

Turning slightly on the stool, Sandra caught the man at the rear of the diner watching them intently. *What are you looking at, asshole?*

He was a big man with broad shoulders and cropped black hair. His face wore the lines of a hard life, and he had the blackest eyes Sandra believed she'd ever seen. He returned to his plate and took a bite from his sandwich.

Sandra turned back to Emalyn, trying to put the stranger out of her mind, but the pulsing of her missing finger concerned her. *Why was he watching them?*

"This is such a neat place," Emalyn said, looking around. "I've never been in a fifties diner before. It's so retro."

"There's nothing retro about this place. It's vintage."

"You mean it's authentic?"

Sandra nodded. She glanced at the man in the booth again. He was concentrating on his meal and didn't seem interested in them anymore. The thumping of her nub eased ever so slightly.

"How do you know what malt is?"

"Oh, I'm full of useless knowledge, according to your grandmother."

She saw the dejected look cross Emalyn's face and knew she had made a mistake. Her niece hadn't seen the evil that resided in her grandmother. Yet.

"I read a lot."

Sandra spent most of her free time alone in her cabin with only her thoughts to keep her company, which wasn't always good. Joel encouraged them to read topics of interest when they felt depressed or full of anxiety—there were no pills handed out to squash the memory phantoms.

Reading helped distract the mind and forced it to focus so it couldn't dwell on the past. She had spent many nights reading a book alone by candlelight until the wee hours of the morning to combat the worst of her memories.

"Really?" Emalyn perked up. "I like to read, too. Right now, I'm really into Brandon Sanderson." She whipped out her phone like a gunslinger drawing a six-shooter and opened the Kindle app. "He's a fantasy writer!"

"That's what you've been doing on your phone the entire ride up here? Reading?"

Joel was right; she needed to quit passing judgment on others so quickly. But it seemed that Emalyn hadn't changed as much as Sandra had first suspected—she was still into fantasy novels, like when she was little. "I thought you were scrolling Instagum or TicTac—like all kids nowadays."

Emalyn giggled again.

"It's Instagram and TikTok."

"Oh." Sandra knew the real names of the social media sites—she wasn't that cut off from the outside world—but thought it would be funny, realizing how much she needed to hear Emalyn's laugh again.

"His new book came out Tuesday. But Dad didn't give me my allowance until Friday, so I had to wait to order it. I hoped to get a Wi-Fi connection somewhere in town to download it for the weekend. I've read this one twice. Have you read Brandon Sanderson?" Emalyn asked, showing Sandra the digital book cover.

"No. I mostly read non-fiction."

"Oh! What kind of non-fiction books do you read?" Emalyn turned to face her aunt; her big brown eyes lit with enthusiasm.

By God, they were connecting.

Sandra shrugged.

"I like history, art, politics, and modern culture. I read a lot about musicians and their music."

"Is that because you played piano? Mom said you were amazing."

"I guess."

Emalyn was quiet for a moment as if contemplating her next question.

"You don't play piano anymore, do you?"

"No. I can't."

"Because of your finger?"

The nub burned white hot as the memory of the buck knife severing through the flesh, the ligaments, the muscle, and finally, the bone tried to work its way to the forefront of her mind. She felt Emalyn's eyes on her missing digit and covered it with her right hand, rubbing it unconsciously.

"Let's change the subject," Sandra said. "How's school?"

"I don't really like school much," Emalyn said dolefully.

"Why's that?"

She shrugged, and her eyes drifted to the counter as if ashamed.

"I guess I don't fit in with the rest of the girls. They're all into sports, social media, boys, or… makeup."

"And you just like to read," Sandra said, glancing at the phone still open to the Sanderson book. "Escape into a fantasy world."

"I like to write my own stories, too."

It pissed her off that she had missed so much of Emalyn's life because of *him*. She had no idea that her niece liked to write, and Carrie never mentioned it to her on the rare occasions they chatted on the phone over the last five years.

And you never bothered to ask about Emalyn, Sandra, so the fault is yours.

True. She had climbed so far into her hole of despair that she could not see any light, including the brightest one in her life.

"No one understands at school," Emalyn continued. "Most people think I'm strange, and sometimes, they make fun of me."

Sandra wondered if Carrie knew about Emalyn's problems at school. She didn't seem like a shy kid, but she was reserved, and reserved kids tended to hold things in, especially the wrong things.

Sandra knew that from her own experiences. After her father, George, died from a chest-stopper heart attack, she'd bottled all her hurt and sadness up. Janis sure as hell wasn't going to comfort her through the loss of her father, whom Sandra adored. Instead, she focused on studying piano and getting good grades to get into college and get the hell away from her spiteful mother.

Still, the lasting effects of losing her father—the only person who truly loved her—loomed over her like a murky shadow, a trauma she wasn't sure she'd ever fully overcome.

"Fuck 'em," Sandra said bluntly.

Emalyn looked up at her, shocked at first, but then a smile spread slowly across her lips.

"Don't let anyone tell you that you're strange for what you love to do. If reading and writing are things you enjoy, do them. It doesn't matter what the other kids say or think. You live your life your way, on your terms. Fuck what everyone else thinks."

"Eff what everyone else thinks."

This time, Sandra didn't correct her—she nodded.

The door to the kitchen opened, and the waitress came out with a milkshake heaping with whipped cream and a large, bright-red cherry on top. She sat the glass down in front of them, along with two straws.

"Anything else?"

"Thanks. We're good for the moment."

After placing their straws in the glass, Sandra watched Emalyn take the first sip. Her eyes widened and grew glassy with pleasure as the malt and cream hit her tongue.

"O-M-G, that's soooo good," she squeaked. "Sooo good!"

"Told ya." Sandra took a sip. The milk and sugar struck her bloodstream and surged through her body like a bullet. She had been at the Compound for so long that she'd forgotten the small pleasures of life, like the taste of a milkshake with malt, and this one was exceptionally delicious.

The diner's door opened. The bell *dinged*.

Sandra looked up to find the man with the beard entering, still holding onto the papers she'd seen him with outside the church. He glanced around the interior; his intense eyes held a troubling gaze that perturbed her.

"Help you?" the waitress asked, approaching the counter.

"I was wondering if you'd seen these people?" He pulled a sheet of paper from the stack in his hand and placed it on the counter.

Sandra couldn't see the paper from her vantage point, but she suspected it contained photographs of those he was searching for.

The waitress studied the sheet but gave no indication one way or another.

"Sorry, no," the waitress finally said.

"My brother, his wife, and their two daughters came up this way a few weeks ago on vacation. We haven't heard from them since. I'm asking around town to see if anyone might've seen them. Besides the grocery store, you're the only place open."

"Didn't pass through these doors," the waitress said, ignoring the obvious question: why everything was closed.

His face tightened with desperation to learn his family's whereabouts.

What happened to them?

"What about you two?" the bearded man asked, turning the paper around so Sandra and Emalyn could see it.

There was only one picture on the sheet of paper, showing a family huddled together in front of a fireplace—husband, wife, two little blonde girls—all smiling wide for the camera, their eyes shining and vibrant. Sandra wondered if it was taken for a Christmas card from the black and red flannel pajamas they wore.

Under the photo was more information.

MISSING!

THE HIBBARD FAMILY

Lewis (42), Rose (43), Mika (10), Kaylie (8)

Last Seen:

6/08/2025

The last line was contact information for the State Police.

"Sorry, we haven't," Sandra replied, looking back at the bearded man who still held the same vacant stare she'd seen in his eyes earlier. Now she understood why, and her heart bled for him.

"Is there anything else I can help you with? A cold drink, perhaps? It's hot out there, and you look like you could use one," the waitress said.

"No. Thank you," he replied, shifting his gaze to the waitress. "Would you mind if I put one of these up in your window? Maybe someone in town will recognize them."

"That's up to my boss."

"Could you ask him?"

"He's not here right now."

The gloomy look told Sandra he must have been hitting the same roadblock in town—at least to those he *could* speak with. No one had seen his family. No one knew anything. Now one of two open businesses in town didn't want the missing person's flyer in their establishment.

Why? Bad for business.

What business?

"Well, thank you for your time."

He turned and headed out the door. The bell *dinged* as he exited. Sandra watched him continue down the street, hoping he would find his family. What happened to them? Were they okay? The phantom pain ached through her palm as if it knew they were not.

Behind Sandra, she heard the man rise from the booth. He dashed past them and burst through the door—*ding*. He looked down the street in the direction the bearded man had gone for a moment before he turned and headed in the opposite direction, nearly in a run.

What's that all about?

A slurping sound brought Sandra's attention back to Emalyn. She had sucked down the malted shake.

"I had a sip," Sandra said, teasing.

"Hey, you snooze, you lose."

The waitress returned, writing on her pad.

"Anything else I can get yas?" she asked.

"No. Just the check."

She finished scribbling on the pad, tore it off, and laid it down on the counter—$ 9.50 for the milkshake. Again, Sandra couldn't believe the prices of everything. Pulling a ten from her pocket, she handed it to the waitress, telling her to keep the change.

"You better eat dinner tonight. Your mom will pitch a fit if she finds you had a milkshake and ruined your appetite."

"I can keep a secret." Sandra's stare hardened. "Cross my heart," she said, making an X over her chest. "I didn't say anything about your gun."

"Let's keep it that way."

Stepping back outside, the heat was more oppressive than when they entered the diner. *Stupid hot,* Joel would say.

"Hurry before they come back out," whispered a voice next to William's SUV.

Sandra saw the four scruffy teens she'd seen earlier kneeling beside the passenger side door. The sound of metal-on-metal scraping needled her ears. They were carving something into the side of the SUV.

"Hey!"

The boys turned at Sandra's voice.

Sandra charged toward them.

"Run!" the redhead yelled.

All four jumped to their feet in unison and bolted. Sandra chased after them, but by the time she came to the rear of the SUV, they were already across the street and running for a trail that led into the surrounding hills.

You little shits!

Three of the four boys disappeared into the thicket of the trail, but the redhead stopped at the mouth of the trail and turned back, smirking maliciously. He raised his hand, showing her the flathead screwdriver he'd used to vandalize the SUV, and made a stabbing motion as if it were a knife.

Sandra's right hand, her gun hand, twitched as if awakened. *Put 'em in the dirt,* the archaic voice of her internal monster spoke suddenly in her head. *Kill the little fucker before he grows up and hurts someone like us.* For a split second, she considered listening and putting a round in his freckled face.

"Sandra?" Emalyn's agitated voice came from behind, snapping Sandra from those pleasant thoughts of putting this punk, who just threatened her and Emalyn's lives, six feet deep.

Turning, she found Emalyn standing beside the SUV's passenger-side door, staring at it with a mortifying glare that raised the hackles on Sandra's neck. The boys had carved a word into the paint that stood out on the side of the black SUV like a flashing neon sign.

LEAVE.

"You two okay?"

Sandra spun around. A police car had stopped in the middle of the street. Behind the wheel sat a distinguished-looking cop wearing a cowboy hat. She guessed his age to be around sixty by the salt-and-pepper beard and matching thick eyebrows.

"We're fine. But those kids vandalized my brother-in-law's truck," Sandra shouted, pointing in the direction they had run off.

The officer looked where she was pointing. His eyes sharpened with annoyance.

"I was just coming back into town when I saw them running across the street. Figured they were up to something."

"Who are they?"

"Oh, they're just a bunch of local kids looking to cause trouble."

"What kind of trouble?" Sandra asked.

He ignored the question and said, "I'm Earl Craven, the sheriff of Little Hope. And you two are?"

"Sandra. This is my niece, Emalyn."

"Hello, Emalyn," Craven said with a wave.

"Hi," she replied timidly.

"You're the folks staying at the Bemyer place, right." He said it as fact, not a question, and pulled off his hat, revealing his receding gray hairline and hawk-beak nose. His eyes held a thoughtful, caring quality, giving him the astuteness of a college professor rather than the sheriff of Little Hope. He dabbed his wrist on his brow before returning his hat to his head.

"That explains why Lew and his cousins Hatch, Tuck, and Conrad were targeting you." Sandra was at a loss, but the Sheriff continued. "Some of our—how do I want to put it—local heathens are all worked up like a bunch of yellowjackets about tourists coming to town."

"From the looks of this town, it could use a shot of life," Sandra replied.

Craven nodded.

"When the quarry closed, a lot of people left to find work, and Little Hope, well, had little hope of surviving. That was until R&R showed up."

"So I've heard."

"You must've been talkin' to Peggy," Craven said with a smile. "Old girl sure does like to spill the beans to anyone who'll listen. Anyway, the locals don't understand. Like it or not, we need R&R if Little Hope is going to survive by bringing in tourists like yourselves. But it's a hard sell to some of these knuckleheads."

"You should rain them in, Sheriff," Sandra said. "If word gets out that locals are hostile to tourists—and it will get out—it'll be just like you said, little hope for Little Hope."

"True. I'll chat with them. Change isn't easy, and it takes time."

Sandra nodded. *Ain't that the truth.*

The sudden urge to get out of town beckoned. She'd had enough of Little Hope's way of greeting its guests.

"Thanks for the help, Sheriff," Sandra said, looking back at the word scratched into the paint. *Not that you did anything.* "But we best be going."

Craven touched the brim of his hat with his index finger.

"That's what I'm here for. To keep the peace. You drive safe now."

He waved goodbye and drove off. Sandra wondered if he would talk to the boys or if it was just an act. He could believe the same as those brats, that tourists were a disease that needed to be eradicated from their town at all costs. Her nub hummed with electoral impulses.

"Think I'm ready to go home now," Emalyn said.

"Yeah, me too."

CHAPTER SEVEN

Back at the house, Sandra parked the SUV next to the porch and killed the engine. Emalyn hopped out.

They had not spoken on the way home, Emalyn staring out the window, watching the passing forest, lost in her own world, while Sandra thought of the vandalism done to the SUV and how William would react to the news.

LEAVE. Was it a warning? That if they stayed in Little Hope, at this house, their lives were in danger. Her thoughts shifted to the bearded man looking for his family—had they faced the same opposition from the locals? Had it turned… deadly?

She swallowed the thought, watching Emalyn run up the steps as the front door opened and Lacy trotted out. She had changed into blue shorts and a white tank top. A Nikon camera dangled from a strap over her right shoulder. Her makeup had been freshened since

Sandra had last seen her, and she looked picture-ready for a photo shoot with the Nikon.

"Hey, you guys are back," she said as Emalyn rushed into the house.

Lacy walked down the steps, her flip-flops slapping against the heels of her feet, while holding her cell phone in the air and waving it back and forth. Sandra got out with the supplies.

"I can't get a signal." Lacy looked at Sandra. "Are you getting anything on your phone?"

"I don't have a cell phone."

"What?" Lacy exclaimed, trying to determine whether Sandra was joking or not. "Wait. You're serious."

Sandra nodded. Before the attack, she wouldn't have gone anywhere without her cell phone and would have thrown a fit if she couldn't get service. It wasn't until after she abandoned the usage of a cell phone, fearing that *he* could use it to track her down, that she realized how dependent she had become on it in her daily life— a technological drug she was addicted to, like most people in the world.

She was happier without being attached to it. If she needed to be contacted, Carrie had the Compound's number, and the staff would make sure Sandra was notified.

"Wow," Lacy said. "I don't know how you do it. I couldn't get by without my phone. Besides, my job depends on me having it."

"What do you do for a living?"

"Devin and I are Instagram Travel Vloggers. It's how we met."

It made sense. Lacy had a bubbly, outgoing personality that would certainly attract followers. She was also easy on the eyes— anyone could see that, even Sandra.

"Our handle is *thetravellife* if you want to follow—"

"I don't have social media," Sandra interrupted. She wasn't in the mood to listen to Lacy squawk after what happened in town.

"Oh." This seemed to amaze Lacy just as much as Sandra's no cell phone policy—maybe more so since not being on social media was seen as a faux pas in today's world.

Fuck what the world thinks.

"Anyway, this sucks." Lacy lifted her phone again, hoping to find a signal. "I planned on posting some shots of this place and doing a livestream later. It's so beautiful, I just had to share it."

Sandra nodded like she understood Lacy's woes—if one could even call them that. But she didn't care. It wasn't a big deal in the grand scheme of real-world problems. Lacy and her followers would make it through the weekend without her posting anything. Sandra knew from experience that it was healthy to disconnect. She just wished more people understood that kind of freedom.

"How'd it go?" Carrie asked when Sandra entered the kitchen.

"Got what we needed," Sandra said, laying the plastic bag on the island. Her sister and mother dug into it, pulling out the contents.

"*Plastic*?" Janis looked as if Sandra had insulted her.

"That's what the store had."

"If you needed money, Sandra—"

"I have my own money—"

"I would have given you enough so we wouldn't have to use *plastic cutlery*."

Sandra took a deep breath, about to tell her mother where she could stick the *plastic cutlery,* when Carrie intervened, sensing the rising tension. She'd always had an intuition to know when to defuse a brewing argument between them.

"It's fine, Mom. We'll survive the weekend with plastic silverware."

"Okay. But don't blame me when you can't cut through your veggies tonight. William always undercooks the veggies," Janis said, turning to the refrigerator to get the salmon.

Carrie's jaw clenched at the dig toward William's cooking. She curled both hands into claws and shook them back and forth, pantomiming strangling their mother. They had only been there a few hours, and already Janis was working on everyone's nerves. Sandra wondered if William and Devin were outside to avoid being around the lovable Janis Leigh.

Smart men.

"We ran into some troublemakers in town," Sandra began. "They damaged the paint of the Sequoia."

"Oh, no. What happened?" Carrie asked, placing a piece of tin foil on the countertop and dumping a bag of carrots onto it to be grilled.

"Four boys carved a word into the paint," Emalyn said, snatching a carrot. "Leave."

"Leave?" Carrie asked, furrowing her brow. She looked at Sandra, the corners of her mouth tightening. "Why would they do that?"

"They don't want us here," Sandra said.

"Who doesn't want us here?" Janis asked, turning around.

"The locals."

"Why wouldn't they want us here?" Carrie asked.

Sandra gave them the Cliff Notes version of what she'd learned in town from Sherriff Craven.

"So, what… they vandalize the Sequoia as some sort of retaliation against tourists?" Carrie asked.

"I believe so," Sandra said. "But that wasn't the only strange thing."

"Oh?"

"Everyone we spoke to seemed to know where we're staying."

Carrie's face turned a shade paler.

"How could they possibly know where we're staying? We didn't talk to anyone."

"Except for the mechanic at the gas station," Sandra replied.

The room grew silent for a long moment. She had no proof that Pappy had spread the word about them around Little Hope. But it could be his way of retaliating because Sandra confronted him for leering at Emalyn. He could've slipped the brats a few bucks to vandalize the SUV.

"Are we safe here?" Carrie asked, gripping the sides of the counter tight enough to turn her knuckles white.

"I don't know…"

LEAVE, scratched into the SUV's paint, flashed through Sandra's mind.

"You don't think…" Carrie stood rigid. "… they'll try something, do you?"

"I think it's best if we don't go back into town—"

"Oh, stop it, Sandra," Janis said.

"—and we make damn sure the alarm is set at night and the doors are secure."

"You're just being paranoid… like before you left. Worrying about things that aren't there," Janis said.

"I'm not paranoid," Sandra replied, shaking her head. "I'm telling you what happened—"

"Stop, Sandra." Janis held her hand up like a crossing guard slowing traffic; all she needed was the whistle. "Just stop. You'll scare Emalyn."

"I'm not scared," Emalyn said, bringing the carrot to her mouth and snapping it in half.

Sandra pinched the bridge of her nose in frustration. "Look, all I'm saying is that precautions must be taken. If our being in town, in this house, has upset the locals, there's no telling how they'll react."

"What do you think they're going to do?" Janis asked. "Chase us out of here with pitchforks and torches?"

Sandra was about to tell them about the bearded man looking for his missing family.

"There was this guy—"

"Enough." Her mother cut Sandra off. "I won't let you spread panic through this house."

"I'm not scared," Emalyn said again. "Sandra has a gun, and she'll shoot anyone who tries to hurt us."

Sandra's eyes flicked to Emalyn.

You. Stupid. Girl.

"Wait. What." Carrie's eyes fluttered like hummingbird wings, something they did when she was genuinely pissed. "Are you... do you have... a gun?"

"Oh, good, Lord," Janis gasped. "Emalyn, dear, come to me."

Emalyn obediently slipped off the stool and went to her grandmother, who pulled her close, making a dramatic show of protecting her granddaughter as if fearing the gun would go off.

Oh, for fuck's sake!

"Why do you have a gun, Sandra?" Carrie asked, her voice raising, demanding an explanation.

"I always carry a gun," Sandra replied. She felt her face redden, the anger working its way across her skin like hot wax. *Goddamnit, why couldn't you keep your mouth shut?* "For protection."

"You know how I feel about guns," Carrie said, her eyes sharp like blades, blades Sandra felt slicing through her, exposing a vulnerability she didn't realize she had.

"I know. But—"

"But nothing! You were carrying around a loaded weapon while you were with my daughter. Did you think about her safety?"

"Of course! That's why I have it," Sandra said in a matter-of-fact tone. She knew how to handle firearms proficiently from her extensive training with Joel—revolvers, semi-automatic pistols, rifles, shotguns, and full-auto machine guns—who had years of knowledge under his belt from time spent with the SEALs.

Carrie's eyelids fluttered again.

"What about the repercussions if someone knew you were armed?"

"So what if they did? Do you think the people around these parts have never seen a gun before? And besides, I have my concealed carry license on me."

Carrie shook her head and closed her eyes, the muscles in her face jumping.

"You could've put Emalyn's life at risk," she said, opening her eyes. The Carolina blue had drained away, and only a cold gray tint remained. "Suppose those vandals had overpowered you, Sandra, and taken your gun. They could have killed you. Or… Emalyn?"

Carrie shuddered at the thought.

"That wouldn't have happened," Sandra said. "I train for situations like this. Believe me when I say they wouldn't have gotten the chance."

"Oh, please," Janis said. "You train at some survivalist, right-wing militia commune where they teach you the world is ending."

"That's not what it is," Sandra snapped back.

"I've heard about *those* people on CNN—the same ones who attacked the capital on January sixth. Hilary Clinton was right when she called them deplorables."

"It's a rehabilitation—"

"And now you bring this… this… filthy way of thinking here to poison young Emalyn's mind. You're supposed to be her aunt, a role model. Yet here you are teaching her that guns solve everything." Janis continued relentlessly.

"What? No."

Her mother was so wrong it wasn't even funny. *Violence is the last resort.* Joel instilled this in them during their combat training

93

sessions. *Always try to defuse, disarm, disengage. Taking a life is your last resort.*

"Yes!" Janis insisted. "And I'll bet you told Emalyn not to tell anyone about the gun. Is that what she did, dear? Make you promise not to tell your mom and dad, or especially me, that she had that... weapon of war?"

That's a bit dramatic.

Emalyn looked from her grandmother to Sandra with the scared eyes of an animal that knew it was caught in a trap. She lowered her gaze to the floor, and her body seemed to wither like a dying flower. Still, her body language made it clear to everyone that Sandra had asked her to keep quiet about the gun.

"You're a sick, sick girl, Sandra. Shame on you for manipulating Emalyn. You need professional help."

Sandra wanted to defend herself, but somehow, everything she had learned to defuse, disarm, and disengage a situation leaked from her mind, creating a pool around her that she was sinking into, desperate to cling onto whatever she could so she didn't drown.

"Look, my weapon is secure." Her mind was racing, and she was trying to think of anything to make them understand her position on why she carried it. "No one is going to get hurt. I think you're both overreacting about this."

"Overreacting?" Carrie's eyelashes fluttered, and her face twisted, making her resemble their mother. "I'm an elementary school teacher, for god's sake. There have been eighty-eight school shootings in the last year alone. And nearly forty percent of unintentional shooting deaths of children occur in the home by a relative or friend—that *is* a big deal, Sandra."

Her lips pursed and her jowls twitched with conviction that guns were evil.

"If Congress had the guts to pass stricter gun laws, it would help prevent mass shootings as well as accidental ones. So, don't you dare stand there and tell me I'm overreacting when people are dying every single day at the end of a gun."

"Carrie—"

"No," Carrie snapped. "I want that gun out of this house. You can lock it in the back of the SUV until we leave."

"Carrie, we have to consider that being so remote and with the locals—"

"Enough. Just stop!" Carrie balled her hands into fists. "When are you going to let it go, Sandra?"

Sandra felt her defenses slam down faster than a watertight door on a sinking ship.

"What's that supposed to mean?"

"When are you going to let *him* stop haunting you? Making you into this person that you've become."

"You weren't there, Carrie… you don't know…"

"And you're not there anymore, either. Look around, Sandra. You're here, with us, safe."

"Safety is an illusion we tell ourselves."

"And that's what I'm talking about." Her voice lowered. "*You* left us to go to that place, to recover, to learn skills that would help you to cope with what happened and live a normal life. But you haven't gotten over it—that's why you haven't come home and why you have that gun. You still fear that one day *he* will track you down."

Sandra said nothing, and her silence filled the room's void. Carrie was right. It was precisely why she continued to train at the Compound: so she would be ready for him if he did come. *He* would never hurt her again.

No one would.

"That's not fair," Sandra was finally able to mumble.

"You know what isn't fair, Sandra? How you've alienated your family when we could've helped. How you cut your niece—who adored you—out of your life so you could go to some self-fulfilling survival training camp that you believed would fix all your problems. What you need, Sandra, is therapy. Real therapy."

"I know someone, dear," Janis said.

"Oh, I'll bet you do," Sandra said, rolling her eyes.

"I want that gun out of this house. I mean it," Carrie said, tapping her forefinger on the counter.

Sandra took a breath and considered reinforcing her stance about the unfriendly locals but decided against it. She was on the losing side in this battle. Defeated, she turned away like a puppy that had been scolded, but not before catching the smirk on her mother's lips. *Bitch!* She headed back down the hallway, knowing she'd screwed up yet again.

Who's really the stupid girl?

She should have been more mindful of her weapon so Emalyn didn't see it. But the vivid nightmare had lowered her fortifications and opened her up to an overlooked weakness. It was funny how *he* still had control over her life.

Outside, the evening was cruelly hot and muggy. The smell of lime hung faintly in the sticky air. There were no sounds of bugs in the grass, animals hopping through the brush, or birds in the trees—the surrounding forest was as quiet as an abandoned cemetery.

Again, Sandra found this odd. She lived deep in the woods at the Compound, and it was never this quiet. It was like the land was cursed, and even the animals didn't want anything to do with it.

Descending the porch steps, she noticed Devin and Lacy by the firepit while William worked on lighting the logs. Devin was snapping pictures of Lacy posing against the setting sun, showing off her tanned body, gorgeous smile, and perfect hair.

The sudden urge to leave again pounced on Sandra. Everyone was happy being there—everyone except her. She thought about grabbing her rucksack and starting for home on foot, hitchhiking back to West Virginia, back to the safety of the Compound, where she didn't have to deal with any drama.

You should've never come.

Still boiling from the argument, she moved to the SUV, where she'd lock the inside—against her better judgment—for the weekend to appease Carrie.

Reaching for the door, the crudely carved word radiated on the side.

LEAVE.

It wasn't meant as a warning, Sandra feared.

It's a threat.

CHAPTER EIGHT

Sandra read the word repeatedly—*LEAVE*—until her eyes began to burn and the letters blurred.

How far were the locals willing to go to prove their point? Was this just the beginning of things to come?

She and Emalyn were treated decently enough in town. Peggy came off as a lonely middle-aged woman who liked to run her mouth to anyone who would listen. As for the waitress, Sandra had gotten no bad vibes from her other than that she'd had a hard life— in this day and age, a hard life wasn't as uncommon as it should have been.

Then there was Sheriff Craven, who said he would talk with the vandals. He, too, seemed sincere but irritated that he had to handle the matter.

But people wear masks to hide their true faces.

Could that be what was going on? Were these the type of people who hid behind false personas? People who were bullies and threatened outsiders to scare them off. Hypocrites—many of them were coming out of the woodwork in recent years.

You're being paranoid.

The word carved into the side of the SUV didn't prove they were targets.

But it doesn't disprove it either. She felt queasy.

She thought about speaking with Carrie again but feared broaching the subject at the moment would escalate her already flared emotions into a fight. Carrie was normally level-headed and would listen to reason, but after finding out about the gun, Sandra wasn't sure Carrie even wanted to see her, let alone speak to her. Avoiding her was the key until she calmed down.

Still, there was someone she believed would listen: William. He was a reasonable, understanding guy. He could at least assess the situation from his insurance point of view mind.

William stirred the roaring fire with a metal poker, oblivious to Sandra's approach. She saw Devin was by the forest wall about twenty yards away, snapping pictures of Lacy, who had her back to the house.

She could hear the shutter click in the muggy, still silence surrounding the property and thought again about the absence of wildlife.

Strange.

William looked up from the fire.

"Hey, want a cold beer?" he asked, reaching for a small metal bucket filled with ice and Coors Light. The ice sloshed inside, reminding Sandra of how her stomach felt.

"No. I'm good. Can we talk?"

"Sure." He sat the bucket down. "What's up?"

"I have some bad news." His eyebrows tightened with unease. "Someone vandalized your truck in town."

"You can't be serious?" He studied her closely, hoping for a gotcha moment. When it didn't come, he said, "Oh, you are."

She told him everything, including her chat with Peggy and Sheriff Craven.

"I think it's a threat, William."

Something played across his face that Sandra hadn't expected—doubt.

"They're just trying to scare us. It's like the sheriff said: the locals aren't happy about the influx of tourists and are trying to prevent what's coming."

Sandra shifted her weight uneasily. She wasn't convinced it was just some tomfoolery hoping to scare them off. There was more to it. The phantom pain ached and deepened into her third knuckle. She rubbed it.

"Sandra," William said in a calm, understanding tone. "I know why this is concerning to you. I get it. But you must look at this reasonably."

"This has *nothing* to do with what happened. What they carved into your truck *is* a threat." Sandra replied, pointing back to the SUV.

"That isn't a threat."

"Then at least admit that it is concerning nonetheless."

He nodded. Though she could tell he still wasn't convinced they were in danger. The majesty of this place had blinded him to a possible danger lurking under its glossy surface, she felt.

"Maybe I should go back into town and speak with the sheriff," Sandra said. "Express my concerns."

He sighed.

"Don't do that. Leave it be, at least for the night." He took a sip of beer. "Tomorrow, you and I will go back into town, talk with the sheriff, and see if we can get this matter straightened out. Okay?"

It wasn't the bolt-the-door, lock-the-windows, and turn-out-the-lights she wanted, but it would have to do.

"Thank you."

She turned to leave, but William asked, "What was all the commotion about inside?"

"My gun. Emalyn saw it under my shirt in the bedroom earlier."

"She let it slip in front of her mother?"

Sandra nodded.

"Shit," he said. His eyes drifted past Sandra to the large window off the deck. Sandra followed his gaze. The sun had dipped behind the tree line, and she could see Carrie and her mother in the kitchen preparing food.

She noticed for the first time that the deck didn't have stairs, adding it to her mental list of odd things about the house's construction. *There's only one way in and out of the house. The front door.*

"Carrie's going to be spittin' venom tonight about this."

"It was my fault. I should have concealed my weapon better in front of Emalyn," Sandra said, turning back. "I'm so sorry. Carrie asked me to lock it in the SUV."

"Yeah, well, what's done is done. Look, do as she asks. Hopefully, I can calm your sister down and try to make her understand."

"She won't."

"No. No, she won't." He shook his head.

Sandra got the feeling William wasn't as anti-gun as his wife and understood why she felt the need to carry a weapon. Had it led to some heated debates in their marriage?

Laughter from Devin and Lacy broke Sandra's thoughts. William turned to them as they approached.

"Get a few good shots?" William asked, his tone and mood shifting quickly to hide their discussion.

"Think so," Lacy replied.

"Good. Hey, Devin, why don't you help your old man get dinner on the grill."

"I was going to go—"

"Nonsense," William said, ushering his son toward the house.

As Sandra watched them walk away, she could not shake the trepidation prickling the back of her neck. Since they had arrived, she'd felt uneasy about the house's construction. Why didn't it have any rear doors or windows in the bedrooms? Why weren't there stairs leading off the deck? Now, the vandalism to the Sequoia.

Something is rotten with this place. And no one sees it but you.

CHAPTER NINE

After locking the gun in the rear of the Sequoia, much to her despair, Sandra returned to the house. It felt as if a part of her was removed without the heft of the gun. A nakedness.

She dodged her mother and sister in the kitchen prepping dinner and slipped into her bedroom. With their combined wrath coming down on her like the Walls of Jericho, she couldn't handle another confrontation.

Emalyn was lying on the bed opposite hers, propped up on a pillow, reading the Sanderson novel on her phone. The bedside lamp on the nightstand lit the room to a dim yellow, turning the blue walls a sickly green color like mold on a cave.

Again, she found it odd that the room had no windows, and that electrical charge Sandra had felt earlier still crackled in the air, causing the hairs on the nape of her neck to stand.

Emalyn watched her anxiously, tapping her finger on the phone as Sandra crossed the room to her bed and sat down.

"It's not your fault," Sandra finally said.

Emalyn sat up in a lotus position, reminding Sandra of the little girl who used to sit in front of the television watching *SpongeBob* while eating mac and cheese. *Aunt Sonnie makes the best mac and cheese,* she would tell her mom. Sandra had just followed the directions on the box; there wasn't much skill involved.

"I'm sorry. I should have kept my big mouth shut. It just kinda… slipped out."

"Nothing we can do about it now."

Emalyn nodded, but her apprehension told Sandra she felt bad about how things had transpired.

"Look, I should be apologizing," Sandra said. "For snapping at you earlier. For not telling you why I left five years ago."

"I know why you left. Because of what happened."

Her eyes drifted to Sandra's left hand, lingering on the missing finger. This time, Sandra didn't pull it out of her niece's sight. She wanted her to see and understand that what *he* had done to her had changed her not only physically but mentally as well.

"You deserved to hear it from me. But you were so young, I didn't think you would have understood." Sandra shook her head. "I could barely understand what I felt then—I was all twisted up."

"You were confused?"

Sandra nodded. "And scared."

"Of what?"

"That the man who did this to me"—she held up her left hand, wiggled the nub—"would come back and finish what he started."

"They didn't catch him?"

"No. He's still out there."

Emalyn considered this with a tremor.

"That must be an awful feeling knowing he's still on the prowl and might attack other women."

"It is. And that was why I had to leave. I couldn't go on living in fear of him or others like *him*. Where I live, the Compound, isn't like what your grandmother says. It's a good place. A place where people like me—people who have been through a traumatic incident—go to get rehabilitated. The man who runs it, Joel Conrad, is a licensed therapist who was an ex-navy SEAL. He started the place to help people suffering from PTSD. Do you know what that is?"

"It's something that people who go to war get?"

"Yes, but not just combatants. I have PTSD because of what happened. It doesn't go away, Emalyn. Joel has helped me understand it."

"Then why do you still carry the gun?"

"Like I said, PTSD doesn't go away."

Emalyn's young eyes shifted behind her glasses as if she were starting to understand.

"Is it like Mom said? That you fear the man who hurt you will return someday?"

"Yes," Sandra said, admitting to her niece what she already knew deep down out loud. "I suppose your mom was right about that. But what I fear more is not being able to defend myself if I'm ever in that situation again."

Sandra sat back on the bed and took a breath.

"What happened to me had nothing to do with my love for you. I know you didn't understand that then and probably still find it hard to accept." Sandra sat up. "I love you with all my heart, and if you allow me to get to know you and rebuild what we lost, I believe we can have the relationship we used to. I saw a little bit of it today."

"I'd like that," Emalyn said.

"Me, too."

That wasn't as hard as Sandra had thought, and she felt some of her guilt for leaving release its hold.

It wasn't all gone. There was another person she owed an apology to—Carrie.

"I'm going to go talk with your mom for a bit. See if I can smooth things over."

"I hope so. I don't want this to ruin our weekend."

LEAVE flashed through Sandra's mind.

"Me either."

Sandra stood and went to the door.

"Sandra?"

She turned back. Emalyn wanted to say something. It was on the tip of her tongue, Sandra could tell. But whatever it was, she couldn't get the words out.

"Never mind."

Give her time.

Sandra closed the door behind her and headed to the bathroom. She needed to compose her thoughts in solitude before speaking with Carrie. She would apologize for having the gun and for asking Emalyn to keep it a secret. That was her fuck-up, and she wasn't too proud to own it.

Still, Carrie needed to understand where she was coming from. She wasn't the sister Carrie had known—she'd never be that person again. *He* had taken that from her.

Opening the bathroom door, she found Devin bent over the sink, sniffing a powdery white line up his nose.

"Shit! Don't you knock?" he shouted, running his palm over the sink and wiping away the residue. He sniffed and rubbed his hand across his nose, trying to get any leftover powder. Some remained in the corner of his left nostril.

"Sorry," Sandra said, quickly closing the door.

She stood outside the bathroom, embarrassed and contemplating what she'd inadvertently witnessed by her stupidity of not knocking before entering.

Devin was a cocaine user. An addict. She remembered when he first showed up at the house that afternoon, he was sniffing and rubbing his nose. She thought the lime dust in the air was affecting him, just like it had Emalyn. But that wasn't the case.

Does William know? She doubted it. Otherwise, Devin wouldn't have been invited this weekend. William wouldn't want Emalyn subjected to such behavior. Neither would Carrie.

She moved away from the bathroom door, wanting to distance herself from what she knew, and stepped into the kitchen. Carrie was by herself, working on cutting some potatoes to put on the grill. Several broken plastic knives lay on the counter beside her. Janis's shrill voice rang like a bell between Sandra's ears. *Don't blame me when you can't cut through your veggies.*

"You know, you could wrap them in tinfoil and put them on the grill to soften them. It would make them easier to cut with a plastic knife."

"There isn't enough room. The grill's full," Carrie said with a touch of hostility.

This is going to be fun.

"Can I help?" Sandra offered.

Carrie said nothing and kept her eyes on her work; her face was as tight as dried leather. Sandra had seen this look before when Carrie was upset, a look that reminded Sandra of their mother when she was deliberately cruel and mean—*I swear, Sandra, every time you laugh, it's like nails across a chalkboard to my ears.*

"Carrie, I'm sorry, okay? I fucked up. Please forgive me."

Carrie slammed the plastic knife down, snapping it.

"I always defended your choices to everyone—Mom, William, Emalyn." She shook her head, eyes blazing with fury. "I reassured them it was what you needed, that going to that *place* would help you overcome… *him.* I shouldn't have."

"I needed to go, Carrie. It was the only way I could heal."

"You call what you've become… healthy? For Christ's sake, Sandra, you were a liberal college student who loved playing the piano just five years ago."

The missing nerve endings tingled as if trying to recall what it was like to strike the keys.

"Look at you now."

"I apologize for Emalyn seeing the gun and me asking her to keep it a secret from you. I'll take your punishment for that. But what I won't do is stand here and let you tell me that I'm not trying to move forward. You don't have the right to tell anyone how they should or shouldn't deal with their trauma. I'm dealing with mine the way I feel is best for me. You may not like it. You may not accept it. But it is what it is, Carrie, so get the fuck over it."

Carrie looked at her now, eyes wide and glassy with hurt.

"What was I thinking inviting you this weekend?"

"I asked myself that same question when you called me. But do you want to know why I came, why I decided to put myself through all of this, knowing what everyone thinks about me, about my choices? I came to repair what was lost between me and that little girl. And our relationship. This isn't easy for me. Being here. And now that Mom's in the mix, it's even harder. But I'm sucking it up. I'm dealing. Now, it's your turn."

"I've been *dealing* with it since that night."

"Yeah, you've been dealing with it. But I live with it."

Sandra stormed past Carrie. *So much for smoothing things over.*

She was done apologizing for her decisions. They weren't the ones who suffered, who foresaw their death at *his* hands as clear as a high-def television screen. They didn't have to deal with the reoccurring nightmares. Nor did they understand the phantom pains, a constant reminder of *their* night together. *This night belongs to us.*

No one had the right—not Carrie, not her mother—to tell her how she *should* deal with the aftermath of the attack. There wasn't a right way to deal with trauma, Sandra had come to understand, and there certainly wasn't a goddamn timeline to recover from it, so fuck those who thought there was.

Knowing she needed to leave the house before she said something she'd ultimately regret, something she'd never be able to take back, she headed for the deck, passing Janis on the sofa in the living room. Her mother was about to open her mouth to say something, but Sandra beat her to it.

"Not a word out of you."

Flinging open the deck door, the warm air rushed over her body like a boiling wave of water that scolded her skin. The sizzling sound of meat filled her ears, and the smell of the cooking salmon crept up her nose. William stood by the grill.

"Everything okay?" he asked.

"It's fine."

If only that were true.

CHAPTER TEN

William had grilled the salmon with a sweet and tangy Thai sauce to perfection, and it paired well with the grilled veggies and corn on the cob—one of Sandra's favorite summer foods—cooked over an open flame, which brought out the corn's natural sweetness.

But she had little appetite that evening and sat quietly during the meal, feeling Carrie's scorn the entire time while she pecked at her food like a bird picking through a mound of seeds.

After dinner, Sandra returned to the deck while everyone gathered by the firepit to chat, roast marshmallows, and make S'mores, which Emalyn insisted they had to have after dinner. She'd had enough family time for the day and was eager to get away from the group to be alone and clear her head.

Sitting on a lounge chair, sipping a Coors, the evening air was hellishly steamy. The fire's warmth and smoke, mixed with the smell of melting marshmallows, seemed to add to the oppressiveness.

The bearded man materialized in her mind, along with the picture of his missing family—the bright eyes and big, innocent smiles of people who hadn't foreseen what awaited them—and tightened her shoulders with apprehension. She wished she could have helped, but as awful as the situation was, there wasn't anything she could do.

She heard the deck door open and footsteps coming up behind her. Her muscles tensed with the thought of engaging in conversation.

"Another beer?" Carrie asked, stepping beside her with a frosted Coors bottle.

Sandra didn't want another beer. The alcohol was making her sweat, and her clothes stuck to her skin like glue. A cold shower was in her future before slipping into bed.

"Thanks," Sandra said, taking the bottle from Carrie to be polite. She polished off the one she was drinking and set the bottle on the deck beside the chair.

"Mind if I join you?"

She hadn't seen Carrie slip away from the group; her mind was too focused on her thoughts to see anything past them.

"Sure."

Carrie slid another deck chair beside Sandra's and eased down into it. She popped the top of her beer bottle and took a pull.

"Emalyn said the two of you had fun today."

Sandra took a sip of the beer and felt her blood pressure rise. *Where's this going, Carrie?*

"We did."

"That's good. She missed spending time with Aunt Sonnie."

Sandra said nothing. She took another sip of the beer; it tasted sour and bitter, and she wanted to spit it over the railing. She knew her sister well enough to know when she was beating around the bush. There was something else on her mind. That was the real reason she was here.

"Get to the point, Carrie," Sandra finally said. "If you came to scold me about the gun again, you can save it. I locked it in the SUV, like you asked."

"I didn't." Carrie took a breath and looked at the firepit, the flames shimmering over her soft olive skin. She had always been the pretty one of the two of them—something Janis never let Sandra forget. "I came to apologize to you. For earlier."

Sandra hadn't expected that.

"After you came to talk with me in the kitchen, I should've been willing to listen. I didn't because I was mad at you about the gun. I know you'd never put Emalyn's life in danger, but with that gun on you, I feel it was asking for trouble."

"Some apology, sister." Sandra looked back at the firepit. Emalyn was putting another marshmallow on her stick. *How many was that now? Five?* William was poking at the fire. Flaming embers floated into the air like fireflies.

"Let me finish," Carrie continued.

Sandra took a deep swig of the beer, feeling she would need it if this were Carrie's idea of forgiveness.

"I wasn't looking at things from your point of view—I never have—even though I said I did. I should've been more perceptive of your decision to leave, to join that… place. And I should've been the one to explain to Emalyn why you needed to go so she understood that you didn't abandon her. I didn't because I was so mad at you for leaving—for not letting me help you."

"You couldn't help me."

Carrie nodded knowingly.

"But I should've supported you, no matter what. I just wish you would've come to me first."

"You would've tried to talk me out of it if I had."

"I would have," Carrie admitted. "Since you were little, I've always looked out for you. After Dad died, I felt it was my priority to make sure you were okay, that his death didn't distract you from getting into college, from playing piano for some big symphony like you always dreamed."

Sandra felt that familiar pang of loss at the mention of their father. One moment he was there, and the next, he wasn't. He loved to play the piano to relax after a long day's work, a skill taught to him by his father.

Sandra used to sit on his lap when she was little, watching his slender fingers slide from key to key effortlessly. Her father taught her the foundations of playing, which she would use for the rest of her music life. Until the night it was stolen from her.

"And with Mom, I always tried to protect you from her hatefulness. But then I was thrust into a situation where I couldn't protect you. The attack. The hospital and surgeries. I felt I was failing my big sister responsibility to keep you safe, like I had done my entire life."

"What happened wasn't your fault," Sandra said. *It was his.*

A deep sorrow darkened Carrie's face as if she understood that fate had set a date for Sandra, which was beyond anyone's control. *This night belongs to us.*

"What I'm trying to say is that I need to let you be who you are now. As much as I want to pretend things will someday return to normal, I know they never will. The sister I had before the attack isn't the same person sitting beside me. Because of... *him.*"

Carrie's acceptance of her decision to leave and undergo radical therapy and training made the back of Sandra's throat tight with emotion. She wanted to say something, but the words caught behind a dam of hardness that had developed in the years since the attack. Nothing was going to hurt her, not even her emotions.

"I love you, Sissy," Carrie said. "I need you to know that."

"I… love… you, too," Sandra said. The words felt strange coming out of her mouth but oddly familiar, like how muscles remember to move weight, even if they haven't done it in years.

Carrie leaned over and wrapped her arms around Sandra. The embrace had been a long time coming, and Sandra had to admit it felt good. The past was easing its clasp, though she knew it would never let her go fully.

When they pulled apart, Carrie's eyes glistened with tears.

"Look at me. I'm crying like a baby," she said, pushing the tears away with her fingertips. "I'm going to go and join the others. Why don't you come down?"

"No. I'm good up here. I need a little break."

"I get it. It's a lot for you."

"It is. But I like being part of this family again, even with Mom here."

"Yeah." Carrie's voice dimmed at the thought of their mother.

"What?"

"I don't know. She's just been acting strange all day."

Sandra looked at her mother by the firepit, sipping a glass of red wine. A shawl was draped over her bony shoulders, and the flames danced across her face, making her appear skeletal, with sunken eyes and cheeks. She looked worn out and tired.

Emalyn came up and sat beside her grandmother, pulling stringy strands of the roasted marshmallow from her stick and stuffing them into her mouth.

"What do you mean?" Sandra asked, watching her mother begin to coddle Emalyn like it was the last time she would ever hold her.

"She's been… nice. Kind."

"She hasn't been that kind," Sandra said, eying Carrie skeptically.

117

"Kind for her, anyway. Like bringing all that food for the family. Emalyn's allergy medicine. Helping me in the kitchen. When has she ever done anything like that before?"

Sandra couldn't remember. Janis wasn't the helping-others type.

"I feel like she's hiding something from us," Carrie said.

"There's always an ulterior motive," Sandra said matter-of-factly.

Carrie nodded. Her eyes burned in thought, trying to figure out their mother's angle. Sandra knew it was a lost effort. Janis was a chameleon at masking her true intentions. Finally, Carrie blinked and looked back to Sandra.

"All right. I better get back. I promised William that I'd get him another beer. He'll wonder if I got lost and come to investigate."

Carrie stood, but before stepping away, Sandra asked, "What's the deal with Devin?"

Her gaze shifted to Devin, who had his arms wrapped around Lacy. They were both staring absently into the fire like lovebirds lost on a deserted island with no hope of rescue.

"Why do you ask?"

"I don't know. I get the sense that he doesn't want to be here."

"He doesn't."

"So why'd he come?"

"I think because of Lacy. We were talking while you were in town, and she mentioned that it was her idea to come this weekend. Devin was going to blow it off. But she insisted on meeting his family and thought it would be good for him to hang out with his dad for the weekend."

"Lacy told me they're Instagram Travel Vloggers. Is that what they do for a living?"

"Yeah. They have a huge following and make a decent living off it, allowing them to travel worldwide."

"So, what, they're like nomads?"

"Pretty much. It's one of many points of contention between William and Devin. William wants him to get a real job and keeps harping about it anytime he sees Devin. But Devin has no interest, and now that he's with Lacy, it looks more and more like he's found his calling—if he can keep her with his other issues."

"Other issues?"

"Substance abuse. He's been in and out of rehab nearly a dozen times over the last few years."

I don't think it's working.

"Hey, honey," William called up. "I'm getting thirsty down here."

"I'm on my way."

With that said, Carrie turned and headed back inside.

Sandra sat on the chair, listening to the conversation and laughter around the firepit until she finished the second beer. She then headed inside to take a shower before the others came in.

Inside, she deposited the empty bottles in the trash and was about to turn away when she saw Lacy's Nikon camera on the island. Interested in seeing what they had shot, Sandra picked up the camera and turned it on.

She began flipping through the photos on the small digital display screen. All of them were of Lacy at various points around the property. The girl was gorgeous, and she could have made a career as a model if she wanted to.

Sandra stopped when she came to a particular one on the reel that caught her attention.

In the picture, Lacy stood in a normal pose, expressionless. It appeared Devin had mistakenly snapped a picture in between her posing shots. Behind her, the house loomed, the blistering setting sun deep orange on the log siding.

Is that…

Though the viewing screen was small, Sandra thought she could make out the shadowy shape of someone standing by the window in her mother's room, looking out from behind the sheer white curtain, watching.

Was it her mother?

No.

Sandra remembered Janis being in the kitchen with Carrie while Devin and Lacy took pictures around the property.

Looking at the functions on the side of the camera, she wondered if there was a way to magnify the photo to see the window better. But if there was, Nikon didn't make the navigation easy to understand without the user's manual guiding her step by step.

The basement door opened, and footsteps approached the kitchen. She replaced the camera on the island, where she found it, just as Devin entered. His eyes met hers, and Sandra knew from the suspicious look he was wondering what she was up to standing in a dark kitchen alone.

"You can turn the lights on," he said.

"I was just throwing my bottles away and heading to bed."

He nodded. His stare held her captive. Sandra's nub tingled with anticipation—did he not believe her?

"What are you doing?" she finally asked, breaking the thick silence.

"Getting Lacy's camera. She wants to take some night shots around the firepit for the Instas."

His eyes flicked past Sandra to the camera on the island, studying it like Sandra might have been looking through the pictures.

Sandra waited for him to say more, but when he didn't, she broke the tension that was quickly building between them. "Well, I better be getting to bed."

She moved past him, eager to escape the strange encounter.

"Are you going to rat me out to my dad?"

Sandra stopped. Now she understood. It wasn't about the camera. Devin hadn't thought she was going through the camera like a snooping perv hoping to find dirty pictures. He was afraid she was going to tell his father about his drug use.

Turning back, she saw Devin stood hunched over and meek; his face was drawn, and the swollen purple bags under his eyes made her wonder when the last time he had gotten a good night's sleep was.

The thought of telling William about his son's usage had crossed her mind, but in the end, she hadn't. She understood what it was like to live with a monster inside and how controlling it could be if one allowed it to take over.

Telling William wouldn't change Devin's substance abuse. Devin needed to face his monster and decide who was in control of who.

"No."

A small, relieved smile creased his lips.

"Thanks."

Sandra nodded and headed into the bathroom, locking the door behind her. With her back resting on the door, she closed her eyes, thankful to be out of the uncomfortable situation she had found herself in.

But the confrontation with Devin wasn't what haunted her mind's eye. The strange picture on Lacy's camera rested there uncomfortably. She wished she'd gotten a better look at it, been able to zoom in, and put her worries to bed. Was it just a shadow? She wasn't sure.

As she started to undress to take a cool shower, she couldn't shake the feeling that she was being watched. It was a similar feeling to that night when she felt *his* eyes on her.

Had someone been standing by the window on the second floor earlier that afternoon? Watching? Lurking?

Someone who didn't belong in the house?

CHAPTER ELEVEN

Sandra awoke the next morning to the smell of coffee. Rolling onto her side, she picked her watch off the nightstand and saw it was ten after eight.

When was the last time she slept in? She couldn't recall. At the Compound, everyone was up by six—routine was the key, according to Joel. *Keep your mind busy on the present, and you don't have time to focus on the past.*

Looking at Emalyn's bed, she found it empty, the covers strewn about. Had she snuck out without Sandra noticing? She was normally a light sleeper and easily awakened by the slightest peep. But not last night. Last night, she'd slept like the dead for the first time in years.

Is that a good thing?

She sluggishly pulled herself up. Her head felt heavy, and her body dehydrated, like she'd spent the previous night slamming beers like she had back in college with friends before her innocence was peeled away layer by layer. Rubbing the sleep from her eyes, she didn't recall having any dreams—good or bad.

Progress?

She hoped so. After she and Carrie cleared the air, and with Emalyn warming to her presence, Sandra knew a light was at the end of her dark tunnel.

Throwing her feet out from under the covers, she stood and stretched the sleep from her stiff muscles. She was about to head to the door and join the others for breakfast when something caught her attention next to Emalyn's bed.

At first, she thought her eyes were deceiving her, that what she was seeing was just her sleep-clouded brain projecting images that weren't there. Inching closer, Sandra realized it wasn't the case.

A boot print marred the polished wooden floor, directly beside Emalyn's bed.

The outline was faint but visible to the naked eye, as if someone had stood there watching Emalyn sleep. Sandra's stomach knotted. The image she'd seen on Lacy's camera the night before shot into the forefront of her brain: the human shadow in the upstairs window of her mother's bedroom—the Watcher.

After showering and while the others were still out by the firepit, Sandra had searched her mother's bedroom—under the bed and the walk-in closet—but found no sign that anyone other than Janis had been there. She'd then checked Devin and Lacy's room and the adjoining bathroom with the same result. Downstairs, she'd done the same.

There was no one in the house... but them.

This footprint said otherwise.

Or did it? Was her ever-present paranoia rearing its ugly head already this morning?

Don't jump to conclusions.

William could have come in to wake Emalyn for breakfast, wearing boots, tracking in a light dusting of dirt that settled onto the floor as he tried to quietly rouse his daughter without waking Sandra.

He had been outside most of the time since they arrived—at the grill or the firepit, avoiding the house drama. He could've been walking the grounds or hiking the trails surrounding the property— he was, after all, a fitness junkie.

Yet, with all the weird stuff going on, Sandra had to be sure.

Opening the door, she heard voices coming from the deck. The smell of eggs, bacon, and coffee made her stomach growl. She'd eaten so little last evening that her stomach pangs were almost as bad as the phantom pains.

Almost.

After using the bathroom, she entered the kitchen and poured coffee into a paper hot cup before going to the deck.

William and Carrie sat at the outdoor table, chatting. The sun was on the eastern side of the house, casting the deck in the morning shade, but the air was thick enough with humidity to cut with a knife, and the shade provided little reprieve. From the mess left on the table, it was obvious that everyone had eaten and was already going about their day.

"Morning, sleepy head," Carrie said, smiling.

"Morning."

"Here, have a seat," William said, pushing out a chair with his foot. He wore hiking boots with thick treads made for rough terrain. William could have made the boot print beside Emalyn's bed.

Sandra wanted to relax and let the weight of her worry go. She couldn't.

"Where you in our room to wake Emalyn?"

"No."

"You sure?"

"I'm positive. I was in the kitchen," William replied. "Why?"

"There's a boot print beside her bed."

"Maybe it was Emalyn's," Carrie said. "She had boots on yesterday."

"Cowboy boots. This was like combat boot tread or..." She looked down at William's feet. "Hiking boots."

"Well, it wasn't me," William said, shaking his head.

"Maybe it was Emalyn," Carrie said. "She and Mom went hiking a little bit ago, and I know Emalyn brought her hiking shoes along."

Sandra hadn't considered that. She'd jumped right to the worst-case scenario. Nevertheless, after yesterday's events in town and the picture on Lacy's camera...

"Sit down. Have some breakfast," Carrie said, breaking Sandra's train of thought. "We have pancakes left."

"And I can whip up a few eggs if you'd like," William added.

Sandra saw a plate with a half-eaten omelet on the table as if waiting for its consumer to return.

"I don't want to take someone's seat."

"Don't worry. Lacy and Devin are trying to find her camera," William replied.

"What do you mean?" Her nub began to tingle.

"She misplaced it somewhere last night," William said with a shrug.

"I saw it on the island before bed," Sandra replied. "Devin came to get it. Didn't he come back with it?"

"I wonder if she left it down by the firepit then," Carrie said, looking across the yard as if she could spot the camera from the deck.

"I'll bet she did," William said, nodding. "She was pretty drunk last night. She probably forgot that Devin brought it to her and left it down there."

Sandra took a sip of coffee. It was too light, too smooth. She was used to the cowboy coffee made at the Compound, where the grounds were brewed at the bottom of a pot full of boiling water, providing a strong caffeine jolt that would wake even the heaviest sleepers. She needed some of that high-octane java now to get herself moving.

"You said Mom and Emalyn went on a hike?" Sandra asked.

Carrie nodded. "Mom's idea."

"Really?" What was going on with their mother? "Mom's not the outdoorsy type."

"I know." Carrie shook her head and looked at her plate, a culinary Rorschach test, as if the answers to their mother's sudden strangeness lay within the messy blotches of egg yolk, ketchup, and small bacon remnants.

Sandra glanced at William, but he remained mum. He had been in the family long enough to know better than to wade into the waters regarding their mother and her antics.

"I'm going back into town," William said, changing the subject. "I'd like to speak to the sheriff about the vandalism and see what he's doing about it."

Carrie's brow pinched.

"You think that's a good idea?"

"I think those boys need more than a slap on the wrist, don't you?"

"Sure. I just…" Concern passed through Carrie's eyes, and her lips thinned into a white line. "I don't want to cause a fuss while we're here, William. If they're willing to vandalize the SUV, what else will they do? And, with us being way out here in the boonies, without cell service or the internet—"

"That's exactly why I *need* to speak to the sheriff. I want to know that he's handled the situation and can ensure our safety."

"If the sheriff can be trusted," Sandra said, sipping her coffee.

"You don't think we can trust him?" William asked.

She shrugged. "His loyalty may lie with the town he's sworn an oath to."

William mulled it over for a moment, chewing his bottom lip. "Sandra's right. I think it's best if we don't make waves."

"What about the damage, Carrie? Are we just supposed to let that go?" William's tone sharpened.

"No. I guess not," Carrie replied, though she didn't sound so sure.

William nodded, looked at Sandra, and said, "You up for another trip back into town?"

"Geez, William. Let her at least have some breakfast first."

"I'll grab something light," Sandra said. "Let me put on some clothes, and we can go."

William stopped in front of the sheriff's office. Sandra slid out of the SUV and walked to the curb. Looking around, she saw Little Hope was deserted as ever.

Pappy's Garage was quiet and shuttered like some derelict building left to rot for the last half a century. It was a quarter to eleven, and the diner and the grocery store were still closed. The birds chirping and the cicadas buzzing in the weeds were the only signs of life.

"Place is hoppin'," William said, stepping onto the curb beside her.

Sandra had expected to see people mingling around since it was Saturday, but if there was any life left in these parts, it certainly was mingling elsewhere. There was something off about Little Hope, and it wasn't just the lack of people. Something unspoken lurked under the surface that Sandra felt in the marrow of her bones.

What is it?

"Let's go have that chat with the sheriff, shall we?" William said.

Entering the sheriff's office, Sandra expected to find Craven inside, sitting at his desk, maybe dipping a doughnut into his morning coffee. But to her surprise, a good-looking blond-haired man in a brown police uniform shirt and blue jeans sat at a desk pushed up against the wall.

He was writing up paperwork; the pen tip clicking was the only noise in the quiet office. Another desk was in the middle of the room, placed in front of a single cell to hold prisoners. Sandra figured it was Craven's.

"Can I help you?" the man asked, looking up from his paperwork.

"Are you Sheriff Craven?" William asked.

"No. The sheriff's out on town business. I'm Deputy Allen. How can I help?"

"My sister-in-law"—William glanced back at Sandra—"had a run-in with a few local kids who vandalized my SUV yesterday afternoon. I wanted to talk with the sheriff and see what was being done about it."

"I heard about that. You're the folks renting the Bemyer place, right?"

William nodded. Sandra's nub twitched. Yet another person knew where they were staying.

The deputy continued. "I'm sorry about your vehicle. We've been trying to wrangle those kids in. Stop 'em from harassing the tourists. But those little bastards are slipperier than a water snake."

"Who are they?" William asked.

"Just some local punks. The sheriff's having a little heart-to-heart talk with those boys and their families now."

"Well, I'd still like to speak to him," William said. "You know when he'll be back?"

The deputy looked at his watch.

"Shouldn't be too much longer."

"Fine. We'll come back."

"Suit yourselves."

Exiting the sheriff's office, the morning sun disappeared behind an overcast sky, making the town seem even more depressing. They strolled back toward the SUV.

"What do you think?" William asked.

"There's something strange about this town, with the house we're staying in."

His eyes met hers, and she felt William didn't share her concerns. She needed to convince him that something was off about Little Hope.

"When I was in town yesterday with Emalyn, a man came into the diner looking for his family. He wanted to put a missing person's flyer in the window, but the waitress refused. Why wouldn't she help?"

"Good question."

"And that's not all. Last night, I saw a picture on Lacy's camera. It was on the island, and I was snooping through it—but only to see the photographs she and Devin took earlier that afternoon. In one of the photos, I could've sworn I saw a shadow of someone standing by the upstairs bedroom window. Then, this morning, I found the boot print beside Emalyn's bed, and the camera was missing."

She studied William's face, trying to read what he was thinking, but it was impossible. He had years of practice keeping his emotions under control in front of clients.

"William, if the locals don't want outsiders in their town, there's no telling how far they'll go to get rid of us. The vandalizing of the SUV was the warning. And now these strange things are happening around the house."

"The boot print could have been Emalyn's," William said.

"Okay. Fine. Maybe it was. But what about the missing camera?"

"Lacy misplaced it."

"She didn't misplace it. She's a travel vlogger who makes a living photographing her trips—it's not something she'd misplace, even drunk."

"You're being paranoid, Sandra."

"I'm not."

"You said it yourself: that what you saw in the photograph was a shadow."

"But I'm not sure it was. I didn't get to look at it long enough because Devin interrupted."

"Well, maybe Lacy will have found it by the time we return. We can check it out then."

They said nothing for a long moment, the lingering dread of the town encapsulating them. Sandra couldn't take it.

"How did Carrie find this place?" she asked.

"How does everyone find someplace nowadays? On the internet."

Duh. Stupid question.

"Okay. But *how* did she know about R&R? Did the company come up in a search?"

"Your mother."

"What?"

William turned to face her.

"Your mother sent us the link to R&R."

"I thought this was all Carrie's idea."

"It was. While looking for a place, Janis replied that she couldn't come due to prior obligations. However, in her email was a link to the R&R website. That's how we found the house."

Something wasn't making sense. Why would Janis say she wasn't coming and then offer to help them find a rental home? She didn't do kind things out of the goodness of her heart unless it served her. What was stranger yet was her sudden change of plans that allowed her to show up anyway. *Surprise. Momma's here.*

Sandra saw a police car pass by from the corner of her eye. Inside, she caught a glimpse of Craven behind the wheel.

"Sheriff's back. Let's go."

When they entered the sheriff's office, Craven was pulling his hat from his head, his swept-back gray hair damp with sweat. Deputy Allen still sat at his desk.

"Howdy," Craven said. His dark eyes flipped past William to Sandra, and his bushy, gray brows rose with recognition. "Sandra, right? So nice to see you again."

If the thumping in her missing finger was a tell, a sixth sense, Sandra felt she was the last person Sheriff Craven wanted to see that morning.

"Hi, Sheriff. My name's William Campbell. I'm the owner of the SUV those boys scratched up yesterday."

Craven looked at William, his face softening with sympathy.

"Mr. Campbell, please accept my deepest apologies for how some of the residents of Little Hope have treated you and yours. And let me assure you that I spoke with those boys this morning. It won't happen again."

"Thank you for that, Sheriff. But all that aside, my vehicle still needs repairs. Who's going to pay for them?"

Craven licked his lips fretfully. He either hadn't thought about the repairs needed or didn't care. Sandra thought it was the latter.

"Well…" He hitched his gun belt up under a small pot gut. "Under normal circumstances, I would say that those boys need to pay for the repairs, but these ain't normal circumstances."

"What's that supposed to mean?" William asked.

"They ain't got no money, Mr. Campbell. Hell, their families are barely getting by as it is."

"So, what? They get off with a warning?" William asked, his voice rising.

"It was more than that, I assure you," Craven replied incredulously.

"Sheriff, please excuse my brother-in-law's sharp tone. He's upset about the damage to his vehicle and wants it handled properly. You can understand that."

Craven nodded, and the tension in the room simmered.

"But our visit this morning isn't just about the vandalization. We've also been experiencing some strange things at the house we're staying in. I spoke to William about it, and we decided it was best that we bring it to your attention."

"What kind of *strange things?*" The sheriff's eyes grew into thin slits.

"A photograph was taken of the house. I believe someone was standing in the upstairs window, watching."

"Do you have this photograph?"

"That's the thing, Sheriff. This camera went missing overnight."

Craven looked to William to confirm the story, which irritated Sandra. Could she not be believed because she was a woman?

"We don't know what happened to the camera yet," William replied.

"So you have no proof of what you saw?" Craven asked, returning his gaze to Sandra.

"No." *Fuck, Sandra, you stepped right into that landmine.* "But I know what I saw."

Craven studied her for a long moment, contemplating something.

"Look, I can see you're both concerned. But I spoke to Lew, his cousins, and their families just minutes ago. They're going to mind themselves."

"I don't understand why they targeted us in the first place," William said. "We didn't do anything to them."

"It's because of the land you folks are staying on," Craven said.

"I don't follow," William said, confused.

"It used to belong to Lew's dad." His eyes flipped to Sandra. "He was the redheaded boy she caught yesterday carving that word into your SUV."

"The Bemyers?" Sandra asked. The missing nerve endings of her finger began to pound like a toothache.

Craven nodded.

"Are we safe out there, Sheriff?" Sandra asked as a harsh fear rose in her chest, one she hadn't felt since *he* slammed the trunk closed on her, trapping her. *This night belongs to us.*

"Yes. You're safe. I promise you that." Craven's stern look was meant to reinforce Sandra's confidence in him and his abilities to handle the situation. But all it did was cause the dreaded feeling to rise from her chest and settle in the back of her throat like a lump of ice.

"So that's what this is about? They're upset because R&R bought their land, and now they're getting retaliation by harassing people staying there?"

Craven glanced at Deputy Allen, who sat with the sheepish face of someone who knew a secret but was afraid to divulge it.

"How far are they willing to take this, Sheriff?" William asked.

"I put a stop to it, Mr. Campbell."

"And if they don't listen?" William asked.

"Then there will be repercussions."

"At who's expense? Ours? Or theirs?" Sandra asked.

Craven's jowls twitched.

"Sheriff, a man was in town yesterday looking for his missing family. Do you think their disappearance has anything to do with

134

what's happening to us? Maybe they were also staying at the Bemyer place?"

"No. I do not," Craven replied confidently.

"But how can you be so sure? I mean—"

"Because I spoke to the man you've mentioned. His family didn't stay at the Bemyer house. Nowhere near it, in fact. They were five miles away at another rental property owned by R&R. I confirmed with the company. Their records show that the family checked in on June first and checked out on June eighth—just like they were supposed to. Whatever happened to them happened after they left. And far outside my jurisdiction."

CHAPTER TWELVE

"The sheriff didn't seem too alarmed about that missing family, did he?" Sandra said to William as he drove them out of town.

"That's the thing about small-town police," William replied. "If it's outside their jurisdiction, it's someone else's problem. Most of these local yokels are only here to keep the peace and make the occasional arrest. They wouldn't understand the laws even if you placed the book in front of their faces, pointed, and said *read here*. I see it in claims all the time, Sandra."

"That's encouraging."

"All I'm saying is that Craven and his deputy aren't going to stick their noses where they don't belong. The sheriff didn't seem like a dumb man to me, nor did his deputy, but I doubt they've dealt with many crimes—I mean real crimes—around Little Hope."

"So that's it. We're just supposed to forget about everything. Enjoy the rest of the weekend with all this strange shit going on?"

"I didn't say that, Sandra. Calm down."

"I am calm, goddamnit! I think you're brushing this off too quickly."

"And maybe you're making a mountain out of a molehill."

"I'm not."

"Look at this rationally for a moment. If they intended to scare us, well then, they succeeded. But we did the only thing we could do, and that was to alert the police."

"It's not the only thing we *could* do. We *could* pack up and leave before this goes any further."

He sighed. Sandra felt irritated, and she wanted to slap some sense into him. She held back, balling her hands so tightly that her fingernails dug into her palms.

"It's not going to get worse," William continued. "Craven said he handled the situation."

Sandra felt her neck reddening. William only saw what was right in front of his eyes—what Little Hope wanted him to see.

They drove silently as the woods tightened around the narrow, winding road, choking them off from the rest of the world. The overcast sky was barely visible through the thick canopy of dark green leaves, most of which had turned over, showing their lighter underbellies—signs of an approaching storm.

If a storm did hit, Sandra wondered if they would lose power at the house. *Way out in the sticks as we are, it isn't ideal.* The phantom pain burrowed deep into the top of her left hand with the thought.

She knew they were in a bad position. The house had a landline, but if the power went down, so would the phone. There was no internet or cell service to call for help. They would be on their own. If they wanted to leave, the only way was to drive out. But what if they couldn't do that? What if the storm took down trees, blocking their escape?

William turned off the main highway and started down the driveway. The house emerged through the trees like a monolithic monster awaiting their return. Sandra felt a strange feeling overwhelm her, making her skin itchy—they weren't returning to their vacation home…

but to their tomb.

William pulled the SUV beside Devin's Nissan Z and parked. He killed the engine and shifted in his seat to look at Sandra.

"Don't bring any of this up in front of the others. I don't want to scare anyone or cause panic, understand? We're leaving tomorrow." He checked his watch. "That's in about twenty-two hours. Then we'll never have to return to this place again, okay?"

He opened the door and slid out before Sandra could respond, leaving her speechless in the already-warming SUV.

She couldn't believe William was brushing this off like it wasn't a big deal. Their safety was at risk. Didn't he see that? Or was she the only one whose eyes were open to that fact? The only one who saw things as they were?

Or are you just being paranoid? Seeing what you *want to see?*

Feeling a sweat break out across her body at this thought, Sandra opened the door and hopped out. She knew her paranoia was an ongoing issue she had yet to resolve—the gun she always carried proved that much. Was it getting the best of her imagination now?

The image on Lacy's camera came into focus, sticking there like a fishhook in her gray matter. The camera had gone missing overnight. Had Lacy misplaced it? Or could an intruder have snuck in while the house was dark and taken it? If that were the case, why hadn't the alarm alerted them?

Was the alarm even set? She had gone to bed before everyone else last night, so she had no idea whether the system was armed. The adults were all drinking, so it could have been forgotten. However, she didn't think her sister would turn in for the night without ensuring everything was secure, especially in a strange house in a strange town.

But if this was the case and someone had snuck in overnight, why would they steal the camera?

Because of what you saw—the Watcher.

This thought raised another question in Sandra's mind: How would anyone know what she'd seen in the photograph? She was alone in the kitchen while looking at it. And she only mentioned it to William when they were in Little Hope.

Get a grip, Sandra.

Maybe William was right; she was making a mountain out of a molehill. Perhaps nothing was happening except a bunch of pissy locals trying to run a big corporation like R&R off by scaring their guests—a just cause in their minds.

Inside, she checked the door lock and alarm in the foyer. The buttons glowed, and the screen display was on. She punched in the door lock code and watched the numbers appear on the digital display screen: 4-3-1-1-5. The deadbolt snapped into place.

Then she typed in the alarm code—8-3-1-1-5—and saw the display screen flip from green to red, meaning it was armed.

The system appeared to be working correctly.

"Everything okay?" Carrie asked from the kitchen.

Turning, Sandra found her sister and William standing by the counter with packs of uncooked hotdogs and burgers ready to be grilled for lunch.

"Do you know if the alarm was set before you went to bed?" Sandra asked.

She felt William's eyes burrowing into her, but she didn't meet his scornful gaze. It wasn't that she was trying to create panic throughout the house, but Sandra couldn't let this rest until she knew for sure.

"Yes. I locked it myself. Why?" Carrie asked, with a cock of her head.

"Just making sure." Sandra glanced at William, but his irritation hadn't abated.

To Sandra's left, she saw Devin and Lacy sitting together on the sofa, watching some old eighties horror flick picked out from the collection of DVDs on the living room bookshelf. Both looked incredibly bored. She guessed without their phones to keep them connected to the internet La-La-Land, real-world entertainment was a letdown.

"Hey, Lacy," Sandra said, entering the living room. "I heard you couldn't find your camera this morning."

"Oh, we found it," Lacy said with a disappointing tone that caught Sandra off-guard, causing her muscles to wind tight like a turn of a screw. Sandra thought Lacy would've been thrilled about finding her camera, but her voice said otherwise.

"That's great! Where?"

"It was in our bedroom," Devin replied. His eyes were bloodshot and watery. He must've had a bump or two already. "Under the bed. We must've kicked it as we got in last night."

"Oh, well, at least you found it," Sandra said, smiling. "I'd love to see some of the pictures you shot yesterday. It was a beautiful sunset, and you looked fabulous, Lacy."

Devin sniffed and rubbed his fingers under his coke nose. His watery eyes shifted to Lacy, who now looked devastated.

Something else had happened, Sandra knew.

"I would show you, but…."

Sandra felt her insides shift uneasily.

"The SD card wasn't in the camera when we found it this morning."

"It wasn't in the camera? Like someone took it out?"

"It probably fell out," Devin said.

"Is that even possible?"

He didn't seem to have an answer to this question and looked to Lacy for help.

"The SD card loads into the side of the camera," Lacy said. "If I bumped the camera on something, it could have ejected the card and fallen out somewhere."

"A few beers make her loopy," Devin added with a smirk.

"Shut up!" Lacy punched him playfully on the shoulder. "It doesn't."

"Sure." He looked back at Sandra and mouthed playfully: it *does*.

They both laughed. Sandra didn't. There was nothing humorous about this. She needed to see the photo again to put her thoughts to rest or confirm them.

"Did you look for the SD card?"

"Most of the morning, once we found the camera. No luck." Lacy's face dropped like a child who had lost their favorite toy.

Devin pushed himself off the sofa, sighed, went to the wall of windows, and looked to the south at the darkening sky.

"There's a storm coming in," he said.

Sandra felt a storm was brewing, but it wasn't the one outside that worried her.

CHAPTER THIRTEEN

After a late lunch, Sandra wandered to the covered porch to think. The wind had picked up, ripping the trees this way and that. Thunder rumbled over the rain-hazy mountains to the south, and orange lightning flashed through the dark, low-hanging clouds. The storm would be over them very soon, maybe by dusk.

The world felt off-kilter, as if she'd entered an alternate reality where some malevolent being would spring forth any moment and grab her in its maw, consume her, consume all of them.

She couldn't shake the feeling that whatever was happening wasn't by accident. The bearded man searching for his family. The photograph. The missing SD card. Everyone in town knew they were staying on the land once owned by the Bemyer Family, the same family who just so happened to vandalize the SUV. Coincidence. *I think not.*

Something was coming their way, as slow and methodical as the storm crawling over the mountains.

She glanced at her watch. There were only twenty hours until they left. Her missing finger began to pulsate. *Thump. Thump. Thump.* She rubbed the nub, but it didn't help alleviate the discomfort. Twenty hours was a long time. Anything could happen.

Thump. Thump. Thump.

"Hey, there you are." Emalyn's voice broke her thoughts.

Sandra turned and watched her niece cross the porch.

"Finally back from your hike, huh?"

"Yeah. Whatcha up to?"

"I'm just relaxing." It was a lie, but it would do. She was anything but relaxed. Nonetheless, there was no need to scare the fourteen-year-old.

Emalyn plopped down in a chair beside her.

"What are *yoooou* up to?" Sandra asked in a playful tone, trying to mask the worry in her voice and nerves.

"I'm bored," she sighed. "Mom and Dad are cleaning up in the kitchen. Grandma's getting a bite to eat since we missed lunch. And Devin and Lacy are upstairs in their bedroom. I think they're sleeping off last night's indulgences."

Such large words for a fourteen-year-old.

"What about your book?"

"Finished it."

"Already?" Sandra was gobsmacked. "That was fast."

"I can read most books in a day or two."

No wonder she has such a big vocabulary.

Sandra and Carrie were fast readers, and she wondered if this was where Emalyn had inherited the skill from. Of course, Carrie, being the consummate schoolteacher, had started reading to Emalyn when she was first born, cementing the love of stories into her mind when it was soaking up everything like a sponge.

"You want to play a game with me?" Emalyn asked. "Beats sitting out here in this soup."

Sandra studied her, wondering if this was a joke. Or was it a test? A test to see if Aunt Sandra was becoming Aunt Sonnie again. Aunt Sonnie would never have turned down a chance to play a game with Emalyn.

"What kind of game?"

"I saw a deck of cards and poker chips on the bookshelf in our room. You know how to play poker?"

"Yes. Do you?"

"Sure. Dad taught me." Emalyn stood, a mischievous smile forming. "But I have to warn you, I'm pretty good."

"Oh? Well, I must warn you." Sandra sat up and pointed at herself. "So am I."

"Great. You'll be a challenge. Dad hates playing with me anymore because I take all his money."

With that, Emalyn skipped back into the house. Sandra sat, momentarily listening to the rain, the thunder inching closer to the property, the festering anxiety that all was not as it seemed, making her feel edgy. Finally, she stood, staring absently past the firepit to the forest wall.

Only twenty hours, she reminded herself, then we're gone. Maybe playing poker with Emalyn would ease her mind.

A movement in the forest grabbed her attention—a shapeless figure slipping behind a tree, almost like a shadow disappearing behind a wall.

The door to the basement closed behind her.

Turning, she found Janis standing there, looking frail. Her normal dark olive complexion was pasty, as if she had the flu.

She hadn't spoken to her mother since last night and had hoped to avoid her for most of the evening. Tomorrow, she would say *bye-*

145

bye and wouldn't have to deal with her until the holidays if she decided to go to Carrie's home for Thanksgiving or Christmas.

"I need to talk with you," Janis said in a no-nonsense tone.

"So talk," Sandra replied, glancing back where she believed she'd seen the movement. It could have been an animal—a deer, perhaps? But she'd neither seen nor heard any animals.

"Can we sit down?" Janis walked to the table, pulled out a chair, and slowly sank into it, wincing as she did, like someone with a bad back.

Sandra looked back at her mother. Something *was* off with the normally put-together Janis Leigh, and it wasn't just her thin frame and pale pallor. It was under the surface, like whatever Little Hope was hiding.

"Okay." Sandra returned to her seat

Janis folded her hands on her lap, her rose-gold wedding ring disappearing under her palm. The anger of never being able to wear a ring sliced Sandra's heart in two as it always did. *This night belongs to us.*

Janis took a full breath as if preparing herself for the gallows— to bravely walk up those stairs and accept her fate at the end of a noose.

"There's something I need to tell you. Something I should've told you a long time ago."

Her mother's eyes filled with regret, a foreign look that Sandra had never seen before. She had always been such a stone-cold bitch that Sandra believed nothing could penetrate her hardened exterior and icy soul.

Even at her father's funeral, Janis had held her composure throughout the entire service. Not a tear. Not a wallow. Not even a sniffle. The only sign of emotion was when she kissed the casket before the pallbearers moved it from the church's crossing to the hearse waiting outside to take him to the cemetery. That was it.

"I guess there's no easy way to say it, so I'm just going to get it over with. I had a doctor's visit yesterday morning." She said it robotically. *Prepared*. "I have stage four breast cancer."

Sandra studied her mother for a long moment, unsure how to respond. She had spent nearly twenty-seven years of her life trying to please this woman, trying to win even the tiniest bit of respect and affection, only to be treated like dog shit in return.

Now, here her mother was, spilling this in her lap. Was it why Janis had decided to come this weekend? Not because her schedule had freed up or because she wanted to spend time with her family, but to tell them of her diagnosis.

Sandra cleared her throat.

"I'm sorry to hear that." Her words came out flat, detached.

Janis's face tightened.

"I'd at least thought you'd feel… something for me." Her eyes flicked away to a spot on the floor.

"What did you expect? For me to hug you? Tell you it's going to be okay? That… I will be here for you, and you won't have to face this alone?"

Janis's head snapped up; her eyes looked like a wounded animal begging for mercy.

"Fuck that!"

Janis blinked as if she'd just been slapped across the face.

"I'm your mother."

"Sure, you gave me life." Sandra shook her head. "But you were never a mother."

Janis studied her daughter for a long, unflinching moment. From her mother's expressionless gaze, Sandra knew she was working something around in her head.

"I decided to come up for the weekend so I could spend time with you girls and—"

147

"And get our sympathy?" Sandra slammed herself back in the chair and crossed her arms. She wanted to feel something—shock, dread, maybe sick to her stomach—but those feelings wouldn't manifest. They were long dead, buried in the darkest part of her heart—a part she wouldn't allow her mother, or anyone else— access to.

"No."

"Then what? Did you come to apologize? For the way you treated me my whole life? Because if you don't do it now, you may never get the chance."

Janis met Sandra's intense glare with her own.

"Save it. If you couldn't bring yourself to do it when you were healthy, then don't say it to me now that you're sick."

"I came here this weekend to... confess something to you, Sandra," Janis said, spinning the wedding band around her finger.

"Confess?" That surprised her. But it shouldn't have. The cunning old bitch was always scheming. *How did Daddy ever marry you, let alone love such a horrible person?*

"Whatever you need to confess, go tell it to a priest. I don't care."

Janis glowered. Anger twitched at the corners of her hateful eyes.

"You really are like your father. Hard as nails," Janis snapped back.

"Hardly."

The insult was so asinine that Sandra almost laughed. Her father was a warm, kind man who loved his family and went above and beyond for everyone. He provided everything they needed— food and clothing, a nice house, money, cars... college tuition for his girls. *His only mistake was marrying you.*

"Oh, you thought I meant George?" Janis shook her head. "No, dear. I didn't."

What the fuck is the old bat talking about? Sandra searched her mother's face, hoping it would be the window to answers yet revealed. But Janis sat like a stone. Unreadable.

"George wasn't your father." Janis's eyes gleamed as she said this, almost like she had been waiting a lifetime for this moment. To unburden herself with the truth.

Something her mother said moments ago struck Sandra like a brick to the side of her head, causing a sharp pain to flower through her skull. *There's something I need to tell you. Something I should've told you a long time ago...*

Swallowing, Sandra found her throat burned like she'd taken a shot of battery acid. Untethered thoughts raced wildly through her mind, trying to comprehend the bombshell her mother had just dropped on her.

"What... what do you mean... Daddy... isn't... my father?" The words choked out of her as though she were trying to speak through a vat of thick, black sludge.

Janis smiled wolfishly, enjoying watching her daughter squirm, toying with her emotions like some twisted puppeteer.

"I guess I should explain myself," Janis said, deadpan. "In 1998, I had an affair with a man."

She let her words hang in the thick, muggy air.

"You were the result of that affair."

The room spun—round and round—and Sandra felt something slip loose from her mind and slither through her body like a slimy slug. Her stomach twisted, forcing an unpleasant salty taste onto the back of her tongue. She thought she might be sick.

"You look so much like him." Janis's gaze shifted to the approaching storm as if she couldn't bear looking at her daughter.

"What... was his name?" was the only thought Sandra could articulate.

"Cullen McCleary," Janis said, facing her daughter. "You have his eyes. His red hair."

Her voice darkened then. "But what you have most of all -what I can't stand—is that you have his smile."

Janis blinked her eyes back to the dark sky with pure contempt. The orange lightning strikes inside the clouds were like flashbulbs going off inside a wad of dirty cotton, and thunder rumbled—closer now—as if the storm reflected her mood.

Sandra's life came into sharp focus in that instant. For the first time, she understood why she was the brunt of her mother's anger. She was the biggest mistake of Janis's life...

"George and I were going through a tough patch around that time," Janis continued. "Carrie was ten. I was always home, taking care of the house and your *half-sister*. George was working sixty hours a week sometimes. I grew lonely, felt unseen—was unseen. Until I met Cullen, who had moved into the apartment across the hall from ours, a battle-scarred ex-Marine from two tours in the First Gulf War. At first, it was just a friendship that started with a *hello* or *nice to see you.*"

A small smile creased the corners of her mouth. Though Sandra was certain it wasn't because she was fond of the memory, but the pain that it brought her daughter by telling her.

"Soon, it became chatting for a few minutes, then a few hours. Before I knew it, we were having lunch and dinner together some nights when George worked late. But then, one day..." She paused and looked at her hands, where she absently twisted the wedding band.

Sandra's nub was hot with fury.

"...I found myself in his bed." Janis sighed. "Nine months later... you were born."

"Daddy... did he... know?" Sandra asked, on the verge of tears.

Janis shook her head. "No. He went to his grave believing his favorite daughter was his blood." She shrugged. "What good would it have done if he had known the truth? He loved you like you were his own. It was better that way."

"Who was it better for? Him? Or you?"

Janis said nothing. She didn't have to. Sandra knew the only person who benefited from keeping her affair and love child a secret was her mother. Her eyes drifted back to her mother's wedding ring, knowing she only continued to wear it because it was beautiful and expensive, not because it expressed her devotion to her father since his passing. Her mother wasn't devoted to anyone other than herself.

"I need you to forgive me, Sandra."

There it is! The real reason Janis came this weekend. To seek Sandra's forgiveness for not telling her sooner that she was the product of an affair. A bastard child.

"Forgive you? So you can die with a clear conscience? No. I'm not going to give you that satisfaction. Let your guilt follow you wherever you land after you croak."

With that said, Sandra charged off, her eyes filling with tears so blinding she nearly tripped out the porch's screen door, heading for the woods.

CHAPTER FOURTEEN

Sandra couldn't contain the burning tears any longer and felt them run hot down her cheeks as she crossed the grass toward the forest. She'd thought her emotions were guarded from her mother, hardened into a callous. She was wrong. Janis had breached her armor like the sharpest sword, gutting her.

Slipping into the forest, she stood behind a tree, away from sight, balled her hands into fists of anger, and clenched her jaw so tight she could hear her teeth cracking.

An animalistic rage swelled through her, causing more tears to spill from her eyes. She wanted to slap her bitch of a mother so hard it would knock the cancer from her body.

Her monster was eager to accommodate.

But what good would it do?

Just breathe. Defuse. Disarm. Disengage.

No amount of lashing out would change the facts. The sins of the past were laid bare. But they were not her sins. They were her mother's. *May she rot in them.*

Yet, the urge to run back to the Compound was like the need for water to survive. No one could hurt her there, not even her mother, with the truth. Her entire existence had just been upended; the world she knew was rubble at her feet, a lie she'd been led to believe. The father she loved and adored wasn't even the man who gave her life. That person was Cullen McCleary—a *hard-as-nails ex-marine,* her mother had called him. Who was Cullen? Where was he now? Was he even still alive?

Does it matter?

She wasn't sure it did. Cullen had never tried to reach out to his biological daughter, so why worry about what happened to him when he didn't care about her?

Fuck him.

But was she being too hard on a man she'd never met? Maybe Cullen didn't know about her. This thought brought Sandra a small measure of solace. She wouldn't have put it past Janis not to have told Cullen about their love child—she'd risk losing control of the narrative if she did, and her infidelities could be exposed, possibly costing her everything.

The rose-gold wedding ring sparkled in Sandra's mind, and her anger flamed like Napalm exploding in the jungles of Vietnam.

Here she stood, crying, heart ripped out, soul crushed by her mother's devastating admittance, unable to wear a wedding ring because some masked madman hacked the symbol of a couple's love from her body.

And then there was her mother, who didn't deserve to wear such a beautiful ring, supposedly devoted to a man—a great man who loved her and his daughters—who was long cold in his grave.

Talk about a slap in the fucking face.

Rain began to tap on the leaves above.

As much as she didn't want to return to the house, she had no choice. Besides, she couldn't abandon Emalyn again, not after making such progress with their relationship.

She wiped the tears off her sticky cheeks and stepped away from the tree, steeling her resolve, knowing she'd be back at the Compound in a few hours and wouldn't see her mother again until her funeral—if she bothered to show up.

About to turn away, Sandra remembered the movement in the trees she'd seen from the porch. Was it an animal, as she'd suspected? The forest's absent silence reminded her that wasn't the case.

Moving further into the forest, she came to the spot where she believed she'd seen the shape, but there were no signs that someone had been there—the forest floor was covered with too much debris.

Until her eyes fell to the base of a large red oak, where the forest's dead remains had been washed away from runoff, exposing the roots and dirt.

Hunching down beside the tree, she saw the indentation of a bootprint in the dirt. Her nub began to *thump, thump, thump* again.

It matched the one she'd found beside Emalyn's bed that morning. She was sure of it.

That could only mean…

Someone had been out here, watching the house, watching… them.

A bloodcurdling scream from inside the house cut through the forest, raising gooseflesh across Sandra's entire body.

That's Emalyn!

CHAPTER FIFTEEN

Sandra rushed up the basement steps, taking them two at a time, and burst through the door into the hallway.

Breathing hard from hauling her ass back to the house, she found Carrie standing in the kitchen, her face pitched with fright, her hands folded between her breasts as if she were trying to keep her heart from leaping out of her chest. William was kneeling before Emalyn, white as a sheet, with tears glistening on her cheeks.

Clasped in Emalyn's hands was a large black book about the size of the Encyclopedia Britannica copies their mother used to get when they were kids, but nowhere near as thick.

"Emalyn. What is it?" William asked, taking his daughter by the shoulders and looking her over as if expecting to find her harmed somehow.

The atmosphere of the house had changed since Sandra was last inside. Now, it felt as if something that should have remained dormant had been awoken.

Carrie looked at Sandra with a worrying gaze before shifting her scared, wide eyes to Emalyn and William.

There were no bruises—physical ones that Sandra could see—but something *had* traumatized the child; it was apparent she was on the verge of falling into hysterics from the shaking of her body, the twitching of her right eye behind her glasses, and the quivering bottom lip. Something had *spooked* her. What?

"Emalyn, answer me," William said, shaking her. "What is it, honey?"

Janis was coming down the stairs from the loft, looking as bewildered and horrified as Sandra felt.

The door to the loft opened again, and Devin and Lacy stepped out. From their sleepy look, they must have been taking a nap.

"What's going on?" Janis asked.

"D-daddy." Emalyn's voice croaked, like a little girl scared out of her mind.

"I'm right here. What is it, sweetheart?"

She pushed the book at William as if she were forcing a gift upon him, a gift that, by the puzzled expression on his face, he didn't know if he wanted to accept. Taking the book from her apprehensively, as if touching it would cause him bodily harm, William studied it. A single word stood out on its leathery, black cover in large white lettering.

GUESTBOOK.

"It's just the guestbook," William said, looking back at his daughter, trying to understand why it scared her.

"No. It's not. In-inside, Daddy." Emalyn pointed to the book with a trembling finger.

Sandra stepped closer as William opened it. To her surprise, to all their surprise, it wasn't the one from the foyer that they all had signed. Sandra's skin drew tight to her bones. She saw four names written on the first page.

John Preston
Mary Preston
Suzie Preston
Anna Preston

"Where did you find this?" William asked, puzzled.

"It was… behind the bookshelf," Emalyn replied nervously. "In my room."

William looked back at the names in the book and said, "Honey, I don't see anything here. Why are you—"

"T-the n-next page, Daddy."

William turned the page.

He and Sandra collectively gasped.

THEY CAME AT NIGHT

The words were scrawled in large black letters across the next two pages as if they had been seared into the book like a brand on a cow's hide.

Sandra felt the air dissipate in the room, making her lungs feel heavy. What the hell was going on? Why was there a second guestbook in her and Emalyn's bedroom? And who in the hell would write such terrifying words inside?

The boot prints she saw moments ago filled her mind's eye.

We need to leave. NOW!

Devin inched up beside Sandra. Leaning forward, he read the frenzy-written inscription.

159

"What the fuck?"

"Devin! Language," Carrie snapped.

"Sorry. But seriously, W-T-F?" Devin rubbed his finger under his nose and sniffed.

Lacy came to the bottom of the steps, her soft features tight with consternation, making her look years older than she was.

"What… is it?"

"Emalyn found another guestbook behind her dresser," Carrie said, glancing at her before returning her eyes to the book. "It has a scary message written inside."

Not a message. A warning...

William looked back at Emalyn and asked her calmly, "Honey, how did you find this?"

"I was getting the cards and poker chips from the bookshelf. Sandra and I were going to play. But when I pulled the deck off the shelf, the bottom flap opened, and some cards slipped underneath. I slid it away from the wall to get them, and that's when I saw… it." She nudged her chin at the book in William's hands. "In the floor vent."

"It was hidden in the floor vent?"

Emalyn nodded, and another tremor worked itself through her small frame.

"But why?" Carrie asked.

"Someone put it there," Sandra said, "for the next guests—us—to find."

"They came at night," Carrie said, reading the words aloud like some incantation from the Necronomicon—the Book of The Dead. "Who's *they*? And *who* was it that *they* came for?"

"The last people who stayed here, presumably," William said. He flipped back to the first page with the four names, reading them aloud to the group.

The bearded man! He was looking for his brother and his family, The Hibbards, who disappeared under mysterious circumstances. Could something similar have happened to the Prestons when they stayed in *this* house?

"There was a man in town yesterday…" Sandra began.

All eyes turned to her like she was standing on a stage in a bright spotlight.

"Sandra… don't," William pleaded.

"He came into the diner where Emalyn and I were getting a milkshake, searching for his family. He wanted to put a missing persons flyer in the window, but they wouldn't let him."

"Wait. What?" Lacy said.

"Are these the people he was searching for?" Carrie asked, looking back at the names written in the guestbook.

"No. This is a different family. But according to the sheriff, when William and I spoke to him, the man's family, the Hibbards, were staying in a house five miles away."

"You *knew* about this, too?" Carrie said, her scornful gaze shifting to William; anger and betrayal etched her skin like granite, and her eyelashes fluttered. "Is this somehow related to what happened to the SUV?"

"I believe so," Sandra answered.

"We don't know that, Sandra." William looked at his wife apologetically. "I thought it best if Sandra and I kept what we learned in town to ourselves. I didn't want to frighten anyone."

"And what exactly did you learn?" Devin asked. Lacy came up beside him and hooked her arm around his, pulling herself into him as if for protection.

"The family who used to own this land… are the same ones who vandalized the SUV," William said.

"If the sheriff is to be believed, and if the missing family was staying in a house five miles from here…" Sandra's gaze shifted from face to face in the room. "Then what happened to the family in that book?"

The air was thick with heightened tension as they looked at each other. No one dared speak about what they were all now considering. What would be so obvious if it were true.

"Are you saying that there's another missing family?" Devin finally asked.

A crack of thunder broke overhead, rattling the house to its foundation. The wind howled, making the house creak and groan. Rain began to pelt the windows with such force that it sounded like marbles being thrown against the glass.

The storm had arrived.

"That's precisely what I'm saying," Sandra finally said.

"Oh, god," Carrie cried, covering her mouth, horrified.

"Daddy, I'm scared," Emalyn said.

"C'mere, baby," William said, wrapping his arms around her slender shoulders. "There's nothing to be afraid of."

"And what if there is?" Janis said.

This was the rare occasion when Sandra agreed with her mother.

"I think we should leave," Carrie said. "Before anything happens to us."

"Calm down. Nothing is going to happen," William said. "We're all together. And there's a security system. If anyone tries to break in, we'll know. We're safe."

Safety is an illusion.

"Tell that to the missing family," Devin said.

William's eyes cut to his son sharply. Devin wasn't helping the situation by pointing out the obvious.

"Is this just another tactic to scare us off?" William asked, though even as the words left his mouth, Sandra saw doubt wrinkle on his brow.

"I don't think so," Sandra said. Something odd *was* happening in Little Hope and at this house, but she didn't think it was theatrics to scare them.

"Just a little while ago, I saw someone moving around in the woods. I found bootprints in the dirt out there. Someone's been watching the house and has been inside. Those prints in the dirt match the ones I found this morning by Emalyn's bed. We should leave. Whoever we're up against isn't friendly."

"I agree," Carrie said.

"We can't go out in this," William said.

"Then as soon as it clears."

"Honey, just calm down."

"Don't tell me to calm down, William! I'm concerned about our safety."

"As am I. But going off half-cocked isn't going to solve anything. Let's all take a breath and think through this."

As much as Sandra wanted to leave, she had to agree with William. They needed to stay calm and think rationally before making a move. If someone was stalking around out there, looking to bring harm their way, they had to stay one step ahead of them. But she also agreed with Carrie.

"You're both right," Sandra said, and all eyes turned to her again. "We must assume that whoever is doing this has deadly intentions. We should have our bags packed and be ready to move as soon as this storm lets up."

That unrelenting feeling of being watched grew to a fever pitch, a poison spreading through Sandra's body and mind. *We're not alone.*

A flash of sharp lightning illuminated the outside of the house, allowing Sandra to see the tree line at the yard's edge through the living room's glass window. This was followed by a crack of thunder that sounded like the earth was splitting apart. She didn't see anyone, but that didn't mean *they* weren't out there, hiding amongst the trees.

"I want to leave," Emalyn pleaded.

"So… do I," Lacy said.

Sandra looked at her mother.

"How did you come across the R&R website?"

"It was in my email the morning after Carrie sent me the invite about renting a summer place. It offered what Carrie and William wanted—secluded rental homes for families. So, I sent it over to her."

"You opened spam?" Carrie said, shaking her head. Janis looked confused. "Not the canned meat, Mom—Jesus. Spam mail—unsolicited junk emails sent in bulk to an indiscriminate list of recipients."

"I don't see how this has anything to do with what's going on," Janis replied, not about to take the blame for their situation.

Had the previous family also rented this home from R&R? A thought occurred to Sandra that frightened her.

"If Craven told us the truth about the other missing family, and now we've come across this book alluding that another family is also missing, that's our link," Sandra said.

"And what exactly is that link, Sandra? Don't keep us in the dark, dear." Janis's voice was patronizing.

"We all rented from the same website—R&R. Rest and Relax."

The room fell silent, except for the rain tapping on the roof, the glass, the deck, and the wind making the eves rasp a protesting tune.

"So, what… the locals are attacking everyone who rents from this company?" Devin finally asked, breaking the silence. He sniffed. "I don't get it."

"The locals don't want R&R here," Sandra said. "So, to hurt the company—"

"They scare the renters," Carrie said.

"Or maybe it's worse than that," Sandra said gravely. She looked back at the book, still in William's hand.

"Didn't you vet this place before booking it?" Lacy asked, looking at Carrie.

"Of course!" Carrie replied. "They had high ratings and good reviews."

"And you believe everything on the internet?" Lacy replied, crossing her arms.

Carrie was about to say something, but her mouth slowly closed. Sandra knew that ratings and good reviews could be doctored to make a website or a business look more favorable than it was, like a filter on one of Lacy's Instagram photos.

Lacy said, "Wouldn't it have gotten out if this company— R&R—knew this was happening to their customers? Someone would've talked to the police."

"Not if there was no one left alive to tell their story," Sandra said matter-of-factly.

A chill rose through the house like a cold wind. Sandra shivered and wrapped her arms around herself; she couldn't help it.

"We need to get our stuff together and plan to leave as soon as the storm lets up," Sandra said. "The longer we stay, the more danger we open ourselves up to."

CHAPTER SIXTEEN

Sandra and Emalyn returned to their room to pack their bags while the others gathered their things. Emalyn's sobs were the only sound in the windowless room. Tears dripped from her chin and hit the bed with a *pat* as she hurriedly threw her belongings into her suitcase.

"S-Sandra, are we…" Her voice broke.

"No," Sandra replied, throwing her dirty clothes on the bed beside her rucksack. "We're going to be fine."

You know that may not be the case. One family was missing. And maybe, after finding the guestbook hidden in the vent, another one, too.

How many other families fell to a similar fate?

"I'm… I'm really scared." Emalyn's voice broke again, and with it, so did Sandra's heart.

She turned to the teenager, who resembled the child she remembered before left—so grown but still such an adolescent. Sandra wrapped Emalyn in her arms. Emalyn buried her head in her aunt's chest, sobbing, her hot tears soaking through Sandra's shirt and onto her skin.

"I'm not going to let anything happen to you," Sandra said soothingly, running her hands through Emalyn's long brown hair. But the juddering working through Sandra's body belayed her confidence in her ability to keep Emalyn—to keep them all—safe.

I need my gun.

After deciding to pack and leave, Sandra had thought about retrieving it from the SUV but knew Carrie would protest. Even under the current circumstances, where their lives were possibly at risk, Carrie couldn't fathom the need for a gun.

Sandra kicked herself now for being unable to ignore her sister's views and going straight to the SUV. She'd feel better knowing she was armed.

Taking Emalyn by the shoulders, Sandra gently pushed her back, looking into her big brown—terrified—eyes.

"We're going to be okay. You have nothing to be afraid of."

"What happens… if… if *they* do come?"

"They won't. This is all probably to scare us away."

IT'S NOT! Her mind screamed as if trying to get her to wake up from the daydream she was living in—the denial—and see what was happening right before her eyes.

"We didn't do anything to *them,*" Emalyn spit. "Why are they doing this to us?"

Sandra wished she had a simple answer. But there wasn't one. Still, she felt she had to say something to help Emalyn understand.

"Some people just aren't accepting of others. It doesn't matter if you're a good, kind person. They will dislike you because of some ingrained perception that you are their enemy."

"That's a stupid way of thinking," Emalyn said, wiping a tear from her flushed cheek.

"It is." Sandra brushed a strand of hair off her niece's forehead. "Finish packing. I'm going to go to the bathroom and get our toiletries." She saw a moment of petrified fear that she would leave her pass through Emalyn's eyes. "I'll keep the doors open and be right around the corner in the bathroom. Okay?"

This didn't seem to quell Emalyn's worries, but she nodded and returned to her suitcase and began stuffing more things inside.

Sandra stepped into the hallway. William and Carrie's bedroom door was open. They were hastily throwing their clothing into their suitcases, not saying anything to one another, and the noiseless, intense emotions emanating from the room told Sandra that Carrie was fuming at William, maybe at them both, for keeping secrets.

She has a right to be pissed. You should have told her what was happening when you got back this afternoon.

There was nothing she could do about that now. She had let William control the situation against her better judgment. Turning into the bathroom, Sandra flipped on the overhead light and gathered their toiletries around the sink—toothpaste and brushes, Emalyn's hair ties, and comb.

Outside, the thunder cracked, and the house shuddered. Glancing down the short hallway, she could see into the living room and the large wall of windows that led out to the deck. Lightning flashed again, catching the driving rain and the tree line beyond in the dusky light. Her nub pinged with discomfort like someone was driving needles into it and scraping what bone was left in there.

She didn't like their situation. They were in the middle of nowhere, without cell phones or internet, and trapped—at least momentarily—by a raging storm.

We need to get out of here.

Gathering all their toiletries together, Sandra sat them on the sink's countertop, then threw back the shower curtain to get their shampoos and Emalyn's loofah, hanging over the top of the spray nozzle by the fabric loop. She was about to pull it off when a glassy reflection caught her eye inside the ceiling vent above the shower.

What is that? Her nub drummed with her rising heartbeat.

Using the tub's sidewall as a step, she could see something hidden behind the plastic slats. Sandra felt her heart rate kick up— a harder *bump, bump, bump* against her sternum. Reaching up to the vent, she grabbed the plastic cover and wiggled it free. Dust fell from inside and sprinkled into her eyes. She blinked the dirt away and coughed.

When she returned her gaze to the vent, Sandra was horrified at what she saw.

A small camera.

The lens aimed to capture the entire bathroom.

Violation spread across her like a psoriasis flare-up—burning and raw on her skin.

Someone *had* been watching them since they arrived. They'd seen them undressing, using the toilet, and showering. And if there was one camera, that had to mean…

The phantom pain rose to a crescendo through her left hand.

There are others…

With a crack of thunder, the lights went out.

CHAPTER SEVENTEEN

"MOM!" Emalyn screamed.

Sandra stepped out of the bathroom into the dark hallway between the two bedrooms. The house was still and quiet, and the air felt unnatural and dead. A foul aroma—perhaps body odor—permeated the house like a black cloud, causing her nose to wrinkle at its stench.

Something's not right.

"It's okay," Carrie's voice cut the gloomy silence. "It's just the storm. Hold on, I'm trying to find…"

Her cell phone flashlight blinked on, casting a wide arc of white light across the bedspread and onto William, who stood with a handful of clothes and looked as concerned as Carrie sounded.

Three lightning flashes strobed through the house, illuminating its contours before the suffused darkness regained its hold. Thunder cracked, and the house quivered to its bones. Sandra could relate.

"William," Sandra called. She needed to tell him about the camera in the bathroom, but emotions were already running high, and fear was seeping in like a virus. Soon to infect all of them. She didn't want anyone to lose their shit, especially Carrie and Emalyn, who were already on the brink of panic from the message in the guestbook.

William put the clothes in his suitcase and walked around the bed. Carrie provided him with light so he wouldn't trip over anything as he went. Emalyn came to the bedroom doorway behind Sandra.

"Mom, I can't see anything and still have a few things to pack."

"Emalyn, stay where you are," Sandra said sharply. Jolts of pain shot from the tip of her severed finger and into her elbow like she'd just stuck it in a light socket. The house felt heavy with malevolence, like an evil presence was among them, lurking in the shadows, a creature waiting, watching for the right moment to strike.

"Sandra? What's wrong?" Carrie asked, picking up the unease in Sandra's tone.

Sandra remained mum, trying not to express her concern with her glance. William stepped into the hallway, his face shadowed by the light at his back.

"What's up?"

She leaned in and whispered, "Someone's been watching us. There's a camera in the bathroom vent. There might be more around the house."

"Dad?" Devin's voice called from the loft. "What happened to the lights?"

"It's okay, Devin. It's just a power outage. How are you guys making out getting your stuff together?" He tried to hide the distress in his voice, but Sandra heard the cracks, the shakiness—the dread—as he spoke.

"We're trying to get everything together," Devin called back.

Pack light. Always be ready to move. With everything Devin and Lacy brought, getting it from the house to the car would take time, slowing them down.

"We need to get out of here," Sandra whispered. "Now!"

"I know. But the storm—"

"Fuck the storm, William. We need to go."

William agreed with a silent nod.

"Devin, hurry up. We're leaving in five," William shouted.

"Yeah, but—"

"No buts."

"William? What's going on?" Carrie asked, moving to the bedroom's threshold, the phone's light broadcasting into the hallway. Sandra couldn't see her sister's face behind the beam, but she didn't have to know how afraid Carrie was—the terror encapsulated in her voice told Sandra everything her eyes couldn't.

"Do you have your stuff together?" William asked, looking over his shoulder.

Carrie shifted the beam of light to the ceiling, reflecting it down onto the three of them so they could see one another—three ghostly faces in the dark.

"Most of it, yes."

"Hurry up. Like I said, we're leaving in five."

A sharp crack of thunder split overhead. Carrie jumped, causing the tendons and muscles in her neck to form into ropy bands.

"But... but the storm." She looked back to William with concern at the thought of leaving amid such nasty weather.

"I'm getting my gun." Sandra finally relented.

The floorboards creaked down the hallway.

Sandra's and William's heads snapped toward the sound. At the same time, a bright light clicked on at the end of the hall, shining directly into their eyes and blinding them. Sandra squinted and held up her hand, trying to see past the light.

"Who's there?" William asked.

At first, Sandra thought the roaring crack was thunder. A crack so close, so powerful that she felt the shockwave pass through her body and cause a dull ringing inside her head.

When she looked back at William, he was no longer standing there. It was like he had vanished into thin air. *Where in the hell?*

Her gaze caught Carrie in the doorway, her face twisted with horror, her mouth agape in a scream, but Sandra couldn't hear anything over the ringing.

She felt something wet dribble off her chin. Reaching up, she touched her skin, her fingertips sliding through something sticky and thick like warm motor oil.

A sound other than the ringing was starting to come to her now, a low, far-off wail, like a foghorn to sailors at sea, warning them of danger as they neared the coastline.

Pulling her fingers away, she looked at them under the light coming from the end of the hall. Something dark red, almost black, stained the tips. She rubbed her thumb and forefinger together, trying to make—the wailing was getting louder—sense of what she was—*what happened to William?*—seeing.

Her focus shifted from her fingers to the floor, where the same substance streaked the polished wood.

Is that…

Slowly, the ringing in her ears began to die, and the wailing started to rise as if someone were manipulating the soundtrack in her mind.

BLOOD!

Sandra's eyes snapped back to Carrie. The sound coming out of her sister was unlike anything she had ever heard before; even her cries the night of her attack paled in comparison to the shrill, distressed screeches coming from Carrie.

The next sound was as familiar as a lullaby. She had heard it many times while at the shooting range.

A shotgun racking!

God, help us.

"Carrie, get down!"

Sandra lurched forward and pushed her sister back into the bedroom, her foot slipping in William's blood as she did. She went down, hard, onto her knees and elbows just as another blast from the shotgun erupted and blew a hole the size of a basketball in the drywall beside the bathroom door.

Had Sandra not slipped, she would've been cut in two. The hallway quickly filled with chalky dust and the hot smell of gunpowder.

The shooter at the end of the hall racked another round into the chamber. Sandra knew she only had seconds to get to cover. Spinning around on the bloody floor, she saw Emalyn in the doorway directly in front of her, frozen in panic and shock at seeing her father ripped apart right in front of her by the business end of the shotgun.

The beam settled on Sandra, and she swore she could feel the light on her skin like a vampire might when exposed to the sun. *I'm in the crosshairs. This is it.*

She closed her eyes and hoped she wouldn't feel anything…

"Dad!" Devin screamed from the loft above.

The beam swung away from Sandra, the arc of light slashing off the wall, and quickly extinguished. The shadows snapped forward, reclaiming their rightful place in the house, other than around the soft white light from Carrie's phone, now on the floor, knocked from her hand when Sandra pushed her into the room.

Sandra darted for the bedroom, grabbing Emalyn as she passed through the threshold. She pushed Emalyn onto the bed and then moved back to the doorway. *Where was the shooter?*

"Dad? What the hell was that?" Deven cried.

"Carrie? Emalyn? Is everyone okay?" Janis asked, distressed.

Carrie was no longer screaming. Her cries had turned into heart-wrenching whimpers that cut deep into Sandra's chest. Her husband, Emalyn's dad, had been taken from them in the blink of an eye.

Sandra choked back her emotions. There would be time to mourn later. Time to cry. Time to console each other. But right now, Sandra knew she had to stay vigilant and focused. Their survival depended on it.

On you.

The house had grown eerily still again. Sandra peeked around the corner of the door and down the hallway. Another lightning strike lit up the house. She didn't see the shooter, didn't hear him moving around. The only sound she heard was the rain pelting the glass. If the shooter was still there, they had taken cover somewhere out of Sandra's line of sight, keeping very still and very quiet.

"Dad!" Devin's screamed from the loft.

"Answer us!" Janis demanded.

Thunder cracked overhead.

Sandra heard their feet cross the loft above, nearing the steps. She knew they were about to descend the stairs to investigate what had happened. If they did, they'd walk into a carefully laid trap and meet the same fate as William.

You can't let that happen.

"Get inside your rooms and lock the doors!" Sandra hollered. "There's someone in the house with a gun."

"What?" Devin shrieked.

"Oh, my god!" Janis's voice trembled. "Is Emalyn okay? Carrie? Please, talk to me, babies."

Sandra noticed her mother didn't ask about her bastard child. *Surprise. Surprise.*

"Get back in your rooms!" Sandra screamed. "Now!"

Across the hall, Carrie sobbed uncontrollably on her hands and knees, her face wet with tears and ghastly white in the phone's soft light.

"Carrie," Sandra whispered. "Where are the keys to the SUV?"

Carrie didn't register Sandra's words. She was lost in a world of confusion, shock, and loss; her entire life had just gone through the blender. Sandra understood. She'd been there, paralyzed by the fear, handicapped by the trauma.

"Carrie! Snap the fuck out of it!"

Carrie's bloodshot eyes shot onto Sandra. She blinked—once, twice—and came out of her trance.

Good, you have her attention.

"Where are the keys to the SUV?"

"On-on the nightstand in-in our room."

"Get them."

Carrie nodded. Using the doorframe, she slowly pulled herself up. Her legs were unsteady, knees quivering. For a moment, Sandra thought she would collapse until she grabbed the doorframe for support.

"You can do this, Sissy," Sandra said.

Easing her hands away from the doorframe, Carrie's right knee buckled. Sandra's breath caught in her throat. But she didn't crumble back to the floor. Instead, she turned on her heels and disappeared into the dark room. Sandra let out a long sigh.

Getting Carrie out of the room was Sandra's number one priority; she'd be defenseless against the armed attacker when he came for them. *And he will come.* Inching back from the door to where Emalyn sat, Sandra grabbed her niece and jerked her off the bed.

"What are you doing?" Emalyn whispered, her eyes glassy in the dim light seeping in from the hall.

Sandra picked up the single mattress, threw it aside, pulled the box spring from the frame, and stood it on end.

"I'm getting your mom out of that room. Then we're getting out of here."

"How? There are no windows."

No windows.

It was clear to Sandra why there were no windows in the bedrooms, no rear entrance, no stairs leading off the deck, and only one way in and out of the house—the front door. The entire house was designed so no one could escape.

A kill box.

With what they suspected about the missing families and the warning left for them, whoever was behind this couldn't let them leave. If they wanted to get out of this house, Sandra knew, they were going to have to fight their way out.

"Get over here. Tuck yourself into a ball in the corner," Sandra ordered.

Emalyn hurried into the corner and ducked down, making herself as small as possible. Sandra then placed the box spring against the wall, covering Emalyn. It wasn't much, and it wouldn't stop a direct blast from a shotgun, but it would provide her with some protection. *Better than nothing.*

"Don't come out until I say. Understand?"

Sandra turned, grabbed the mattress off the floor, and moved beside the doorway. She suspected the shooter was still at the end of the hall, basking in the darkness from which he came.

He no longer needed the flashlight to see her; the light from Carrie's phone on the floor made her easily visible. He would need one evenly leveled blast with the shotgun to knock them down like pins at a bowling alley.

The mattress wouldn't protect Sandra from the shotgun's wrath, but that wasn't the point. If she stayed low in a crouch and hurried across the hall with the mattress held upright, she hoped that the shooter would aim for a center mass or headshot, thinking she was standing up, dumb enough to believe a mattress could stop a slug from a shotgun.

If the shooter made the miscalculation, like she believed he would in the rush of adrenaline to get off a shot, she would have milliseconds, as he rechambered the shotgun, to get Carrie across the hall before he could get off a second shot.

And if he aims low?

She flung the thought from her mind. There was no other way. It was just a matter of time before the shooter came down the hall, looking for them. He'd find Carrie in the room and execute her as easily as shooting a scared rabbit in a cage.

Then, he would turn his sights on her and Emalyn.

But if they were together, in one room, that might give them a fighting chance of executing the plan already forming in Sandra's mind.

But let's not get ahead of ourselves.

She looked back to her niece, hidden behind the box spring. She could hear her crying, and Sandra's heart broke for the second time that evening. It wouldn't be the last.

"I love you, Emalyn," Sandra said, knowing this could be the final moments she spent with her niece. She had missed so much of Emalyn's young life because of unforeseen events over which she had no control. Now, she might never see her again because of events she had no control over. *How sickeningly profound.*

Looking across the hall, Sandra saw Carrie had returned holding the SUV's keys. Sandra pointed at herself, made a walking gesture with her fingers, and then pointed at her sister. Carrie nodded, understanding Sandra's intentions to come and get her.

Getting into a crouch, Sandra took hold of the mattress and pulled it away from the wall. She felt it tilt forward and then back the other way. She shifted her grip up the sides so it wasn't top heavy and didn't flop around as she crossed the hall, giving her trickery away to the shooter.

Speed was her concern. The sooner he discharged the shotgun, the sooner she could drop the mattress, grab Carrie, and get them both back into the room.

Swallowing whatever had formed in the back of her throat away, Sandra rushed into the hall.

She was a foot away from the door when the shotgun erupted, blowing a large hole through the center of the mattress with enough force it took all Sandra had to keep ahold of it. Stuffing littered the air and slowly see-sawed like snowflakes back to the floor.

She had turned her face away from the blast out of pure instinct. Now she saw William in the bathroom, a spectral form visible in the soft white light from the phone. The shotgun blast had blown his body into the tub, where he lay crumpled like a discarded doll. His legs dangled over the tub's bloody wall, twisted and broken.

The shooter, pulling back the fore-end, racking another round into the shotgun, broke the dead silence.

Sandra threw the mattress away and reached for Carrie. Pulling her sister from the threshold of the door, she launched her into the opposite room like a pro wrestler slingshotting an opponent into the ropes, just as she heard the round in the shotgun hammer home.

Sandra charged toward the bedroom door. A sickening premonition radiated through her body that she wouldn't make the short distance unless...

She leaped through the air towards the doorway just as another round barked. This one missed obliterating her from existence by mere inches and blew the bathroom door apart in a shower of wood shrapnel. She came down hard inside the bedroom, feeling the meat peel and roll back like sushi from her right elbow. Pain instantly shot into her shoulder, neck, and back, its fangs sinking deep into the muscles.

Carrie and Emalyn were beside her almost instantly. They helped her to her feet. A violent crack of thunder, as loud as the shotgun blast, broke overhead, and Emalyn nuzzled up to her mother.

"Are you okay?" Carrie asked, holding her terrified daughter close.

Sandra nodded. She shook her arm and circled her neck, feeling the discomfort from the sudden stop. *Put it out of your mind.*

Moving around the room, she began looking for anything she could use as a weapon. But the room was bare. A sickening realization settled over her: anything they could use to defend themselves had never been in the house in the first place. No silverware. No knives. No tools in the work shed.

The forethought put into this operation must have been massive. Someone had gone to painstaking ends to ensure they did not leave this house alive. Why?

Think, Sandra, think.

"How did he get inside?" Carrie whispered. "The alarm never went off."

"Maybe it didn't go off because the power went out," Emalyn said, burying a knuckle into her watery eye.

"Most security systems have backup batteries," Carrie said. "That's how ours works at home, anyway."

Sandra had wondered the same thing. How *had* he gotten in without them hearing?

"All right," Sandra whispered. "This is what's going to happen. He'll be coming down that hall any moment. I want both of you to stand in the middle of the room."

"What are you going to do?" Carrie whispered back. Her bottom lip quivered as she spoke.

"He believes he has us trapped. His confidence will be his downfall. As soon as he comes around the corner, I'm going to disarm and secure him—"

"Secure him?" Carried butted in, eyebrows raising.

"We should lock the door. Wait for the police," Emalyn said. "Someone had to have heard the gunshots. Right?"

"Not in this storm. Not way out here. There's no one coming," Sandra said gravely.

"Oh, God," Carrie moaned, pulling Emalyn into her.

"Once I have him disarmed and disabled, we bolt for the front door. Stay low to the floor. Move swiftly but cautiously behind me. There could be another shooter out there that hasn't made himself known yet. Once we reach the front door, I want you two to head to the SUV while I get Mom and the others. Have it fired up and ready to go by the time we're coming out. Got it?"

Carrie's eyes shifted back and forth like her mind was short-circuiting and hadn't heard a word Sandra said. Sandra grabbed ahold of her sister and shook her forcefully.

"Snap out of it. You have two jobs: protect Emalyn and yourself and get to the SUV. Understand?"

Carrie nodded, shaking more tears loose from the wells of her eyes.

"He's coming!" Emalyn cried in a panicked whisper.

Sandra turned and saw that the shooter's flashlight was on again. Her heart hammered in her chest. *You have to stop him.* The beam made a large circle on the wall, floating up and down like a fishing bobber in a stream. The shooter *was* creeping toward them, his steps as silent as Death's, the circle of light growing smaller and smaller the closer he got to the room.

Suppressing the fear trying to solidify in her veins like steel, Sandra pushed Carrie and Emalyn into the middle of the room. They needed the element of surprise to survive. The shooter, she suspected, wouldn't expect to find two helpless females just standing there, awaiting their fates. In the moment of his disbelief, Sandra would strike.

Tiptoeing back to the door, Sandra pressed her back against the wall. Everything Joel had taught her was kicking into overdrive. She was acting on reflexes, on instinct.

The ball of light, no bigger than a baseball, had now stopped bouncing on the wall. Sandra held her breath and felt her blood pumping in her ears. He was just outside the door.

Another flash of lightning strobed the darkness, and Sandra saw the end of the shotgun pass into the middle of the doorway; a tactical flashlight was mounted on the sliding fore-end, where a large, gloved hand retained its levelness.

She focused her mind, trying to visualize the fight before it happened, playing different scenarios and their outcomes. A hundred things could go right. A thousand could go wrong.

She felt her muscles tense, readying themselves for her surprise attack. She would only get one shot.

The shotgun barrel turned into the room, and the bright light swept through the darkness in a streak and fell onto Carrie and Emalyn, huddled rigidly in each other's arms like two deer caught in the headlights of an oncoming car.

The shooter barged into the room, wanting to get close to his targets so he didn't miss when he pulled the trigger. He wore dark pants and a hoodie that concealed his appearance.

Sandra sprang from her concealment beside the door.

She grabbed the barrel and the fore-end with her left hand while her right arm simultaneously slipped between the shooter's outstretched arm, which held the shotgun level, and his body.

Wrapping her right forearm around the frame of the shotgun like a boa around a tree branch, she pulled both the frame and the barrel close to her body, mindful to keep the bore pointed at the floor, away from her, away from Carrie and Emalyn, just in case it went off.

"Get down!" she yelled at them.

She locked herself in place, pinning the shooter's outstretched arm against her own body. The shooter tried to wrestle the gun free from her grip, but even though she was smaller, the shooter didn't have enough control of the weapon to wiggle her off.

Sandra knew the shooter had two options. One: he could let go of the grip and try and grab or punch her, hoping she'd release her grip on the weapon. Two: he could drive her into the wall and try to knock her free like shale from a crumbling rock wall.

The dumbass took option one.

As soon as he took his hand away from the trigger, Sandra twisted her body down and pivoted on her left foot, easily sliding the shotgun from his grasp.

As she came around to face him, ready to blow him to kingdom come with his own weapon, she realized she had underestimated one thing: his speed.

He was on her before she could even get the shotgun level, swinging a fast right hook. Sandra saw the blow coming and got her arm up just in time to protect her head. The strike landed hard across her forearm, and with such force, it felt like she'd just been hit with a baseball bat.

The powerful blow knocked her one-hundred-and-twenty-pound frame across the room and sent her crashing into the nightstand; its four legs broke under her weight. She hit the floor hard; the shotgun flew from her grasp and slid between the shooter's feet.

FUCK!

The shooter went for the gun.

She couldn't let him acquire the weapon again. Her eyes fell onto one of the nightstand's broken wooden legs lying beside her.

Snatching the leg from the floor, she swung out just as the shooter's hand wrapped around the shotgun, connecting across the knuckles. A man's voice screamed out in furious pain and he clutched his hand to his chest.

She arched back again with the nightstand leg and brought it around as hard as possible. This time, clobbering him behind the left knee. His knee buckled, and his large frame dropped to the floor, shaking the room.

Sandra kicked out, her foot striking the gun's stock, and it slid under her bed, far out of reach. His head snapped around to her, his features still hidden in the dark of the hood, only to have the wooden leg raked across the side of his face. The makeshift club shattered into pieces, and he was driven to the floor, growling in pain, holding his head.

"Let's go!" Sandra screamed, not worrying about trying to retrieve the shotgun under a dark bed that would cost them precious time—time they didn't have.

Grabbing the cell phone off the floor, Sandra, Carrie, and Emalyn rushed to the end of the hallway. There, Sandra glanced around the corner.

Darkness.

A flash of lightning streaked across the sky, giving enough illumination for Sandra to see that the living room and foyer were clear.

Was it only one shooter? Or were there more of them?

She didn't know.

From the bedroom, Sandra heard the shooter moan. It was just a matter of time before he got back in this fight. She assumed he would go for the shotgun under the bed before coming after them.

"Move," she ordered.

Quietly, she led the three of them to the foyer. A crack of thunder caused her to jump, thinking it was the shotgun going off, but it was only the raging storm outside.

Carrie hurried to the security system and punched the code to unlock the door. It *beeped,* and a red screen flashed three times, indicating she had entered the wrong code in her haste. She punched in the numbers again.

Again, it *beeped*, and the red screen flashed three times.

Sandra hurried to the monitor on the wall and typed in the door code and slammed her finger into the enter key. The deadbolt snapped open with a *click*.

Carrie grabbed her daughter by the wrist. But Emalyn ripped her hand from her mother's grasp.

"You need to come with us," she pleaded to Sandra.

"I'm getting the others," Sandra said, walking toward the steps. "I'll be right behind you. Go. NOW!"

Carrie yanked Emalyn away before she could protest again and threw open the door.

A sharp flash of lightning illustrated another hooded figure standing on the porch.

Carrie and Emalyn screamed.

He lunged through the door, grabbing ahold of Carrie by the shirt and yanking her forward into him. Something long and sharp in his hand gleamed wetly in the dim light.

A knife.

A knife he was going to bury deep into Carrie's stomach if Sandra didn't stop it.

She bolted forward and grabbed his wrist in mid-thrust, stopping the knife from penetrating Carrie's stomach by inches. Relief was short-lived. She had saved Carrie's life but at the risk of her own.

Sandra's free left hand shot into the blackness of the hood before he could turn the knife on her and found an eye with her thumb. She dug her nail into the socket. He cried in furious agony and tried to pull away, but her hold on his wrist prevented him from moving.

She burrowed her thumb in deeper, feeling the squishiness of his eyeball moving around, the tears; it didn't take much pressure to pop an eye from the socket. With a grunt, he yanked his wrist from her grip, his feet backstepping through the doorway and out onto the porch, rubbing his eye.

Sandra saw her opening.

She sprinted through the door, and just as he looked up, she leaped off the ground and caught him in the chest with a Muay Thai knee strike that sent him careening back into the porch railing. He hit the railing with his lower back, his momentum flipping him over it and tossing him onto the soggy ground below.

"GO!" Sandra screamed.

Carrie grabbed Emalyn, and together, they rushed past her into the deluge, heading for the SUV.

Sandra hurried back into the house to the base of the steps leading to the loft.

"Let's go!" she called.

Both doors at the top of the loft opened. Lacy, Devin, and Janis materialized from the darkness inside their rooms and stepped cautiously onto the balcony like frightened spirits emerging from the underworld.

"W-where's m-my d-dad?" Devin asked, stuttering.

"We need to go, Devin," Sandra replied. She didn't want to be responsible for delivering that awful message to the man's son, though she supposed she would eventually have to be the bearer of bad news.

Devin came around the banister to the top of the stairs, looking down at her. The phone's light made him look pale and sickly with sweat; the house had grown ungodly hot inside.

"W-where's my dad?" He swallowed deep; his throat made a sound like grinding rocks.

Sandra said nothing. She didn't have to.

"Oh, Jesus!" He hurried down the steps as if he was going to be able to save his father. "Dad!"

"You can't..." Sandra trailed off when her eyes caught something: shiny tips of the steel barbs gleaming in the dark about halfway up the steps. It took her a moment to realize what she was looking at. "No! Devin, wait!"

But it was too late. Sandra was helpless to do anything other than watch the horrific scene unfold as Devin, in his panic to save his father, charged right into the barbed wire strung across the steps.

The barbs sliced into his ankles and wrapped around them, tripping him. He screamed as the razor wire cut into his flesh, and his body heaved forward, his arms pinwheeling as he tried to grab onto the railing to stop his fall. But his hands came up empty, with only fistfuls of air. He faceplanted on the wooden stairs.

The bottom half of his body—ankles bound together by the barbed wire—bent backward over itself. A slow crack, like a dry tree branch breaking, fractured the silence, and Sandra knew the sound was Devin's head snapping from his spinal column.

His lifeless body tumbled down the steps, arms flailing like pool noodles, head lolling back and forth like a bobblehead doll; the ligaments and muscles were the only things keeping it connected to his shoulders.

Devin's body came to a rest at Sandra's feet, blood leaking from his ears, mouth, and nose. His eyes were open, but the life force that gave them their shine was dull, vacant.

Gone.

Lacy's scream brought Sandra's appalled attention back to the loft, where her mother stood, preventing the young woman from rushing down the steps to check on her now-dead boyfriend.

A sharp flash of lightning cut across the house's interior, revealing another hooded figure standing in the upstairs hallway as if he had materialized like an unclean spirit from the shadows.

They came at night.

"Behind you!" Sandra screamed, already rushing up the steps to intervene before Lacy and her mother were harmed.

As Sandra rushed the steps, the hooded figure charged Janis and Lacy. Something reflective and sharp slashed up from his right side.

A tomahawk!

Lacy screamed, and in her fright, pushed herself from Janis's arms, thrusting the old woman toward the rapidly advancing killer in the process.

Oh, no! Sandra pumped her legs as hard as she could up the steps, trying to get to the top before... before...

The gleam of the tomahawk's blade came down in a wide arc and struck Janis's upper right arm, peeling away a chunk of flesh. Janis cried out, eyes pinched shut, and grabbed the gash. Thick, dark blood poured through her fingers and hit the floor with a *SPLAT.*

Sandra was almost at the top of the steps now, repulsed at what she was witnessing, powerless to help, as Janis backpedaled from the third attacker.

Her mother's eyes were wide with disbelief, and she made small sucking sounds that sounded like *no no no,* as the tomahawk

189

rose again. The hooded attacker advanced on her quickly, ready to strike her down this time.

You have to do something!

Without thinking, relying on reflexes alone to save them, Sandra reared back with Carrie's cell phone and launched it. The phone flipped through the air, the light flashing off the walls in a circular pattern.

It smacked the attacker on the side of the head. An *oof* seeped from his lips. The blow knocked him off balance, causing him to sidestep and grab his head.

Coming to the landing, Sandra yanked her mother to the stairs. "Run!"

Janis stood petrified with fear, her eyes locked on the attacker, slowly regaining his wits after the wallop with the phone.

"RUN!" Sandra screamed again in her mother's face, snapping her from her stupor.

Sandra thrust Janis down the steps and then turned back to find Lacy crumpled on the floor with her back pressed against the wall. She had worked herself into a dead spot on the loft's landing. There was nowhere for her to go. Looking to her right, Sandra saw the hooded attacker coming toward them, the booted feet slamming onto the wood like hammers.

Sandra turned and grabbed Lacy by the wrist and tried to drag her away from the wall. But she protested. Her fear kept her rooted in place, even as a killer bore down on her with a weapon that could easily cut her into bits of bloody meat.

Sandra knew there wouldn't be enough left to send home to her parents if that happened.

Knowing she had to head the attacker off before he could strike, Sandra turned and charged him. The tomahawk rose over his right shoulder, and in the dim light from the phone, she saw the chin of a bearded male underneath the hood; his lips cocked with a sinister smirk. The confident look told her he believed he would take her out with a single swing.

What he didn't expect, what he never saw coming, was what Sandra did next.

Using her momentum, she dropped down, kicking her feet out in front of her like she was sliding into second base, and took both his legs out from under him. She felt his weight crash down on top of her. His hard kneecap struck her in the right eye socket as she slid. Pain blasted through her skull, and she could already feel it growing warm and swelling.

Working herself out from under his heavy legs, Sandra rolled to her side and saw the tomahawk in the middle of the hallway. It must have been knocked from his grasp in the fall. He was already going for it, his hands clawing at the floor, reaching. Sandra's eyes shifted to Lacy, still hunkered down, glued to the wall.

"Lacy! Get out of here!" she screamed.

Lacy's watery eyes snapped to Sandra's with recognition—the light bulb of her mind switching on, understanding the magnitude of their situation. Forcing herself to stand, Lacy hurried down the steps to where Janis waited at the bottom, holding her bloody arm.

Using the railing, Sandra pulled herself up. The world swayed around her, and her vision became splotchy with black dots. The shot to the eye socket had rocked her more than she thought.

Her body pitched forward into the banister, and for a moment, she thought she might go over until she tightened her grip on the railing for stability. She shook her head and blinked several times to clear the spots floating through her vision.

She knew there wasn't time to stand around and fully recover. Still loopy, she tugged herself along using the railing toward the stairs like a diver on a tether to the surface.

Rounding the banister at the top of the steps, Sandra saw her mother standing by the open front door. *Was she waiting?* Behind her, lightning strikes lit up the yard and woods beyond, exposing the force of slanted rain.

Lacy was hunched over Devin's lifeless body, sobbing. No tears would bring him back.

Starting down the steps, Sandra's head began to clear just as she heard the shooter clomping into the hallway. He must have found the shotgun under the bed. He was back in the game, back on the hunt.

The shotgun-wielding madman came into view beside the stairs, directly below Sandra. He brought the shotgun to his shoulder and aimed the barrel at Janis. Sandra felt every fiber of her being wiggle in dread. He had her mother in a dead-bang shot.

Knowing there were only milliseconds before he squeezed the crescent-moon trigger and cut her mother in half, Sandra launched herself over the banister.

The weight of her body drove him into the wall. The shotgun went off with a howling report, blowing a large hole in the ceiling, instead of her mother. Drywall and insulation rained onto the floor, the tac flashlight catching the dusty particles and small microfibers of insulation floating through the air.

Sandra jumped up and reared her left foot back to smash her boot into the shooter's face, but he grabbed ahold of her right ankle and ripped it out from under her before she got a chance to deliver the blow. She came down square on her back. The air exploded from her chest in a giant *whoosh*. Her lungs seized, and when she tried to pull a breath, she couldn't.

Before she knew what was happening, the shooter was on top of her, wrapping his hands around her throat. Squeezing. Squeezing. Tighter. Tighter. She felt her esophagus constricting and her tongue being forced out of her mouth involuntarily as his determination to suffocate her increased.

"Get away from my daughter, you son of a bitch!"

Sandra's bugging eyes flipped to her mother standing next to them. She swung something back over her shoulder and brought it forward into the side of the attacker's head. It shattered into a million pieces on impact. He slumped off Sandra and fell onto his side.

Sandra gulped air. It tasted metallic and chalky but was sweeter than any candy that had ever hit her tastebuds. Her eyes found her mother, her arm a bloody mess, her chest heaving up and down; pieces of the vase from the table in the foyer were in her hands.

At that moment, Sandra saw everything that had happened before that night—the animosity between them from her mother's infidelities—fall from Janis's eyes.

For the first time, she did not see the spiteful woman who had raised her but a mother who would do anything to protect her.

Out of the corner of her eye, Sandra saw the shooter sit up with the shotgun in his hand and aim it directly at her mother. He squeezed the trigger before she could move a muscle to stop the unstoppable.

The shogun went off.

And Janis was violently ripped from Sandra's life.

"NO!"

She sat up, tears burning behind her eyes, to find what was left of her mother lying on the floor. The shotgun had not just taken her life; it had eviscerated her from existence.

The re-racking drew Sandra's attention back to the shooter who was bringing the barrel of the shotgun around toward her. She pushed herself away and rolled under the open loft steps just as he fired. The round blew the railing and part of a step away. Splinters of wood flew into the air in all directions.

"Son of a bitch!" he shouted.

"Did you get her?" the one upstairs hollered down.

"No! She's harder to kill than a fucking cockroach."

Jumping to her feet, Sandra beelined toward the front door. She didn't see Lacy and figured she had made it to the SUV while Sandra was dealing with the shooter. She prayed Lacy had made it. Her mother, William, Devin—none of them would be joining their trip home.

The racking of another round seemed louder than the thunder to Sandra as she blew through the open front door and immediately tripped over something on the porch. She fell into a roll, slamming her back into the railing, bringing her to a sudden stop.

"The bitch is outside," one of them yelled.

Flipping onto her side, Sandra found Lacy lying there. Blood leaked from a gash along her hairline like she'd been clubbed over the head. She couldn't tell if she was alive or not. It was too dark.

"Not getting away this time," a male voice said from behind.

Sandra looked over her shoulder. The second attacker was back, covered in mud, and soaked through. She had forgotten about him after knocking his ass off the porch. She saw the knife he held clearly. It was a tactical model with a tantō blade.

His fingers flexed over the black handle excitedly.

Sandra tried to spin around and defend herself, but he closed the gap before she could raise her hands to fight him off.

"Hey, asshole!"

He spun to see who had spoken, only to be met with a shot to the face by Carrie with a large piece of wood from the firepit. The strike knocked him back over the porch railing and down into the wet muck of the yard for the second time that night.

Sandra jumped to her feet, grabbed her sister's hand, and rushed them through the rain toward the SUV. Angry shouts came from inside the house, but Sandra couldn't understand them. The SUV was in sight. Just a few feet away. If she could get to her gun, she could change their situation in a heartbeat.

"Get behind the wheel, Carrie, and get us out of here!" Sandra said as they came alongside the SUV. She ripped the rear door open and climbed in. Emalyn was hunkered down on the floor in the back, terrified and crying.

"Sandra, the tires…"

Sandra launched over the back seat to where she had hidden the gun.

"Sandra!"

She moved things out of the way, searching.

"Sandra!" Carrie shouted.

"What?"

"The tires. They're flat. All the cars have flat tires."

Sandra studied her sister's face until her words finally clicked. All hope of them making it out of there seemed to sink from her like someone had opened her up and was bleeding her dry. They were stuck. Their only chance now was to go through the woods on foot and hope and pray they could use the darkness and the brush to lose their attackers.

But Sandra knew the odds were against them if they at least didn't have some protection. *My gun*! She turned back and moved more stuff, searching desperately for the weapon.

But it wasn't there.

They had been watching and listening to all their conversations. They knew Sandra had put the gun in the SUV. *And they removed it before anyone could get to it.*

"Let's go!"

She hopped out of the SUV, pulling Emalyn with her. Past Carrie, she saw the attacker in the muck beside the porch, pulling himself up just as the other two came stumbling out the front door.

"We need to get into the woods and disappear," Sandra said, pulling her sister and niece along.

Thunder rumbled overhead, and lightning lit up the entire area. The woods were no more than fifteen feet in front of them.

"Go! After them!" one of the attackers shouted.

"Come on!" Sandra screamed, trying to pull Emalyn and Carrie along. But neither could keep up with her and were quickly slowing—the rain, the mud, and the violence sapping their energy.

Sandra heard a familiar pop echo through the forest and realized it was her Smith & Wesson discharging. The bullet zinged by her head and cracked into a tree somewhere in the woods.

"Hurry!"

They were almost to the tree line. Just a few more feet…

We got this. We got this.

POP! POP!

POP!

Carrie screamed. Sandra felt her sister's hand go limp and slip from her grasp and heard her fall hard into the muddy, wet ground. Spinning, with Emalyn at her side, she saw Carrie lying in the mud, trying to claw her way back to her feet. But there was something wrong. A terrible feeling rose through Sandra.

Oh, God. NO!

"Emalyn, run for the woods," Sandra said, looking at her niece. "Don't stop. Don't look back!"

"But my mom," Emalyn cried.

"I got her. Now run, sweetheart. RUN!"

Emalyn turned and bolted for the woods.

Sandra hurried to Carrie. She hooked her hands under her sister's arms and tried to pull Carrie to her feet, but the muddy, wet ground caused her feet to slip out from under her, and they crashed back down. On her hands and knees, covered in mud, Sandra crawled to Carrie.

"Sissy?" Sandra could hardly see through the tears that had suddenly built in her eyes. "Get up. You need to get up. Please, Sissy."

Carrie's eyes were dull, the lids heavy. Her face was the color of wet ash. A dark, crimson sheet stained her white blouse. Blood pumped from a small black hole in the center of her chest. Sandra knew then that a bullet had entered her back and exited through her breastbone, most likely severing her spine.

Sandra pressed her hands to the wound, hoping to stop the bleeding. But she knew. God, help her, she knew.

It was already too late.

"Don't you... don't you leave me, Sissy!" Sandra wallowed.

Carrie tried to say something, but Sandra couldn't understand what she was trying to articulate. Her lips moved, but nothing came out. Then Carrie grew still, eyes opened, and her last breath seeped through her lips in a low *hhhhhh*.

No. No. No. No. This can't be happening. This can't be... it...

The cocking of the revolver drew Sandra's attention away from her sister.

The three of them stood before her in a triangle formation. Lightning streaked across the sky at their backs. The one in the middle had her Smith & Wesson 442 pointed at her.

They came at night.

He squeezed the trigger.

The last thing Sandra saw was the muzzle flash of her gun going off.

CHAPTER EIGHTEEN

Sandra was vaguely aware that she was being moved as she came to, her body a pendulum swinging back and forth above the ground.

She tried to drag herself back to the surface from that dark place she had found herself in after the gun—her gun—went off, but she was trapped just below the waves of consciousness. But when the gloom began to envelop her again, pulling her back into that murky abyss, she didn't fight it.

He was there, waiting in the darkness.

This night belongs to us, he wheezed excitedly through the KN95 mask.

Sandra was shaken awake.

She slowly peeled her eyes open and saw blurry trees passing above her, the leaves stained red. *Am I on my way to hell?*

The thought caused a sharp pain, like someone was slowly driving a knife directly behind her eyes. Warm, sticky air rushed past her body, and even in her semi-conscious state, she realized she was in the bed of a pickup being taken somewhere.

But where?

A bump in the road rocked her forward into something soft and mushy that felt like a saturated, rolled rug. She tried to focus on the object, but the ax-slice of pain that cut through her cerebral cortex forced her to close her eyes.

Once more, she fell back into the trench, into *his*...

cage.

She was inside the cab of *his* tow truck. Hot, sticky tears burned her cheeks and tasted salty on her quivering lips. He ogled her from the open driver's side door like a pervert at a peep show, wheezing behind the KN95, not from exertion but from the delight of finally capturing his rarest quarry.

Her.

No! No! she screamed.

He slammed the door...

The pickup's tailgate falling jolted Sandra back from that uncomfortable place. It sounded so much like the tow truck door in her mind that momentarily, she thought she was back with *him*.

Something dead saturated the air around her, making it nearly impossible to breathe without gagging. Her head still pounded, but it seemed to have dulled since her last bout of consciousness - the synapses of her brain were beginning to fire correctly.

Keep still. Keep quiet. Don't let them know you're awake. Alive.

"Get the two on the left first," a male voice spoke.

Sandra felt the truck dip as someone climbed into the bed. She kept her eyes shut, held her breath, and remained still. A foot landed directly next to her arm and then stepped past her to the front of the bed.

"There has to be an easier way to do this," the man beside her said.

"Quit whining, Derick," a third voice said.

A Zippo lighter flicked open, and the flint wheel rolled. A second later, the smell of cigarette smoke wafted past Sandra's nose, mixing with the rancid smell of death that polluted the air.

"Easy for you to say while you stand around and smoke, barking orders at us," Derick said.

"Gary, you grab one foot, and I'll get the other," Zippo said. "I don't want to be here all night listening to Derick piss and moan about being overworked."

"Eat my ass."

All three men laughed.

They felt no empathy for what they had done to Sandra and her family. They chit-chatted and joked nonchalantly like they were standing around the cooler in a breakroom commiserating.

Sandra felt an ache so deep in her heart that she thought it might implode under the emotional duress. Slaughtering her family *was* just a job to them. Another day in their lives. Nothing more.

How many others have they done this to?

The truck rocked as they moved whatever lay next to her. Peering through her eyelashes, she saw William's body slide past. His eyes were open in a death stare, his face speckled with dried blood. She realized she had rolled into him earlier when she momentarily regained consciousness, thinking his dead body felt like a wet rug under her fingers.

They're getting rid of our bodies.

William was yanked off the tailgate and hit the ground with a heavy, wet splat. Raising her head slowly—which caused the intense stabbing pain behind her eyes again—Sandra saw two men in dark clothing and hoodies pulling him by the ankles down a narrow trail surrounded by woods bathed in red from the pickup's taillights.

The third man, Derick, remained on the bed watching them. They dragged William for about twenty yards before they dropped his legs, turned him on his side, and gave him a push with their feet. He rolled out of Sandra's sight.

Glancing over, she saw Carrie on her stomach, her head facing away, her auburn hair matted to her skull in long, wet strands. Tears built in Sandra's eyes, and the need to scream rose in the back of her throat like a volcano about to explode.

She swallowed her anguish. Her grief.

Her rage.

You motherfuckers are dead, the archaic voice of her monster roared from deep inside.

Gary and Zippo started back to the truck while Derick began to turn around. Sandra quickly lowered her head and closed her eyes before anyone saw she was alive.

She felt Derick's weight shifting the truck under her. As he worked his way toward the cab, he stepped on her right forearm, his boot digging into the flesh, twisting it, scraping it away like a road rash. Gritting her teeth to suppress the pain, she knew she was nothing more than trash to be disposed of. Insignificant.

Who are these guys? She'd only seen glances of their faces, but it was enough to tell her they were men in their late twenties to early thirties. She was certain it wasn't the boys who vandalized the SUV. Trained killers—mercenaries, perhaps?

Were they also responsible for the mysterious disappearance of the Hibbard and Preston families?

"This one will be lighter," said Derick.

"Pretty little thing, wasn't she?" said Gary.

"Shame. We could've had some fun with her," Zippo said.

"Still can," Gary said.

There was a moment of silence. And in that silence, Sandra suspected all three of them were considering the unthinkable, the unimaginable. But when they all laughed jovially, it seemed to break whatever unholy thoughts percolated in their minds. Maybe molesting her sister's corpse was a step too far, even for three cold-blooded killers.

Carrie's body was ripped from the bed like a slab of meat. Sandra heard them dragging her sister through the forest, the twigs and leaves snapping and crunching as they walked. She was the only one left. Where was Lacy? Her mother? Devin?

Where was Emalyn?

Oh, God. Emalyn?

Did she make it to the woods? Was she able to hide before they found her? Had she made it to a safe place and told someone what had happened? Maybe town? Maybe the sheriff's office? Craven? Could he help? Could he even be trusted?

Sandra didn't know.

Whatever was going on had to be stopped. Exposed. If Emalyn made it out, maybe help was on the way.

If she's alive…

The thought caused Sandra's chest to constrict, and the blood rushed to her temples, making her head thump with each thunderous heartbeat—she might never see her niece again.

"Last one," Zippo said, returning.

Hands wrapped around Sandra's ankles and pulled her forward. For a moment, she felt weightless as she came off the bed and tried to prepare herself for the sudden stop, but it did little upon impacting the soggy ground.

Tentacles of pain spread to the far reaches of her body like she'd been struck with a sledgehammer between the shoulder blades. At least the wind hadn't been knocked out of her. They would have known she was alive and very much awake if it had.

She kept her eyes closed as they dragged her through the forest. Her shirt rolled up to her neck, exposing her chest and back. Sticks and rocks sliced her bare back like she was being run over razor blades.

Put it out of your mind.

Something in the ground, maybe a rock or a tree root, snagged her bra strap, and they halted their pulling when they realized she was hung up.

"What the hell?" Zippo said.

She could feel their eyes leering on her toned belly, on her breasts covered by the black bra. Revulsion sank past her flesh and into her bones. She wanted to move on them. Wanted to kill them. Her monster was awake and ravenous with bloodlust.

Yet, she knew she couldn't take on three men in a fight, no matter how good her combat skills were, especially now that she was wounded. Her head thumped again as if hammering this point home. She needed the element of surprise on her side before she attacked.

There was a special place in hell for these three.

Sandra was the deliverer.

"Her bra is caught on something," Gary said.

"What's going on?" asked Derick, still by the pickup.

"Nothing. Bring the bags up here."

"'Kay."

Sandra remained completely still as one of them straddled her. She felt the cold steel of the knife slide under her bra, and with a quick pull, the blade cut through the fabric. The cups fell away, exposing her small breasts. Still, she didn't move. Didn't breathe. She lay bare, exposed. Then he cut the straps around her shoulders.

They started to pull again, and this time, she didn't get hung up on whatever had snagged her bra.

"That did it," Zippo said.

They dragged her a few more yards and then dropped her feet.

"I'll be glad to get rid of this little bitch. She put up quite a fight. You see that kung fu shit she was doing?" the one named Gary asked.

"Yes," Zippo replied.

"Took the shotgun right out of my hands like she was a female Steven Sea-gal. Bitch was lethal."

"We were worse," Zippo said. "Push her down, and let's get this over with."

Sandra felt a pair of hands on her bare side. She tried not to recoil at their touch, which was harder to do than she expected.

You're dead men.

They pushed her away, and she began to roll down a muddy embankment, side over side, until she came to a sudden stop at the bottom, slamming into Carrie's body.

She began to sink into a thick, wet substance that made up the basin, a gritty sludge that smelled of decomposition. The sludge slowly began to swallow her like quicksand, rising over her left eye and her mouth until her body settled on the rocky bottom, half buried.

She tilted her head just enough to keep her nose above the sludge line and one eye to survey her surroundings.

Carrie lay in front of her on her back, sunken into the muck, nearly up to her open eyes. She stared at the dark sky, not seeing it, not seeing anything. Sandra's tongue pressed to the roof of her mouth, and every muscle in her body tightened with the finality of the loss of her big sister.

Prying her horrified gaze away, she saw her mother—what was left of her—lying face down at Carrie's feet. William's body was next. He lay on his right side. His head had disappeared in the gritty liquid like it was slowly absorbing him, becoming one. Devin's body lay past his father's, facing away from Sandra, the barbed wire still wrapped around his bloody ankles.

Were Emalyn and Lacy also down here, out of her sight, their bodies already resting on the bottom of this heinous pit of death?

If that were the case, her entire family was down there.

But Sandra was the only one alive.

"Get those bags up here!" Zippo ordered. "These suckers are ripe."

"I told them, but they didn't listen," Gary said, "This pit is used up. We need to cover it over and dig a new one."

"That's not our call," said Zippo.

Though she couldn't see what was happening above her, Sandra heard the squeaking of a wheel. Derick must have been pushing a wheelbarrow or a cart to the pit.

What was in those bags?

"Jesus Christ! Ugh," Derick said.

"The humidity's lifting the smell," Zippo said.

"Let's get this done before this stink drifts too far," Gary added.

"Grab the hook from the tree and attach one of the bags. Where's the cutter?"

"Oh, shit. Back in the truck."

"Go get it," Zippo growled. "For fuck's sake."

"Right."

Sandra heard Derick run back up the path. The other two stayed behind, working together. *What are they doing?*

"Okay. Swing it over the pit," said Zippo.

The rope twisted and stretched like leather, and the tree creaked from the bag's weight. Dried, brown leaves rained down, settling on top of the sludge and the bodies in the pit like petals left for the dead.

"Where the hell are—"

"I'm right here. Step aside so I can cut the bag open," Derick said.

Overhead, Sandra heard the seams of a fabric bag being sawed apart. Something started to sprinkle down from above. She felt it dust her cheek and tickle her ear.

More started to fall—a heavy, thick, white, powdery substance that quickly covered Carrie's face, making her look like a painted corpse in an old-time horror film.

What the hell are they...

Sandra's thoughts were knocked from her when she was hit by something from above all at once, like a fist of air that nearly drove her under the sludge—a dusty substance that smelled earthy and moldy.

Lime!

They were covering their bodies with lime to keep the smell of decomposition down.

When they'd first arrived at the rental home, they'd smelled lime. Sandra had thought it had come from the nearby lime quarry.

But the smell was emanating from the pit of death itself.

She figured the pit must be close to the house if they had picked up the scent.

"Get the other bag hooked and cut it open. That should do it for tonight," Zippo said. "We'll deliver the girls, and I'll say something about this hole being used up to Richter."

The girls! Did that mean they had Emalyn? Lacy? Sandra believed it did. Emalyn had not gotten away as she hoped, but it also meant she was still alive. *Where are they taking them?*

"I'll finish up and be along shortly," said Derick.

Sandra listened as Zippo and Gary headed back up the path while Derick worked on getting the second lime bag attached to the hook. She heard a diesel engine rumble to life and gathered that they had driven there in two separate pickups if they were leaving their buddy behind to finish the job.

All the bodies couldn't fit into one pickup.

The bag was hoisted overhead, and Sandra once more heard the sawing of the fabric being cut away. Another geyser of lime powder slammed into her. But she had braced herself for the impact this time.

At the lip of the pit, she heard Derick reattach the hook and rope to a nearby tree before turning away and starting back up the path.

Pushing herself out of the sludge, the stabbing pain exploded across her forehead. She felt a furious burning sensation along the left side of her scalp as if someone had opened her up and poured salt into the wound. Sucking chalky air through her teeth, Sandra dug her fingers into the sludge, balling them into tight fists of anguish.

Now, on all fours, she looked over the expanse of the death pit.

The night had cleared, and the moon shone blue over the forest. The pit was about ten feet around and nearly six feet deep. White lime powder coated the walls like paint.

The hard rain from earlier had washed sections of the soil away from around the opening, causing mudslides that made streaks like dirty tears through the white walls, turning them the color of the sludge—a reddish brown.

She could make out other bodies in the blue moonlight cascading over the pit, besides her family. Her repulsion swelled, choking off her airway. A leg, a foot, an arm, or a hand stuck above the surface here and there. Some of the bodies were on their sides, on their backs, or face down, being slowly consumed into the pit.

How many families are down here?

Anger replaced her disgust, causing the burning along her scalp to flair like gasoline thrown on a fire. She wanted to make them pay for what they had done. And they *were* going to pay.

With their lives.

First, you have to get out of this hole.

Turning away, she tried to crawl back up the sides, but the rain had made the walls slick and muddy. Unable to get a grip, Sandra slid back into the basin, kicking Carrie's corpse in the process.

Abhorrence clutched her. The need to break down threatened to pin her under her emotions. She didn't have that luxury right now; she couldn't allow herself to fall into despair. Emalyn and Lacy were still alive. She had to save them.

On your feet, her monster growled in her head.

Climbing back to the muddy wall, Sandra punched into the earth, sinking her fists so far into the wet clay that she anchored herself to the wall. She did the same with her feet. She repeated the process, using her buried fists in the mud to pull herself while her feet propelled her up the wall like a rock climber scaling a snowy cliff.

She was nearly halfway to the top—punching, pulling, kicking, pushing—when she paused. Exhaustion, immense pain, and fatigue threatened to stop her.

Keep going. You must keep going for Emalyn and Lacy.

She reared back and punched her aching fist back into the mud. This time, she struck something buried under the surface that she instantly recognized shouldn't have been there.

Sandra ripped her hand from the hole, pulling a chunk of the wall out. She nearly screamed—she couldn't help it—but held it in even though what she saw buried only inches from her was horrific, barbaric.

A man's corpse. The mudslide had buried him in the wall.

A strange sensation that she'd never felt before—not even that night—worked through her body. She knew his face! She'd seen him yesterday. In town. The bearded man who was looking for his family.

Oh, God! Whoever was behind these crimes had discovered he was snooping around, asking questions. They sent the wolves to silence him before he learned too much.

She swallowed the bile away.

What did we stumble into?

To even attempt to process such a thought was impossible. Her head and body hurt too badly to form thoughts of such magnitude. What energy she did have, she needed to get out of that fucking hole.

She began to climb again.

At the top, she took ahold of the firmer, though damp, soil. Looking like a corpse rising from the grave, Sandra dug her fingers into the earth and began to drag herself onto solid ground.

She rolled silently onto her back and lay looking at the trees overhead. Her muscles burned and twitched. Her lungs heaved oxygen. She tasted death on her tongue, and lime granules stuck between her teeth made her mouth feel like it was full of sand. Her heart pumped with such ferocity she felt the blood surging down her left arm and into the tip of a finger that was no longer there.

A voice.

Ahead, Sandra saw Derick standing beside the pickup. His back was to her, talking to someone on a cell phone.

If he were talking to someone, there had to be reception. She could call for help.

I need to catch my breath first.

The burning along the side of her scalp was worse than the headache now. It must have been where the bullet struck her, she realized. She wanted to rub it, to try and soothe the discomfort away. But she didn't want to touch it. *How bad is the wound?* Did she even want to know?

Rolling onto her side felt like she was trying to move while twisted up in a blanket, bound and restricted. Her body suddenly craved sleep, and her mind wanted to shut down. She couldn't allow that to happen. She needed to get up. Get moving.

Her monster said: *you must find out where they took Emalyn and Lacy...*

And the only way she could do that was to ask Derick.

...I have no plans on asking, her monster said.

Inching herself to her feet, she looked for something she could use to beat the truth out of Derick. Her eyes fell onto the hook and rope secured to the tree. A heavy metal pulley system was mounted to a large branch that extended over the pit.

They used the hook to attach the bags of lime and then used the pulley to swing the bags over the pit before cutting them open, allowing the lime to spill out over the bodies below.

Helping to keep the smell down.

She unwound the rope from the tree and ran it back through the pully until it was free. Turning, she saw Derick was still talking on his cell phone with his back to her. He hadn't noticed her movements. *Good.* She wound the rope into her left hand, leaving enough dangling in her right that she could use the metal hook like a scorpion tail when she swung.

The smell coming off her skin made her nauseous. Half of her body was covered in the viscous juice lining the pit floor, and the other half was coated in the thick lime powder, giving her the ghoulish appearance and fragrance of a reanimated corpse.

If she could smell herself, Derick might be able to smell her, too. She couldn't risk giving herself away. She would have to do this quickly so he didn't catch her scent as she snuck up on him.

At first, she moved wobbly up the trail. Her equilibrium was off from the shot to the head, and she teetered back and forth like she was drunk, nearly falling but catching herself before she went down.

Still, Derick hadn't noticed her approach, too consumed in his conversation. As she drew closer, she could hear him talking to someone—maybe his lover—on the other end.

"I told you I'll be home a little after midnight."

Distracted by his conversation, Sandra knew this was her opportunity to strike. She compartmentalized the pain as best she could and hurried toward him, bringing the rope and hook back as she neared.

"'Kay. Bye," Derick said.

She was within a foot of him when she brought the rope around. The heavy metal hook lashed out like a weighted whip and connected with the left side of Derick's head.

There was a crunching sound of his ear cartilage breaking. A shrill howl broke across the moist forest. He grabbed the side of his head, blood flowing between his fingers from the busted ear, and fell into the pickup, his shoulder denting the metal door.

Taking the rope in both hands like a garrote, Sandra sprung forward and looped it twice around his neck, pulled it taut, and then yanked on the rope as hard as she could. A wet *yak* shot from Derick's lips as his body was wrenched backward onto the forest floor.

With everything she could muster in her battered and bruised body, Sandra dragged him across the ground toward the bumper. Choking gargles seeped from his mouth as he gasped for air and clawed at his neck, fingers trying to pry under the rope to peel it away. She tied the rope around the bumper.

Heaving and sweating as exhaustion gripped her body and pain dimmed her focus—*stay with it,* her monster's voice ordered—Sandra turned and saw him reaching for something at his waist.

The tomahawk!

She kicked his hand away from the tomahawk before he could grasp it and then dropped her left knee into the center of his chest.

Any air that remained in his lungs shot out through fluttering lips, his hot spittle dotting her skin.

Reaching down, she grabbed the tomahawk from its sheath, spun it around in her hand so he could see the –point—his eyes widened in –terror—and sunk it into the meat of his left thigh.

A strangled scream rolled from his open mouth. Tears wetted his bloodshot eyes and leaked down the sides of his face. He flailed under her for a few seconds, but without oxygen, the fight quickly went out of him. Soon, he grew still on the ground.

Ten seconds.

Ten seconds was enough to render a man unconscious from strangulation.

But Sandra didn't want to kill him. Not yet, at least.

She unwound the rope from his neck, and he sucked in a large gulp of air as he snapped back to life. Just so he knew where he was and the situation he found himself in, Sandra pulled on the tomahawk to get his attention.

He screamed and went to sit up, but she slugged him in the jaw with a left jab that put him back down.

Now, up close, she saw he was a good-looking guy with short dark hair and a neatly trimmed beard. He definitely wasn't one of the boys who vandalized the SUV. And he wasn't someone she had seen in town.

"Where are the girls?" Sandra asked.

"W-what?"

Sandra wiggled the tomahawk's handle, the sharp point moving around inside him. He cried out.

"By my estimation, I sunk that blade close to your femoral vein. You don't tell me what I want, I'll open you up. Let you bleed out right here. Got it?"

He nodded frantically.

"Y-yes. P-please—"

213

"The girls. Where were they taken?" Sandra interjected, caring not for his pleas for mercy.

"The quarry," he said. His face was ashen and sweaty, and his lips were the color of parchment paper.

Sandra remembered passing the Sewyer Lime Quarry just outside of Little Hope. She had been told it was abandoned, but that wasn't the case if the girls had been taken there.

"Why were they taken to the quarry?" Sandra asked.

"If I tell you, they'll kill me."

"I'll kill you if you don't." Sandra wiggled the tomahawk again. He screamed through his clenched teeth and reached for his injured leg. She slapped his hands away. There would be no reprieve from the pain, no amnesty shown, just like they had shown none to her family.

"Okay! Okay! Just stop."

Sandra eased the pressure on the Tomahawk.

"Who are you?" she asked. "A local? From Little Hope?"

Derick shook his head.

If he wasn't from Little Hope, then who in the hell was he?

"I'm part of a squad assigned to your rental home."

"Why us?"

"I can't tell you that."

She wrenched the tomahawk's handle and heard the meat of his thigh rip like a zipper. He let out a scream that cut through the muggy air as sharp as the tomahawk's point slicing through his flesh.

"Why!" Sandra screamed. Droplets of the sludge from her face dripped onto his cheeks.

"My team and I were hired to dispose and collect." He made it sound normal, as if they were a repo crew there to repossess a sofa or a car. "After we're done, we take the collected items to the quarry. Whatever happens to them after that, I have no idea."

Sandra struggled to control her monster's pulsing anger, which wanted to unleash itself on Derick and tear him apart limb from limb.

I can take it from here, Sandra, it said. She ignored the voice, the urge to set her monster loose.

"Where would I find the girls?"

"It doesn't matter. You won't get within ten feet of that place. It's heavily guarded."

Sandra wiggled the tomahawk.

"Please! Please, stop," Derick begged.

"Tell me, or it'll get worse."

"Okay! Okay." He took a breath and swallowed thickly, working his tongue around his dry mouth. "They'll be in the holding pens—underground."

"How do I get in there?"

"The elevator. It'll be in the building directly beside the communications building toward the front of the complex."

"How will I recognize the communications building?"

"There are satellite dishes on top."

"Thanks."

Sandra's grip tightened on the tomahawk's handle as her rage—her monster—took full control. With a jerk, she ripped the tomahawk downward, opening his leg like a splayed fish at a wet market. Blood sprayed like water from a broken winter pipe.

Derick screamed, eyes bugging out of his skull at the sight of his spurting blood.

He begged her. Begged Jesus. Begged God to save him.

None of the three were in a merciful mood that evening.

CHAPTER NINETEEN

Sandra wanted to remove their bodies from the death pit. Her family didn't deserve to lie there... *in that... that slop.* It was the least she could do for them. But it was an impossible task, she knew. Hell, she had barely gotten out herself.

Sharp talons of grief ripped into her, tearing open her encased heart, causing emotions she thought long dormant to flood out. Tears formed in the cups of her eyes, stinging. Her loved ones would have to remain saturated in that grimy sludge. She wanted to roll into a ball and scream.

What good will that do? asked her monster. *It won't bring your family back, even if you scream until your throat is raw. The dead are dead.*

The voice in her head—her monster, now fully awake—was right.

217

Focus, her monster said. *Conserve your energy to get back to the house. You need first aid. You need nourishment. And if we're going after Emalyn and Lacy—we are— we need our rucksack. Now, check that cell phone.*

The cell phone.

Derick had been talking to someone on it. If he was getting a cell signal out here, she could use the phone's GPS to find out where she was.

She began searching the forest floor and found the phone about five feet from the pickup, in a mudpuddle, floating screen up. *Fuck!* It must have flung from Derick's hands when she attacked him and landed in the puddle. With hope dwindling, she rushed to the phone and lifted it out, chocolate-colored water draining out the bottom. She tapped the phone's dark screen. As she feared, it was as dead as Derick behind her.

She dropped the phone back into the puddle and returned to the pickup. She could use it to get the hell away from this godawful place, at least. But where in the hell *was* she?

Pulling open the pickup door, Sandra heard the hinges *rrreeek,* and the conversant recollection of that night raised goose pimples on her skin. *His* door had *rrreeeked* like that, too.

Stop it! Her monster's voice boomed in her head, scaring the memory away before it took root. *Remember your training, goddamnit!*

Focus on the present. Not the past.

Using the steering wheel, Sandra pulled her aching body into the cab, dropping the tomahawk on the seat beside her. The musky smell of man's sweat stunk up the inside, making her eyes water like she'd huffed Clorox.

She checked the ignition and saw the keys dangling from the switch. A small measure of relief washed over her. It was short-

218

lived, knowing she was most likely the only survivor ever to leave this place.

Choking the realization down, Sandra pushed in the clutch and turned the key. The heavy diesel engine rumbled to life, shaking the entire truck. She slammed the gearshift into first and punched the accelerator. The rear tires spit dirt, and the pickup tore off on a narrow path cut through the forest.

The rough terrain bounced her around in the bucket seat, making every bone and muscle in her body cry out. Overgrowth and low-hanging branches scraped the pickup's metal exterior, a grating sound that worsened her headache.

She drove for what felt like forever through the dense forest before a paved road materialized, the double yellow line reflecting the headlights like a caution sign.

She didn't know where she was or how far from the house she had been taken. It couldn't have been too far, remembering how strong the lime odor was in the air yesterday. That meant the house had to be within a few miles of her current position.

But which way?

Closing her eyes, she tried to visualize where she was standing on the lawn when she first caught a whiff of lime in the air. It seemed like a forgone memory now. So much had transpired since yesterday; so much had changed in her life that it no longer seemed real. Something she made up in her mind, convincing herself it was reality when, in fact, she had never escaped *him* that—

Knock it off! There is no time for self-pity or wallowing. Pull it the fuck together. Mourn later!

Her monster was right. She forced her mind to concentrate, causing the blood to pound into her scalp and make the laceration fester like a boil. If she could remember which direction the breeze had been coming from, bringing the scent of the lime with it, she'd be able to find her way back to the house. But how could she…

The clouds! They were coming in from the rear of the house. She sank deeper into her memory, the blistering pain stalking across her skull, making her wince. She recalled Emalyn sneezing; the smell of the lime had irritated her allergies. Sandra saw herself walking to the edge of the lawn to pick the peppermint leaves to use as a tea. The sun was on her back.

Her eyes snapped open. If the sun was on her back and the clouds were rolling over the house from the rear, the breeze had to be coming from the southwest.

Looking at her watch, Sandra saw it was covered with pit sludge. She rubbed it away with her thumb. The compass's dial pointed northeast. If she was facing northeast, the house had to be somewhere to the left of her current position. She gunned the pickup, praying her memory was correct and that she was hopefully heading in the right direction.

As she drove the lonely road, with the warm air blowing through the cab, drying the sludge to her skin, the dreaded thoughts she had momentarily sat aside rushed back into her broken mind. The torment of losing her family, watching them brutally slain, wrenched her soul as if Death's hand had reached in and taken hold.

They're all gone. All gone. Her world had been stripped bare like bark from a tree, an exposed wound, open to the elements, that would never heal.

She screamed for the first time that night. Pounded her fists on the steering wheel. Tears flowed thickly down her face, hot and scalding her skin like bubbling cheese. She screamed again. And again. And again, until her throat constricted, and the scream morphed into a strange, disembodied sound she didn't recognize.

Memories flashed through her mind like snapshots: Carrie and William's first kiss at their wedding, holding Emalyn minutes after she was born, getting ice cream with her mother at that shop in Mechanicsburg—*God, what was it called* – where they had talked and laughed like a loving mother and daughter do—if only that were true.

And it had all been ripped away.

The road stretched like a black serpent twisting and winding around the forest. She didn't recognize anything. The woods made everything look the same as if she were stuck in a repetitious nightmare—a road to nowhere in her subconscious.

Another sobbing bout hit her like a dagger to her stomach, twisted and then driven further in until it nicked her spine. She doubled over in the seat. Grabbed at her stomach.

They're all gone. All gone.

Focus, her monster's voice screamed. *You have a mission. There isn't anything you can do about what is done.*

She wanted to. But it was too hard. Her mind was crippled with the unfathomable loss of… everyone she loved.

She started crying again. Her eyes burnt like someone had poured iodine into them. A repeated *knock, knock, knock* inside her skull caused an aggravating discomfort that made her sick to her stomach. Her bereavement worked its way through her body with electric pulses, making her think of bugs frying in a zapper. *ZZZZ. ZZZZ. ZZZZ.*

Was it possible to die from sorrow, she wondered?

She ran her hand over her runny nose and sniffed back a glob of snot leaking onto her upper lip.

You can't give up. If you do, they win, Sandra, her monster said. *He… wins.*

But she was up against an enemy far bigger than she ever expected to face.

She had gone to the Compound so no one could ever harm her again. Despite all the years spent working on her hand-to-hand combat and weapon training, she had failed to protect herself. And, especially, those she loved.

How well did that work out for you? This time, it wasn't her monster's voice that spoke, but a familiar wheezing one.

More tears came with her new certainty, and the truck began to drift toward the side of the road.

You failed, the wheezing voice said.

Ahead, a large tree came into view as the truck veered further off the road.

You couldn't save them.

The voice wasn't coming from inside Sandra's head. It was in the cab, next to her. When she looked, *he* was sitting in the passenger seat. And even though she couldn't see his face behind the KN95 mask, she knew he was smiling, soaking up her misery like a sponge.

Let go, Sandra, he said through the mask.

The tree was closer. Coming up quickly.

God help her, she agreed with *him.* It would be so easy. All she would have to do was close her eyes and let the truck guide her into the next life. It would be over in an instant—a blink of an eye. The pain, the suffering, the loss, the memories—good and the very bad—would be gone as soon as the truck struck the tree.

I have your cage waiting for you.

But if she did that, then *he* would win. *He* might not have gotten her that night along the side of the road, but in the end, if she gave in now and let the truck smash into the tree, *he would* win—they *would* win.

Don't be a victim…

No! She had Emalyn to think about. If she gave in and succumbed to the weight of her emotions, she'd be letting her niece down, abandoning her to… *them.*

This night belongs to us. He laughed behind the KN95 mask.

"Fuck you!" Sandra screamed at the empty space beside her and cut the steering wheel hard to the left, snapping the pickup back onto the road. The tires screeched, and the cab rocked back and forth, throwing her battered and bruised body around.

She had to be strong—if not for herself, then for Emalyn and Lacy. Someone had to save them.

That's my girl, her monster's voice returned.

Sandra slammed on the brakes when she caught a familiar sight. The tires locked on the wet pavement as the pickup's ass end fishtailed to a shuttering stop.

She stared at the covered driveway to her left, blinking slowly, her lids heavy with exhaustion and confusion. Was it the driveway to the house? She believed it was.

Cutting the wheel to the left, she stomped the accelerator, and the pickup barreled down the lane. Soon, the headlights revealed the rental home, bleak, static, and deathly mute—the life that had been there only hours ago was nothing but a foregone memory now.

She slid the pickup to a stop next to the porch and killed the engine. Slipping out of the pickup, her feet almost went out from under her from sheer exhaustion. Holding onto the door to avoid crumbling, she turned to the cab and pulled the tomahawk out, glistening with Derick's blood.

Though she intended to rescue Emalyn and Lacy from the quarry, she was in no physical shape. Before going after them, she needed to repair, refuel, and resupply.

Stepping inside the foyer, the house smelled of the atrocities that happened there. The stench of gunpowder. The coppery tang of spilled blood. And the sourness of fear-sweat and utter despair.

The smell was so strong, so overpowering, that Sandra stood immobile as the tears welled again, pinning her. Just a few hours ago, everyone she loved was here with her, alive. Now, they were all gone. Some of them lying in a gross burial pit where the dead slept, others taken.

Use it! Her monster's voice spoke between her ears.

Swallowing the hurt was like swallowing a bitter pill that was too big and too nasty-tasting down her throat. But swallow it, she did. Yes, she would use her emotions when the time was right, unleashing her monster on those who had wronged her.

And her monster was awfully hungry.

She closed the front door and moved through the house, her feet crunching broken shards of glass and wood, in a daze—a waking dream-like state as if she were on a drug.

The world around her swayed, and she fell into the wall, nearly collapsing. The burning of her scalp radiated down the left side of her face; her ear felt like it was being held to a blow torch.

Carrie's emotionless face, her once bright Carolina-blue eyes now dull and lifeless, staring at the sky from the bottom of the pit, shot into Sandra's mind.

Use it!

Pushing herself off the wall, she teetered like a toddler through the dark, heading to the bathroom. She felt her way along the wall until she came to the smaller hallway, where she paused to catch her breath before moving onto the bathroom.

Once in the bathroom, she laid the tomahawk on the sink and began feeling through the dark for the tub wall. Were they still watching? She doubted it. The house had been cleared of guests.

But Sandra couldn't take that chance.

Finding the tub in the dark with her fingertips, her hand sliding through William's congealing blood, she snatched her hand back and shivered. *Use it.* She stepped onto the wall, nearly slipping on the blood coating the side, but caught herself before going over. She fumbled her fingers across the ceiling until she found the vent, felt the camera inside, ripped it from its nest, and dropped it to the floor.

She turned on the shower. The cold spray hit her in the face, scaring her, and her heart leaped into her throat at its chill. She stripped her clothing, piling it at the rear of the tub, and began rubbing the grime away.

The cool water stung the abrasions on her back where the rocks had sliced her open. The muck fell off her body in thick clumps that began clogging the drain, the dirty water pooling around her ankles. She forced the congealed mass down with her toes.

When she ducked her head under the spray, she felt the sting of the laceration and screamed at the blinding pain that shot across her scalp like a lightning strike.

All of this was too much for any one person to handle.

Folding her arms around herself, Sandra squatted in the tub and began to sob. She could feel herself crumbling, her defenses breaking down little by little.

Use it, her monster said. *Use this pain to hunt down those motherfuckers and kill them for what they did.*

When the sobbing stopped—there were no more tears to be shed, at least that night—she gathered herself up and stepped out of the shower. After toweling off, she fumbled into her and Emalyn's bedroom and found her rucksack on the bed where she had left it.

Inside was an emergency first aid kit—*like American Express, don't leave home without it*—and a few Chem Lights, military-grade glow sticks that worked up to twelve hours. Ripping open the pack with her teeth, she pulled out a glow stick and cracked it. A green hue rose around her. It would allow her to move around undetected and without garnering outside attention.

She returned to the bathroom with the glow stick and the first aid kit. Nude and shivering with shock, she stood in front of the mirror.

The bullet had grazed the left side of her head, ripping a straight fissure along her scalp, leaving a flap of skin hanging. A small portion of her skull gleamed in the green light. Black blood oozed from the wound and dripped onto her shoulders and bare chest. It would need to be sewn shut. The bleeding wasn't going to stop on its own.

She removed a small bottle of extra-strength ibuprofen from the kit, popped six tablets into her mouth, and chewed them up. The taste was unpleasant, but chewing the tablets would get the medicine into her bloodstream faster—the pain ravishing her body was worsening as the adrenaline began to subside.

She then took out a bottle of antiseptic, gauze, needle, and thread. Knowing how to treat field injuries was something Joel pounded into their heads. Once, she'd fallen and sliced her hand open on a rock while hiking in the bush; they were miles from the Compound on one of Joel's weekend hikes into the forest. The cut needed a stitch to close. Sandra did it herself.

Cleaning the scalp wound with antiseptic felt like she had dumped acid into the open wound, a harsh stinging that caused her to suck air between her clenched teeth and made her double over and death grip the side of the sink.

When the discomfort began to subside, she stood and dabbed the frothing blood away with the gauze. More blood oozed. And it would continue until she closed the wound. But that was the least of her concerns. She had no idea what could have gotten into her bloodstream with such an exposed wound while in the pit. She could become septic. Could die.

Not until I see this through.

We see this through, her monster reminded her.

Her hands shook so badly—from the shock, the pain, the emotional grief—that she couldn't get the thread through the tiny sliver in the needle's head. After a few failed attempts to thread the needle, she succeeded and went to work at closing the gash. She gently laid the scalp flap back across her skull and pushed the needle through.

It was like getting stung by a giant wasp. And each subsequent push and pull through the flesh felt like another sting. Doing this wasn't just pain. It was self-torture.

Suck it up, buttercup, her monster said.

When she finished, and her head was sewn back together, she tied off the suture and cut the thread with the small scissors from the first aid kit.

Looking in the mirror at herself, her eye swollen, her scalp sewn back together, the black blood staining her skin, she no longer saw the woman known as Sandra Ann Leigh. Something else stood there now. Something that had been growing inside her for years, waiting to be unleashed like a great wrath upon the world.

This thing staring back at Sandra would show no empathy and would kill anyone preventing it from rescuing Emalyn and Lacy— for taking her family.

They had no idea what was on its way.

CHAPTER TWENTY

After cleaning blood from her flesh for the second time that evening, Sandra moved, still nude, from the bathroom and back into her and Emalyn's bedroom. Dumping the remaining contents of her rucksack onto the bed, she took inventory of what she had inside—dirty clothes, tampons and pads, twelve .442 shells in two moon clips, a small flashlight, riggers tape, Chem lights, a pack of waterproof matches, a Bic lighter, and a multipurpose tool. It wasn't much.

You need more.

She decided to go through Emalyn's things but found nothing useful.

Crossing the hall, she threw open Carrie's suitcase, smelling her sister's scent on the clothes. She had never noticed it until that moment, reminding her of the life cut short. She rummaged up underwear and a sports bra. A pair of black cargo pants, a black tank top, and black hiking boots.

Though she and Carrie are—*were*, a depressing reminder to Sandra's new existence—the same height, she was more muscular than her sister, causing the clothes to fit snugly across her chest, butt, and thighs. The boots were her size—no problem there.

You need to refuel, her monster said.

Later.

Now, Sandra!

She ignored its voice.

Next, she went through William's luggage, looking for anything useful. She threw the clothes aside and found his toiletry bag at the bottom of the suitcase. Opening it, a folded stainless steel straight razor gleamed in the morbid green light from the glow stick. Unfolding the blade from the handle, it was sharp, able to cut through a man's throat easily.

Her monster wiggled with glee.

She placed her foot on the bed and slipped the straight razor down the inside of the right boot.

But one straight razor wasn't going to be enough. She needed more.

Heading upstairs, she went through Devin and Lacy's bags. She found a small baggie of cocaine in Devin's suitcase but nothing useful. Next, she went through Lacy's pink bags, finding one thing that brought a sly smirk to Sandra's face.

A makeup kit.

She could use it to camouflage herself.

Then, she went through her mother's neatly packed things, sitting outside the door of her room as if waiting for Janis to retrieve them. She wasn't. None of them were ever coming back for their belongings. They were all *gone.*

Use it.

Going through her mother's bags, she didn't find anything useful. Janis had packed only for the weekend—her blood pressure pills, toiletries, and two extra outfits.

A tear spilled from Sandra's right eye. The small things that belonged to her loved ones—the mundane objects they used — made the realism of losing them hit her again.

Use it.

She was about to turn away, to head back downstairs when she thought of something.

How did they get in without us knowing?

The picture on Lacy's camera flashed so strongly across Sandra's mind that the laceration along her scalp spasmed. She tried to line up her thoughts, but they ran wild until one flashed from the recesses of her mind that made sense.

They didn't need to sneak in…

Because they were already inside.

Sandra thought of the picture on Lacy's camera again. She'd seen what she believed at the time was a human shape standing in her mother's bedroom window. Had her bedroom been the access point to the rest of the house?

But you checked everything in the room. You looked under the bed, behind the dresser, around the vents, and…

The closet.

Her chest tightened with a terrible thought.

She turned and headed to the walk-in closet of her mother's room. Throwing open the door, the closet was long and narrow, about seven by eight feet long. It was bare of clothes and smelled of new carpet. Nothing looked unusual, just like last night.

Until her eyes landed on the back wall and drifted down to the floor, where a fan pattern disturbed what should have been unmolested carpet. Sandra had checked the closet after fearing what she saw in the picture was a person. But she hadn't really looked, had she? She hadn't seen what was right in front of her eyes.

You could have prevented this.

Coming to the rear wall, Sandra noticed no handle or latch to open the doorway, which she believed was concealed in the back of the closet. Why would there be? It was meant to be inconspicuous. Sandra figured it might be pressure sensitive. Push on it, and the door would release.

She did.

A *click*. A seam opened in the wall.

Taking hold of the side, she slowly inched the door open, revealing a dark and narrow corridor leading to a concealed part of the house, a part the guests were never meant to see or find. The green light from the glow stick pushed away the shadows, allowing Sandra to see that the corridor led to a small room built within the house walls.

Their hideaway.

Stepping into the room, she smelled the tang of man stink—a mix of body and rotten ass odor that reminded her of the boy's gym locker room she was once in during high school. She couldn't recall why she had been in the boy's locker room; it was too far back, but the smell had kicked the memory from her mind all the same.

Along the far wall was a desk with a computer on top; the green light on the computer indicated that it was still on, still working. *This room has its own power source, separate from the rest of the house.* A flat-screen television was mounted on the wall. Cables connected it to the computer.

She ran her fingers around the TV frame, searching for the power button. Finding it, she switched the television on, fearing what she suspected all along was about to be true.

She tried to prepare herself. Still, what she saw gutted her.

The screen was split up into twelve different camera angles. Six on the top. Six on the bottom.

The six along the top of the screen showed various camera views around the second floor: Lacey and Devin's bedroom, her mother's bedroom, and the adjoining bathroom between the two bedrooms. One camera faced the loft's hallway. Another one overlooked the hall downstairs. The last one viewed the living room from above.

The six on the bottom were similar. One camera view in each bedroom, one in the kitchen, one facing the front door, and one covering the living room and the kitchen. There was only one angle that was snowy. Sandra knew it was the camera she had ripped out of the bathroom earlier.

The entire house was covered with surveillance cameras powered by this room. They had been watching them the entire time, hearing every conversation. They had lay in wait up here until they were ordered to strike.

But who gave the order? And why?

She remembered thinking how odd the house's shape was when she first saw it—too big on the outside and too small on the inside. Then there was the electromagnetic buzz she felt in her room, like she had at the computer labs in college. Now she understood why— to hide these men inside the walls so they could spy on them with carefully hidden cameras placed around the house.

We walked right into their trap. Their kill box.

Sandra felt lightheaded.

Refuel, Sandra, her monster's voice ordered.

It was right. She needed to get something into her system, or she would pass out. There was nothing she could do about her discovery now. It was far too late.

Back downstairs, she opened the fridge and pulled out some leftover burgers and hotdogs from earlier that afternoon. Her appetite was nonexistent, but she needed to eat. She had lost a lot of blood, and with it, energy. She needed sustenance if she was going to see this night through.

She tore into the cold meat like a bear ripping into a frozen deer carcass. There was no decency, no politeness in the way she ate, devouring the meat, not tasting anything. It was fuel. Nothing more.

She popped the top of a soda can and chugged half of it in one swallow; the sugar and caffeine hit her bloodstream like an adrenaline shot, making her head buzz and the nub tingle. She burped. Wiped her mouth with the back of her arm.

Just then, a pair of headlights cut the darkness of the kitchen.

Someone was there.

CHAPTER TWENTY-ONE

Hurrying to the front door, Sandra saw a police cruiser parked beside the pickup. Sheriff Craven stepped out from behind the wheel, and Deputy Allen rose from the passenger side.

What the hell were they doing here? Sandra wondered. Were they somehow involved? Did they know she had escaped the pit? Had they returned to the house to finish her off? If so, how?

Her hands balled into tight fists, fists that she wanted to use as hammers to turn their faces into pumice if they were connected to whatever was happening in Little Hope.

"Doesn't seem like anyone is here, Sheriff," Allen said.

"That's what concerns me," Craven replied. "Let's check the house."

The pair started toward the porch. Allen pulled his flashlight off his belt and shone it into the pickup's open door.

"Sheriff," Allen said, his voice wound tight. "There's blood in the cab."

A current of headlights washed over the wet grass and front of the house. Craven and Allen looked up as a pickup and a white Ford Econoline van came barreling down the lane, pulling to a stop behind the police cruiser. The engines cut. The headlights dimmed.

No one got out.

"I'm Sheriff Craven with the Little Hope Police Department. Step out of the vehicles and identify yourselves."

The stillness was palpable, as if time had ground to a stop. Sandra watched Craven glance at Allen with unease creeping across his face. Craven hadn't been expecting anyone, she believed. Maybe he and Allen weren't a part of what was going on.

The passenger side door of the van popped open, and someone hopped out from inside.

"Evening, Sheriff," said a man, slinging his arms through the open window while keeping his body hidden from their view.

That voice...

"You guests of the Campbells?" Craven asked.

"No, sir," the man said. "We're with the rental company."

"R&R?"

"Yes, sir."

"Is there a problem?" Craven asked, his voice lit with suspicion.

"We got a call that the power failed. Came to see what the trouble was," the passenger said, reaching into his breast pocket and pulling out a pack of cigarettes. He popped one into his mouth and lit it with...

Zippo!

Now Sandra knew who he was and why she recognized his voice. He was one of the men who had helped slaughter her family and dispose of their bodies. That's why they were here, to clean up

236

the place and prepare it for the next unsuspecting family. Only they hadn't expected to find Craven and Deputy Allen snooping around.

Craven glanced at Allen, their eyes meeting suspiciously.

"The power is still on in town. This place is on the same grid," Craven said. "How could it have failed here but not in town?"

Zippo said nothing this time. He looked back into the van's cab at the driver and nodded as if he was giving him a signal. From the uncomfortable tightening of Sandra's chest, and the pinging sensation of her nub, she felt something bad was about to happen.

"I asked you a question," Craven barked, his voice edged with authority.

The driver's side snapped open, and another man slid out, keeping himself hidden behind the door.

"It would be wise for you and your deputy to get in your car and drive away, Sheriff."

"We came out here to check on the Campbells. They raised concerns about feeling threatened. My deputy just found blood in the cab of that pickup." Craven paused, and his hand went to his sidearm.

"And I'm starting to suspect, now that you're here, that what they told me was true. So, let me make this clear for you, son: I'm not going anywhere until I know what's going on. Why are you here? And is that family safe?"

Craven and Allen weren't involved. Sandra was sure of that now. Every fiber of her being wanted to intervene, to warn them what she knew was coming, but if she did, she'd expose herself, most likely ending in her death. *You have Emalyn and Lacy to think about.*

"Suit yourself. Gary."

A deafening roar of a shotgun blast broke the quiet evening and echoed through the forest like cannon fire. Sandra saw Deputy

Allen go down, holding his stomach. She shifted her gaze back to the driver, the bore of the shotgun smoking in his hands.

Craven jerked his sidearm free of the holster, but the driver swung the shotgun and fired another round before Craven could even bring his weapon up. The sheriff's chest exploded in a shower of sinew and his body was thrown violently back into the police cruiser, and he crumbled to the ground, dead.

Sandra watched in horror as Zippo stepped from behind the passenger-side door. He wore a set of tac knives on each leg, like a gunslinger, and crossed the lawn to where Deputy Allen lay in the grass holding his bleeding belly, moaning and crying in pain with a gut shot—the most excruciating of places to have been hit, Sandra had learned from Joel.

Stepping beside Allen, Zippo pulled one of the tac knives and thrust it to the hilt into his throat. A strained gargle emanated from the deputy before he finally grew still and quiet on the ground.

The van's door opened, and four men dressed head-to-toe in white hazmat suits jumped out. Their faces were covered with KN95 masks. Sandra felt a shudder work its way through her body.

This can't be happening.

But it is happening, Sandra, her monster said. *It's time to face your past, once and for all.*

"Why is Derick's pickup here?" Gary asked. He, too, had taken her family. Sandra's monster wiggled with glee at the thought of killing them.

"I don't know," Zippo said, running the bloody blade through the wet grass before sliding it back into the sheath.

"He was supposed to return to the quarry after he was done at the pit."

Zippo straightened and looked at the men in the hazmat suits. "Get the sheriff and his deputy loaded into the trunk of the police cruiser, and then one of you dispose of them in the pit. Then, take the police car back to the quarry for cleaning. We'll need it to complete the infiltration of the town."

Infiltration of the town?

Zippo flicked the cigarette away and approached the house with Gary while the other four men snapped into action behind them.

Sandra turned and hurried to the bathroom, grabbing the tomahawk off the sink. It wasn't much to defend herself with, but it would have to do. There was nowhere to run or hide, and escaping wasn't an option since there were no exits from the house except through the front door. She was in a kill-or-be-killed situation.

Returning to the corner of the short hallway, she peered around the wall just as the front door banged open. Zippo's large silhouette filled the entrance, searching the darkness before stepping into the foyer and flipping on the first-floor lights.

Sandra ducked out of sight behind the wall before he saw her. They had restored the power to the house at some point. Like everything else in the house, they must have had control of it from their hideaway.

"Derick?" Zippo called out. "You here?"

When Derick didn't reply—*I bled him out back at the pit,* her monster said—Zippo started down the hallway, his wet boots squeaking on the hardwood floor with each step.

Sandra pushed herself against the wall and brought the tomahawk beside her sweating face, readying it to swing, to coat its sharp blade in Zippo's blood as he came around the corner.

"Where the hell is he?" Gary asked, also in the house.

"I don't know. Derick?" Zippo called.

Sandra heard the alarm in his voice. *You should be alarmed.* None of them knew what they had unleashed, and her monster was eager to introduce itself.

"If he ain't here," Gary said, "then how did his truck get back here?"

"Jesus Christ." A third muffled voice spoke. It sounded like *his* voice—*this night belongs to us*. A chill raced up Sandra's spine as the past and the present collided. "What the hell did you guys do to this place?"

"We had an issue," Zippo said.

"You shot the shit out of everything."

"Like the man said: we had an issue," Gary added.

"What issue? It was a family. How much of a problem could they have caused?"

"Enough to draw the sheriff's and deputy's attention," Gary grumbled. "Just do your job."

"We clean the wet stuff. We're not carpenters. This is going to take a whole team to fix. Je-sus Christ."

"Whatever," Gary replied.

"No, not whatever," Muffled-voice continued. "Richter is going to be pissed when he finds out you shot this place to shit. Repairs will have to be made before this unit is functional again."

Who the fuck is Richter? Is he the guy calling the shots? What did he mean by functional unit? What is this place being used for? Why had they killed everyone but kidnapped only Emalyn and Lacy?

"Let us handle our end, and you handle yours, okay?" Zippo said. "Get your crew in here and do your jobs."

"Fine," Muffled-voice said. "Get the sheriff and his deputy to the pit, Mark, and then head back to the quarry with the cruiser and start cleaning it. The rest of you, inside with me."

Sandra heard the one called Mark start the police car and drive off while two more pairs of feet clopped up the front porch steps and into the house. That put five people inside. Five to One. She bit her lip. She'd have been skeptical of those odds if she were a gambler.

"Where the fuck is Derick?" Zippo asked again.

"We should check upstairs," Gary replied. "Maybe he's in the room."

"If he were upstairs, he would've heard us. No, something is going on here."

"You two start in the bathroom. I'll work on the mess here in the hall," Muffled-voice ordered.

Padded footsteps started down the hallway, getting closer and closer to where Sandra was hidden behind the short hallway wall.

She had to move fast and be accurate with her strikes. She couldn't afford any miscalculation. It would cost her dearly if she did. She held her breath and kept her muscles tense, ready to act like a cat ambushing an unsuspecting mouse.

Remember your training, her monster said. *Attack. Cover. Move. Repeat.*

They were only footsteps away, maybe three to five feet from meeting Death herself, their breaths seeping through the KN95 masks, reminding her of *him*.

Fear sweat seeped into the freshly stitched laceration, causing it to burn and itch, and her heart pounded so hard against her sternum that she thought it could be heard as easily as someone knocking on a wooden door in the middle of the night.

She tightened her grip on the tomahawk, not wanting it to slip from her sweaty palm with the first swing.

Attack. Cover. Move. Repeat.

This was it. Sandra pushed herself from the wall and bent her knees to deliver a powerful first strike with the tomahawk. She took a steady breath. The air tasted salty on her tongue, which she found oddly soothing.

"Wait!" Zippo yelled.

The footsteps ceased. Sandra released her breath slowly.

"What now?" asked Muffled-voice.

"Something's wrong here. Something is very, very wrong," Zippo said suspiciously. Sandra heard his wet boots squeak on the floor, starting down the hall. "Let me check that hallway before you go down there."

"Why? There's no one here. Your man isn't here."

"Then how'd his truck get here?" Zippo asked.

They hadn't connected all the dots, but they were getting there.

"I see what you mean," Muffled-voice said.

"Step aside," Zippo ordered the men in the hallway, just around the corner from where Sandra stood with the tomahawk prepared to draw blood.

She thought about moving back down the hall but knew if she fled, she'd lose the element of surprise. She had no choice but to attack first.

Attack. Cover. Move. Repeat.

Zippo was right next to the short hallway. Sandra readjusted her grip on the tomahawk's handle. She drew in a steady, even breath.

Meet the monster, motherfucker.

She sprung out of the darkness as Zippo was about to step around the corner. He never saw the tomahawk coming, and she sunk it dead center between his eyes with a sickening wet *crack*. His entire body went rigid.

"What the hell was that?" Gary asked, still by the front door.

Zippo's left eye rolled slowly up into his skull. The right one leaked a blood tear. Sandra yanked the Tomahawk back out of his head with a crunch, and Zippo's body fell away from her stiffly onto the hallway floor with a thud that shook the house under her feet.

"Holyshi—" started one of the two hazmat guys standing before her. Sandra brought the bloody tomahawk back over her shoulder, the blade dripping blood. With wide, trembling eyes, they followed the weapon's movement.

She came at them then, screaming like a demon set free from hell and looking for retribution. The closest man to her held up his arms to protect himself, fearing she would strike him in the head.

But Sandra had expected him to do that, so she went low with her swing instead and caught him with the tomahawk across the right knee. There was a horrible chomping sound like an ax driven through wood as the knee was both shattered and split in two, the leg nearly severed off. Blood spattered across the floor and onto the wall.

He screamed and fell to the floor, grabbing at his leg, blood pouring out of him and painting the white suit crimson.

Sandra wasted no time taking out the next one, catching him below the chin with the tomahawk in an uppercut swing that split his face in half. The blow lifted him off the ground and threw him back into Muffled-voice behind him. Both tumbled to the floor next to the loft stairs.

In the same movement, she spun on her heels, brought the blade back around, and buried it into the head of the one behind her on the floor holding his nearly amputated leg.

The blow drove him to the ground, blood shooting from between his wet lips along with his last breath.

The shotgun racked behind her.

Looking over her shoulder, she saw Gary already had her locked in. There was no way he could miss. And there was nothing Sandra could do to stop the onslaught. She saw him tighten his finger around the trigger…

…and slowly start to squeeze.

She wasn't afraid of death. She welcomed its release at this point.

Muffled-voice shot to his feet in the middle of the hallway, looking to flee, just as Gary pulled the trigger. The shotgun spat fire, and buckshot ripped through his white outfit, creating small reddish-black pebble-size holes. The blast knocked him to the floor like his feet had been ripped out from under him.

"FUCK!" Gary screamed.

Sandra brought the tomahawk back over her shoulder while Gary racked another round. The only question in her mind was who was faster. The man with the gun. Or the woman with the tomahawk.

She pitched forward, releasing the tomahawk. It flipped through the air like a spinning missile, embedding its blade in Gary's upper right thigh, just below his pelvis, before he could get the shotgun leveled on her again.

He screamed out. His body twisted, and he fell to the floor, cupping his hands around the tomahawk's blade deep in the meat of his thigh.

"You fuckin' bitch! You fuckin' bitch!" he screamed. "Ahhhhhhh!"

As Sandra darted toward the kitchen, she grabbed one of Zippo's tantō knives. Staying low, she ducked behind the island, out of Gary's sight. Peering around the corner, she saw him lying on his side, still holding his leg, rocking back and forth like a baby in its crib. Soft whimpers floated up the hall. She felt nothing for him. She licked her wet lips like a wolf hungry for the taste of blood.

Attack. Cover. Move. Repeat.

In a crouch, she advanced into the living room, taking cover behind the sofa. She planned to flank Gary and take him out before he knew what hit him.

Peeking around the corner of the sofa, she saw Gary roll onto his side, looking for his weapon. He reached for the shotgun, but it lay just beyond his grasp. He slammed his fist down onto the hardwood floor.

"I'm going to kill you!" he screamed, spittle flying from his lips.

He reached out again for the shotgun, coming within a half inch of grabbing it.

She couldn't let him regain control of the weapon. She had to move on him. Now.

Gary heard her coming and sat up to try and defend himself. It was too late. Sandra was already bringing the tantō blade around to slash his throat open. He screamed a high-pitched wail that would have been funny in normal circumstances and held up his hands, fingers splayed, to protect himself.

But Sandra had underestimated the distance of her swing slightly. The knife's blade came up short. It didn't entirely miss, though, taking nine of his splayed fingers off in one violent slash. They flipped from his hands like dominos and plopped one by one to the floor.

He screamed again, his eyes stretched with horror when he saw nine geysers of blood squirt simultaneously from the cleanly cut nubs.

It was the last thing he ever saw.

CHAPTER TWENTY-TWO

There was nothing but death inside—the lives *they* took and those Sandra's monster took in its vengeance.

She'd heard stories about so-called houses of horror on the news, but she believed the looming monstrosity behind her lived up to its name as she made her way to the pickup. Her monster urged her to burn the atrocity to the ground. But the smoke from the fire would be seen miles away. Someone would be alerted—possibly whoever was behind this... whatever *this* was.

It was a risk she couldn't take, not with Emalyn and Lacy's lives hanging in the balance.

Now, with her face, arms, and hands camouflaged in blue and gray from Lacy's makeup kit and armed with Zippo's lighter and his two tantō knives strapped to each leg, the tomahawk tucked into her belt, and the shotgun with extra rounds, Sandra solely focused on her mission: finding Emalyn and Lacy and getting them back.

There were no thoughts of her family, the attack in 2020, or the lives she had taken.

Her transformation was complete.

The monster was in full control.

She wrenched open the pickup door, threw in her rucksack, jumped in, and fired up the engine.

She did not look back while heading toward the main road.

Ten minutes later, she cut the lights and pulled into the woods, far enough from the road that anyone passing by wouldn't see the pickup. The quarry road was a half mile directly in front of her.

Staying tucked into the darkness of the woods and using the trees and brush as cover, she crept along so as not to make too much noise until she saw the Sewyer Lime Quarry sign through an open pocket of the forest. Hunching down in the cover of shadows, she inched closer until she was behind a thick maple tree.

The gate leading to the quarry was open, and the road was lit by dusk-to-dawn lamps attached to the trees.

A man built like a linebacker, dressed in a black suit and tie, stood guard. From the bulge on his right side, Sandra knew he was armed. A curly wire running back over his left ear and down the inside of his blazer indicated they had coms.

It was not something she could bypass. Her mission just got a lot more complicated.

A pair of headlights approached, slicing through the dense forest like laser beams.

Sandra shot behind the tree. A tightness settled across her shoulders, and she wondered if she'd been spotted. The car turned onto the quarry road, its tires crunching the gravel under the tread before coming to a stop. Gazing around the tree, she saw a black limousine idling there. The guard was bent by the driver's side window, talking. She relaxed ever so slightly. He hadn't seen her.

What the hell is going on here?

The guard stepped back from the limo's door and motioned for it to proceed. He brought his left cuff to his mouth and said, "Please let Mr. Richter know his first evening guest, Mr. A., has arrived."

What's a Mr. A.? And why is he here? An icy feeling tiptoed up her back. Something important and highly secretive was going on. Was it government-related? Or a foreign shadow organization operating in the heart of where the Declaration of Independence was written? And who was Mr. Richter? She'd heard his name several times already.

The sound of an approaching automobile, this one coming from behind Sandra, caused her to turn. Another limousine rolled past and pulled to a stop by the guard, who spoke with the driver. After a moment, he waved it on too.

"Ms. W. has arrived." He spoke into his cuff, watching the limo driving off. "Please let Mr. Richter know."

Whoever these people were, they had the money to arrive in such luxury. *And where there's money, there's power.* But who *were* they? And why were *they* coming to a supposed abandoned quarry in the middle of the night? Why had *they* taken Emalyn and Lacy and brought them back here?

It doesn't matter. Get in, find the girls, and get out. Nothing more.

Sandra considered executing the guard. She could do it efficiently by driving the Tanto knife into the base of his skull—lights out. But it was a bad idea. She'd expend too much energy flanking and killing him and then hiding his tree trunk of a body—energy she needed.

No. She'd leave him be.

For now.

Sandra approached the quarry through the woods, following the road. Each step was carefully placed, trying not to rustle too many

249

leaves or snap the dead twigs and branches littering the forest floor. One loud crack would give her away, possibly causing the guard to get curious and investigate.

As she inched along, she wondered how far from the road the quarry was. She figured it had to be deep enough in the woods so whatever they were doing wouldn't attract unwanted attention.

Not that there was a lot of life in these parts besides the wild animals and a few locals that still called Little Hope home. Still, precautions would have been taken to ensure their activities remained hidden.

She wormed from tree to tree until the forest began to grow thin. Soon, bright white lights radiated from the ground and through the trees, catching the moisture in the soupy, lime-tainted air. The smell reminded her of the death pit—of Carrie lying there, her eyes open, staring blankly.

Use it.

She came out of the forest at the top of a crater. Large boulders lined the rim, and she ducked behind one. Below, she saw the sprawling complexity of the quarry spread out in front of her.

It was split into two levels. The old, rundown buildings used when it was operating were on the first level. A twisted road of compacted dirt and stone led to the underground maze of tunnels, where the earth had been stripped.

In the center was the largest building, at least five stories high. From all the rusted tubes and conveyor belts running to it, Sandra suspected it was where the lime was sent after it was processed in the various buildings around the quarry for packing and loading.

Floodlights burned around the top of the structure, illuminating the floor, though there were pockets of darkness where the light did not invade beside buildings or equipment left to rust. She could use the shadows to her advantage and disappear into them as she worked her way inside.

Sandra noticed two brick buildings, sitting side by side to the left of the hulking structure. The first building had windows across the front, and three satellite dishes were mounted on its roof; SATLINK was written across the front of them. Was it the communication building Derick mentioned?

What the hell kind of operation is this?

She counted fifteen guards in tactical gear moving about the complex, carrying machine guns, but suspected there were more embedded in the quarry tunnels like an ant colony. From her vantage, she couldn't tell what kind of rifles they were. Did it matter? Any machine gun could cut her in half.

At the front of the complex, two elevated covered towers and a chain-link gate with coiled barbwire running along the top blocked access to the quarry. Two guards were in each tower. One guard manned a roaming spotlight that swept the perimeter, while the other manned a mounted M60 machine gun aimed at the road. They were both trained on a third limo that had arrived. No one was getting past the front gate without the guards noticing.

And no one was getting out, either.

Whatever they were doing here, Sandra figured they had chosen the quarry for its natural barrier. Anyone trying to sneak in or out would have to scale the hundred-foot lime rock wall, which would be impossible for the average person, including herself.

The gate began to roll open, the fencing *chinging*. The limo passed between the guard towers and pulled to a stop by a building no bigger than a shack just aft of the towers. From inside the shack, a well-dressed man stepped out. Four guards lingering nearby followed the well-dressed man to the limo. Two of them held long poles. The other two held a small device.

Was this some paramilitary group? With the rise in hate and distrust in government over the last several years, Sandra knew those kinds of groups were popping up all over the country: men

251

and women looking for any excuse to go to war with the United States government. Her mother, after all, had accused her of being in one—which she wasn't.

If this was some right-wing paramilitary insurgence, they must be a well-funded organization, with the amount of people and firepower. What Sandra still didn't understand was why they kidnapped Emalyn and Lacy. Most of the people in these types of groups felt they were standing up to a tyrannical government that was looking to brainwash them and their children into becoming slaves.

So, if it wasn't a paramilitary group, then what was going on?

She turned her attention to what she believed was the communications building. Derick told her she'd find an elevator inside the building next to it that would lead underground to the holding pens. But to get there, she'd have to pass the front gate, the guards scattered about, and into the building without being seen.

Scaling down the cliff was out. There had to be another way in.

Think, Sandra, think!

Movement by the limo pulled her eyes in that direction. The four guards were along both sides of the car. Those with the poles looked underneath the limo using mirrors that flipped out on the ends. The other two ran their devices along the limo like a carpenter would a stud finder searching for a two-by-four hidden behind a wall. She realized they were looking for tracking devices. They didn't want anyone catching wind of their operation.

When they were done, the guards stepped back.

The rear limo doors opened, and two large bodyguards stepped out, followed by a short man wearing a suit and white dress shirt with an open collar. A gold neck chain gleamed in the overhead lights, as did the rings on his fingers. His head was square, and his dark hair was closely cropped.

"Mr. P." The well-dressed man spoke. "Would you and your bodyguards lift your arms and allow my men to scan you?"

She watched Mr. P. and his men raise their arms while the guards scanned their bodies with the devices, much like they had the limo.

"They're clean," said one of the guards when they were finished.

"Right this way, gentlemen," the well-dressed man said. "My guards will lead you to the lounge."

Mr. P. checked his watch—gold, just like everything else he wore. "How long until the show starts?" he asked in a thick Russian accent.

A Russian? *Was that important?* Sandra wondered.

"We are waiting for two more guests to arrive," the well-dressed man replied. "There are refreshments in the lounge while you wait. Please enjoy yourself."

The two guards who had swept the limo, Mr. P., and his goons, led them toward the communication building. The limo pulled forward and parked beside the other two Sandra had seen arrive. Shifting her attention back to Mr. P., she watched them enter the space between the two buildings and disappear.

That confirmed what Derick told her. The elevator to the underground had to be in that building.

I need to get in there.

Walking through the front door was out of the question. The gunners in the nest would spot her and cut her in two.

What she needed was a diversion.

Sandra believed she had what she needed in her rucksack to do the trick.

CHAPTER TWENTY-THREE

From her rucksack, Sandra pulled out matches and the rigger's tape. Using the multipurpose tool, she began cracking the match heads from the sticks with the pliers onto the sticky side of the tape. Once finished, she rolled the tape into a short four-inch strip.

Next, she cut open a shotgun shell and removed the slug and wad from inside, leaving only the gunpowder. She slid the rolled tape into the shell, ensuring it was inserted into the gunpowder, and then repacked the wad to keep everything tight before securing it with the rigger's tape. She had essentially just made an M-80 in under five minutes.

Making her way silently through the woods, Sandra came to the side of the road, far enough from the towers that the guards, even with the spotlights, wouldn't be able to see her, especially when she was wearing dark clothing and camo makeup. She dropped down in the small gully beside the road and concealed herself under wet leaves, sticks, and branches.

She planned to toss the explosive underneath the next limo that passed, hoping the charge would create a loud enough bang and shockwave to trick the driver into thinking a tire had blown.

She had just settled into position when the headlights of another approaching limo illuminated the woods, and her heart rate kicked into overdrive. For the diversion to work, she had to light the fuse and toss the explosive perfectly as the limo drove over it.

The limo was less than ten feet away and closing fast. Sandra pulled the Zippo from her pocket and spun the flint wheel. It sparked but didn't catch.

Eight feet from her position.

She tried again. Still, there was no flame.

C'mon!

The limo was now six feet, the headlights growing bigger, brighter by the second.

C'mon! C'mon!

She flicked the Zippo again. The flame caught, and she held it to the makeshift fuse. The limo was so close Sandra felt its motion reverberating through the ground and into her body.

The fuse caught.

Sandra tossed the shell, which exploded just as the limo rolled over it. The limo cut sharply to the left and then back to the right. The tires ground on the dirt road, kicking up dust and spitting rocks into the air as the driver tried to regain control.

Sandra shot to her feet, leaves and sticks falling off her, watching the limo fishtail out of control. She didn't have time to gawk but darted through the woods toward the front gate, not worrying about being quiet—the runaway limo masked any sound she made in the woods.

She was halfway to the gate in a dead sprint by the time the limo swerved off the road and slammed into a tree about ten feet from hitting the right guard tower. The loud crunch of metal folding shot through the woods, and the horn burped twice upon impact. A hiss cut through the muggy air and white steam billowed from underneath the hood of the smashed radiator.

Sandra slowed to a steady pace, inching closer and closer to the front gate. The hiss of steam and the confusion of the crash would hide her movements. The spotlights on the guard tower swept through the woods and landed on the crashed limo—all attention would be on it now.

Still, she cursed silently, knowing that if the limo had hit one of the guard towers, it would have taken out a spotlight, an M60, and two guards and caused quite a commotion that would have disoriented everyone, perhaps, allowing her to slip in unnoticed.

Perhaps not. Beggers can't be choosers, her monster said.

As the hiss from the radiator whistled out, Sandra dropped down onto her stomach and stealthily crawled across the forest floor, sticks and rocks jabbing into her bare forearms and elbows. Once concealed in a thicket of brush directly in front of the righthand guard tower, she observed men rushing to the gate. Someone inside ordered it open.

The electric motor kicked on, and the chain-link gate started to move. The fencing shook with a *ching, ching, ching* as it rolled open. Five armed guards rushed through the opening. She scanned the quarry floor. The entire complex was awash with activity from the accident, with guards rushing to the gate.

With everyone distracted, including the guards in the tower, Sandra felt it was her best opportunity to infiltrate the quarry. The base of the right-hand tower was submerged in blackness, and Sandra knew she could use it to vanish.

A ghost.

Easing herself from hiding in the brush, she hurried into the shadows and ducked down. Hugging the wall and crouching, she moved to the corner just as two more guards rushed to the accident.

The well-dressed man followed them. He was talking into a CB, reporting to someone unseen about the crash. This close, she recalled seeing his face somewhere recently. *Where?*

Suddenly, it hit her: the diner. He was the man in the back, eating a sandwich alone. Sandra remembered his eyes lingering on her and Emalyn while ordering their milkshakes.

Cleve, the waitress had called him.

A disturbing thought began pecking away in her brain, and Sandra felt something awful climb up from her stomach and settle in her chest like a bad cold.

She remembered Zippo saying something about completing the infiltration of the town. Was Cleve a plant to monitor those still calling Little Hope home and the tourists coming in? She had suspected that the entire town was involved at first.

But with Sheriff Craven and Deputy Allen's execution back at the house, this idea was starting to seem less of a possibility.

It didn't matter. What mattered was that she found Emalyn and Lacy and got out of there as quickly as possible.

Peeking around the corner of the guard tower, Sandra saw the coast was clear. The communications building was about ten to fifteen feet from the main entrance. She looked around for lingering guards but didn't see any. She was about to step out from the shadows…

…when the door to the guard tower burst open.

Sandra sucked in a breath and ducked back around the wall into the dark, her heart in her throat.

Another guard rushed by her. He was in too much of a hurry to pay attention to anything other than the wrecked limo.

Sandra stood and moved into the quarry unnoticed. Behind her, men shouted that they needed to get someone called the Sheik out of the limo. Paying their voices little mind, she hurried across the open complex and ducked behind some rusted equipment just as another guard sprinted around the communications building.

Pulling the tomahawk, she prepared herself to take him out quietly and efficiently, but only if she had to. She didn't need a trail of bodies leading them right to her.

But he passed her by without even a glance. She released her breath in a low sigh. Looking back at the communications building, she saw it was connected to the building beside it by what appeared to be a conveyor belt. She could use it to access that building, knowing she couldn't go through the front door to get to the elevator—it was also bound to be guarded.

Jumping to her feet, she dashed across the open space to the communications building and dropped into the shadows, as thick as black ink, lingering beside the door.

In front of her, she had a clear line of sight of the wrecked limo. The area was a beehive of activity. Cleve ordered his men to set up a defensive perimeter if someone tried to get past them.

Little did they know; Sandra was already inside.

The limo doors were open, and the driver and a man of Middle Eastern descent dressed in a thawb stood beside it, both looking baffled as to the cause of the accident.

Sandra understood the reference to the Sheik she had heard moments ago. Who was he? Why was he here?

Doesn't matter.

It wouldn't be long before someone found the brass head of the shotgun shell. They would put two and two together and know someone was trying to access the compound or had already breached it. When that happened, all hell would break loose, and this place would be locked tighter than Fort Knox.

As quietly as a black cat, Sandra opened the door and slipped into the building. Staying low, concealed in the shadows around the floor, she smelled coffee and found a lone man seated at a computer terminal with his back to her. He hadn't heard her enter. He sported a laid-back attire of blue jeans, a black t-shirt, and flip-flops.

Sandra knew he wasn't a guard from how he was dressed. He was typing what looked like code into the computer. Maybe some technical support?

Will he know where Emalyn and Lacy are?

He finished typing and smashed his finger into the enter key. *CLICK!* A smaller window appeared out of the black screen. On it, Sandra saw a video feed of what looked to be a stage. Silhouettes moved hurriedly around in front of the camera as if rushing to finish whatever they were doing before they went live.

A stiffness crimped Sandra's chest, making it hard to breathe. *That's exactly what they are doing!* Whatever was going on, they were filming it and sending it across the internet using the Max Satlink Satellite Dishes mounted to the roof. *You sonsabitch—*

The tech picked up a CB next to the keyboard and pressed the button on the side.

"Live feed is up. Everything is running smoothly for tonight's show."

"Roger that," a voice crackled through the speaker.

Along the side of the video feed, Sandra saw usernames—to keep their true identities a secret—starting to appear as guests entered the feed. She wondered if this was going out on the Dark Web. She'd heard about the Dark Web but had never seen it before; she was not someone who ventured into such depravity.

"Our online guests are starting to join in," the tech said into the CB.

"Perfect. Keep me updated, Neils. We will start as soon as all our guests arrive."

Sandra understood now why the limo guests were being addressed as Mr. A, Ms. W, Mr. P, and the Sheik—to keep their identities a secret, even from the guards working in the compound.

"Ten-four," Neils replied.

Neils placed the CB down, picked up a coffee mug, and brought it to his lips but found it empty.

"Bugger," he groaned.

Sandra's eyes flipped to the half-full coffee pot sitting on the stand. *Oh, shit.* If he turned around, and he would, he'd spot her and maybe sound the alarm.

He kicked off one of the chair's legs, spinning the seat around, and was in the process of getting up for a refill when Sandra lunged from the shadows, cupped her hand over his mouth, and placed the tantō blade across his throat. His eyes widened with fright and shock, trying to process who she was and how she'd gotten past the guards to him.

"I'm only going to ask you once," Sandra whispered, pulling lightly on the blade, creating a small slice into the soft flesh of his neck. She felt him stiffen, and he began nodding vigorously. "Two girls were brought here tonight. Where are they?"

"They've been taken down to the pens," he said with a tremble after Sandra removed her hand from his mouth.

"Where are the pens?"

"The building next door. Inside, there's a lift that leads to the underground facilities. The pens are beside the stage on Level Two."

Sandra slowly lifted the knife away, letting Neils think he was off the hook. He sighed and closed his eyes, thankful to still be alive. He wasn't for long.

Sandra quickly drove the knife through his left temple, killing him instantly. She guided his limp body to the floor so he didn't make any noise. She left the knife in his head so as not to leave blood all over the place when she hid his body.

After stuffing the corpse under the computer desk, she replaced the chair by the terminal. If anyone entered, nothing would look out of place. They'd think Neils had gotten up to go for a leak or to get something, nothing more.

Sandra was about to move but dropped out of sight as two guards rushed past outside. She had kicked the hornet's nest. The hive was swarming.

You need to hurry.

Staying low, she moved into a room filled with old, dust-covered office furniture, which had been left there since the quarry closed. A stairwell was to her left. She quickly took the steps, entering a large vacant room that smelled heavily of lime dust, making the air repugnant and hard to breathe. She wondered what this room was originally used for. A small square slot was cut in the wall, leading to the conveyor connecting the two buildings.

Wiggling through the hole, she slid onto the shaky, rusty conveyer. On her stomach, she inched herself forward. The conveyor swayed slightly from her movements, and she heard the eroded metal securing brackets squeak and groan in protest.

Move slow.

Easing herself onto her hands and knees, she began to crawl. The ground was a good twenty feet or more below. If the conveyor gave way, or she lost her balance and went over the side, the fall could seriously injure her. Or worse, kill her. She had to be—

She stopped, sucked in a breath, when a door opened directly below her. Peering over the side of the conveyor, she saw three men step out. The leader was dressed in a suit. He was bald, and his dome reflected the overhead lights. The two following him were the guards who had escorted Mr. P. and his goons from his limo.

"As soon as everything's secure at the front gate, we'll bring the Sheik over," one of the guards said.

"Right," replied Baldie.

The guards started away. Sandra flattened onto the conveyor so neither saw her if they turned around. The door below banged closed. Baldie had returned inside, and the guards had walked out of sight.

She got back up on her hands and knees, edged her way across the conveyor, and rolled through the slot in the wall and gently down onto a catwalk, the steel grating digging into her.

On her stomach, Sandra scanned the room. Baldie had returned to a desk beside a mine shaft lift—the kind she'd seen in countless movies and TV shows. The catwalk made an H shape across the top of the building. She could use it to slip on top of the lift, hopefully without anyone noticing her presence, and ride it into the underground.

The door opened, and a fury of words she didn't understand flooded the room. The man at the desk shot to his feet as if he were about to salute a superior officer.

Looking to the door, Sandra saw two armed guards enter first, followed by the man they referred to as the Sheik, ranting and raving—most likely about what had happened—in his native tongue. Both guards looked concerned, as if they suspected something was amiss.

Had they found what was left of the shotgun shell? Or had Sandra gotten lucky, and it had been blown into the woods when it exploded? She didn't know. But, since no alarms had gone off, and there was no sign that anything was wrong—outside of the obvious—Sandra felt luck might be on her side tonight.

Luck only counts in horseshoes and hand grenades, her monster said.

The Sheik was still screaming, spittle flying from his mouth, white foam collecting at the corner of his lips and tangling in his thick, black beard.

"Please settle down," the one guard said. "We understand you're upset, but what happened was an accident."

Baldie came around the desk, holding a black wand. He motioned for the Sheik to raise his arms so he could scan him.

"Get da fuck outta here wit dat," the Sheik spat. "You already check me."

"This is precautionary," the other guard said evenly.

"You know who I am?" The Sheik pointed at himself. He turned to Baldie. "What 'bout you? You know who I am?"

"It doesn't matter who you are," the first guard spoke. "No one goes below without being scanned a second time. Now, if you lift your arms so we can do our jobs, we can escort you down."

The Sheik hissed like a cat and rolled his eyes, but he lifted his arms to be scanned with the wand.

It was now or never. Sandra quietly crossed the catwalk, keeping her eyes on the men below as she moved toward the lift. None of them looked in her direction because no one expected a threat from above.

"He's clear," Baldie said.

"Of course I am," the Sheik spat.

She approached the railing directly above the lift. There was about a foot of space between the wall and the catwalk that Sandra could slip between to get on top without anyone seeing her. She climbed over the railing and stealthily lowered herself onto the caged roof while the Sheik stepped onto the lift; it rocked from their weight, but he didn't seem to notice as he checked his diamond-crusted watch impatiently.

The two guards stepped into the lift beside the Sheik and closed the door.

The three of them were directly below her. The first guard pushed a button on a panel on the right-hand side of the lift, and its motor engaged with a *click*.

They fell below the surface faster than Sandra expected. Her stomach rose into her throat, and the sudden jolt of movement almost caused her to lose her balance as the lift descended into the underworld.

The vertical lime walls of the shaft were lit with square lights that cast a beige glow, making everything look dingy. *Sickly.*

What the hell was she going to find when she got down there?

Sandra unslung the shotgun from around her chest. If either of the guards happened to glance up and see her, they'd be able to shoot her as easily as a bird on a wire. But not if she had the shotgun ready. She aimed the barrel between her feet, knowing from this range she could kill all three of them with one round.

"Please allow me to extend my apologies for the mishap," the first guard said.

"Unacceptable. Fucking unacceptable," the Sheik spat.

"I'm sure Mr. Richter will compensate you for the trouble," said the second guard.

"I come all dis way—nearly sixty-five hundred miles—to have dis happen to me. A flat tire that almost get me killed. He better compensate well."

"I'm sure Mr. Richter will."

"The price I'm paying him, he damn well better."

"Mr. Richter's services are one of a kind. He also makes sure his clients are taken care of. I'm sure you will leave tonight forgetting all about your... incident."

What would be offered to the Sheik as compensation? Her monster stirred with savagery. Squeezing the trigger and making these three into mincemeat would be rewarding.

Problem. Fucking. Solved.

But she couldn't. Not yet.

Getting Emalyn and Lacy out came first and foremost. Everything else, including her monster's lust for vengeance, was secondary.

The lift settled to a bumpy stop. The second guard opened the door for the Sheik.

"He better compensate me," the Sheik angrily said and stepped out, followed by the guards.

Sandra watched them start up a tunnel from atop the lift, their footfalls echoing off the walls.

Reslinging the shotgun across her back, she opened the small hatch in the cage roof, dropped into the lift, and moved to the opening.

The tunnel was lined with light bulbs running along the walls as far as she could see. Ahead, it veered to the right. Small alcoves had been hacked into the limestone.

Sandra figured the miners probably used them to store things needed to strip the earth when this was still a financially prosperous vein.

There was no one in the tunnel that she could see.

Hugging the wall, she started down the tunnel. She expected it to smell of dust and lime, but the air was pure and fresh. Whoever ran this operation had spared no expense in ensuring top-notch ventilation.

Richter? Who in the hell was this guy?

She was almost to the bend in the tunnel when a human shadow cast over the wall, coming in her direction.

Sandra froze.

The shadow grew bigger as it neared. Sandra felt her pulse quicken. If the person came around the corner, she would be fully exposed.

Her eyes fell onto one of the dark alcoves cut into the wall.

She ducked into it just before one of the guards who escorted the Sheik rounded the bend, passing so close the musk of his aftershave tickled her nose.

Where had they taken the Sheik? What was really going on? Only God knew.

But Sandra was in the devil's factory, and these men were the devil's laborers. Could God's divine power even reach this far?

She waited in the shadows of the alcove until she heard the lift begin its assent back to the surface.

Then, she stepped around the bend and ran directly into the chest of the second armed guard she hadn't noticed returning from delivering the Sheik.

CHAPTER TWENTY-FOUR

The guard was surprised as Sandra was. But his shock quickly turned, and his face morphed into alarm. She could practically hear *INTRUDER! INTRUDER! INTRUDER!* going off inside his head like a warning siren.

He went for the UTAS rifle slung off his shoulder.

She punched out with her right hand, catching him in the Adam's apple between her thumb and index finger before he even had the weapon unslung. *A man can't fight if he's struggling to breathe.*

The guard's tongue shot from his mouth like a large, uncoiling pink eel, and a choking sound crept out of him. Sandra hit him a second time. She felt his larynx crush and his hyoid bone break.

He fell to the floor on his back, gasping for air. He dug at his throat as if trying to tear the flesh away, to open himself up and allow oxygen to rush his lungs, to save him. His feet flailed around like a swimmer trying to get to the surface, fearing drowning. No matter how hard he kicked or tore at his throat, his efforts were futile.

As the guard slowly suffocated at her feet, Sandra looked down the hallway. It split into a Y about twenty feet from where she stood, but it was clear of further guards and quiet as a church. How had she not heard him approaching?

Get your shit together, her monster's voice growled in her head. *This isn't any training exercise.*

It certainly wasn't.

A final choking gurgle came from the man at her feet, and then he grew still. His face was blueish purple, and his eyes were rolled up into his head, the whites showing. *Dead as a fucking doornail.* She thought about spitting on him but decided he wasn't worth the wasted bodily fluid.

Stepping over his dead body, she moved to where the hallway split. At the end of the tunnel was a single door painted dark red with a light above—a beacon to the entranceway of hell itself.

Perhaps it is.

She turned her attention to the left hallway. Unlike the right, this tunnel dead-ended at a lime-rock wall. Two gray doors were on either side of the hall, and at the end, a green door led to places Sandra wasn't sure she wanted to venture.

There was a more pressing matter, however, that she needed to attend to. The guard's body. She couldn't just leave him in the middle of the tunnel; he'd be found, the alarms would sound, and they'd be searching for her like a drug-sniffing dog.

Hide him!

She tried the first door in the right-hand tunnel. To her surprise, it was unlocked. Inside, it was dark and smelled sterile, reminding her of the hospital she'd spent weeks recovering in. The phantom pain surged through her at the memory.

Hurrying back to the body, she grabbed ahold of his arms and dragged him into the room. Normally, dragging a full-grown man would have been nearly impossible for someone of Sandra's size, but the sled-pulling drills Joel had them do over and over made the task somewhat easier.

He harped that they never knew when they might have to drag an injured person from a ditch, a car accident, a fire, or God forbid, someone during or after a mass shooting.

Once the guard's body was pulled into the room, she closed the door. The room fell into a thick, silent darkness that she felt squeezing her. Sandra needed a moment to catch her breath before moving on.

Turning on the light wasn't a good idea. Even though there were no windows in the steel door, the light could seep out, giving her away. She didn't need another surprise visit.

Unslinging her rucksack, she reached in and grabbed a glowstick. Cracking it, the green light revealed a medical bay with all the bells and whistles. But what grabbed her attention was the gyno table in the middle of the room.

Why did they have a gyno table?

She had read books about experiments the Nazis did on their prisoners in concentration camps—a therapeutic exercise to help her deal with her trauma, which paled in comparison to the atrocities the Jewish people went through. Could that be why they had taken Emalyn and Lacy? To conduct some radical medical experimentation on them down here?

Did she want to know?

Pushing the awful thought away, she unslung the rifle from the dead guard's shoulder, popped the magazine, and checked the load. Full. She slid the magazine back into place, slammed it home with her palm, and then pulled the slide back, arming it.

Taking the two ammo magazines on his belt, Sandra stuck them in her left hip pocket to reload faster, allowing her to keep the weapon in her dominant firing hand.

She patted him down, finding a pack of cigarettes and a Bic lighter. The lighter and cigarettes could come in handy—lighters were full of fuel, and cigarettes made good, slow-burning fuses in a pinch. She dumped the glowstick down the sink before stepping out. Opening the door, she checked both ways—clear.

Now armed with an automatic rifle, Sandra moved up the hallway with a proficient shooter's grace: knees slightly bent, rifle tucked tight—but not too tight—into her shoulder, eyes sweeping the hallway back and forth, the barrel following her gaze.

Moving to the red door at the end of the hall, her hopes of finding Emalyn and Lacy behind it rose with each step closer.

I'm coming, girls. Aunt Sonnie is coming.

But as she reached out to grasp the handle, the lift's motor *clicked* on, and the cage rattled as it descended the elevator shaft. Someone was coming. A guest? Another guard? Both? With her heart in her throat, she spun around, grabbed the door handle, and charged through.

Little did Sandra know what kind of hell she was walking into.

CHAPTER TWENTY-FIVE

The red door led her into a large, dimly lit, cavernous stone room modified into an amphitheater. It looked like something straight out of Greek culture. *Or something the Nazis would have created in a secret cavern.*

Three sections of stone seats had been chiseled into the earth in a semi-circle, each separated by stairs leading to the staging area. A podium sat on the right-hand side of the stage, lit by lights suspended above. The backdrop was a velvety maroon curtain that oozed sleaze like a dank bordello's wallpaper—a prickling sensation across Sandra's nub caused her hand to cramp at the nasty image in her mind of gross men with young girls.

Ducking into the shadows at the back of the amphitheater, Sandra saw three people sitting in the first row of the center section for a prime viewing experience—the guests she'd seen arriving earlier in the limos, she supposed.

Two servers, dressed in white blazers, black slacks, and shoes, came out from a doorway to the left of the stage with trays full of drinks and hors d'oeuvres for the guests to pick at as they waited for the show to begin.

But what kind of show was this?

The lights around the theater dimmed to near darkness, and the servers quickly shuffled back into the room they came from. The show was about to begin.

The velvet curtains parted, and a man dressed in an expensive black suit stood there with his hands folded at his waist like he was about to teach a class. He was tall with a natural athletic build, strikingly handsome European features, blond hair, and the bluest eyes Sandra believed she had ever seen.

"Welcome, guests." He spoke in an eloquent German accent, which explained the European looks. "I'm happy you are with us this evening. Please let me apologize for the delay. It seems we're having some unforeseen issues tonight. And we've been waiting for one more guest to arrive, but since he has not, we will begin this evening's festivities without him. For those of you watching and are maybe new to these events, I'm your host, Deitch Richter."

Richter directed his blue eyes onto a particular guest in the front row and smiled.

"Sheik, please let me apologize for what happened with your escort. It was an unforeseen accident that no one could have predicted. However"—his voice rose—"to make this right, I have an item to compensate you for your troubles. How does that sound?"

Item? The chill broke into a cold flop sweat across Sandra's body, numbing her like she was sitting in an ice bath.

"Perfect," the Sheik said.

"Wunderbar." Richter clapped his hands together with a wide smile. His eyes shone excitedly, darkening them to the color of the Hope Diamond. "Helga?"

To the right of the stage, a woman twice Sandra's size stepped out from behind the curtain. Her unnaturally muscular physique was poured into a black leather onesie that zipped up the front, allowing the contours of her well-developed muscles to pop under the overhead lights.

Her blonde hair was stick straight and stopped just above a square jaw that Sandra knew could only be obtained using synthetic steroids. She turned, reached behind the curtain, and pulled a young woman onto the stage beside her.

Sandra's heart clutched in her chest.

Lacy!

She looked like she'd been through a war. Her blonde hair was a tangled rat's nest. The abrasion on the right side of her head where the attackers had struck her at the house had been patched up, but the dried blood droplets remained on her summer dress. Her blue eyes were large and round.

Fright and confusion caused her body to tremble as Helga took hold of her upper arm and escorted her to the front of the stage. She was walking with a bad limp.

"Now, Sheik, because of your unforeseen event with your transportation, I am offering her to you free of charge in compensation. I'm sure you can find a place for her in your organization, yes?"

"She's... dirty," the Sheik said as if he'd been offered a pig covered in shit as reparation.

Richter looked at Lacy like a seedy car salesman would a used car. "I apologize for her appearance. I did not intend to gift her to anyone this evening. But after what happened, I thought it was only right. She just needs a bath before being put to work."

He talked about Lacy like she was a mangy dog. A fire in Sandra's belly ignited—what kind of work did they have lined up for her?

"Okay. Fine," the Sheik said. "I take. You wash her before I take?"

"Of course."

"Very good, dis. Very good."

"Wunderbar!" Richter turned to the others.

"Now, lady and gentlemen, guests watching around the world, we can get started with tonight's auction."

Auction? A bitter chill nipped at the base of Sandra's skull. Whatever was being sold—auctioned off—was of great value and secrecy to these people, people with money and power. Her nub thumped with repulsion, and her upper lip rose in a snarl.

Richter stepped back and looked toward the curtain.

"Martin," he said.

Another man emerged from behind the curtain and crossed the stage to the podium. He was a short, slender man who looked like a strong wind could blow him away. His dark hair was slicked back over his head, pasted there. A pencil-thin mustache matched his tiny, straight mouth. Round glasses magnified his dark eyes.

The auctioneer. And he's going to sell...

"Good evening," Martin said with a wolfish grin that made Sandra's skin crawl. "Tonight, we'll begin with the sale of two vintage items. Mr. A?" His eyes shifted behind the glasses, searching the faces before him through the dark. "Ah, there you are. I believe you will be very happy tonight."

There were a few snickers from the guests in the front row—an inside joke shared between them that made Sandra shudder. *How long had they been doing this?*

Martin looked to the side of the stage and said, "Helga? Bring the first item out."

"Come. Now!" Helga ordered someone behind the curtain in a thick German accent. "Here. Now. Here." She thrust a sharply filed red fingernail at the floor directly beside her.

When no one appeared, Helga stomped to the side of the stage and pulled a thin girl by the arm from behind the curtain.

Emalyn!

Sandra's need to intervene cooked her blood as Helga paraded her niece across the stage. The fear and turmoil in Emalyn's eyes caused a deep ache in Sandra's chest, rousing her monster.

Let's kill 'em all. Bathe in their blood.

Then, it all clicked into focus, and Sandra understood what they were doing. It was heinous—there was no better word. She felt sick to her stomach.

They are going to... to... sell her.

This was a well-financed and highly organized sex trade operation.

Rage replaced the sickness circling Sandra's stomach. And she willed herself—her monster—from bringing the rifle up, flipping it to full auto, and pulling the trigger until it was empty, leaving all of those sick fucks nothing more than shredded meat.

But as much as she'd like to merge the fantasy into reality, she had Emalyn to consider. She couldn't allow a firefight to break out with her niece standing directly in the middle. Besides, a bullet was too good for people of their ilk—too easy, clean, and quick. They needed to suffer for what their power, influence, and money caused and what it funded.

And suffer you will.

"For a virgin fourteen-year-old, we'll start the bidding at two hundred thousand dollars," Martin said.

The gyno table flashed into Sandra's mind, and she knew that Emalyn had been *examined* on it to see if she was... a virgin.

Revulsion shot from Sandra's nub like a jolt of epinephrine. *Disgusting. Sick. Fuckers.* They would pay more for a virgin.

A silhouetted hand rose in the dark.

"Very good, Mr. A. Now, how about two hundred and fifty thousand?" Martin asked, his eyes sweeping the guest sitting before him.

"Three hundred thousand dollars?" A slender hand rose at the far end.

"Very nice," Martin said, adjusting his spectacles. "We have a bidding war between Mr. A. and Ms. W. Four hundred thousand dollars?"

Mr. A's hand shot in the air as if he were trying to be the first one called on in class.

The hand on the end also rose, and Ms. W. spoke with a Texas drawl, "Four-fifty."

"What da fuck you doing?" shouted Mr. A, his Italian accent echoing across the cavernous room.

"I'm just trying to make things interesting," the one known as Ms. W. replied snootily.

"Dis is my brand. Back off."

She laughed in that fake posh way that only rich people can get away with and not get slapped across the face.

"Oh, darling. I don't want anything to do with *your* brand."

"Den why you drove da price up."

"I was just having a spot of fun. At your expense, of course. You can afford the price tag." She looked back at Emalyn on stage. "Then again, I think you overpaid, myself."

"*Bitch!*" Mr. A snarled.

Ms. W. laughed.

"Do I hear five hundred thousand?" There were no takers this time. "Ms. W? Mr. A?"

"Fine. Five hundred," Mr. A relented.

"Back to you Ms. W." Martin said, looking at her over his round spectacles.

"No. I'll pass. The item is too... *vintage* for my tastes."

"Sold. For five hundred thousand dollars to Mr. A."

The guests, along with Richter and Helga, applauded as if Mr. A had just bought some rare antiquity—but not as rare as it should have been in today's world. The thought profoundly disgusted Sandra, causing her thumb to rub over the full-auto switch at the side of the rifle.

Helga stepped forward and grabbed Emalyn's arm, pulled her from the stage, and shoved her behind the curtain. Then she pulled another child onto the stage. This one was a male in his early teens with dark hair. He wore only white briefs, and his narrow bird-like chest was concaved with fright. It appeared he'd been stolen right out of the safety of his bed.

They Came At Night.

"YES!" Mr. A said, excitedly jumping out of his seat.

"Settle, Mr. A," Martin said calmly, as if he were addressing librarians sitting around a discussing Tolstoy's works. "Bidding will start at seven hundred thousand dollars for the vintage item. Please allow others—"

Martin touched his ear; someone was talking to him through a Bluetooth earpiece. Sandra hadn't noticed the device until now. "We have an online bid of 1.5 million dollars. And since the bidding has started, Mr. A, would you like to offer more?"

"Two," Mr. A said eagerly.

"Three." The Sheik this time.

"Three-fifty?" Back to Mr. A.

Martin touched his ear again. "The online bidder has dropped out. It is between Mr. A. and the Sheik. Do I hear four million dollars, gentleman?"

279

"Yes," the Sheik said. "Four."

"Very good, sir. Very good." Martin looked to the other side of the room. "Mr. A?"

"Agh! No. Out." Mr. A sat down, disappointed. He threw his hands in the air. He had wanted the boy even more than Emalyn.

That deeply troubled Sandra. She wondered if it should. Why should their sex mean anything? These children were nothing more than prime meat—to be consumed. Were they purchasing these kids as commodities to force them into their sex trade organizations, or for... personal use?

Sandra shivered at the thought.

She was pretty sure she understood how the operation worked. They murdered the families in the houses and then kidnapped the children. Then, they brought them back here to be auctioned off to the highest bidder—someone either present or on the Dark Web.

But how were they doing this without the law catching wind? How were they getting away with it? How were they...

"Sheik, you're the winner."

Another round of clapping.

"We will take a short break while we prepare for the next round. Please take advantage of our fine selections of wines and hors d'oeuvres in the lounge—the shrimp is to die for," Richter said.

CHAPTER TWENTY-SIX

Sandra backed out of the amphitheater and into the hallway without anyone seeing her. Neils, the tech she'd driven the tantō's blade into, had said they were holding Emalyn and Lacy somewhere near the stage.

It wasn't practical for her to slip past everyone, grab them, and sneak back out. They were sure to be caught in the process—killed. Or worse.

You have to find another way back there.

A voice echoed through the tunnel.

"When you speak to Mr. Richter, please tell him I'm sorry for my late arrival. I did not mean to hold the auction up."

Sandra heard approaching footsteps. There was nowhere for her to hide except back into the amphitheater. But if she did that, she'd expose herself to those entering. It was a bad spot to be in, and she had no intention of dying like a rat trapped in a cage. She had made up her mind a long time ago that if she were ever in a situation like what she had endured that *night*, she would fight until her last breath.

"You know Mr. Richter doesn't like to be behind schedule, especially on auction nights. He has other clients whose time is more valuable than yours, Mr. C."

Sandra made a beeline up the hallway. She had to cut them off before they saw her and sounded the alarm.

"Surely, Mr. Richter will understand. I was caught up with work. My company—"

"Your problems are not Mr. Richter's concern."

The voices were so close Sandra felt their words reverberating in her eardrums. Since she heard only two voices, she prayed that was the case. Still, she had to prepare herself for more. She was knee-deep in the shit now and had no choice but to make a stand, though she didn't plan on killing both of them. She needed one alive long enough to tell her where they kept Emalyn and Lacy.

She slid the tomahawk from her belt.

"If you are late again," a guard was saying as he and another man in a three-piece suit rounded the corner of the tunnel, "Mr. Richter will have no choice but to—"

His lecture was cut short when Sandra swung the tomahawk, the handle catching the guard across the bridge of the nose. An expulsion of blood burst from his face, and he instantly dropped to the floor with his nose shattered, eyes filling with water, in so much pain he was unable to make a sound other than a small whimper.

She turned and swung the tomahawk at the person the guard had been escorting. In the moments before she notched the blade into the side of his face, cutting his left eye in half, she thought she recognized him. She yanked the blade out of his head with a wet sucking sound, and he crumbled like a marionette with its strings cut.

Turning back to the guard on the floor, her chest heaving, she saw his hand pressed to his face, thick dark blood seeping through his fingers, moaning in pain. This was her chance to find out where Emalyn and Lacy were.

The injured guard held his bloody hand out in front of him and began inching himself away from Sandra when she started coming toward him. His scared eyes flipped to the blood-dripping tomahawk in her right hand.

"Please! Please!" he begged.

"Where are the children being held?"

He pointed down to the left hallway, his finger shaking uncontrollably.

"The green door on the left will lead you to another hallway. Follow it until you reach a dead end. There will be another door on the right. Through it is another hallway that will lead you to an intersection. The holding pens are to the right, but you'll need a key card to access them."

He rooted in his front pocket, pulled out a small plastic white card, and held it out to her, his blood smearing its glossy surface.

Sandra snatched it from him.

"Please, don't kill me. I have a family," he said with pleading eyes and a quivering bottom lip.

"So did I."

Sandra raised the tomahawk and brought it forward, sinking the blade to the hilt in the middle of his head. He went cross-eyed, and the light in his eyes dimmed. She kicked him in the face to knock him free of the blade's penetrating hold.

The thought of moving the bodies crossed her mind, but what was the point? Their blood had been spilled everywhere. A blood trail would lead someone right to them, and once their bodies were discovered, word would go out across the complex that an intruder had infiltrated.

She prayed that no one would find them until she found the holding pens.

Sandra began searching the guard for anything useful, finding a Kimber revolver in a shoulder holster. Standing, she tucked the Kimber into her belt and looked back at the man in the three-piece suit. Again, she thought she recognized him like the face of an old friend unseen for years.

And then, it hit her like a fist, causing the laceration to hum. Even with his left eye socket caved in and his face twisted with the last moment of fear he felt just before she ended his life, she knew him.

Lawrence Maxwell .

Her heart began to beat hard, and something broke in Sandraa. It was as if everything she had come to believe about the world was a lie.

Lawernce Maxwell was a tech industry titan who created Max SatLink, providing customers with lightning-fast satellite internet. She remembered reading an article about him in *Outdoor Life* a few years back. At that time, he aimed to provide wireless, high-speed internet to anyone, anywhere, at any time.

Max SatLink was not quite as big as Starlink, owned by Elon Musk, but Max was gaining a foothold in the industry while making himself a household name. Max was the new kind of celebrity—the billionaire whose charm, wit, and salesmanship could win over millions, getting them to buy cars, the internet, or subscribe to an ideology.

Was he down here for the same reason as everyone else?

The lift's motor clicked. It was starting down again.

Move! her monster screamed.

284

CHAPTER TWENTY-SEVEN

A strange electricity now charged the honeycomb of underground tunnels. Sandra didn't know if this feeling was in her head or if it was some external uneasiness because she left two dead bodies in the middle of the hallway to be discovered eventually.

It was bound to happen—*impossible not to break a few eggs while making an omelet*—but she wished when the shit hit the fan, she would have been on her way out, not still searching for her niece and Lacy.

Now, the question riddling her mind was: when she did find Emalyn and Lacy, could she hold off their pursuers long enough to get them out alive?

Coming to the green door, she pushed through it, finding the subsequent hall empty. She ran until she came to the dead end, where she found another green door, just like the guard had said there'd be. *Good!*

She pried open this door and peeked into the hallway beyond. It, too, was vacant, and she proceeded until she came to an intersection where four hallways met. To her left was another hallway that led to a larger lift, maybe a freight elevator, used at one time to get equipment down there. To her right was another green door with a keycard-operated lock.

Scanning the keycard, the lock *clicked,* and Sandra pushed it open. Twelve doors lined the narrow hallway. Each door had its square viewing window with a metal grate—the holding pens.

A heat rose through her. Emalyn was held against her will like an animal in one of these pens. At the end of the hall was another red door, like the one she had seen earlier. It must've led into the rear of the amphitheater. She realized the doors must have been color-coded to avoid confusion in the labyrinth of tunnels.

Moving to the first door on the right, Sandra stood on her toes to peer into the prison. Inside, two children—a boy and a girl—sat in a room no bigger than a closet with their backs pressed against the wall. They held each other close as if they could ward off the monsters inevitably coming for them. Impossible. From their miserable, drawn faces and absent stairs, they saw little hope of being saved.

Sandra dropped away before the children saw her, not wanting to rile them up, thinking she was there to free them, to save them. After she had Emalyn and Lacy out, she could contact the police and tell them about this awful place.

She moved to the next pen, finding two girls between the ages of eight and ten sitting on the floor with their legs drawn up to their chins, rocking back and forth.

In the next pen, Sandra found two males—between the ages of five and eight—before moving to the last one on the right side. Another girl—this one couldn't have been more than four—held a stuffed animal and was so scared out of her mind that her entire body shook.

It was horrific.

A sneeze brought Sandra's attention around.

Emalyn!

She had been allergic to the lime dust. Down here, it must have been agonizing for her.

She hurried along the pens on the left side, peeking into each room as she passed, finding them empty except for the teenage boy she'd seen on stage during the auction—*a vintage model like Emalyn*. Her skin slithered. In the next pen, she found Emalyn and Lacy.

Emotions, ones Sandra couldn't explain, flooded every part of her as if a dam had crumbled. Tears of joy, of anger, of outrage at what *they* had done to her niece burned her eyes.

"Emalyn," Sandra whispered.

"Aunt Sonnie!"

Emalyn ran to the door. Lacy followed, slower, limping. Emalyn's small hands clawed at the steel grating of the viewing window, her fingers sliding through the metal holes. Sandra took her niece's fingers and felt the icy fear trembling through them.

"I'm getting you two out of here," Sandra whispered.

Lacy winced as she eased herself to the door beside Emalyn.

"Can you walk?" Sandra asked her.

"I twisted my knee during the attack back at the house. But I'll keep up."

"If you slow us down, I'll leave you behind, understand?" Sandra replied.

Lacy studied the woman who resembled Sandra with horrified eyes, dreading being left to those animals. Sandra knew they planned to get Lacy hooked on drugs and then put her to work in the sex industry. It was the only reason Lacy had been spared, taken.

She was still young enough to be useful to them but too old to sell to one of the sickos at the auction.

"What about the others? We can't leave them down here," Emalyn said, breaking Sandra's thoughts.

Sandra knew she couldn't sneak all the children out of the tunnels, past the guards, to safety. The three of them would be hard enough.

"Just you two," Sandra finally said.

Emalyn stepped back, appalled at the thought of leaving anyone behind. Sandra understood her objection. Still, the others were not her concern—not even Lacy. Her injured leg was a liability that Sandra couldn't risk Emalyn's life over.

Sandra looked away from Emalyn's disappointing gaze. She scanned the keycard, and the door unlocked.

"Let's go," she said, throwing open the door.

"We can't leave the others," Emalyn pleaded. "We can't leave them down here to…"

Sandra tugged Emalyn's wrist, but she ripped herself free. Turning back, she saw the anger flame across her niece's face.

"You can't do this," Emalyn cried. "You can't leave them here."

"We don't have time for this."

"Please," Emalyn begged.

The pleading in her eyes was like a hot drill going through Sandra's stone-encased heart, reaching whatever remained of her that still felt emotion. But she couldn't let it in. She had a mission to see through.

And that mission was to save Emalyn.

"Get your ass moving. Now!" Sandra growled, grabbing Emalyn's wrist and yanking her forward. She couldn't be the savior of all these kids. But she could save one of them. *The one that counts most.*

Emalyn tried to protest, but Sandra kept pulling her up the hallway. When they reached the door, she opened it, scanned the tunnel before them, and pushed Emalyn through.

"Please, don't leave us," a small voice said from inside one of the cells.

Sandra tuned it out, pretended she hadn't heard it.

"Hurry," she said, stepping aside as Lacy limped past.

Her gaze shifted when the red door opened, and Richter, Helga, and two guards armed to the teeth entered. Sandra locked eyes with Richter like two gunfighters in an old Western, and she saw anger twist his face into a sinister snarl. His once-blue eyes were now a deep black, large and round, leaving very little of the whites visible, like a demon possessed him.

"ALARM!" Helga yelled, hitting a large red button on the wall that Sandra hadn't noticed.

A loud *BERP, BERP, BERP* echoed through the tunnels.

"Get them!" Richter ordered the guards.

The two guards rushed past Richter and Helga.

Time to go!

Sandra shot through the threshold, pulling the door shut behind her. She scanned the keycard, locking the door. Stepping back, she pulled the Kimber and fired at the security lock. It exploded in a shower of twitching sparks and flames; the unpleasant smell of burning electrical wires filled the air around her. Shooting the lock would only slow them down for so long. *Like water, they'll find a way in.*

"Let's go," Sandra said.

She hurried them to the freight elevator, hoping they could use it to reach the surface. But just as Sandra went to open the sliding gate, the lift started to rise. *Fuck!* With the alarm sounding and the gunshots, the tunnels were about to get crowded with armed men.

"We need to move! Follow me."

Sandra led them back through the tunnels the way she had come. Behind her, she heard the lift settle back into place, the door open, and the pounding boots of their pursuers echo off the tunnel walls.

Coming to another green door, Sandra cracked it and looked into the hallway. She saw Maxwell and the guard she had cut down still lying there, but there was no one else.

Not yet.

Sweat dripped into Sandra's left eye, and she quickly rubbed its burning away. She knew they couldn't outrun them, not with Lacy's bum leg. It was just a matter of time before they were captured unless they got out of the tunnels and made it to the woods first. If she could get them back to the lift and the building directly above, they could use the conveyor to escape. It was the only way.

Pushing through the door, Sandra stepped out into the hallway, motioning for Emalyn and Lacy. As Emalyn came through the threshold, Sandra saw a movement out of the corner of her eye up the hall.

Two guards had found them.

Three rounds coughed through the dry tunnel, one cutting so close to Sandra's right ear it threatened to take it off—the other two embedding into the wall next to her. Sandra shoved Emalyn back through the doorway before a bullet could cut her down.

Spinning, she brought up the automatic rifle and fired blindly back at the guards, causing them to duck and dodge for cover.

It was the distraction Sandra needed to give her the time to duck behind the green steel door just as three more bullets knocked on the other side with a hard BONG, BONG, BONG that sounded like a bell tolling. The steel was thick, at least an inch. Unless they were using armor-piercing rounds—which they weren't—Sandra knew she had taken up a decent defensive position.

She flipped the gun to full auto—*my turn*—and came around the door. The closest guard was already advancing on her. He never knew what hit him as a burst of rounds spat from Sandra's rifle, the bullets opening his chest into three red blooming flowers before he fell to the floor face-first, dead.

Shifting her attention to the second guard, Sandra saw him fire his Glock .9mm. She ducked behind the door. His shots were misplaced in the adrenalin rush of the firefight; only one of the four rounds impacted the steel door.

She came around again and opened fire. Two rounds shredded his left leg into bloody lunch meat, while four others ripped through his torso. By the time he hit the floor, he was no longer moving.

She stood and came out from behind the door. Emalyn and Lacy gingerly stepped into the hallway, looking shell-shocked from the cacophony of gunfire. Sandra's eyes shifted back down the hall and saw six more guards—the ones pursuing them from the freight elevator—approaching.

She squeezed the trigger and sent rounds downrange, hitting only one of them in the leg and dropping him.

"Hurry!"

Running for the lift, Sandra ejected the magazine, knocking it free with a strike to the side of the rifle with the palm of her hand. She grabbed another one from her left hip pocket, jammed it home, and chambered a round.

Once back at the lift and inside, Sandra hit the button on the panel, and the elevator began to rise. She figured the shots had been heard topside and knew they would be met with more resistance as soon as they reached the surface.

As the elevator rose, Sandra thought only of getting them out of there alive. Nothing else mattered. She could feel the waves of anguish coming off Emalyn for not springing the other kids.

She felt bad for having to leave them behind—to die or worse. But they were not her concern. Emalyn was. Once they found help, she would report what they found to the authorities, and the kids could be rescued.

A grim realization began to form in Sandra's mind: *this operation would be long gone when the police arrived.*

Focus on the mission. The mission is Emalyn—no one else.

"There are going to be guards when we get to the top," Sandra said, looking from Emalyn to Lacy. "I'm going to have to kill them. I want you two to stay behind me, understand? When I move, you two move. When I duck, you two duck. When I run, you two run. Got it?"

They both nodded with fear dancing through their eyes. "Keep your heads down and your eyes focused on where you're walking. I don't need either of you tripping."

Sandra didn't have time to let either of them think about the onslaught coming their way.

Pushing them into the corner, they hunched behind the lift's control panel.

The carriage shook to a stop when it settled into position on the top level.

"Check it out," said a voice.

"Fuck that. You check it out, man."

"I'm your boss."

"Fine."

The metal elevator door slid open. No one entered.

"Looks empty," said one of the men.

"Check the blind spots," said the other.

Footsteps neared. Sandra's grip tightened around the handle of the machine gun. She breathed out slowly, and as soon as the guard crossed into the lift, she fired a single round, hitting him behind the left ear.

Before he hit the floor, Sandra was already moving toward the opening, her shadows sticking with her. She came around the side of the door and fired two rounds into the bald guard's chest. Two fleshy red mushrooms exploded from his white shirt, his tie jumped like a snake shot in the sand, and he fell back over the desk and onto the ground, leaving a messy blood trail in his wake.

"Moving," Sandra told them.

She led them to a ladder leading up to the catwalk. There was no doubt in her mind the gunshots were heard all over the compound, and more armed guards were already on their way there.

They could use the catwalk to get back onto the conveyor belt and shimmy across it to the other building, keeping them moving and from being seen. They also needed somewhere to hole up for a few moments before attempting to escape. The second floor of the building adjacent to this one was empty, and it hadn't looked to Sandra like it was being used for anything—a great place to catch their breath.

"We're going up to the catwalk, and then we will follow the conveyor outside and back to the building directly across from us. Got it?"

Emalyn and Lacy nodded.

"I'll lead the way."

Sandra took hold of the ladder and started climbing the rungs. Emalyn was next, and Lacy brought up the rear. At the top, Sandra hauled Emalyn off the rungs and onto the catwalk and then helped Lacy up.

Assisting Emalyn onto the belt, Sandra saw it sway; the brackets screeched in protest from the added stress.

"It's fine," Sandra assured her niece when she saw the dreaded *will it hold my weight?* look in her eyes.

"It's how I got in here. Stay below the lip of the belt so no one sees you. Once you're across and inside, keep out of sight below the windows. Got it?"

Emalyn nodded and started to crawl across the belt toward the other building. Sandra would send Lacy across when Emalyn reached the building and was inside. There was no telling when the old brackets and rusty screws would give out, and Sandra didn't want to risk a collapse.

Still, she had no idea how long, or even if, the belt would hold, but it was a risk they had to take. If one of them did fall to their death, Sandra knew it was better than being auctioned off to those vile creatures below.

This thought gave Sandra pause. Emalyn was right. She couldn't leave the others down there to be sold off like human cattle. If she did, she would be no better than those running this operation. A sin she would never recover from.

You have to go back for them.

Focus. The Mission. Emalyn. Safety. That's all that matters right now.

And it was.

It's the only thing that matters.

And it is.

Sandra turned her attention back to Emalyn just as her foot disappeared into the building, the darkness slurping her up like a spaghetti noodle.

"Lacy, you're next."

Climbing up on the belt, Lacy got down on her belly and began to crawl slowly.

There was commotion below. Men were running around, shouting at one another, searching, hunting. How long until they were smoked out? Sandra didn't know. She just prayed they could make it to the forest and disappear before they were found.

Those kids. What about those kids?

Shut up, she told herself. *Just shut the fuck up.*

Lacy was to the other building.

Wanting to make this place a distant memory, Sandra hopped on the conveyor and started crawling.

She was nearly halfway across when she heard one of the wall-mounted brackets make an *urrrt* sound as it pulled free from the wall. The conveyor dipped from the rear and threw Sandra to the left. She gripped the sides so she didn't get tossed off, as if it would do any good if the conveyor gave out and she crashed twenty feet to the ground below.

But it held… for the moment at least.

She knew she had to move even slower now. She'd be done for, injured, or worse if another bracket gave way. Also, the commotion of the conveyor belt crashing into the ground would draw the guards' attention, and they'd swarm the area, finding Emalyn and Lacy.

You can't allow that to happen, her monster said.

Sandra would die to prevent them from getting their grubby hands on Emalyn again. This thought rotted in her mind, saddening her. If it came down to that, and there was no chance of escaping the clutches of this horrendous place, she would do what needed to be done so they weren't captured again.

Moving slower so as not to rock the proverbial boat, she inched across the old conveyor belt to the other building, climbed through the opening, and dropped beside Emalyn and Lacy, hidden in the shadows.

"How you holding up, kiddo?" Sandra asked.

"I'm okay."

"You?" She looked at Lacy.

Lacy nodded. The pain tightening her face told Sandra otherwise.

"We're not out of this yet."

"Won't they come after us?" Emalyn asked.

"They'll try. But we'll be long gone by that point."

"Do you have a car nearby?" Lacy asked.

Sandra nodded.

Voices shouted just outside the building, and they ducked farther into the darkness. Sandra breathed a sigh of relief when the voices faded out. Looking at Emalyn and Lacy, she said, "Let's move. Stay behind me, right on my ass."

The fear in her niece's eyes pulled at her heart. She wanted to wrap her in a hug and assure her that everything was going to be fine. But she couldn't. That part of her needed to remain locked away. She couldn't let her emotions seep in or interfere with the mission.

You need to go back for the others.

She shook the thought away.

Emalyn watched her with a strange gaze.

"Aunt Sonnie?" she asked.

"I'm fine."

Staying in a crouch, keeping to the shadows, Sandra led them across the room. Coming to the stairwell wall, she cleared the steps and motioned for them to follow her.

Bringing the machine gun up, Sandra led the way down the stairs. They creaked under their feet, and if anyone were in the building, they would have easily heard and taken advantage by shooting them in the stairwell, where there was no cover and nowhere to hide.

But the building remained still, vacant, lifeless.

Coming to the bottom of the steps, Sandra peeked around the corner. The room was empty, and as far as she could tell, so was the room where she found the tech guy setting up the video link on the

Dark Web. His body was still tucked under the desk; he hadn't been discovered yet.

That's good.

She led them to the door leading back outside. Looking through the glass, Sandra didn't see any guards mingling around. But when her eyes fell onto the gate, she felt her breath catch in her chest.

It was closed, and the sentry guards were again watching from the towers. She wondered if most of the guards had been pulled into the tunnels, searching for them. Possible. Her missing finger thumped maddeningly. Were they walking into a trap? That, too, was a possibility. A well-laid trap that she had led them into.

Ensuring Emalyn didn't end up back in their hands chilled Sandra. She didn't want it to come to that. But if it did, she would have to do the unthinkable. How could she look Emalyn in the eyes, knowing she might have to…

Sandra threw the thought away. *Focus! Worry later.* She was the only person who could lead them out of there. Until then, those horrible *what-if* thoughts would stay locked away.

Turing the door handle slowly to avoid any noise that might alert a roaming guard, the latch popped free, and Sandra pulled the door open.

Shouting to her right.

Two guards ran to Cleve, who was stepping out of the small security shack behind the guard towers.

"We think the intruder got out, sir," one guard said. "We found Stone dead next to the desk. And Kline down inside the elevator with his head blown off."

"Get everyone topside. I want this cunt found," Cleve said.

"Yes, sir."

The two guards turned and ran back in the direction they'd come from. Cleve returned to the shack but stopped before entering and looked around as if he might spot the intruder himself. The phone inside rang, and he hurried to it.

Sandra's eyes shifted back to the sentry guards in the tower. They were the gatekeepers to the kingdom. Sandra knew she had to go through them if they wanted out. She also suspected the mechanism to open the front gate had to be inside the guard towers. She needed to get inside.

"Let's go," she whispered.

They hurried out of the building and ran about ten yards before ducking behind the old quarry machinery to avoid detection. Sandra scanned the area around them. They were alone, except for Cleve in the shack talking on the phone, his back to them. They could make it to the guard towers without him seeing them if they moved quickly.

Sandra led the charge. As they covered the ten-yard gap to the tower, she kept her eyes on Cleve. She'd put him down if he turned around.

Luckily for him, he never did.

Along the guard tower, Sandra pressed Emalyn and Lacy down into a crouch against the tower wall.

"Stay. Don't move. I need to go inside and open the gate," she whispered. "As soon as you see it opening, I want both of you to run for the forest. Don't stop. Don't look back. And whatever you do, don't wait for me. Understand?"

"But…"

"This isn't debatable, Emalyn. You guys run, and you keep running in that direction." Sandra pointed to the west. "You'll find a pickup parked in the woods near the road. Wait there for me. If you don't see me in ten minutes, take off. Avoid Little Hope. Head to the nearest state police station."

Emalyn's eyes were wide and wet, trembling with lucid fear. Though Sandra wasn't showing it, not outwardly anyway, she was just as scared. Swallowing it away, she turned and moved to the guard tower entrance.

Cracking the door, she peered inside but found the room built into the structure empty. She slipped in unnoticed.

Above her head, she heard two men talking, but their voices were indistinguishable through the thick wooden floor. Stairs on the left-hand side led to the lookout platform. The room had a metal table and chairs. There was nothing else in there—no lever to open the gate, no electronic button to push. That meant the gate had to be operated above, which made sense. Both towers probably had buttons to operate the gate in case one tower wasn't occupied.

The shotgun or the rifle would make too much noise and attract too much attention.

She was going to have to do this the old-fashioned way.

Hand-to-hand.

Pulling the remaining tantō knife from the sheath, she stalked up the steps slowly, like a serial killer about to strike an unsuspecting family. When she came even with the floorboards, she saw one guard standing beside the mounted M60 E6, the upgraded version of the M60.

A push-button switchboard was mounted to the front wall—a green button to open the gate and a red one to close it. The other guard, by the spotlight, was closer to the stairs, sweeping the beam across the dark forest.

He turned in her direction, and Sandra ducked back down onto the steps before he saw her.

While crouched on the steps, she heard the guard manning the M60 ask, "See anything?"

"No. All quiet on the western front."

"Funny. Just keep your eyes peeled. There's a lot of chatter over the coms. They haven't found our guest yet."

Sandra needed to draw the closest one to her. She was in a defensive position and couldn't just charge the nest.

She began tapping the knife on the step.

TAP! TAP! TAP!

"You hear that?"

"Hear what?"

"That tapping sound?"

TAP! TAP! TAP!

"Yeah. What is it?"

"I don't…" *TAP! TAP! TAP!* "Sounds like it's coming from the stairs."

"Check it out."

Sandra heard the guard's feet shift on the floor and dust sprinkle down from between the boards.

TAP! TAP! TAP!

"There it is again."

"Careful. It could be our guest."

Concealed in the shadows, Sandra saw the guard bend and peer into the lingering darkness of the stairs. He reached to his side for his flashlight, but before he could pull it, Sandra sprung, with the knife leading, and penetrated the guard's left side.

He tried to scream, but the knife pierced his lung, collapsing it before he could muster a sound other than a wet, raspy gurgling that seeped from his already bloody lips. Before he could comprehend what happened, Sandra stabbed him five more times and pulled him over the side. He was dead before his body slammed into the steps below, bounced off, and hit the floor.

She shot up the steps and charged the machine gunner. Taken by surprise, he was trying to turn the M60 toward her. But it was too big and heavy to swing easily, so he went for his sidearm.

Rearing the knife back over her shoulder, she whipped it forward, but not before the guard freed his .9mm Glock. The blade found its home in the man's face and he involuntarily squeezed off a round before he fell back into the wall, dead.

Sandra felt the bullet rip through her right side as if someone had just run a drill through her flesh. She went down, pain swelling through her body like fire.

Pain is just an illusion, she heard Joel say in her mind.

Yeah, fuck you very much, Joel. She could feel the blood leaking from her body, and she found it hard to breathe.

"Hey, is something going on?" The voice brought Sandra back from the brink of agony.

Open the fucking gate!

Pushing through the pain, she pulled herself to her feet, her right hand pressed to her bleeding side. Across from her, she saw the men in the adjacent tower, staring at her, wide-eyed with shock—they were as surprised as she was to have gotten this far.

"We got her, sir," one of the guards said into a CB, his face shifting into something sinister.

Sandra looked back at the M60.

Wanna bet, fucker.

Grabbing the M60, she heaved the nearly thirty-pound weapon into her arms, swung it toward the guard tower, and squeezed the trigger. The bullets ripped from the M60 like a buzzsaw, and the two tower guards were torn in half in a spray of blood and body parts; the bullets split the wooden poles of the tower roof, causing it to crash down into itself like a deck of cards.

"She's topside!"

Looking to her right, Sandra found Cleve standing by the shack doorway. The phone was pressed to his ear, and he stared stupidly at her.

Jabbing her thumb into the green button on the switchboard, she heard the gate roll open.

"GO!" she screamed to Emalyn and Lacy as she moved to the rear of the guard tower and placed the M60's tripod on the banister. She aimed the gun directly at Cleve. His face went ghostly white. He tried to duck for cover, but it was too late.

The M60 roared to life, spitting round after round into his body, tearing him apart as if he were made of nothing more than papiermâché full of red liquid.

Movement toward the rear of the quarry caught Sandra's eye. At least a dozen fully armed men were charging toward the gate. They must have used the freight elevator to get above ground. As they rushed the tower, they started shooting blindly. Bullets zinged past her head, some hitting the trees, others into the tower above or below her.

She had to hold off the onslaught of men, allowing Emalyn and Lacy time to make it to the woods. But that would only last until the ammo ran out. This was it. This was her stand, her sacrifice.

She squeezed the trigger.

And the M60 spoke for her.

CHAPTER TWENTY-EIGHT

Every fifth bullet on the ammo belt was a tracer, so the gunner could tell where the bullets were going while firing at night. Sandra saw one of these fiery rounds strike a guard in the head while charging the tower, exploding it into a fine red mist.

Guards scurried around below her like cockroaches scampering from sunlight. Sandra was the exterminator, and the M60 was the bug killer.

The hollow *ratatat* sound of lead embedding into the tower, splitting the wood and spitting fine dust into the air to Sandra's right, caused her to swing the lunky M60 onto two guards who had taken cover behind one of the parked limos, firing and ducking, firing and ducking.

She opened up on the limo, sending round after round into the side, peppering away the black paint. The tires blew out with a *BOOOF* and the car fell onto the rims with a heavy clack of metal against metal. The smell of gasoline from the ruptured tank permeated the air, and Sandra concentrated her fire on the fluid trail below the car.

A tracer round ignited the fuel, the blue fire followed the trail of gas back up into the tank, and the limo exploded in a giant fireball, killing the guards who sought it to take cover.

Swinging the gun back around, she shot at a man trying to advance his position, taking both his legs below the knees with a single burst of fire.

She knew she couldn't hold out forever. They would overrun her sooner or later. But she would take as many as possible before they got her.

Continuing to spray bullets until the M60 clicked dry, with nearly a dozen dead or wounded on the ground, the remaining guards—*Christ, how many are there?*—started all firing at once, the bullets striking the tower all around her.

Dropping onto her stomach, Sandra crawled over to the stairs and slipped onto them as the bullets *zinged* and *whizzed* overhead, ripping through the structure and decimating it.

She was bleeding badly from the gunshot wound to her right side; the blood soaked through her shirt and stained her thigh, sticky like warm honey. She had to stem it.

Knowing she only had a few minutes of respite before the guards rushed her position, she unslung her rucksack and grabbed a tampon from inside. She ground her teeth hard as she worked the tampon into the gunshot wound—it wasn't the best source of field dressing, but on the fly, it would do.

Trying to force the pain away, Sandra unslung the machine gun from around her chest, knowing she was down to her last magazine. The shotgun still had five rounds. So did the Kimber. She could take a few of them if she made every round count before they got her.

If they wanted her life, they would have to work for it.

Moving down to the middle of the stairs, she aimed the machine gun at the door. Her elevated height gave her a momentary advantage over those looking to get inside—that is, until they figured out she was above them. Once that happened, she'd have to change her position quickly if she hoped to keep up the attack.

"Get that door open," someone ordered outside. "Make sure that bitch is down. If she's not dead, Mr. Richter wants her kept alive."

Alive? For what?

The door kicked open, and two guards hustled inside. She fired twice in the cover of darkness on the stairs and dropped them like potato sacks where they stood.

From outside, around the corner of the doorway, someone sightlessly fired, none of the bullets coming remotely close to hitting her. She still had the advantage of the higher ground, for the moment. But it wouldn't last. If she were lucky, she could take out one or two more before they put it together where she was.

"Go!" one of the guards outside ordered another.

Another one charged through, and Sandra squeezed the trigger, sending him back out through the door, riddled with bleeding bullet holes that made him look like a piece of bloody Swiss cheese rolling across the dirt.

"She's on the steps!" someone else yelled.

That's my cue.

Leaping from the stairs, she landed on her feet and rolled behind the metal table in the room. Pain tentacles shot through the far reaches of her body. Pressing her hand to her side, she felt the sticky, warm blood seeping through and around the tampon.

From under the table, Sandra watched a man enter, spraying a wad of bullets into the darkness of the stairs.

Bringing the machine gun up, she fired a single round. The bullet ripped through the guard's shins, taking his legs out from under him. She pulled the trigger again and shot him between the eyes as he fell.

Her rifle was empty, and she knew she didn't have time to grab a magazine from one of the dead guards or even his rifle before more of them entered, looking to take her out or capture her.

Tossing the machine gun aside, Sandra tipped the table over, hoping to trick them into thinking she was taking cover behind it. With a *bang*, the table crashed to the floor, and she quickly took position along the wall just as two more guards charged in and began firing into the table.

They never saw Sandra when she fired the shotgun at nearly point-blank range. The first guard was hit in the side of his torso, blowing him into his buddy and knocking him to the floor. Sandra racked another round into the shotgun, stepped forward out of the shadows, and fired as the other guard was trying to roll the dead body off him.

His head became a red paint splash across the floor.

Rushing to the door, Sandra looked out. She didn't see anyone. The air smelled hot and full of gunpowder. Had she killed all the guards and brought this operation to its knees? She doubted it. Whoever these people were had tons of money; with that much money came a lot of reach. What she'd done tonight was a flesh wound to the bigger giant.

She stepped out and was struck across the back by something hard. She came down into the dirt face first. Dust and grit kicked into her mouth and eyes, blinding her. Through her watery vision, she saw a wavy shape stomping toward her.

Rolling on her back, Sandra tried to get the shotgun up but was too disoriented from the blow. The figure kicked out, striking the end of the shotgun's short barrel. It flew from Sandra's hands like God had taken it from her. She went for the Kimber, but he was on her before she could grasp the handle.

He raised his foot and stomped it directly onto her bloody right side. She screamed as pain shot through her body with lightning-fast speed. Falling back into the dirt, holding her side, tears leaked from the corner of her eyes, making slick, wet trails down both sides of her dirty face.

The guard reared his foot back again and then buried it deep into her right side, just below where she'd been hit. Any remaining oxygen in her lungs was forced out in a grunted cough of air. Intense pain consumed her.

Curling into a ball, her mind began to sink into a deep black well from the lack of oxygen. Her heart blasted in her chest, ears, and temples. Then, just as Sandra was on the verge of passing out, she saw the guard step forward and aim his rifle at her.

This is it—time for checkout. See you soon, Sissy.

"STOP!" a voice screamed.

The guard halted, his finger already applying pressure to the trigger. He eased his tension, lowered the gun, and stepped back.

Sandra felt herself beginning to slip away—from the pain, from the exhaustion, from the lack of oxygen—into that void of nothingness. But just before she succumbed and the darkness took her, someone stepped up beside her—a face she recognized, loathed.

Martin. The auctioneer.

"Mr. Richter wants to deal with her personally."

CHAPTER TWENTY-NINE

When Sandra came to, she found herself staring into an overhead light shining directly into her eyes. She winced in discomfort and pulled her watery gaze away. It took a moment for her eyes to adjust, for her mind to focus on the fact that she was alone in a stone room.

I must be back underground.

The air was sour with despair. It was ungodly hot, and her skin was tacky with dirt, sweat, and blood.

Her body ached badly, not just from the physical abuse but from a fever that had developed since she lost consciousness. She wondered if she was in the beginning stages of sepsis from being in the pit. If she didn't get antibiotics into her system, she'd be a dead woman in a matter of hours.

That's if they don't kill us first, her monster said. *Which they're likely going to.*

A short, grim future, Sandra thought.

She tried to sit up but found her wrists and ankles bound to a table by leather manacles, like the kind used in mental hospitals to keep patients from harming themselves. She tried to swallow the terror working its way up her throat but was unable to.

Everything she had been through, fighting tooth and nail to get her life back, to move on from the attack, from that night with *him*, it all came back around to this.

A cage.

Had this been her destiny all along? What had she done to deserve such treatment? Or was it her doing at all? Was it her mother's sin—of infidelity, for bringing a bastard child into this world and keeping it a secret—being passed on to her?

God's cruel plan?

Looking around the small room, Sandra tried to find something she could use to cut the leather, but the room was bare except for the table she lay on and her rucksack in the corner.

The *click* of a lock releasing and the door opening grabbed Sandra's attention like a heart attack. Two guards entered, holding machine guns. They took positions on either side of the door just as Richter entered, followed by Martin, the auctioneer.

Richter's dark, blue eyes leered at Sandra splayed on the table. His lips pulled over his straight, white teeth. The urge to knock them from his gums and down his throat—*choke on 'em, motherfucker*—beckoned.

Then he laughed as if something had suddenly struck him funny—an unnatural sinisterness that raked her nerves like scratching metal with a butterknife.

"I must admit, you have surprised me, *Mädchen*. Truly. I never would have expected someone like you, a *Hündin*, would be able to take out as many of my men as you did. Truly remarkable."

"Happy to help rid the world of scum," Sandra replied.

He walked alongside the table, looking her bloody and battered body over. His dark blue eyes twinkled with delight, toying with her, enjoying her agony.

"Who are you?" Richter finally asked.

"A ghost," Sandra replied.

"A ghost? A ghost who just happened to take out, what?" Richter looked at Martin, who mouthed a number to his boss. "Nearly sixteen of my men."

Sandra wiggled around on the table and pulled at the restraints, hoping to break free.

"There is no use fighting, *Kätzchen*. You can't get free."

Sandra grew still. Richter was right. No matter how hard she pulled, kicked, and wiggled around, she wasn't going to snap the bindings. She'd only tire herself out. She needed to conserve her strength for when an opportunity arose—*if an opportunity arose*—to break free.

"Who are you?" Richter asked again.

"Instead of retreading the same question and getting the same answer—like I said, I'm a ghost—let me ask who you are. And why you're doing this?"

He sneered at her like he smelled something awful permeating from her skin. Maybe he did. She was dirty and sweaty and bloody—hers and others; she had to be ripe by this point.

Still, the look was of a man dubious about divulging his secrets to outsiders.

"C'mon, Richter. I'm a dead woman lying here anyway. Why not at least tell me what's going on?"

He smiled and tapped his forefinger on his chin as if considering.

"Okay."

"What?" Martin said, looking at his boss. "Sir, I must—"

"Shut it, Mr. Klus." Richter's eyes snapped at him with a harshness that Sandra remembered seeing in a coyote's eyes just before it sank its teeth into a helpless hare.

"Like she said, she's a dead woman anyway."

Richter rounded the table to Sandra's right side. He placed a cold hand on her bicep, causing her to jerk from his touch. He rubbed her arm. "Your skin is tough, leathery, unlike Emalyn's."

The mere mention of her niece's name coming out of his mouth made her see red.

We'll take your tongue for that, her monster said.

"But you want to know, *Kätzchen*, what's going on." He bent close to her face, his breath smelling of peppermint, nearly making Sandra gag. "I'll share. Besides, it's the least I can do for a dead woman."

He straightened. And as he did, Sandra noticed something sticking out from inside his jacket's interior pocket. Was it a small knife? A pen, perhaps? She wasn't sure.

"I own towns across Europe, the Middle East, Russia, Asia, Mexico, South America, and several right here in the good ol' U.S. of A. You would be surprised by the abundance of dying towns worldwide and how easily they can be acquired—banks want money, and they don't ask many questions when handing them cash."

He smiled, proud of himself, of his accomplishments.

"Once the town is under our control, we start weeding out the locals and inserting our people and reconstruction to fit our needs. We set up a main area of operation, usually in a nearby abandoned warehouse, mill, or, in this case, a quarry. Then, with the help of the internet, my company attracts vacationers looking for rental homes near one of our towns."

It all fell into place in Sandra's mind, causing a cascade of anguish to nearly flatten her under its abundance and deviousness.

"You're the mastermind behind R&R. After you lure unsuspecting families to one of your rental homes with fancy ads and good reviews, you murder them, and then your goons kidnap their children, and you sell them into the sex trade?"

"Or a private collector."

She thought about Lawerence Maxwell being there. She had questioned his involvement, not until after she killed him, of course, but she had questioned it, nonetheless. Now she understood.

On the outside, to the public, Maxwell had presented himself as an upstanding billionaire looking to right some of the world's wrongs with his satellite internet company, money, power, and influence. But all of it was a self-serving act. Like so many other famous billionaires around the world, he was full of shit, capitalizing on a broken system and the people who were suffering within it.

And Richter was their dealer, their supplier.

This operation made Epstein's Island look like Disneyland in comparison.

"I have clients all over the world. Some of them were watching tonight when you interfered with the auction. Luckily, for us—and them—we hadn't gotten to what everyone came for." Richter's upper lip rose in an evil snarl that disgusted her.

Sandra didn't need him to verbalize his thoughts to understand what he was talking about—the selling of the most innocent. These people had so much money they could buy human beings to do with as they pleased without ramifications.

"I must confess that I had reservations about taking you and your family. You might think everyone who uses R&R falls victim, but that wouldn't be the case. Orders are placed from our clients, like on Amazon, and we deliver the goods."

"Is that why you tried to scare us off? Because we didn't have anything of value to you?"

313

Richter smiled at this.

"On the contrary, that's not the case at all. Attacking every family that stayed at one of the rental homes would attract too much attention. Plus, we need honest online reviews and positive word of mouth to keep the merchandise flowing in.

"Those boys who vandalized your brother-in-law's SUV are not part of our operation. They are members of the families who oppose R&R taking over the town. They believe that if they scare off enough of our guests, R&R will look elsewhere to set up. They are a small thorn in my paw."

He mimed pulling a thorn from his palm.

"See, this kind of people—small-minded folks who cannot see the bigger picture—don't understand that a corporation like R&R will revitalize their town and make it more prosperous than ever. Those willing to turn a blind eye—and there are many willfully ignorant people—will be rewarded for such ignorance."

Richter's face took on a menacing sneer.

"Those who oppose will be dealt with, like the sheriff and his deputy, like those boys and their families. After those problems are solved, I will place men or women—I'm not a sexist—into positions of power to keep the town running smoothly as any good boss does. Bezos didn't become the richest man in the world because he knew everything—he was smart enough to surround himself with people who followed his lead and knew how to accomplish his vision, like me."

"So why'd you send the dogs after us?"

"You were sticking your nose where it didn't belong. After you found the photo on the camera, catching one of my men in the window, they were supposed to dispose of the SD card and eliminate you and your family while you were sleeping."

Sandra remembered the boot print beside Emalyn's bed. *They* had been in their room that night, awaiting their orders to kill.

"But I decided against it at the last moment, thinking we had everything under control once the SD card was in our possession and there would be no photographic evidence. But when your niece found the hidden guestbook in the house, I knew I had made a grave mistake letting you and your family live. I couldn't risk exposure to the public—my clients expect their identities to remain a secret."

"Sex trafficking isn't a secret. You're all being exposed. One asshole at a time."

Richter smiled as if he knew something that Sandra didn't.

"It is when it comes to who my clients are."

How high up the ladder does this go?

"Your niece and the other girl were on the older side for most of my clients."

Richter leaned down so close Sandra could feel his peppermint breath tickle her ear.

"But with the right handler, like Mr. A. or the Sheik, they'll be able to work in the industry, making me and my clients money."

Sandra snapped her teeth at him, like the jaws of a shark coming in for a bite of a tasty seal. Richter pulled back before she could sink her canines into his flesh.

Lucky bastard.

"You still have a lot of fight left in you. Good. That will make Helga happy."

Richter straightened his jacket by the lapels, ran his hand through his hair, smoothing a loose strand across his forehead, and snapped his fingers.

Helga strolled into the room, pushing a cart. The wheels squeaked, rolling across the floor until they stopped beside Sandra.

"Hello, dear," Helga said.

Sandra looked at the cart, her eyes catching the gleam of sharp, stainless-steel instruments that belonged in some diabolical

315

surgeon's operating room. She swallowed, her throat dry, grinding. Helga's bright red lips widened into a smile.

"Do my tools scare you? They should. I cannot wait to introduce you to them."

"This is where we part company, *Fräulein*," Richter said. "I will leave you in Helga's capable hands. She will see you through the rest of your evening."

Richter turned to walk out of the room when Sandra called him. "Richter!"

He stopped and looked back down at her.

"My niece? Do you have her?"

"All in due time."

They had not found them. Emalyn and Lacy should have made it back to the truck and were far away from here by now.

Richter turned to leave, but Sandra called out to him again. He turned slowly to face her, annoyed that she was holding him from his precious auction.

"You shouldn't walk away with me still alive. You should stay and make sure I die."

"I would take immense pleasure in that," he said with a smile. "Sadly, I have other matters to attend to."

He stepped from the room and headed down the hallway.

Martin sauntered up to the table and pulled the tampon from inside Sandra's gunshot wound, dropping it on the floor. She wanted to wiggle away, but she wouldn't give him the satisfaction of her pain. Her fear.

To the left of her, Helga was humming a pleasant tune as she arranged her instruments of torture on the tray as if they needed to be in some special order to inflict pain.

"From the moment I laid eyes on you, I wondered what it would be like to be inside you," Martin said, his breath hot and rancid like sauerkraut on her face.

He drove his thumb into the bullet hole in Sandra's right side. She screamed and wrenched around, the leather straps strained and stretched, the pain nearly unbearable as she felt him wiggling his thumb around inside of her like he was searching for something he had lost in there.

As he yanked his thumb from inside her, Sandra collapsed back onto the table with fresh sweat seeping from her pores—a persisting internal pain lingered like an extraterrestrial being had invaded her. Martin studied his blood-covered thumb like a lollypop. Then he slipped it into his mouth and sucked it clean, pulling it out from his mouth with a *pop*.

"Now I know."

He stepped from the room, and one of the two guards followed him. Soon, the room became quiet as their footfalls faded away.

Helga looked at the remaining guard.

"Leave us," she snapped, looking back to Sandra, cold blue eyes brightening in delight. "I like to work in solitude."

As the guard exited the room, pulling the door shut behind him, Helga picked up a stainless-steel probe about five inches long but no thicker than a needle. Sandra had no idea what it was traditionally used for. But as Helga neared and every muscle in Sandra's body grew tense, she understood that the thin instrument was about to bring her immense agony.

"Now, dear, feel free to scream all you want. No one will hear you, and it's music to Helga's ears."

CHAPTER THIRTY

The need to fight Helga off, the will to survive, much like it had on *that* night, caused panic to swell through Sandra like a rising tide. She wanted out of this room—this *cage*—but with her hands restrained, she was helpless to do anything other than watch as Helga neared holding her instrument of torture.

Helga's free hand snapped out and grabbed ahold of Sandra's left wrist with a grip so tight she felt like it might snap, causing her to wince.

"I see you're already missing a finger. So, what I'm about to do shouldn't hurt too bad. But like I said, feel free to scream for Helga."

Before Sandra could protest, the sharp, steel probe was driven under her left index fingernail.

Blistering pain bloomed that she believed was worse than when her finger had been severed. She didn't think that was possible. Yet, it was. She ground her teeth, not wanting to give Helga the gratification of her agony. *Sick bitch!* But when she heard her cries coming out of her mouth, Sandra knew there was nothing she could do to stop them, despite her willpower.

"That's it, dear," Helga said, pushing on the end of the probe, driving it further under the fingernail. "Let Helga hear you scream." She closed her eyes, tilted her head, and swayed back and forth as if she were listening to classical music performed by some acclaimed orchestra.

Helga pressed harder on the probe, pushing it further under the fingernail, and Sandra felt her stomach lurch and her mind slip into some hazy reservoir between suffering and death—she welcomed the death part; it would be so much easier to bear, especially now that she had gotten Emalyn out.

The pop of the probe's tip bursting through the top of Sandra's nail, and the blood that squirted up onto her forearm, snapped Sandra back into the room with Helga, with the searing discomfort. She heard a scream again, but she didn't recognize the sounds coming from her own mouth.

Pain is an illusion, remember, her monster said. *USE IT!*

Helga released her death grip on Sandra's wrist and stood back to admire her work. With an evil grin, she licked her red lips hungrily, enjoying the taste of the torture she had inflicted.

"Hang in there, dear. Only eight more to go." She turned to the cart and lifted another sharp probe, the light gleaming off its stainless-steel surface. Delicately, Helga ran her fingertips down its side like she was touching a religious artifact, fascinated with it.

Sandra's breath came in a hyperventilating wheeze, her chest rising and falling heavily. Sweat dotted her forehead and face. Scanning the room, she tried to find anything to aid her in an escape.

"Are we ready to proceed, dear?" Helga asked.

"Wait!" Sandra said. "The right one."

Helga resembled a dog that's just heard a strange noise, cocking her head to the side.

"Please. I-I can't take another one in that hand. Do the right one. Please."

Helga smiled devilishly, and her eyes shone bright with pleasure.

"I think I can accommodate you."

Helga rounded the table, passing by Sandra's head, strolling like she was heading to the pharmacy to pick up a prescription, humming again.

"Now. Are we ready to proceed, dear?"

Sandra nodded and closed her eyes, swallowed. Her throat ground like sand in a mixer and was just as dry. She wanted the pain to end, and it would as soon as she killed Helga and could retract the probe. But first, she had to get Helga closer.

Right where we need that twisted, sick bitch.

Helga reached out to take Sandra's wrist.

"Wait."

"What now, dear? I will not give you another reprieve."

"No. I'm not asking for that. I was, well, I was just wondering if I could have a cigarette?"

Sandra had seen her rucksack on the floor shortly after she came to. It had most likely been ripped from her back and tossed there when she was dragged into the room unconscious.

"They're in my bag. If I could have one last smoke before…."

Helga took a long breath, brought the probe to her bottom lip, and tapped it with the pointed end.

"Sure. Why not? Besides, who am I not to allow a prisoner one last smoke?"

Helga crossed the room to where the bag lay in the corner, her back to Sandra.

Sandra flipped the concealed pen in the palm of her right hand around so the ballpoint was up. She had pulled it from the inside of Richter's jacket when he bent over and spoke into her ear. He hadn't noticed her remove it when she snapped her teeth at him, scaring him away; any thought concerning it would have dissipated in his mind, feeling lucky he hadn't been bitten.

Even with her restraints, Sandra believed there was enough wiggle room that she could drive the pen into a vital spot—an eye or Helga's jugular. As Helga started to turn around, Sandra tucked the pen back into her palm and closed her fingers around it.

Helga returned with the pack of cigarettes and the lighter Sandra had taken off the dead guard.

"This is a very nasty habit," Helga said, pulling one from the pack and slipping it into Sandra's mouth.

So is kidnapping children and selling them.

Sandra slid the pen into a stabbing position in her hand as Helga focused on the lighter and lit it. Her grip tightened on the pen; she needed to make sure she drove it deep into Helga to stop her long enough for Sandra to get free of the restraints; a superficial flesh wound would not do.

Helga bent carefully, watching the flame so it didn't go out. With her gaze diverted, she didn't see Sandra's right hand coming up like a piston to the maximum reach of her restraints. But she sure felt it when Sandra buried the end of the ballpoint into her throat.

Helga lurched backward, eyes wide with pain... with fright. One hand went to her neck while the other wrapped around the end of the pen and yanked it free.

A thick spray of arterial blood squirted from the small, black hole. All the color instantly drained from her face, and she cupped her hand over the hole in her neck, blood spraying from between her fingers. She stepped forward, her eyes trained with a wild craziness. She wanted Sandra's life.

But before she could reach the table, Helga's body gave out, and she toppled forward; her forehead caught the side of the table on the way down with a terrible crunching sound of her skull caving in. She did not get back up.

Lifting her left hand, Sandra tilted her index finger back as far as possible so the probe faced her. Taking the end of the probe in her mouth, she ripped it out from under her fingernail. Warm blood bubbled from her finger and pooled in her palm. She felt light-headed and queasy.

Pain is an illusion! her monster yelled.

With the probe in her mouth, she wiggled it into the cuff's straps and pried the leather from the metal clasp until it was a small mound she could grab with her teeth. Spitting the probe aside, she craned her neck and began to work the strap free.

Once the loop was free of the metal clasp, she worked her teeth to the end, careful not to lose it in her mouth. She pulled hard at the end of the leather strap, slipping the pin from the notch. The cuff loosened enough for her to slide her hand out.

Now free, she went to work on the other wrist. Then, the binding around her ankles.

Swinging her feet over the side, she saw Helga lying in a pool of blood. Dead as dead could get. Her eyes were open in a death stare, panic tacked across her face at the idea that she was about to meet her maker.

Hope you made your peace with God.

Sandra turned her attention back to the door. Now, she had to figure a way out of this room.

But how would she open the door and get past the guard waiting outside?

Then the answer became so clear. And Sandra couldn't stop herself from smiling.

CHAPTER THIRTY-ONE

Dragging Helga's body around the table, she placed her beside the cart. Next, Sandra grabbed a scalpel and then got onto the floor, wiggling herself under Helga's already chilling corpse.

She hoped to make it appear that she'd broken free, and they'd gotten into an altercation that left both of them injured.

She took hold of the cart and tipped it over. It crashed to the floor, scattering the instruments of torture everywhere. She prayed the ruckus would draw the guard's attention, causing him to rush into the room and check on Helga. When he did...

Surprise motherfucker!

"Helga?" The guard's voice came from the other side of the steel door. "Are you okay?"

When a reply didn't come, Sandra heard the lock click, and the door started to open. She lay perfectly still, eyes closed, the scalpel in her right hand.

"Helga!" the guard said, rushing into the room and straight over to the women on the floor.

Kneeling, he rolled Helga off Sandra. She sprang. Her right hand lashed out and she caught him across the face, opening him up from his left ear to his mouth in what looked like a Glasgow smile.

In his shock, the guard grabbed at his gushing face and fell onto his ass. Before he knew what was happening, before he could even let out a scream, Sandra was on top of him, opening his jugular.

Within seconds, he grew still under her.

He was armed with an M4 assault rifle and two extra mags, with one in the gun. A .9mm Glock was strapped into a holster on his right side, along with three clips, and a tac knife was on his belt. Stripping off his gear, including his tactical vest, she moved to her rucksack.

Pulling a fresh tampon out, she inserted it into the bullet hole. She didn't need to bleed out before she saw her mission through. Then she wrapped the rigger's tape around her several times, making sure the makeshift field dressing didn't wiggle out. She then tore off a small piece and wrapped it around her thumping finger, still oozing fresh blood.

After slipping on the tactical vest and strapping the gun and knife belt to her, Sandra cleared the tunnel and stepped out.

The hallway was unfamiliar. Was she deeper in the quarry? The holding pens and the auction were on the second level. She had to get back there, stop the auction, and get the kids out of this hellhole. She remembered Richter and Martin turning right when leaving the room.

What's good for the goose is good... well, all that shit.

Hurrying up the tunnel to where it bent to the left, Sandra pressed herself to the wall and peeked around the corner. At the end of the hallway, there was another green door.

What's beyond the green door? she wondered.

She went to take a step but teetered into the wall, catching herself before she crashed to the floor. The fever made her mind sloshy, causing her muscles to tighten and her joints to ache furiously. The thought of climbing into a soft bed and sleeping never looked better.

You can rest when you're dead, her monster said.

The voice snapped Sandra from her feverish state.

Sucking up the discomfort—it was nothing in comparison to what those children would go through if she left them there—she rushed to the green door.

Cracking it gently, she peeked through the small slit in the door and saw another tunnel stretched out in front of her for about twenty yards before it dead-ended at a lift. LEVEL 4 was painted on the wall.

Bingo!

She stepped through, easing the door shut behind her.

This tunnel was vastly different from the previous ones she had been in. The walls had been carved out on both sides into two large rooms, and glass partitions separated them from the hallway.

To her left, two men—a fat guy in a flowered Hawaiian shirt and a skinny guy with an acne-scarred face—sat facing computer monitors. Fatty's monitor displayed a list of encrypted usernames. She watched him select the name and pound a few commands on the keyboard with his chubby fingers, and another screen popped up with the username's real identity.

"Username: kiddy9isjustfine. Real name: Vern Gabbletone," Fatty said.

Skinny typed the name into his computer, and a screen opened with Vern Gabbletone's personal information.

Sandra understood what they were doing. Anyone who joined one of the video feeds or was a personal guest to one of the live shows was logged into R&R's databanks—a digital black book, so to speak.

Heidi Fleiss, eat your heart out.

The room to Sandra's right was filled with computer servers. From the cold air misting the room, she knew it was climate-controlled to keep everything cool and functioning properly. What was on those servers could expose R&R and their clients to the world.

Sandra pulled open the door and entered. Both men looked up at her with surprise. Their eyes slowly lowered to the rifle she had aimed at them, and their hands rose.

"Which of you can copy all the files you have stored on those computers?"

Fatty quickly pointed to Skinny.

"Get to work, and you two might leave here alive," Sandra said.

Five minutes later, Sandra walked out of the room with a flash drive in her pocket containing everything she needed to expose R&R, leaving two dead computer techs in her wake.

CHAPTER THIRTY-TWO

Sandra took the elevator to the second level and got off, realizing it had returned to where she had found Emalyn and Lacy in the pens. The green door was open like a black maw as if waiting to gobble her up.

She rushed into the room and found the pens empty and the kids gone. They must have been moved into the amphitheater for the auction to resume.

The show couldn't go on. Sandra knew that these children weren't looked at as humans. They were a commodity. A product to be sold into slavery, something they'd never be able to escape—unless they were extremely lucky… or dead. Maybe the dead ones were the lucky ones in the end; they didn't have to endure the horrors of the industry anymore.

She cracked the red door and found that it led to the rear of the stage. To her left was what appeared to be a large dog kennel, where the kids were being held, waiting to be brought forth by the lingering guard. To her right, the red velvet curtain blocked her view of the stage, though she heard Martin driving up the bid of some unfortunate child. The auction had resumed.

The curtain was thrown back, and a second guard escorted the little girl Sandra had seen with the stuffed animal off the stage. He passed her onto the other guard, who returned her to the cage, like merchandise awaiting pick up. That guard then yanked one of the two small boys forward and dragged him to the stage; the kid didn't put up a fight, too scared to do anything other than let himself be dragged along.

With the guards distracted by the child swapping, Sandra slipped through the door, keeping herself low and tight to the shadowy wall.

Soon, she heard the bidding start again.

Sneaking along the wall as the guard returned to his position next to the cage, Sandra pulled the knife from the sheath. She jumped onto his back, wrapped her hand over his mouth, drove the knife to the hilt in his throat, twisted, and rode him down like a sinking ship to the floor, where he bled out.

Once the guard grew still, she moved to the cage with the kids. An older girl, maybe around ten, came forward. Her eyes were brown and large. She appeared petrified with fear. But Sandra also saw hope that their savior was there and would get all of them out and back to their lives—what was left of them.

"What's your name?" Sandra asked.

"Suzie Preston," the little girl said. She turned and pointed to another girl at the rear of the cage. "That's my sister, Anna."

Sandra remembered their names in the guestbook Emalyn had found in their room, hidden in the vent.

"Were you the one who had the foresight to hide the guestbook in the vent?" Sandra asked.

Suzie nodded.

"Anna and I were in bed when they came. I heard a loud bump that woke me up. When I went to see what was happening, I found three men standing over my mom and dad on the floor in the living room. They weren't moving. One of them said, *Get the kids.* I grabbed the guestbook, the only thing nearby, and hurried back to our room and wrote the message."

"They Came At Night," Sandra said.

Suzie nodded. "I had to warn the next guests who stayed at that house. And I prayed that if someone found the book, they'd be able to find us."

She paused, and her eyes grew glassy.

"Do you know what happened to our mom and dad?"

"I'm getting all of you out of here," Sandra replied, not wanting to answer the question she knew the answer to. *They're dead. In the pit alongside my family.* "Suzie, I need your help."

"Okay."

Sandra bent, pulled the cage keys off the guard, undid the lock, and swung the door open.

"Through that door is an elevator. Go to it, but wait for me. I won't be long."

Suzie motioned for the other kids to follow her like a natural-born leader.

Good girl!

Time to take out the scum, her monster spoke.

Indeed, it was.

Sandra came to the stage just as another guard came through the curtain with the child he'd taken a moment ago. Sandra snuffed his light out with a quick thrust of the knife's blade through his left eye. She told the terrified child where to find the others by the elevator. The kid nodded and pattered off.

331

"And for our next item…" Martin trailed off when he saw Sandra step through the curtain.

Richter was to his left and stood to attention. "You? How did—"

Sandra shot Martin through the mouth, blowing his teeth and tongue out the back of his head in a chunky splatter of gore. He crumbled in on himself and hit the floor hard, kicking up dust.

Richter went to run, but Sandra swung the M4 around.

"Don't! Get over here." She looked back at the guests in the front row. They were watching with scared fascination. The events unfolding before them were not what they expected this evening.

Mr. P's goons slowly crept toward the stage, pistols drawn.

"Tell them to get back, Richter, or I'll kill you."

"Do as she says," Richter ordered. "This *Hündin* is crazy."

"Tell them to put their weapons on the ground and move over by the doorway where the servants are standing," Sandra yelled. "Do it!"

Richter did as ordered, and the two goons obliged.

"Now, Mr. Richter, tell your guests to stand and move into the room next to the amphitheater."

"What da fuck—"

"Shut up!" Sandra told Mr. A. "Do it now, Richter, or so help me, I'll blow a hole through your fucking head."

"Do as she says," Richter replied.

"What is the meaning of this, Mr. Richter?" Ms. W. asked, rising to her feet. Sandra had no idea who she was but judging by her southern drawl and pull of the S's, she was from Texas, maybe an oil baron. "I thought you and your men had everything under control."

Richter said nothing. What could he say? He had no control over anything, not his own life or theirs.

"Unacceptable," said the Sheik. "Dis woman!" He spit at Sandra.

Sandra didn't get worked up over it. He would get what was coming to him soon enough—they all would.

At gunpoint, she led the guests and Richter to the room next to the stage. She ordered one of Mr. P.'s goons to open the door and saw it led into an immaculate lounge with comfortable leather furniture atop an Oriental rug. Along the back wall was a bar with a wall of expensive liquor. Behind it was a young man, the bartender, looking petrified.

"Inside. All of you."

Richter, the two guards and servants, and two of the guests did as they were told, fearing Sandra would shred them to pieces with the M4.

The Sheik, however, stood defiant and stared at her with contempt. There was so much hate in his dark eyes that it gave Sandra a chill. Not even the man who attacked her alongside the road five years ago had such a look. Sandra realized there were levels of madness in this world at that moment—the Sheik might've been at the very top.

"I will not be going in there," the Sheik said.

"Fine," Sandra replied and shot him through the brain, dropping him where he stood.

She spun, aiming the weapon at the remaining perverts backed into the small waiting room. They all looked like sniveling rich people begging for mercy—from the public more than anything else—so they could continue to live their lives without any repercussions from their actions.

Not this time.

Sandra was the judge, jury, and executioner tonight.

And she would have her vengeance.

"I'm sure we can work something out," Richter said.

Sandra brought up the M4. Everyone cried and ran for cover behind the furniture or the bar. She squeezed the trigger, and the M4 spat bullets into the wall of liquor. The bottles exploded in a shower of sharp glass and booze.

When she stopped firing, she could hear the liquor running off the shelves, soaking into the rug. It had splashed everything, and the smell of alcohol was so strong it burnt her nose.

Heads started rising from behind the bar and furniture. Mr. A. was bleeding across the top of his head, hit by a shard of flying glass. Ms. W. looked a fright with running mascara, which made her face appear melted. More heads rose, including Richter, who watched Sandra reach into her pocket and pull out the lighter she'd taken from Zippo back at the house.

"What are you…"

Sandra flicked the lighter open.

PING! Rolled the striker.

The flame caught.

"NO!" Richter shouted, coming around from the bar and lunging for Sandra, hoping to stop her from...

Sandra tossed the Zippo behind the bar. The flame ignited the alcohol, rushed up from the floor, and lit the wall. At the same time, the fire caught the saturated Oriental rug and crawled its way to the furniture in a matter of seconds. Everything was ablaze.

Backing to the door, Sandra stepped through and went to slam it shut, but Richter was already there. He hit the door with his shoulder, driving Sandra back, and fell through the threshold and onto the ground, his suit on fire. He screamed and rolled around, trying to put himself out.

Sandra turned and looked back into the inferno. People coughed and cried. Through the thick gray smoke, she saw a few dark shapes advancing on her, hoping to escape the room before they became crispy critters themselves.

This time, Sandra slammed the door on them. She brought the M4 stock down into the door's handle three times, bending it in place, preventing anyone from unlatching it.

Escaping.

She heard fists pounding on the other side of the door. Screams of terror. Of agony as the fire slowly consumed the air and their flesh from their bones.

Burn motherfuckers!

Suddenly, Richter tackled Sandra to the ground like a pro football player.

The rifle flew from her hands and slid across the floor. She was back on her feet before Richter could get to his. She saw the left side of his face was badly burned, and blood oozed from the shrapnel he'd taken. His suit was charred, smoking. She reached for the knife, wanting to see the light go out in his eyes when she cut his heart in two.

Now enraged that Sandra had ruined his empire, Richter reached behind himself and pulled out his own large knife.

"I'm going to see to it that you pay for what you did, *Hündin*," Richter said.

He screamed like a German warrior running across the battlefield in France during WW1, closing the gap between them in three strides, swiping at Sandra's face.

She pulled back but felt the blade come dangerously close to taking off her nose. Before she could counterattack, Richter came at her again, swiping backhanded at her chest. This time, Sandra had to back away so as not to get caught with the knife, but her legs hit the amphitheater's stone seats, and she went down, the concrete edge of the seat driving into her injured side.

Richter was on her again, driving forward with the knife, looking to pierce her heart. She rolled away just before he found his target. His forward momentum took him over the edge of the seat, his knee clipping the concrete with a knock.

Sandra came back around with a swipe of the knife. She caught Richter across the upper arm, laying him open with a deep slash. He cried out and rolled away.

Seeing her opening, she came in for the kill. But before she could deliver him to hell, he got his foot up and kicked her square in the chest. The blow was hard enough to knock her down onto her ass, but the body armor prevented the wind from being driven from her lungs.

Richter staggered to his feet. Blood ran down his right arm and into his hand before dripping off to the floor. His once-styled hair was wild, his eyes crazed, and his face was contorted into a mask of rage. It was clear he wanted nothing more than to see Sandra die a slow and painful death. He charged at her, swinging the knife back and forth, back and forth.

Sandra held him off with her knife, the blades clinking and clanging like a tiny sword fight.

She saw an opening and stabbed forward but missed Richter's chest. Unfortunately, her effort to take him down had also opened her up to his counter strike, which he took advantage of, coming down with his blade across her forearm. Sandra screamed at the burning pain, the blood that reminded her so much of that night years ago when her finger was severed from her hand.

She tried to pivot away before he could land another strike, but Richter slashed out again. This time, his knife caught her across the left side of her face. Blood poured into her mouth, the salty, coppery taste of pennies coating her tongue. She stumbled forward into the seats, blood from her arm and face dotting the white lime floor in her wake.

Looking back, winded and sleepy with blood loss and fatigue, she saw Richter running at her. He bent low and laid a shoulder into her chest, throwing her back onto the rock seats. Coming down hard on her back, the air kicked from her body, and the knife shot from her grasp and skidded across the floor somewhere.

She coughed, and blood blew from her mouth.

"You're too old for the industry," Richter said. "But I have an acquaintance in the snuff film world. He would love you for one of his videos with some of the worst monsters God has ever created. I'm going to contact him. I would take great pleasure watching them tear you apart for one of their films."

He reached down and grabbed a handful of Sandra's hair, craning her neck so he could look her in the eyes. "I will have that niece of yours—Emalyn, I believe, was her name—watch as they dismember you."

Her monster ignited a furious rage when she heard Emalyn's name on his lips for the second time that night. She had thought about taking his tongue the last time he spoke Emalyn's name. Now, she was going to have it. She reached down to her boot and felt the outline of William's straight razor there.

"Go... fuck... yourself," Sandra said as a glob of blood and saliva dripped from her lips. She would've spit in his face but didn't have the energy; she needed what she had left to finish the job—the mission.

Take it home, Sandra, her monster said gleefully.

"I'll never understand how women can bleed so much and not die?"

"We're resilient," Sandra replied.

A condescending smirk creased Richter's lips.

"But there's something else you're forgetting about us women, Richter."

He looked back at her with a cocked eyebrow.

"We're cunning."

She came up with the straight razor. Richter's mouth went slack, forming an O, and from the look of surprise in his eyes, he was shocked to see there was any fight still left in her.

The razor caught him across his open mouth. The sharp blade passed through the thin cheek flesh and severed the tip of his tongue off in one swipe. Blood leaked from Richter's mouth and the piece of disconnected tongue slipped between his lips and hit the floor with a *spat*. He grabbed at his face and reeled back with a gargled howl.

Sandra rose to her feet.

Blood poured from between his fingers, and ran down his fancy suit, soaking it in crimson. He stared at Sandra with the look of a man who didn't understand how his life had taken this unexpected turn of events.

"I told myself that was going to take your tongue for saying my niece's name." She stepped on the piece of severed organ, squashing it like a bug. "Now that I have it, I'll take your life, too."

Sandra pulled the .9mm Glock strapped to her leg and fired two point-blank shots into Richter's chest and two more into his face before he hit the floor.

The door above the amphitheater burst open, and two armed guards rushed in. Sandra turned and fired at one coming down the center aisle, hitting him in the throat. His knees unlocked, his body crashed onto the steps, and he rolled the rest of the way down.

She ran toward the backstage area as bullets chased her, impacting the lime walls and dancing through the curtain. Aiming at another guard coming from her left, she fired, but the shot was wild, and the ejecting shell caught in the breach.

Clearing the breach by pulling back on the slide and letting it spring forward, she punched out with the gun, aimed, and fired again. This time, the bullet caught the guard on the side of the head, twirling him around in the air like a spinning top before falling to the floor.

She cut sharply to the right and darted behind the curtain, through the door, and into the holding pen room. She bolted down the tunnel to the lift and saw the kids huddled by it, waiting for her.

They watched in gaping awe as she neared and slowly stepped aside as if she were a prophet sent from heaven to save them. Opening the door, she let the kids enter before her.

Then, Sandra stepped into the lift—the last woman off the battlefield.

CHAPTER THIRTY-THREE

Sandra pulled the limo to a stop in front of the Compound's main building. Before Joel bought the place, it was an old hunting camp high in the hills of West Virginia. As Sandra stepped out, the smell of pine hit her nose like a dopamine rush.

Home.

As she rounded the front of the limo, the door to the main building opened, and Joel stepped out. He looked relieved to see her. His long, graying beard even seemed to settle back onto his chest. What hair was left on his head had turned a shade whiter since she'd seen him last. But goddamn if he wasn't a sight for sore eyes. A fellow warrior. A friend. A mentor. A brother.

Emalyn hopped out of the passenger side. She hadn't said much since everything had happened. Sandra understood. She had lost her parents. Her grandmother. And had almost been sold into the sex slave trade. How could any fourteen-year-old comprehend that?

After escaping the tunnels, Sandra had led the eight children back to where the limos were parked. Once they were inside, she got behind the wheel. Finding the keys in the ignition, she'd fired it up and gunned it out of there, crashing through the front gate.

About a mile outside Little Hope, she'd found Emalyn and Lacy along the road, trying to flag down passing motorists (according to Lacy, she couldn't drive the pickup since it was a stick shift—something Sandra had not considered—so they'd set on foot for help), hoping to take them to the police.

Pulling the limo over, Sandra had hopped out and run to her niece. Wrapping her arms around Emalyn, the two had sunk to the ground, and Sandra had felt everything inside her break.

Together, they began to cry.

She had taken Lacy and the children to the nearest state police station and dropped them off, speeding away before anyone saw her or Emalyn. They needed to disappear. With the USB drive containing R&R's clientele she carried on her, she could not risk that information falling into the wrong hands.

Sandra trusted no one.

That was twelve hours ago.

Now, Emalyn held a scary, absent gaze in her eyes that Sandra recognized. It was the same look she had seen on her own face countless times since the night *he* attacked her. She knew the horrors of what Emalyn had endured would not fade away easily, and she knew that she was not equipped to help the girl through this tough time.

If anyone could help Emalyn, it would be Joel and his staff. Here, Emalyn would get the help she needed while learning skills that could save her life—just as they had saved Sandra's.

"This is Emalyn. Emalyn, this is my friend, Joel," Sandra said, making the introductions.

She coughed. Her body ached. The fever had set in, and she knew it was dangerously high. She was lucky to have gotten them back there at all. They'd stopped at an abandoned rest stop so Sandra could patch herself up and rest for a while. She'd known even then that the fever was taking hold, and it would be just a matter of time before it overtook her and her body began to shut down.

Joel squatted down and looked Emalyn in the eyes, almost as if he were searching for something there. Finally, he stood, keeping his eyes on the child in front of him. Then Joel turned and motioned to Mary Clemons, his assistant, who helped him run the place.

"Hi, Emalyn. I'm Dr. Clemons. I want to show you around and introduce you to some of our staff and guests. How does that sound?"

Emalyn nodded apprehensively and looked to Sandra as if confirming that it was safe to go with this strange woman.

"She's good people," Sandra replied weakly.

Emalyn nodded and followed Dr. Clemons as she led them away.

"Do you think you can help her?" Sandra asked, looking back at Joel.

"Depends on if she wants it." Joel studied her. "Just like you."

Sandra turned away and breathed in the cool mountain air, sweet with pine. She had missed this place.

"I want her to move on, Joel. I want her to have a happy life."

"Only time will tell if that happens or not, Sandra."

If there was one thing she liked about Joel, it was his brutal honesty.

She looked at him, wishing he had a brighter outlook. But he had seen too many people come through his doors, looking for help, only to find it either at the end of a bottle, a needle, or a gun. Too many of his brothers and sisters had succumbed to their trauma—the devil sure did work in mysterious ways.

Emalyn was no different, Sandra supposed, than when she herself had first come to this place, looking for help.

But Sandra would do whatever it took to make sure her niece overcame the trauma and that she didn't suffer endlessly from the horror of one single night of her life like Sandra had. She didn't know if it was going to work or not. But she was going to try.

Joel reached out and touched her damp forehead.

"You're running a fever. Let's get you to medical and get you checked over."

Joel led her inside the main building.

"Do you still have that hacker contact?" Sandra asked. Coughed. She could feel her body growing weaker by the moment.

"I do," Joel said, his eyes narrowing. She could tell he wondered where Sandra was going with her questions.

She reached into her pocket and pulled out the flash drive and handed it to him.

"I want to know what's on that."

CHAPTER THIRTY-FOUR

Sandra didn't notice summer turn to fall as she spent nearly three weeks in bed recovering from the sepsis that had settled in her body, not to mention all the other battle wounds she had sustained in the fight to save Emalyn.

It was touch and go for a while, Mary and Joel told her when she was finally feeling well enough.

Her fever had spiked, her blood pressure had dropped dangerously low, and she'd had difficulty breathing as the infection ravished her body. They were sure they were going to lose her multiple times. Had it not been for the round-the-clock antibiotic cocktail fed through an IV into Sandra, Mary was sure she would have died. Joel said he never saw anyone fight as hard as she had.

She asked about Emalyn and learned that Joel had kept her busy working around the Compound with light chores, while allowing her to spend time with her aunt in the evenings. He had started therapy sessions already, and Emalyn seemed accepting of them.

By early October, Sandra was on her feet again. She wasn't one hundred percent herself yet, and some of the physical trauma she had sustained lingered in her body, but she was back in the land of the living.

That evening, as Sandra leaned against the railing of the main building, drinking a cup of cowboy coffee after dinner, the snow fell for the first time. Emalyn was by the fire in the courtyard, talking with a twenty-three-year-old guy named Frank Thompson, who had come to the Compound two years after America pulled out of Afghanistan, having witnessed countless atrocities—the death of three of his fellow Marines. Sandra noticed that Emalyn had taken a shine to the young man. However, their relationship was in a big brother-little sister way, much like hers and Joel's.

Joel came up next to her. He wore cammies and a black knit sweater that made him look the part of a captain of a former Navy SEALS unit.

"I heard back from my hacker guy today," he said.

"Oh?" Sandra turned to him. "Took him long enough."

"Yeah. They encrypted the flash drive. He had to find a way around it."

"Of course they did." Sandra shook her head and looked back to Emalyn and Frank.

"He said there are a lot of very powerful names on there."

Sandra said nothing but felt Joel's eyes burning into the side of her face.

"What the hell did you uncover down there, Sandra?"

She watched Emalyn laugh at one of Frank's silly jokes. His jokes were terrible, but they were funny because of the cute way he told them. Sandra was glad to see her niece smiling after everything that had happened.

"Something more insidious than any of us could imagine."

Joel's eyes dimmed. He knew the dark side of humanity better than most.

"With the names on that list, Sandra, it'll start a global shitstorm. Many powerful people will try and sweep their sins under the carpet like they never happened."

"It happened," Sandra said, thinking of Carrie. Of William. Of her mother, even. "They took so many lives. They stole so many children to... to…"

She trailed off and pushed a tear off her face. It wasn't right what wealthy people in powerful positions worldwide got away with. Joel put his arms around her.

They were quiet for a long moment as the snow continued to fall, blanketing the camp. It looked so peaceful, and Sandra had a hard time understanding how there was evil in a world when it could be so serene.

"So, what are you going to do about it?"

Sandra looked at him.

"What do you mean?"

"Are you going to be their victim? Are you going to let Emalyn be their victim?"

"Do you know someone who could get the names out there?" Sandra asked, turning and watching Emalyn again. She was smiling. By God, she *was* smiling, almost like the little girl Sandra knew before.

Almost.

"I do. And I've already spoken with him about making the list public. He's just waiting for the go-ahead," Joel replied.

The people behind these sinister organizations needed to be exposed and their crimes brought to light. Sandra could do that for all those lost souls still out there, trapped in a hellish world not of their choosing.

"Joel?"

"Yes?" he said dryly, without emotion.

"Release the list."

THE END

Westley Smith had his first short story, "Off to War," published when he was just sixteen.

Recently, he's had short stories featured in *On the Premise*, *Unveiling Nightmares*, and *Crystal Lake Entertainment*. He was the runner-up contestant in the *Alfred Hitchcock Mystery Magazine's* "Mysterious Photograph Contest," where his name was featured in the magazine.

He sold his debut thriller, *Some Kind of Truth*, to Wicked House Publishing. His thriller, *In the Pale Light*, was published with Watertower Hill Publishing, as was his next thriller, *They Came at Night*.

He is also the author of two self-published horror novels, *Along Came the Tricksters* and *All Hallows Eve*.

Visit Westley at www.westleysmithbooks.com.